T0221780

ALSO BY ELLEN BAKER

Keeping the House

I Gave My Heart to Know This

The Hidden Life of
Cecily Larson

ELLEN BAKER

The Hidden Life of Cecily Larson

A Novel

MARINER BOOKS

New York   Boston

THE HIDDEN LIFE OF CECILY LARSON. Copyright © 2024 by Ellen Baker Creative. All rights reserved. Printed in the United States of America. No part of this book may be used or reproduced in any manner whatsoever without written permission except in the case of brief quotations embodied in critical articles and reviews. For information, address HarperCollins Publishers, 195 Broadway, New York, NY 10007.

HarperCollins books may be purchased for educational, business, or sales promotional use. For information, please email the Special Markets Department at SPsales@harpercollins.com.

FIRST EDITION

Designed by Renata DiBiase

Library of Congress Cataloging-in-Publication Data has been applied for.

ISBN 978-0-06-335119-6 (hardcover)
ISBN 978-0-06-338071-4 (international edition)

23 24 25 26 27 LBC 5 4 3 2 1

To my mom and dad

The Hidden Life of
Cecily Larson

PROLOGUE

Madeline

November 1924
Chicago

Joe Teague said he would marry her, but he didn't want some other man's brat hanging around.

Though Joe Teague would love Cecily, Madeline just knew!

He'd refused even to meet her. "This is a whirlwind, darling," he'd told Madeline. "Get caught up in it or get tossed."

Now Cecily's little hand was hot and sticky in hers, as Madeline—clutching in her other hand a small suitcase packed with Cecily's extra dress, three little pairs of clean underwear; let anyone say Cecily didn't come from people who loved her!—led her up the walk toward the imposing brick mansion. It had taken an hour and a half and four buses to get here, but the place looked as nice as Rosie from the dance hall had promised. Four stories, rows and rows of windows. That was good. There would be light. Which window would be Cecily's?

Madeline didn't want to cry. She didn't want to upset Cecily.

Only three weeks ago, it was, when Joe Teague had pressed up too close, dance after ten-cent dance, then invited Madeline out for a late, late supper. He was wearing gold cuff links and six-dollar shoes. She'd ordered the pork chops with mashed potatoes, sopping up the last of the gravy with a thick hunk of white bread, and he'd said he liked to see a girl with an appetite. Only three weeks ago, and now her life was about to change. "I'll buy you a house in Oak Park, all right?" he'd promised. "I'll take you to see the Grand Canyon."

Madeline was twenty-two years old, and every day she was aware: her looks wouldn't last forever.

She crouched in the icy gravel drive and looked into the deep blue eyes of her daughter. Tommy's eyes; Madeline loved them. She caught one of Cecily's dark curls and twirled it around her finger. Her gloves were new, from Joe Teague. It wouldn't do for his wife-to-be to have holes in her gloves, he'd said. *Don't you want to leave this whole sad chapter of your life behind?*

She straightened her daughter's wool cap. Tugged at the front of the little hand-me-down coat. Oh, Joe Teague would *see* his mistake! Madeline would *make* him see. This was only temporary, today! He wasn't heartless. He was just a man. Men thought differently about things, but there were ways to set them straight. It just took a little time! And then he would welcome Cecily into their Oak Park home, they would be a family—

A thin woman with gray curls poked her head out the front door of the mansion. "May I help you?"

Madeline stood, alarmed, though she shouldn't have been. She rested her hand on the back of Cecily's head. "Yes! My—my daughter."

The woman's face softened in sympathy. "Come in out of the cold."

Madeline led Cecily forward. There were big pillars on either side of the door, tiny octagons of tile forming a pretty pattern on the stoop, a stained-glass fleur-de-lis window in the door. A classy place, Madeline thought with satisfaction, though tears streamed down her face.

The woman, in a brown sack of a suit, asked Cecily what her name was, and Cecily told her.

"My—my husband died," Madeline said. She had never been in such a soaring room before: marble columns, a wide staircase that started in the middle of the room and split at a landing to go up in two directions. She had never felt so small. "I can't—can't afford—"

"We see all sorts of women in your position, ma'am." The woman did not seem unkind. She picked up a clipboard and asked Madeline for some information, which Madeline, voice trembling, gave. "Don't worry, ma'am," the woman said. "We'll take good care of her."

Cecily tugged Madeline's coat. "Mama?"

"Oh, Sissy!" Madeline knelt down and hugged her like she was dying. Maybe she was. Cecily felt so sturdy, so terrifically *alive*, hot, in her little coat, while Madeline was brittle, cold, drifting away. "You be a good girl like Mama taught you, all right? I'll be back for you before a mare could shake her tail. I'll be back. Don't forget me, Sissy. I'm going to get us everything. It's just going to take a little time. Don't forget me!"

Cecily had started to cry, though Madeline knew it was only because *she* was crying; that Cecily didn't really understand.

"Here." Madeline stripped off her new gloves and fumbled to open the clasps of the suitcase. "Look, I tucked in something from your daddy." She pulled out the prayer card, on which was written *Hope begins with Saint Jude*. Tommy had brought it home one night early on in their time in Chicago—Madeline had no idea why, or where it was from—and leaned it up against the lamp on the dresser. More than once, she'd caught him gazing at it while he fastened his collar, as if he might actually believe praying to the saint could do some good. Madeline had scoffed every time, made terrible fun of him, in fact, and, after he'd died, she'd pressed the card to her chest and told the saint how sorry she was, and deep down she wondered if she'd prayed a little harder, to someone or something or anything, Tommy might've not got killed.

She didn't think Joe Teague would like the card one bit. "Remember how I told you, Sissy? How this was one of your daddy's favorite things?" She held the card out to Cecily, who took it in her chubby fingers and frowned down at it.

A gentle hand on Madeline's shoulder. "It's best if you go now, ma'am."

Madeline's heart pounded. "Her things—her other things are here!" She snatched the card from Cecily and dropped it into the suitcase's inside pocket, then latched the whole thing up and stood with it in her hand, clutching her new gloves in the other. She didn't want to give the suitcase over. "You can see how much I love her!"

The woman reached for the suitcase, took hold of the handle gently. "I know, ma'am. You'll be back just as soon as you can. We can hold her for up to a year before she's put up for adoption. Would you like me to check that option on the form?"

Madeline finally let go. "Yes, yes! I'll be back." She was putting on her gloves. "A year? Don't be insane. I'll be back long before a year goes by."

Cecily was really crying now, though surely she didn't know what a *year* meant—did she?

"It's best if you go now, ma'am."

Madeline knelt before Cecily again. "This nice lady's going to look after you awhile, all right, Sissy? I know it's always been just the two of us against the world, but now you're going to have so many nice friends to play with!"

"Mama!" Cecily shouted, an objection, as if she understood now, and Madeline grabbed her into a hug again, but the woman was yanking her arm, pulling her up, ushering her out the door with gentle force.

"I'll be back, Sissy!" Madeline yelled, then the door shut behind her, and she was out in the cold. A light snow had started to fall.

Madeline screamed into the gray of the sky. She screamed again.

A crow cawed.

Snow drifted down, settling on evergreen boughs.

And Madeline set out walking, wiping the tears from her face before they could freeze.

PART ONE

Firecracker

CHAPTER 1

Tuesday, February 17, 2015
Itasca, Minnesota

I t was a Tuesday morning when Liz got the call she'd been dreading. "It's your mom. You'd better get over here." It was her mother's next-door neighbor Harold, who checked every morning to make sure Cecily had raised the blinds in the kitchen of the big old Victorian by 7 A.M. If not, he went straight over to check on her. "She fell," Harold said. "She's unconscious. I called the ambulance."

Liz tossed her phone onto the bed, shucked off her flannel pajamas, grabbed a sweater and jeans and wrestled into them. Alarm had numbed her limbs, made them hard to manage. As happened most mornings lately, she'd been sipping coffee and staring at the row of Dean's golf shirts still hanging on his side of the closet, telling herself *this* would be the day she'd box them up and take them to Goodwill. People said time slowed after a death, but, for Liz, whole days, weeks, even months, had zipped by in a blur. She could not account for the more than three years that had passed since the day—also a Tuesday—she'd woken up beside him and he simply had not. An aneurysm; there'd been no predicting it. Nor did she understand how the pain could seem to grow worse with time, not better. The initial shock that had shifted to a dull ache for a couple years was now, from time to time, a screaming pain.

And now her mother! A fall. The first slip toward the end, as everyone knew, especially at Cecily's age. Liz yanked on wool socks, grabbed her phone, and ran to the mudroom. She shoved her feet into her SORELs, pulled on her parka and leather gloves.

Car keys, car keys, where?

On the hook where they always were, thank God. And her purse beside them. She dropped her phone into its pocket and hurried out into the cement-cold of the garage, pressing the button for the opener, the door whirring up (*thank you, Dean;* her birthday present, seven years ago). Into the cold Grand Cherokee. She fired it up, then jumped out to grab the shovel and hack away at the six-inch-high drift that had formed after last night's snow. Frozen solid. She tossed the shovel into a much bigger drift against the garage, hopped back into the car, and gunned it in reverse. A big galumph over the bump, but she made it! Out onto the frozen gravel road, sheltered by tall pines. The road was slick, and she was driving too fast.

Slow down, slow down, she heard her own voice, as if she were talking to her daughter, Molly, who always drove *way* too fast, in Liz's opinion, but now it was Liz herself who only pressed harder on the gas. It was eight miles to town—thirteen minutes, minimum, in even the best of weather—and she was half cursing Dean for insisting fifteen years ago that *this* was their dream lake house, where they'd retire, and half thinking how she'd been trying and trying (hadn't she?) on her twice-weekly visits to tell Cecily that it was simply *time* to leave the old Victorian where Cecily had lived for nearly seventy years; where Liz had grown up, and Liz's father, Sam, too. Heartbreaking, yes, but a woman at ninety-four couldn't expect to still live alone, and, if it was independence Cecily wanted—she'd refused even to consider having Molly and Caden move in, saying flatly, "They are *not invited*"—surely an apartment up at the Senior Village would be nice, wouldn't it, when so many of her friends were there?

"The same people I've had to answer to all my life, you mean?" Cecily would say, with a dismissive laugh. And Liz, inwardly fuming—she'd always felt herself the more adult of the two of them, even when she was a small child—would turn to chores that seemed more immediately "pressing": the garbage needed taking out, the steps another sprinkling of Ice Melt, and so on. Honestly, Liz just hated to argue, especially with Cecily, who never failed to win. And, yes, there'd surely been a part of Liz that had been happy to deny that disaster was on their doorstep (just the bare facts: ninety-four; that big old house), happy to let Cecily continue blithely on—or else it had been Liz herself who'd been blithe, pretending this call wouldn't come, when she must have known it would. But—she supposed; and not that this was an excuse—she'd been caught up in her grief, unable to handle things with the practical efficiency she'd always handled most everything before.

Before.

And now see where they were. Knowing Cecily, she'd probably been out shoveling the back steps after last night's snow, even though she'd been told a thousand times to wait for Harold to do it.

CHAPTER 2

Tuesday, February 17, 2015
Itasca, Minnesota

When Cecily woke up, she was in her kitchen being strapped to a gurney, and she recognized the paramedic from church. "Roger, I was hoping not to see you until Sunday," she said.

He smiled, tightening a strap. "I could say the same about you, Mrs. Larson. Now, it seems you may have broken your hip. We're going to get you to the hospital."

"That's impossible. I have so much to do today." But she remembered. She'd simply missed the bottom step of the back stairs that led from the upstairs hall into the kitchen. The stairs she'd climbed up and down at least ten times daily for more than sixty-five years. The ones that her daughter had said recently were too steep for her, telling her she ought to use the wide front stairs and always hold the railing. And Cecily had thought, *Ha.* "I have excellent balance," she'd told Liz. "Nothing to worry about."

But Liz had been right to worry, after all. Cecily had missed the bottom step; had probably hit her head, too, or else why the lost consciousness? She wished Sam were here—he would be able to explain—but he hadn't been here in twenty years.

She reached for Roger's wrist; he stopped adjusting the second strap and looked at her with placid blue eyes. He was suited for this work. So calm. She would write a letter to the department in praise. If she recovered. That was really what was on her mind. The *if.* "Is this the beginning of the end?" she asked.

Roger gave a slight smile and shook his head. "Let's just get you to the hospital, Mrs. Larson. You're in shock now, but it's going to start to hurt."

"Oh, yes. I understand about that," she said, and he laid a blanket over her, and he and the other paramedic—whom she didn't recognize; a Baptist?—carried her through the house and out the front door, where red flashers lit the gray morning sky.

She heard a car pull up and stop, a door slam, footsteps crunching snow. "Mom? Mom?"

Cecily couldn't reach out her hand or turn her head, they had her strapped in so. "Don't worry, Liz, honey! Just a little fall," she called out, as the paramedics bounced her along. They were moving gingerly, with the snow and ice underfoot. The air was frigid on her face; she could see her breath. She heard Roger telling Liz about the broken hip, the shock; that Liz could follow the ambulance to the hospital, and not to worry about red lights, just follow them on through.

Cecily did not think this was good advice at all. Anything could happen! Liz could have an accident on the way to the hospital just as easily as Cecily had fallen. "You be careful, though, Liz, honey!" she called out. Why had she always felt such munificence from Time, when in fact, day by day by day, she was coming closer and closer to breaking the promise she'd made to herself: that she would tell Liz and Molly the truth about their family before she left this earth.

The one time she'd mentioned it to Liz, about a year ago, Liz had just shaken her head, seeming to misunderstand. "You're an orphan, Mom. You don't even know *your* background, right? How do you expect to be able to tell *us*?"

Admittedly, Cecily had brought up the subject only when Liz was on her way out the door, parka and boots on and everything. Also, it had been a day when Liz had seemed particularly out of sorts, her grief bubbling to the surface as it did from time to time.

But Liz had never followed up with any questions. Maybe she just wasn't interested? Cecily could hope.

Still, though. *I was Cecily McAvoy*, she imagined beginning. *Born June 5, 1920, to Madeline and Thomas McAvoy.*

It got a lot more complicated from there.

But she'd always liked the sound of her parents' names—the ones on the papers in the file at the orphanage, which she and Flip had sneaked a look at one day when Mrs. Hamilton had been called away by the sudden alarm of a mysterious (ha) kitchen fire, leaving the big drawer in her private upstairs office unlocked.

Father, deceased. That had been a blow, at age seven, to find out for certain.

Mother, unknown address. (An address beside that was crossed out, with a note: *Attempt to contact "returned to sender."*) Perhaps worse.

Anyway, that was such a small part of the story. And, for some reason, Cecily hadn't even told Liz that much. *Madeline and Thomas McAvoy.* Liz with her permanent pinched frown, these days, and Cecily felt for her, she did, and Dean had been a wonderful man, but sometimes Cecily just wanted to shake Liz and say, *There's a lot more life out ahead of you, so buck up, kid.*

Though, at sixty-eight, Liz was not really a kid anymore, Cecily had to admit.

"I'll be right behind you, Mom!" Liz called back now, and Cecily wiggled her fingers—all she could approximate as a wave, strapped in as she was—and then a feeling that she imagined was grace, or maybe it was gratitude (how *fortunate* she was, to be in such capable hands! to have lived the long life she had!), permeated her body, warming her by degrees despite the frigid air, and she heard the idling engine of the ambulance growing louder with each of the paramedics' careful steps, the creak of the door being opened, and then they were sliding her inside, into the warmth, and, as she saw the dials and machines lining the inside of the metal compartment, she thought, *how interesting*, that this was where she'd ended up, when she had been the girl famous for never falling.

"Fearless, this one is," said Mrs. Hamilton, resting her hand on the back of Cecily's dark curls. "A firecracker. Honestly, we don't even know what to do with her."

Cecily smiled up at the man in the gleaming black topcoat—the orphans were instructed always to be charming to visitors, and never to seem hungry—though her toes were curled inside her too-small shoes with nerves at having been called into Mrs. Hamilton's office. Flip and Dolores had whispered that certainly they'd been found out, before Cecily had shushed them. How could Mrs. H. even suspect they'd climbed out onto the roof again after lights-out last night—and, if she did, wouldn't all the malefactors have been called in? Instead, the other orphans, all seventy of them, had been sent outside to play, with only Miss Oversham and Miss Thompson to watch them, which Mrs. H. rarely allowed to happen, because she said Miss Oversham didn't have the sense for this work. (Cecily disagreed: Miss Oversham had taught her to read, said she was the best seven-year-old reader she'd ever seen and that reading would open up the world for her, then presented her with her very own pocket-size copy of *Around the World in 80 Days* to prove it. Cecily had carried the book in her apron pocket for weeks, sleeping with it under her pillow to make sure it didn't get swiped, though eventually Horace, twelve and a giant, stole it straight from her pocket, ripped out the pages, and stomped them into a mud puddle. In Cecily's view, the only thing Miss Oversham didn't understand was that orphans couldn't have anything nice of their own.)

Right now, Cecily could only conclude that she was *really* in trouble. She just had no idea why.

"Pretty little thing, too," the man said, and the up-and-down look he gave Cecily made the hairs on the back of her neck stand up. He had a thick brown mustache that covered most of his mouth, so it was impossible to tell if he was smiling. "But the price you're asking is awfully high."

"The price is the price. A required donation to the Home," Mrs. Hamilton said stiffly. "I believe she'd be perfect for your needs."

Mrs. Hamilton and the man stared each other down, and the man's mustache twitched, which only intensified Cecily's awful feeling that she'd done something horribly wrong. *You are just the worst troublemaker, child; no wonder your mother never came back for you,* Mrs. H. always said, especially whenever she caught Cecily turning backflips down the hallway, or front flips down the stairs. And what was Mrs. H. trying to sell, anyway, that this man didn't want to pay full price for?

The whirring feeling at the back of Cecily's neck was growing worse.

Mrs. H. spoke first. "Cecily, dear, why don't you show the nice man the way you walk on the railing?"

"But you said I wasn't supposed to—"

"Come now." Mrs. H. tugged her by the hand.

Out in the cavernous hall, Cecily removed her shoes and stockings, more nervous by the second. She'd only ever tried this when no adults were around, and the two times Mrs. H. had caught her, she'd yelled her head off and sent Cecily to The Closet for a whole day. And now she wanted her to walk the rail for this horrible—Cecily had decided he could be nothing else—man?

The Home was an old mansion, and the wide staircase that led up from the broad tiled foyer split in the middle at a landing graced with a weathered statue of a sad-looking woman, then headed up in two narrower flights to the second floor. All flights were lined in sweeping oak balustrades (once a week, the orphans polished every post), as was the upper length of hall that crossed at the rear of the building. It was this rail that Cecily was preparing to cross. The drop to the landing below was a good fifteen feet.

Mrs. H. clapped twice. "Chop, chop. And do that little flip at the end."

Cecily had never, ever seen adults act the way Mrs. H. and this man were acting now.

But what could she do about it? Nothing. Just like she could do nothing about the fact that her mother hadn't come back for her in almost three whole years, even though the box on the form was checked saying she'd intended to come back in one.

So, Cecily tucked her curls behind her ears and boosted herself onto the railing, grabbing the pillar to keep steady. She'd only traversed the rail's length the first time because Flip had said he bet she couldn't do it. The times after that, it had been for fun, to see if she still could. But—having to do it under these watchful adult eyes?

Would she get in trouble if she refused?

What if she fell?

One more look at Mrs. H. said the lady wasn't joking.

All right, then, Cecily thought.

She curled her bare feet around the rail. Let go of the pillar. Wobbled. Held out her arms to steady herself. Took a step. Then another. Another, another, another (it was easiest when you moved fast). She wobbled again; caught herself, heart pounding, as she glanced down to the top of the head of the sad statue below. This was the hardest part: the middle. Her feet were starting to sweat. She took another step. Another, another, another—then sent herself flying off toward the carpeted hall, shooting her heels over her head then around and onto the floor. *Thunk.* She grinned and raised her arms when she realized she'd landed right.

"Bravo! Bravo!" said Mrs. H., applauding, and the man took a handkerchief from his pocket and wiped his brow.

"My goodness," he said. "That *is* promising."

CHAPTER 3

Tuesday, February 17, 2015
Itasca, Minnesota

M om, you can't keep me from seeing my own father," Caden snapped, as he buckled in to Molly's Mazda SUV for the ride to school. The argument had started over breakfast; Molly had hoped he would just let it go.

"Well, pardon me for being surprised," she said, turning to back out of the drive of the rented blue bungalow, craning to see over the snowbanks on either side. There never seemed to be an extra five minutes in the morning to warm up the car, the way her father, Dean, had always told her she should, and she could see the fog of her breath in the cold interior. "When you announce your father's coming to town *this weekend* for your game. You haven't seen him in six months, and I haven't seen him in two years. I haven't even *talked* to him in weeks."

"Yeah, well, he calls me every day. And it wasn't his fault the weather was bad at Christmastime and I couldn't reschedule my trip to Newport on account of hockey."

Molly bit back what she wanted to mutter—the enlightened, positive communication practices she recommended to her clients did *not* come easy—and, at a four-way stop, took her turn, tires crunching on leftover snow. Honestly, the changes to Caden in the six months since Evan had seen him had been *seismic* (six inches, a deep voice, a whole new taste in music, plus he was reading Hemingway!)—would Evan even recognize him?

"Mom, I just really need you to be cool about this," Caden said, and in his voice suddenly was the little boy he'd been—the one whose heart she'd broken.

Instant tears stung her eyes, and she found herself remembering her mom's voice on the phone that terrible morning three years ago—*Your dad's gone,* Liz had said, and Molly had thought, *Gone where?* Already, she and Evan had been struggling, and the idea that someday soon she'd get a similar call about her grandma, or her mom, had sent her careening like a car down a mountainside after busting through a guardrail. There was just no turning it around. None of the dozen healing modalities she'd been trained in could seem to touch the wreckage of her heart; none of her highly-trained-therapist's techniques had managed to bleed over into making her marriage work. Less than a year after her dad's funeral, the marriage was over, and she and Evan were in court to decide whether almost-twelve-year-old Caden would stay in Rhode Island with his father or move with her to her old Minnesota hometown.

Yet—imagine asking a child in court which parent he preferred! ("I love them both equally," Caden had said, with an equanimity that had clearly been rehearsed; it slayed her to imagine him, probably in the privacy of his bedroom the night before, in that voice that had been so tiny then: *I love them both equally.*) And when the decision came down that he'd move to Itasca with her, she'd known instantly that meant she'd be the one making him go to the dentist, do his homework, brush his teeth, take out the garbage, while Evan would be the fun one, the one picking him up at the airport and taking him to the beach, the surf shop, up to Boston for Red Sox and Bruins games. The one Caden would long for, in other words.

Her grandma Cecily had tried to console her: *Some things you never get over. Sometimes life makes you strike poor bargains, and sometimes you just plain don't know what to do. And you just have to go on and do the best you can!*

Honestly, how would Molly have *made it* without Cecily, these last two years in Itasca? Their weekly lunches—Molly brought takeout; dessert was always a slice of one of Cecily's famous fifteen-layer cakes, left over from this or that recent community meeting—were all that had

really *sustained* her. With her mom, Liz, never that easy to talk to in even
the best of times, it was only Cecily who'd made Molly believe that, even
after all that had happened and all she had lost, she could still succeed
in building a new life in her old hometown—and in raising her son on
her own.

"Okay, bud," Molly told Caden carefully now, as she pulled into the
line of traffic in the high school's circle drive. She did *try* to be enlightened. "Just give me a little time to process, okay?"

A big sigh. "K, Mom." And he was gone, slamming the door.

"Have a nice day!" she shouted through the window to his back. His
shoulders were slumped a bit, till a friend came up and they bumped
gloves and disappeared through the sliding glass doors.

Always like a pinprick to the small balloon of her heart, that. And
why did kids these days talk like every utterance was a text message?

Then she had to laugh at herself: *kids these days*. She was just glad
Caden had made good friends when he'd moved to town at the start of
seventh grade—small-town cliques could be so unforgiving—as well
as that he'd inherited his athletic abilities from his father and not from
her, because scoring goals for Itasca Central as a freshman made you a
once and future king, and that was that. She'd been such a nerd in her
day, class of '93.

She sighed at the thought of seeing Evan, put the car into gear, and
inched ahead, close behind the bumper of the car in front of her. Once
she got out of here, it was just a two-minute drive to the century-old
brick building downtown that housed her private practice. Her cell phone
rang in through the stereo; she clicked the button on the steering wheel to
answer. "Hey, Mom!"

"Moll?" From the tinny sound of the Bluetooth and road noise, it
was obvious Liz was calling from the car. She never called at this time
of day, and, as Molly recognized the sound of bad news, her stomach
clenched.

"Moll," Liz shouted through the speaker. "It's your grandma. Meet
me at the hospital!"

CHAPTER 4

October 1927
Chicago

*A*n' then," Cecily whispered to her friends, "he asked me if I'd ever ridden a horse, then he told Mrs. H. that he had to ask his partner and he'd let her know, but he still thought the price was too high."

"What the blazes?" said Flip. They were outside in the barren fenced yard under a pure blue sky, huddled together against the cold wind. Brown and orange leaves skittered past.

"You're gettin' adopted, I guess," said Dolores sadly.

"But the guy didn't have a wife!" Flip said. He and Dolores had gotten a look at the man when he'd come in, before they'd been sent outside. "How could he *adopt* anybody?"

"Shh!" Cecily said, and the other two cocked their heads, then looked around to see who might be listening, but the older kids were playing Kick the Can, and the little ones wouldn't understand, anyway.

After they'd all turned seven—Flip was first, Dolores last—the three of them had made a blood oath to stick together forever, because everybody knew: Once you turned seven, your chances of getting adopted were slim to none, at best. There were always new babies coming in, at least one every month, and they were what grown-ups wanted to take home. (The twenty-nine kids in the orphanage who were nine years old now, babies during the flu pandemic, hadn't had a prayer.)

Cecily, though, had a secret card up her sleeve: her mother was still alive, and intending to come back for her. Flip had scorned it when

Cecily'd shown him the little box checked on the form, but Flip scorned everything except the Chicago Cubs. Cecily had decided privately that, when her mother came back, she'd just make her mother take Flip and Dolores home, too. It was the least Madeline could do, for making Cecily wait two whole extra years. Cecily hadn't told her friends, because she didn't want them always pestering her about *when*. But Cecily had put a lot of facts together. One: the form had also said, *Reason for surrender: Financial. Mother (distraught) cannot earn enough to support the child and care for the child at the same time.*

Two: Cecily had asked Miss Oversham what *financial* and *distraught* meant. "Money-related" and "very, very upset," Miss Oversham had explained.

Three: Cecily had a vague memory of Madeline taking her to Marshall Field's downtown once—how *happy* her mother had been, just walking in through the big doors, seeing the glittering merchandise laid out in the glass-topped counters, though she'd told Cecily, *Don't touch, we can't afford one thing!*

Putting all of these facts together, Cecily had decided that Madeline worked at Marshall Field's now and was saving up so she could afford to come get Cecily. Cecily didn't know how long it would take, though she did think three years ought to have been enough. But what did she know? (Even Miss Oversham didn't know how much a saleslady working at Marshall Field's would make.)

Cecily imagined Madeline taking the 'L' train downtown every morning and home every night. She imagined her helping ladies try on shoes. Maybe hats. Or lipstick. Madeline was gentle and kind, and everyone wanted to buy from her, because she was beautiful. She barely even had to ask.

"I don't know what he was after," Cecily told her friends, about the man. She swallowed. What if her mother came and Cecily wasn't here? Would Madeline think that Cecily had given up on her? "Look, I'll just tell Mrs. H. I won't go with him. And that'll be that."

Flip scoffed—justifiably, in this case; everyone knew you couldn't say no to Mrs. H.—and Dolores just looked at Cecily with big, sad eyes.

That night, after prayers and lights-out, Cecily felt a poke to her shoulder.

"What?" she whispered, without opening her eyes. Dolores had a way of creeping out of her own cot and over to Cecily's without making a sound. She always had something more she wanted to tell or ask before she could sleep; things she maybe hadn't wanted to say in front of Flip, who, this time of night, was stuck over on the boys' side, unless they'd made a plan to sneak out to the roof to meet. Tonight was too cold to bother with that. Anyway, Cecily wasn't in the mood to press her luck about getting caught.

Dolores also had a way of knowing things that were going to happen before they actually happened, which Cecily had chalked up to strange coincidence at first, but now largely found useful. It wasn't as if you could ask her anything you wanted to know, though; more like she'd just get a feeling about things, sometimes. Two weeks ago, for example, she'd suddenly fixed her eyes on Harriet across the yard and said, "She's gonna get adopted."

It seemed ridiculous. Harriet had been at the Home for two years and was six years old. What was more—as Mrs. H. put it whenever Miss Oversham had to call Mrs. H. into the classroom on account of Harriet pitching a fit—her disposition was not attractive.

A week after Dolores's pronouncement, though, Cecily and her friends watched out the front window as a tall man in a gray coat and fedora and a stout, pretty woman in a purple coat and cloche led Harriet out to a waiting Model A, each holding one of her hands and talking to her solicitously. They helped her up into the car, and the man walked around to the driver's side while the woman climbed in after Harriet. Doors slammed, and away the shiny black car went, with Harriet smack in between her new parents in the front seat. "Told ya," Dolores said.

Cecily kept waiting for Dolores to say that Cecily's mother was coming for her, but, so far, nothing.

It wasn't like Dolores knew *everything*, though.

"Something bad's gonna happen," Dolores whispered urgently now. "I don't know just what."

"Oh, hush up," Cecily whispered back. What good did *that* kind of prediction do? "Go back to bed. You're gonna get us in trouble." For once, Cecily was plain tired of being in trouble. She guessed if she hadn't been such a firecracker, the way Mrs. H. had said, that man wouldn't have looked at her the way he had.

"I don't want you to leave me, Ceccy," Dolores said.

"I'm not leaving you." Cecily hoped this was true. But what choice would she have, if Mrs. H. said she had to go?

She recognized then that she wasn't actually fearless. She was afraid of all kinds of things! She was afraid of leaving the Home, because she didn't know what all was out there in the world. She was afraid of being without Dolores and Flip.

Most of all, she was afraid of missing her mother's return.

God, I'll be good, I promise, she prayed. *If only you don't make me leave here, I'll be so good you won't even recognize me.*

Dolores tugged the blanket. "Scoot over." Cecily did, and Dolores crawled under the covers next to her. Cecily was glad for the warmth. She'd just have to make sure Dolores woke up in time to get back to her own cot in the morning. She heard Dolores's stomach growl; after a moment, her own echoed it. They only ever got thin potato soup for lunch and supper, thin Cream of Wheat for breakfast.

For a second, Cecily wondered if, wherever that man wanted to take her, there would be more and better food. Bedtime snacks, even.

She caught herself. *Please, God. I don't want to leave this place.*

"That man is a bad man, Ceccy," Dolores whispered. She was staring at the ceiling, still caught up in her own dreams. "Deep down bad."

"Oh, hush!"

Dolores clutched Cecily's hand.

CHAPTER 5

Tuesday, February 17, 2015
Itasca, Minnesota

When Cecily looked up from where her name was printed on the plastic bracelet around her thin wrist—*hers? this old, liver-spotted thing?*—and saw Liz and Molly standing there, brows knit, eyes pinched, she felt sorry for them more than for herself. Waking up in this steel bed, to this view of the ice-rimmed river and flat gray sky, felt like a bit of an adventure—a break in the routine, so to speak. Though that might have been the painkillers talking.

"I don't want you girls to worry," she said, even as she wondered what time it was. The sky gave no indication. Was it even still the same day? "I'll be right as rain before you know it."

Then, Liz announced that Cecily was going to have to go straight from the hospital to The Pines—the rehab center on the edge of town—on Monday. "Dr. Olson's staff has already made the arrangements."

"That's ridiculous. I'm going home."

"You can't go home, Mom. You won't be able to walk on your own, let alone climb up and down stairs. You're going to need rest, and lots of physical therapy."

The painkillers made Cecily want to laugh. Or cry. "Then Molly and Caden can move in and help me." Why had she been so stubborn on that point? Wanting independence for Molly, yes—but mostly for herself. If she hadn't been so stubborn, maybe this stupid accident wouldn't have happened—

"I'm sorry, Grandma," Molly said, "but you're going to need real nurses' care. At least for a while."

If Molly said it, then it was true. Molly would've done anything for her, Cecily knew.

So much for a grand adventure. She let her eyes drift closed, a dream cascade down.

It was three days later when the man came back for Cecily, during breakfast time. She had no warning at all. Mrs. H. just came into the dining room with a small yellow sweater and Cecily's little suitcase in hand—how did Cecily even recognize it? It had been in storage for so long—and said it was time to go.

Cecily felt the words like a kick to the stomach. She'd been trying so hard to be good! Hadn't God noticed?

She was through trying now. She shoved her bowl away, the last precious bites of Cream of Wheat. "No," she said.

Mrs. H. tapped her toe. A hush fell over the dining room, as seventy orphans realized what was happening.

"Cecily," said Mrs. H.

Cecily folded her arms, pushed out her lip. "No. I won't go."

Dolores and Flip were watching with wide eyes, half-open mouths. Though everyone knew who was going to win.

Mrs. H. came and grabbed Cecily's elbow, pulling her up to stand. She wrestled Cecily's arms into the yellow sweater, which Cecily knew wasn't hers, had never been. She wanted to cry out, but didn't. She wouldn't give Mrs. H. the satisfaction.

So, she just hadn't been good *enough* to suit God. (*You have only yourself to blame,* Mrs. H. always said, when doling out any punishment.)

Mrs. H. brushed her hands together, then grabbed Cecily's arm again, hard enough to hurt. "Dolores, Frank," she said, "you may come say goodbye to Cecily at the door."

Cecily tried to yank her arm free, but couldn't. Dolores started to cry. Mrs. H. began marching Cecily toward the exit, and Dolores and Flip scampered up to follow. Cecily could feel their presence behind her, though there was a rushing in her ears and she wanted to scream. She bit her lip and didn't. The sweater smelled funny, like it had been at the back of some closet for a long, long time.

Near the front door in the high-ceilinged foyer stood the man in the gleaming black topcoat. He was holding his derby hat, turning it round and round in his hands. He smiled when he saw them. "Ah, good!" he said.

Mrs. H. yanked Cecily to a stop before him. "She's a bit sad about leaving her friends, I'm afraid. We don't discourage them from getting attached to one another, though perhaps we should."

Cecily found her voice. "Mrs. H., this isn't fair! You can't make me go! My mother's coming back for me, and I promised I wouldn't leave Dolores an' Flip!"

The man laughed like she was a puppy who couldn't walk straight yet, and Mrs. H. shook her head. "Cecily, this is for the best. You'll see. Now, say your goodbyes."

Cecily scrunched her eyes closed. What choice did she have? She could yell and scream for hours, and Mrs. H. wouldn't budge. Cecily knew this from experience.

The man was handing Mrs. H. an envelope, telling her she'd find the whole amount inside, and Mrs. H. was looking in it, counting.

She's selling *me.* The realization fell on Cecily like a sack of flour, with a dull thud.

Then, she wondered how much she was worth.

Enough that Mrs. H. definitely wasn't going to change her mind, seemed like, from the way she was giving the man the biggest smile Cecily had ever seen on Mrs. H.'s face in going on three years now.

All right, then, Cecily thought.

She turned to face Dolores and Flip. Even Flip had tears in his eyes, and Dolores was biting her pinkie nail. Cecily pulled them into a close huddle. She could smell the Cream of Wheat on their breaths, feel the heat of their tears steaming off their skin.

"I'll come back for you," she whispered. "I'll find some way."

Dolores lowered her hand and sniffed, but her voice was firm: "No. You won't."

Flip gave Dolores a slow blink.

"I will, too!" Cecily objected.

Dolores shook her head. "No. Somethin' big's gonna happen to you. I don't know what. But you're not comin' back here. Not ever."

Cecily wanted to shout every curse word she knew straight into Dolores's face, and tell her once and for all that she did not know everything! How dare she accuse Cecily of being faithless? Of not sticking to her promises?

Flip straightened, wiped his nose with the back of his hand. "To heck with ya, then!" he said, with an angry frown, and Cecily flinched— then saw by the tremor in his lip that he was only trying to be brave.

"Time to go, Cecily," said Mrs. H. "You have a train to catch."

Cecily exchanged electric glances with her friends. A train?

"Goddamn!" Flip said.

All right. She had to be brave, too. Around the world in eighty days. Starting with a train!

She grabbed Flip's hand, then Dolores's, too. "I'm not gonna forget you two, I swear it. If my mother comes, tell her I never gave up. Tell her I said she should take you both home, and then I'll find you, I'll find all of you, I swear I will!"

"Sure, it's all gonna come up roses," Flip said, but he was blinking back tears again, and Dolores was full-on crying without making a sound. Mrs. H. took Cecily by the shoulders and yanked her backward, pulling her hands from her friends', then turned her around to face the man in the topcoat, who was holding Cecily's suitcase. He opened the door to the outside world, and Mrs. H. gave her a little shove.

And she was gone.

CHAPTER 6

Tuesday, February 17, 2015
Itasca, Minnesota

When Liz announced that she was heading over to Cecily's house to pick up a few things, now that Cecily was resting, Molly said, "Are you sure, Mom? I can go." Other than when Molly had left for an hour to see a client she claimed she couldn't cancel on, mother and daughter had been together in the hospital waiting room all day, drinking bad coffee, pacing, making failed stabs at small talk, disagreeing on "Who Wore it Better?" in outdated magazines. Liz had overheard Molly on the phone, rescheduling other client sessions, arranging for Caden to have supper at a friend's house after hockey practice.

"No, you wait here in case she wakes up again," Liz said. "Get the inside scoop from Stacey, if you can." One of the nurses on duty was Stacey Thorson, who'd been a friend of Molly's growing up, which was both reassuring and unnerving, since at the back of Liz's mind ran images of Stacey at slumber parties when the girls were eight, nine, ten, screeching and carrying on. Liz tried to shake off the old pictures; to remind herself that not one of them was quite who they'd been thirty years ago. "It'll feel good to get some fresh air."

She accepted a hug from Molly, though she couldn't relax into it, then got suited up for the cold and headed out into the overcast afternoon. The light was beginning to soften, the day to end.

Some days, you could not imagine in the morning what they would hold by the time they closed.

The Grand Cherokee was cold, and Liz let it idle for a moment to warm up while she checked her phone. Nothing from her son, Eric, though she'd texted him right after Cecily had come through surgery—but that was no surprise. He was in Patagonia, working as a mountain climbing guide, and rarely had access to cell signal. Liz hated to leave him messages, because she always ended up worrying he was buried in some avalanche.

She couldn't think about that now. Wouldn't, anyway. She set her phone aside and put the Jeep into gear, making the familiar drive along the icy streets from the hospital to her parents' house in the neat, squared-off section of town on the other side of the winding river. Her father had been a key player in getting the new hospital built in 1965. State of the art for its time, there'd been no finer one in all of northern Minnesota when the ribbon-cutting had taken place, the same week as Liz's high school graduation. Years later, in 2000, her mother had almost single-handedly raised the funds—including a substantial donation from Dean and Liz—for the large addition and upgrade made in Sam's name. It was on account of this that people like Cecily could get a hip surgery in this town at all, without having to travel by ambulance the ninety miles to the big hospital in Duluth. (Cecily hated to go to Duluth for any reason—Liz had no idea why—and, anyway, Itasca's orthopedic surgeon, Dr. Olson, went to Cecily's church. Cecily would get excellent care here, Stacey Thorson notwithstanding.)

So why did Liz still have this terrible gnawing feeling in the pit of her stomach? It should've been relieved when Cecily had woken up, seeming lucid—seeming *herself*, even. Or else when Dr. Olson had reported he was optimistic that, with physical therapy, Cecily could possibly make a full recovery within months.

Well, that was it, wasn't it? *Possibly. Within months.* When "months" could be presumed to be a large portion of the time that Cecily had left on earth.

And Liz simply did not know how she was going to get along without her mother.

The idea that someday she'd have to had always been a vague one, before today. Yet, some quick research on her phone—after Dr. Olson had answered her terse questions about prognosis with "Let's just take it day by day, for now" and a gentle hand on Liz's elbow—had turned up that, of elderly people who broke a hip, only half would make a full recovery, and more than a quarter would end up dead within a year.

The oldest and frailest patients are most likely to die from a hip fracture; a sudden sharp decline in overall function is a usual result—

No. No, no, no. That could *not* be the case with Cecily.

Liz pulled into the drive at the old house, tires crunching ice, and got out. Before she could pick her way to the back stoop, Harold emerged from his small box of a house next door without a coat on, just his checked flannel shirt. She should've phoned him with news; why hadn't she thought to? "How's she doing?" he called. "She all right?"

Liz turned, trying to compose her face, suddenly aware of her exhaustion; glad to think that the lowering darkness might hide the worst of her appearance. "She had to have surgery. Dr. Olson was able to get her right in, which was pretty much a miracle. I can't thank you enough, Harold. I'm so sorry I didn't call."

"When will she be coming home, then?"

"Not for a while. She'll have to go up to The Pines."

"Ah, well." Harold's sigh made steam in the cold. "Could be worse, I suppose. Bess made a hotdish. I'll bring you a plate."

He wouldn't take no for an answer, even when Liz said she planned to be at the house for only a few minutes, that she had to get back to the hospital, especially with Molly waiting. "Well, then," he said, "Bess'll make up a to-go plate for Moll, too." Finally, all Liz could do was sigh and say thank you.

Inside, the kitchen was cool; Cecily must not have turned up the heat this morning. Liz flipped on the light, revealing the ivory steel-rimmed table and chairs that had been there her whole life. The light blue cabinets and patterned yellow and blue linoleum were even older than that.

Cecily and Sam had moved into the house when Liz was just a few months old. Liz's grandfather—old Dr. Larson—had died, and Sam, who was working out east at the time, had answered his mother's pleas to come home and take over his father's practice. Sam's sisters had moved to Minneapolis by that time, and his mother, thrilled at the chance to relocate to the city, had handed over this house, complete with the doctor's office in the front room and the shingle out front saying DR. LARSON, to the young family. Liz's father had seen patients there until Liz was in eighth grade, when he'd finally merged his practice with the new clinic's.

Ancient history now. Liz shut the door to the back stairs—the scene of the crime. She'd always (inexplicably) hated that narrow, steep, cold passageway. Now she had reason to. In the dining room, she turned up the thermostat, listened to the boiler kick on, and flipped on the light—the globes of the chandelier over the table took on a warm yellow cast—trying to fight the cold, deserted feeling the house had after just one day of Cecily's absence. Yet, Cecily's touches were everywhere. The familiar old Valentine's Day paper cupids and hearts taped on the bay window, catching the last of the light. Red roses in a blue glass vase at the center of the long oak table. A neat stack of stationery and actual letters awaiting return; Cecily's favorite blue pen.

It was all so normal. Home. Yet, Liz felt strangely like a trespasser. She wanted to get in and out quickly, get back to her mother at the hospital.

Heading for the front stairs, Liz passed under the archway into the living room. Cecily had kept this room formal, Victorian, ready to seat ten or twelve at a moment's notice. Two facing sofas were bookended by pairs of well-worn wing chairs, all surrounding a marble-topped oval coffee table. How many of Itasca's most important meetings this room had seen, over the last sixty-eight years! Book clubs, fundraising drives, afternoon coffee after afternoon coffee, Cecily's weekly Prayer and Action Circle. ("Heavy on the action, light on the prayer," as Cecily always advertised it.)

Liz climbed the stairs, her fingers trailing the oak banister, for some reason recalling the night Robby Hanson had picked her up for her first-ever date when she was fifteen. They were going to a dance at the school; Liz still remembered the sateen peacock-blue dress she'd worn, the smoothness of her nylon stockings, the way she'd wobbled in her new white pumps as she'd turned the corner to see a nervous-looking Robby standing there in a jacket and tie, Liz's father beside him. At the sight of Liz descending, Sam had taken off his glasses and wiped the corner of his eye with his knuckle. In those days, he'd thought maybe she'd follow in his footsteps and become a doctor, too—and, yes, he had been that progressive, that he hadn't imagined she could only ever be a nurse.

In the upstairs bathroom, Liz rifled through drawers to find her mother's cosmetic bag, then the medicine cabinet to make a stab at what Cecily might need: moisturizer, eyebrow pencil (Cecily would want to look good for visitors), lipstick, tweezers, prescriptions.

The master bedroom spanned the front of the house, and, walking in, Liz was astounded all over again—she so rarely came in here—by how Cecily had redecorated after Sam's passing: lavender walls; a wild quilt of aqua, orange, yellow, purple; a dozen bright throw pillows stacked halfway down the bed, the large one in front proclaiming, *Life is too short to blend in.* Tall bookshelves in each corner stood full to bursting with neat rows and stacks of fiction. Her parents' older books—over their sixty-eight years in the house, they'd collected literally thousands—resided downstairs in her father's office, up in the attic, in the shelf-lined guest bedrooms. Cecily claimed they were impossible to get rid of—*They're like old friends!*—and knew the location of each and every one.

Lavender walls notwithstanding, it was a comfort to see Cecily's office in the adjoining tower looking as it had all of Liz's life: the desk facing out at the yard and street corner, the angular walls lined with overflowing bookshelves under the windows. Each shelf had a cushion seat on top, the perfect size for a kid to lie down and read. Liz remembered the sounds of her mother's pen, the folding of stationery into envelopes; how Cecily would let Liz lick the stamps and carefully affix them.

But this must not have happened often: in those early years, Cecily had surely spent most of her time downstairs in Sam's reception room, greeting patients, managing records, pulling pennies from behind children's ears to make them smile. She'd taught Liz, at eight, how to alphabetize files, answer the phone, schedule appointments. "Good riddance to those chores!" Cecily had said, upon assigning them fully to Liz, telling Sam that Liz was "fully qualified and much better suited to the work than I am." As Liz grew older still, her father would let her pilfer through *Gray's Anatomy* and answer any question she had. She'd been sorry when he'd moved his office to the clinic, though Cecily had declared herself perfectly happy to let him go: "More time for committee work!"

After that, at least once a week, Liz would come home from school to find Cecily in the kitchen making one of her fifteen-layer cakes on the stovetop. "These things *change people's minds*," she would say. "They open wallets. Work wonders!" Within five years, she'd spearheaded the raising of a million dollars for the performing arts center. (These cakes were Cecily's "secret recipe"; the one time she'd let Liz, age seven or so, "help," layer five had somehow slid off the side into a messy pool of hot icing, leaving them both in tears. Mortified to have made her mother cry, Liz had never attempted to "help" again.)

Now, at sixty-eight, Liz had enough perspective to guess that most children who were fortunate enough to be well cared for believed, as Liz had, that *their* parents were just the way parents *were*; that there was nothing unique or interesting about them. "My parents are one hundred percent conventional," she remembered telling Dean before the first time she'd brought him home from college, senior year. In hindsight, of course, her scorn for the bourgeoisie—her muted so-called rebellion at the time—had been nothing more than going along with a different crowd. Later, when she became a mother herself and she and Dean had moved to Itasca because he said it must be the best place in the world to raise a family "because look how good you turned out, babe," her parents' conventionality, their solid footing in the world, had been a great comfort, and something she'd come to aspire to. (In reality, Dean had been far better at community doings; Liz always ended up feeling off-kilter, like she was the one who came from somewhere else.)

Now Liz grabbed the books that were on Cecily's bedside table—a thin little volume called *Keep Going: The Art of Perseverance,* plus a Laura Lippman mystery—then retrieved a Vera Bradley tote from the closet shelf and headed for the top dresser drawer. She pawed through Cecily's white and pink satin underthings, feeling a little like a burglar, trying to discern by touch which might be the most comfortable.

At the bottom of the pile, her fingertips brushed against what felt like stiff paper. Odd.

She peered into the drawer, parting the pile, uncovering a crisp, plain manila folder.

How strange. What could be inside? Her mother didn't have any secrets.

Liz fished out the folder and opened it. Inside was a small, ancient, black-and-white snapshot, scratched, its corners bent; mottled and a bit wrinkled, as if it had been left out in the rain. It showed a serious-looking boy—maybe seventeen—standing in a nondescript field, leaning on a sledgehammer, wearing a newsboy cap, gazing off to the side. From the shape of his nose and the shade of his skin, he might've been African American, but it was difficult to tell. On the back of the picture was written, in handwriting Liz didn't recognize, *Lucky.*

A hundred times, Liz had seen Cecily rifle through the overflowing bin at The Antique Barn labeled *Unidentified (Know Anybody?).* This photo could've come from there.

But no woman put anything in her underwear drawer that didn't have personal significance, right?

Well, Liz could hardly ask Cecily about it when Cecily was just out of surgery. Besides, to ask would be basically to admit that she'd been snooping—

A distant knock sounded on the kitchen door downstairs, startling her. The door creaked open. "Just settin' it on the table for ya!" Harold called. Liz shouted back her thanks, trying to sound natural—he hadn't *actually* caught her doing anything nefarious!—and heard him go out again.

She let out a breath. Enough nonsense. She needed to get back to the hospital. She stashed the snapshot back where she'd found it, quickly finished packing, then headed downstairs, turning out lights as she went, the faint mystery of the snapshot fading behind the glaring concerns of the present. The house would be empty all night—and for who knew how long afterward. Harold would surely keep an eye on the place, but that wasn't the same as having someone occupying it. This was the time of year when pipes could freeze; when things could go badly wrong in a house in a very short amount of time.

Well, she'd leave the heat turned up, at least—though Cecily would surely find it wasteful and extravagant, to heat an empty house.

Forecasting the weeks ahead reminded Liz of the 114 bowls she'd promised to donate for the Empty Bowl fundraiser in early April. How was she going to finish them now? In the past, the feel of clay turning under her hands had always been what grounded and centered her. After Dean's death, she'd been out in her studio a good twelve hours a day. But, these days, she was plain uninspired. Exhausted, to tell the truth, and aching, somehow, deep in her bones. She'd hardly set foot out there in months. And now there'd be daily drives to town, nursing care to coordinate, this house to manage on top of her own—

She caught herself. Cecily was the one suffering. Liz would just have to buck up.

Back in the kitchen, she pulled the foil off one of the two paper plates that Harold had loaded with tuna-noodle hotdish. Catching the scent made her suddenly ravenous, and she grabbed a fork from the drawer. The first bite of melded egg noodles, tuna, Campbell's Cream of Mushroom, and cheese tasted so good that tears came to her eyes, and she started shoveling the concoction into her mouth—bite after bite after bite, like a starving child. Hot, cheesy sauce dribbled down her chin. Comfort food.

So where were these tears coming from?

Nothing so small as a fall down some stairs could actually *kill* Cecily, could it? (Liz could not let those statistics about hip injuries sink in—just could *not* accept them as fact, as reality. She *would* not accept them as reality, not ever.)

But Liz had overheard Cecily as the paramedics were wheeling her in through the hospital's sliding glass doors: "Roger, all I'm asking is that you *admit* this *could* be the beginning of the end for me. I think Sam is getting impatient, waiting—"

Liz wiped her face with a paper towel and threw it and the paper plate into the under-sink garbage can, though she knew it would probably start to smell by tomorrow. As she passed the refrigerator, where a family photo gallery was arranged with cheerful magnets, a familiar image of her father as a young man caught her eye. Later in life, Sam had worn round tortoiseshell glasses, but this picture had been taken long before he'd needed them; in college, maybe. He was classically handsome in a Norwegian way, blond-haired and blue-eyed. Liz had inherited his big bones, light eyes, and much of his height, though her hair, before it shifted toward gray and she'd taken to coloring it light blond, had fallen between her father's blond and her mother's nearly black at a mousy, nondescript brown.

Looking into her father's eyes now, she wished she could know the things he'd known. Maybe life wouldn't seem like such a great big crapshoot if you were used to thinking in scientific terms, in black-and-white and lab results, diagrams and charts. These days, Liz could see only the flowing of colors, the surprise of glaze and chemistry, the fallibility and mystery of clay and fire.

But then she remembered what her father had said when, with great trepidation, home for Christmas from her sophomore year at the U of M, sporting hippie-straight hair and bell-bottoms, she'd broken the news that she was changing her major from biology to art. That she was going to become a potter. Sam had laughed and started to sing: "To everything, turn turn turn. . . ." (She'd been astonished. Her parents listened to The Byrds?) And, to this day, she didn't understand his laughter. Did he think, in that moment, that she was ridiculous? Or simply that *life* was? Then Cecily had started laughing, too, and said to Liz, "Honey, you must know, in our eyes you can do no wrong." So maybe her parents didn't actually see things in black-and-white terms to the degree that she imagined.

(Still, though—laughing?)

"Dad," she said out loud to the picture. "I'm not ready to give her up."

But he didn't answer.

CHAPTER 7

October 1927
Chicago

T he man didn't tell Cecily his name. He just told the taxi driver to take them to Union Station and settled into his own corner of the back seat, reading a newspaper in front of his face.

Cecily hadn't been off the grounds of the Home since her arrival there almost three years earlier—nor had she ever been in a car, let alone a taxi. Soon, she was craning her neck to try to take in everything they were driving past, even as she wiped hot tears from her face. First, row upon row of small houses; frost-coated lawns in the early morning light; street upon street lined with young, autumn-tinged trees. Then, brick storefronts, the shades being raised to open for the day. Pedestrians, rushing in and out. And then, taller buildings—six, seven, eight rows of windows high. The sidewalks grew more and more crowded with people, and, as the taxi lurched and bumped along, Cecily read the signs above the doors and painted on the walls. P.A. GREEN & SON. 40% OFF. WRIGLEY'S THE FLAVOR LASTS. RED HOT VIENNA SAUSAGE SANDWICHES 5¢. WOOLWORTH'S. SURE-RAISING FLOUR. IRVING'S FURNISHINGS. LACROSSE HOTEL.

She wished Flip and Dolores could see all this. The thought of them crushed her all over again.

Where was this man taking her? And why *her*—?

Then she caught sight, in the distance, of buildings so tall that her mouth dropped open. She blinked. Lost count at twenty rows of windows up. Blinked again. All around, now, were these magnificent buildings, rising toward the puffs of clouds, the sun glinting on their windows as it climbed the opposite sky.

The man lowered his newspaper. "You ever been downtown, kid?"

"No!" Just that one visit to Marshall Field's, maybe. But this part, she did not recall.

"This here's Michigan Avenue." As the taxi crawled south with the noisy traffic on the wide, flat boulevard, the man pointed out the window at a pair of white terra-cotta towers gleaming in the distance. "That there's the Wrigley Building. Baseball and chewing gum, all the good things in life, right?" He pointed again. "The London Guarantee Building. And that's the Tribune Tower, where the newspaper lives."

Nothing he said made sense to Cecily, but there was too much to look at to ask him to explain. Hundreds of people, hundreds of cars. Horns honking, gears grinding, motors kicking and grumbling, newsboys and vendors shouting, businessmen in suits hailing cabs, women in fur coats and fantastic hats clicking down the sidewalks in high heels.

"And this here's the Chicago River," the man said, as they inched onto a metal bridge, tires purring over the grate. "They teach you about any of this at the orphanage?"

"No!"

"You're going to learn about the world now, kid. Hell, you're gonna *see* it. I'm gonna personally guarantee that."

Cecily wanted to poke her head out the window to see if she could make out the glimmering water between the cracks of the bridge. She didn't quite dare, but just imagining it made her grin over at the man. Maybe he wasn't as bad as Dolores had predicted.

"Where are you taking me?" She finally dared to ask.

He smiled, shook his head like he still thought she was a puppy, and raised the newspaper again.

Union Station was colossal. Gigantic arches, soaring ceilings, throngs of rushing crowds. Cecily scurried through the marble foyer after the man, trying to keep up, not to lose him, for how would she distinguish him from the hundreds of other men wearing black topcoats? Her suitcase, small as it was, was too heavy for her. She had to switch hands, back and forth, back and forth, then finally carry it with both, as it bumped against her knees.

"We're meeting up with the show in Belvidere," the man called over his shoulder, taking it for granted that he hadn't lost her. How could he be so certain? And where—or what!—was Belvidere? "Isabelle can't wait to meet you."

"What show?" she piped up, though she was short of breath. "Who's Isabelle?"

He didn't answer, just kept on moving through the crowd, toward where the trains billowed steam.

He let her sit next to the window so she could look out. The seat was a hard bench, and she sat on her hands, feeling the train rattle all through her. She watched the buildings get smaller again, then disappear, replaced by wide fields punctuated with square white farmhouses and big red barns. She wondered about the families that lived in those houses, so far from other people. Did the man live in a big, lonely house like these? Was Isabelle his wife? Did they have other children?

What did they want with Cecily?

The window was partway open, and Cecily felt cold despite the yellow sweater Mrs. H. had foisted on her, plus slightly dizzy from the scenery streaming past. It was odd to be moving so quickly; to be going away. Had she ever even imagined leaving Chicago? Maybe not. At least, not while she was still a kid. She would never have willingly left while there was still a chance her mother would come for her. And certainly, when she'd woken up this morning, she hadn't known that, by noon, she'd have left behind the only city she'd ever known.

She wondered what Flip and Dolores would have to say, if they were in the train looking out the window, too. Just imagining it—*Goddamn!* and *The family that lives in that house is happy; that man isn't afraid of anything, not even of being alone*—made her feel a little better. The man was sitting next to her, reading the newspaper again.

CHAPTER 8

Tuesday, February 17, 2015
Itasca, Minnesota

When Molly finally left the hospital and headed south on the main highway out of town to get Caden from George's house, it was past eight, pitch black, and two below zero. Hoping the heater would take effect soon, she'd just turned up the radio to belt along with "Livin' on a Prayer" when her cell phone rang in through her Bluetooth and the name *Evan Bouchard* displayed on the stereo.

Her heart sped up. She hadn't talked to her ex-husband since Christmas, about Caden's canceled trip, the impossibility of rescheduling—

Today did *not* feel like the day to talk to him again.

No sense avoiding him, though. Caden would hear about it and no doubt lecture-tease her in her own tone about facing life head-on and dealing with people in a grown-up, respectful manner.

She clicked the button to answer. "Fancy meeting you here," she said.

"Hey, you answered!" said the oh-so-familiar voice, the one she'd first heard piping up from the back of her English 120 class, second semester freshman year at Colby; the one that, unfortunately, still caused a tuning fork to vibrate somewhere deep within her. "So, listen, I'll be quick. Cade said he told you I'm coming into town for his game Friday, right?"

"And none too soon." Ha, she seemed to have perfected the haughty ex-wife tone instantly, and with no preparation! "This could be their last game, if they lose."

"I know, Moll. I've been hoping to make it all season, but things have been totally nuts at work, so, yeah, now I'm just breaking away. Only trouble is, every single hotel room in town is booked, so I was wondering if I could crash with you."

The good humor she'd been forcing drained out in an instant, like a stopper had just been pulled. "Are you serious?"

"As a heart attack," he said cheerfully.

She didn't trust herself to keep driving. She pulled into the Home Depot parking lot—it was nearly empty, this time of night—watching for slick spots on the pavement, steering into a space next to a plowed-up snowbank as tall as a two-story building.

"Moll?"

She shifted into Park—and, to her horror, burst into tears. Noisy ones. She couldn't hide or stop them.

"Moll?" Evan said again, this time sounding worried. "I guess I didn't think you'd be *happy*, but—"

"Oh, stop! Stop. Not everything's about you." She wiped her face with her glove, trying to collect herself, feeling his presence in stereo-surround. She'd been trying so hard all day to be cheerful and strong for Liz, not to show how scared she was. Trying not to even *think* about it.

Because, yes: the thought of losing Grandma Cecily was simply *unthinkable*.

"What is it, then?" Evan said. Molly was vaguely surprised that he didn't seem exasperated by her crying. Of course, he'd had a two-year respite from it. That probably helped.

"It's my grandma," she said, swallowing back more tears, and she told him what had happened, trying—though it was obviously far too late—for a calm-cool-collected, got-it-under-control tone. "So, she's got a really long road ahead, they're saying," she finished, digging in her purse for a Kleenex. "Rehab and everything. Full recovery could take up to a year."

"Aw, Moll, I'm so sorry," Evan said, and it was exactly the same tone he'd used when she'd gotten the call about her dad. That time, it had been in person, in their tiny, sunny Newport kitchen lined with the tile they'd ordered from Italy, with his arms around her. Recognizing that now made her stomach ache. "But, you know," he said, "things like this were exactly why you moved back out there, right?"

His tone wasn't unkind, but still. "Salt, wound, Evan. Remember? Didn't we promise no salt?"

"Moll, come on. I'm just saying it's good you're there." The slight catch in his voice made her remember: the few times he'd visited Itasca with Molly, he and Cecily had hit it off, spending hours together listening to Cecily's extensive collection of jazz LPs, which Evan had pronounced "classic" and "first-rate."

It suddenly struck her as so strange to have his oh-so-familiar voice coming through the stereo speakers of her car in the Home Depot parking lot of her old hometown. How did life turn out this way, anyway? That someone you'd once shared the most intimate and precious parts of your life with could be so far gone and far away, and yet, through the miracles of technology and the fact of sharing a child (*children*), still envelop you, be indelibly connected. As though moments of your past lived on and bound you, regardless of any opposite intent you might have had.

Regardless of how much you'd wanted to leave the pain behind.

"Moll?" he said again. A slight prick with an X-Acto knife, every time; a warm blanket, too.

She yanked off her wool hat and ran a hand through her newly bobbed platinum hair. Just last week, Hilda down at the Cut-n-Curl had laughed with delight when Molly'd shown her the recent picture of Jennifer Lawrence, of the transformation Molly wanted, away from her plain-Jane light brown waves. *Oh, yah, that'll shake the dust right off ya*, Hilda had said. *That'll be just the thing.*

Now it was a reminder: She was different. She wasn't who she'd been. *Okay*, she told herself. *Okay.* "Listen, Evan, it's good you're coming, for Caden's sake, but I don't know about you staying with us." Having six-foot-three Evan in the tiny bungalow would be like putting a bear on a bicycle and telling him it was no sweat to ride. "It's a two-bedroom. You'd be stuck on the couch."

A pause. "The couch is fine. I can't get a hotel. Apparently, the opposing team has a *lot* of fans coming down for the game."

Molly squeezed the steering wheel tight in both hands. She should just say no. She should, should, should say no.

But how? She could still hear that lost-little-boy tone of Caden's voice this morning. "All right, fine," she said. "Just text me the details. When you'll be getting in and all that."

"Cool. Great. Thanks. Oh, and, Moll, listen, I wanted to tell you: I'll pay for Cade's honors bio project. The DNA thing? He said it'd be, like, four hundred dollars, but I think it's a great idea."

"What's this?" Molly hadn't heard anything about an honors bio project.

"You know, where he's going to analyze the four generations of your family's DNA? Cool, right? He seems so excited about it. I guess he's really interested in genetics."

"Oh, yeah!" She pretended to know. Now she was light-headed, suddenly. Too hot. She flicked the heater off, tugged at her scarf.

"Anyway, yeah, I guess we can figure it out this weekend, but definitely know I'm good for it."

The car's idle was a soft hum. "It's going to be weird to see you," she blurted, even as she was thinking how Caden should've asked her about this project first, if it was to be *her* DNA, plus her mother's and grandmother's? And why was it so damn hot in this car? She yanked the zipper of her parka partway down.

"And you," Evan said. "It's going to be weird to see you, too." A pause. She somehow wanted to throw something; had no idea why. Then: "But, you know, I'm the same."

She didn't know what to say. Landed on: "How unfortunate."

He laughed. "I see you're the same, too." Then he said he'd text her, and she said sure, and they said goodbye and hung up, leaving her alone in the darkness of the idling Mazda beside the snowbank. She realized she'd forgotten to ask how long he was planning to stay. The weekend? A week? Good Lord, she hoped not.

And—was she really the same? Was he?

She seriously doubted it.

The halos around the Home Depot's floodlights showed tiny flakes of snow drifting down. It was five miles out to George's house. She flipped the heat back on and put the car into gear.

"Yeah, well, Mr. Rasmussen suggested I send in my DNA and Great-Grandma Cecily's DNA, plus maybe the two generations in between, and have it analyzed," Caden said in the darkness on the drive back into town, after Molly had given him a full report on Cecily, and a not-so-full report on her conversation with Evan, and then, trying not to sound too aggravated, asked him to explain about his honors bio project. "He said we'd be able to see how the genes get passed down that way, and trace our ancestry to other countries and stuff. He said it was unique to have four generations in the same town, and the tests are really easy to do now."

Well, okay. This was pretty cool. And, also, the first thing all school year she could remember Caden sounding excited about, outside of hockey. Maybe it was even a first step toward getting into a good college! Molly had sudden, dizzying visions of him in a white lab coat, the letters *Ph.D.* after his name. "That sounds great, bud! Let's just wait a few days to ask Grandma Cecily. Till she's feeling better, you know? But we can talk to Mom first. I'm sure she'd give you a sample. You could at least do three generations, that way."

"K," he said.

She waited. There was nothing more. And, much as she wanted to, much as she tried, Molly just could not read him one bit these days. Was he upset about Cecily at all? Or simply able to coolly accept, with the hubris of the young, that she was going to be just fine?

Molly gave up trying for the moment and just drove, remembering how out of sorts Liz had seemed by day's end, too, going on about the coming cold snap: how the pipes would certainly freeze in Cecily's house; how Liz had to make 114 bowls for the Empty Bowl fundraiser and didn't know how she'd manage. It was strange, come to think of it: Not once had Liz said she was worried about Cecily. Just the house, the bowls, the weather.

Molly watched the swoop of the headlights through the black night. Caden's fingertips drummed his knee. He always seemed to have some private rhythm going lately.

She couldn't help wanting to be let in, and she thought of something. "Hey, bud, you know, this project of yours could be really interesting, because Grandma Cecily was an orphan. Did you know that? She never knew who her parents were, or if she had siblings. So we might have a bunch of relatives out there that we have no idea about."

"Really? Cool."

Sudden tears stung Molly's eyes again; she had no idea why. Beyond her headlights, the stars were pinpricks of light in the black sky. She remembered Evan, shouting once, in one of the bad times: *You talk about the importance of family! You're the one breaking ours! You're the one who thinks you're going through all of this alone, when that's the farthest thing from true!*

She thought of something else. "Hey, bud," she ventured. "Those DNA tests—are they the kind that tell you stuff about your health? Like, can they forecast potential issues, or explain things that have happened?"

"Like why you lost the babies, you mean? I don't think so."

He said it so coldly that it was like a fall into ice water. He said it as if he was tired of the subject; as if it had ruined his whole life. And maybe, in some way, it had: Every two years, starting when he was two, she'd had a miscarriage. Four babies, lost. By the time he was ten, she and Evan had been so broken, they hadn't had the wherewithal to keep trying.

Now Molly was reeling from her son's cruelty, even as she heard her own voice: *Try to understand his pain. In adolescence, every emotion is extreme.*

But then he spoke up again: "It was probably your fault, Mom. You're just going to have to accept it."

Tears flooded her, blurring her vision as she drove.

No, she thought then. *No.* Her son was not going to set her healing back five years; he just was *not* going to be allowed to do that. "How dare you speak to me that way?" she hissed.

"You always tell me we have to accept things the way they are! That's all I meant!"

She swallowed hard. "I thought," she managed, through gritted teeth, "that I had also taught you about compassion. Tell me, Caden. Tell me what you say to indicate compassion."

A sigh. "I see your suffering. I acknowledge your suffering. I am sorry."

"Caden," she said, teeth still clenched. "I see your suffering. I acknowledge your suffering. I am sorry."

"You sound totally sincere, Mom," he said.

"Well," she said. "So do you." Another parenting victory. God help her.

Get me home to the laundry, she thought. *At least that I know how to do.*

CHAPTER 9

October 1927
Belvidere, Illinois

The train clanked and groaned to a stop at Belvidere with a long, slow squealing of brakes that reminded Cecily of when Horace ran his fingernails across the chalkboard, making the other kids shriek and Miss Oversham rap the desk with her yardstick and shout, pink-faced, "Children! Children!" Cecily was sad to think that she hadn't gotten to say goodbye to Miss Oversham, and that sadness lodged, humming, underneath her nerves and discomfort. (She needed a toilet, but she didn't want to say so to the man.) "Ready, kid?" he said, folding his newspaper under his arm, and she just nodded, and stood when he did. He looked like he must ride the train a lot, and she wanted to seem like she had experience, too.

The Belvidere depot was made of red brick and had a wide platform with a long roof running the length of it, to keep everybody dry, Cecily guessed, as she hopped down the grated iron steps behind the man. She had realized two facts about him so far. One: he was always in a hurry. Two: he had confidence in her, though she didn't know why.

He turned and handed her her suitcase, which he had carried down for her. "You hungry, kid? I bet you are. It's gonna be a while before we eat, sorry to say." He started away, and she followed. There wasn't such a crowd here, only a few folks scattered across the wooden platform. Today, the broad roof was just providing a too-cool shade, when the sun would've been nice to feel.

L

The man led her inside—he seemed to know she needed a bathroom without her saying so, and she was grateful. She used it quickly and washed her hands carefully. When she came out, he was sitting on a bench, and looked at her like he wondered if she was going to be more trouble than she was worth. It was only half past ten in the morning. He left the newspaper on the bench, and they went back outside and around behind the building, where there were more sets of train tracks.

They walked a long way, down between two lines of cars, flatcars on one side, boxcars on the other. The man slowed so she could walk beside him, and he put his hand on her back, looking around watchfully now.

Cecily, struggling with her suitcase, heard a frightening roar in the distance, then the blat of some kind of horn, and laughter. The man just kept walking.

Now there was a stock car with its slats painted bright blue, the words SAX & TEBOW CIRCUS emblazoned on the side in yellow. And now a green car with a painting of a larger-than-life tiger: SAX & TE-BOW CIRCUS BIG CATS. One in red with a clown: SAX & TEBOW CIRCUS CLOWNS. On and on, as they walked, Cecily's shoes crunching rough gravel, each car was illustrated with something new: EGYPTIAN CAMELS. ZEBRAS. MONKEYS! LIBERTY HORSES. AERIAL DARE-DEVILS. BAREBACK RIDERS. Even the passenger cars were painted this way.

The orphanage had had a picture book about a circus, but Cecily had never dreamed she'd *see* one. Was the man taking her to one before he even took her home to meet his family?

By the time they reached a little white caboose, on which was painted a giant, red-nosed clown in a derby hat with a purple flower, her heart was pounding. In the distance, she heard breathy, screechy fast-paced music, reminding her of when she and her friends had tried learning to play the recorder after a well-meaning Samaritan had donated a few to the Home, before Mrs. H. declared she had a permanent headache and stowed the instruments away "for good."

"We'll throw your suitcase in here for now," the man said. He opened the door to the caboose, snatched Cecily's suitcase and tossed it up inside, alarming her. Then he grabbed her under her arms, lifted her onto the step, and said, "Wait here. Don't move a muscle." He disappeared into the next car.

Well. What else could she do?

So, she waited, tapping her foot with nerves, listening to the distant music, the occasional shouts and screeches, the banging. The air smelled of roasted peanuts and popcorn, hay and grain, dust and manure, roasting meat, sweet taffy. Her mouth had started to water, her stomach to rumble.

The man came out wearing a red tailcoat, white shirt, red vest, white jodhpurs, and a top hat. His black boots gleamed. "Come on, kid," he said, as he headed for the noise, adjusting his white bow tie. "Keep up."

After the white caboose was a plain red caboose, and that was the last car of the train. The man led her around the tail end of it, where the screechy music grew louder. Some distance ahead in a wide-open field was a massive dirty white canvas tent. Other, smaller tents were off to the side. And lined up in front was a whole parade! A hundred or more people in bright costumes; at least a dozen vivid wagons pulled by matched teams of two or four or six gray or black Percherons; two dozen sleeker horses in plumed headdresses with riders, men and women both, in Arabian-style dress; a dozen made-up clowns on foot in big red shoes and baggy patched pants. In one wagon—just a large cage surrounded by red and gold filigree—paced a pair of tigers, while a dark-haired woman in a short pink dress paced atop it. In another wagon-cage was a sleeping lion, and a handsome man with a whip stood above it, smoking a cigarette. A beautiful young woman in a short red sparkling dress stood on the back of a gorgeous white Percheron, one of three lined up wearing red plumed headdresses. On top of another wagon stood a very tall man, beside a seated fat lady, plus a woman in a flowing satin gown who seemed to have a *snake* around her neck—could that be? Five men in sequined green suits were stretching and unlimbering themselves. Four zebras draped in gold-rimmed purple silks shook their manes. A man placed a monkey in a purple hat and vest on the back of one, and the monkey screeched and grinned. Two camels draped in red chewed their cud like they were bored by the man who held their leads. On top of another wagon, a seal barked and, when a clown set a ball on its nose, held it there, balancing. A chimpanzee in a blue vest pulled a child's wagon with a braying goat inside. The smell of the animals was very strong.

"Come on, kid," the man said, his long legs stretching toward the front of the parade. "You're gonna ride with me."

The man led her to the front of the line, then, without warning, lifted her up onto a huge, brilliantly white horse, placing her ahead of the saddle. He climbed up behind her and grabbed the reins, just as that breathy, screechy music stopped. "This is Blanco," the man told Cecily. "Hold on to his mane."

Cecily grabbed the coarse hair just in time, as the man clicked to the horse. The lurching of the horse's big muscles was a shock and a thrill. The gathered crowd, cheering, opened for them to pass through, and Cecily glanced back to see that all the wagons and animals and people were pitching into motion, and the motion was rough and chaotic at first, as the many parts began to merge into a whole. The wagon directly behind the man and Cecily was the bandwagon, and, with a motion from the red-coated conductor, the brass band burst into quick, cheerful music. When Cecily glanced back again, she and the man had become the bow of a long, beautiful boat, all flowing of a piece.

"Wave to the crowd, kid," the man said, and Cecily did, and people on the ground cheered and pointed and laughed, and she laughed back, as

Blanco's beautiful ears seemed to twitch to the music, and Cecily clutched his mane with one hand and waved and waved with the other, still wearing the little yellow sweater Mrs. H. had given her that morning.

"That's right, help yourself!" the man said, laughing as Cecily stood on tiptoe to heap scoop after scoop of mashed potatoes from the steam table buffet line onto her plate. "You poor starving kid!"

They'd led the parade through the whole town, across the river and through the orange-tinged trees, past the brick facades of the downtown shops and restaurants, and back again, what must've been a mile or more, and all along the route the crowd was a dozen deep and cheering. All together, it was more people than Cecily had ever seen, and they'd all been cheering for *her*. Flip and Dolores were never going to believe it.

Back at the circus lot, the man had helped her down from Blanco and led her straight over to what he called the cook top—another large white tent—where she was first in line for lunch. The wonder of the mounds of food was almost enough to blot out all the other wonders of the day. She loaded roast beef and gravy on top of the potatoes, said why not to the little logs of steamed green beans. There were side dishes of stewed tomatoes, small plates of peach cobbler, plus coffee with cream that the man poured for Cecily, saying she might as well start drinking it today, now that she was in the circus.

"What do you mean?" Cecily said, but the man just led her over to one of a dozen long tables covered in red-checked cloths—a carnation in a bud vase adorned each—and bid her to sit down. The performers were streaming in, lining up and loading their plates, the men in sparkling green, the tiger lady in pink, the very tall man, the fat lady, the clowns.

"Howdy, Mr. Tebow," said one of the clowns, and the man nodded at him, then tucked his white linen napkin into his collar and told Cecily to dig in.

"Ladies and gentlemen," the man—Mr. Tebow—shouted through a megaphone two hours later in the center of the packed Big Top. Cecily bounced in her seat, which was a white-painted folding chair next to the backstage entrance.

Cecily had been scraping her plate clean, while many of the performers were still lined up to fill theirs, when Mr. Tebow had pushed back his chair and told her, "Come on." He'd led her through the maze of backstage tents, where a group of men stood on each other's shoulders, horses waited to have their shoes replaced, and the chimpanzee fed the goat a head of lettuce. Finally, Mr. Tebow flipped up a secret flap in the Big Top, pointed to the folding chair, and again told her, "Don't move a muscle."

So, from here, Cecily had watched everything: workmen wedging extra folding chairs into all the rows, watering the dust with a hose, placing props and putting final touches on the ring and animal cages as the acrobats in green checked the ropes and lines above.

And then the crowd had begun pouring in, finding their seats, munching popcorn, looking up wide-eyed at the scale of things. "You're about to see the most spectacular show on earth!" shouted Mr. Tebow now, and the clowns came streaming from the entrance beside Cecily, walking oddly in their giant shoes and playing tricks on each other as they came, so that already the crowd began to roar with laughter.

There was too much to see, really, though it was just a one-ring circus.

The clowns juggled hoops and balls and bowling pins, and knocked each other down. One balanced a ladder on his chin. There were pies in the face and tricks on ladies in the front row and on Mr. Tebow, who pretended to be very offended. Cecily had never laughed so hard. Next, the lion, all power and grace, stalked past Cecily to get into the ring, where he walked a wire, then yawned, showing giant teeth; when the handsome man cracked a whip, the lion reared, pawed the air and roared, drawing shrieks from ladies in the crowd, then yawned again and got down and padded out of the ring, right back past Cecily, his tamer drawing dust behind him with dramatic cracks of the whip. The Arabian riders thundered in, a mass of noise and glamour and dust that gave Cecily goose bumps as they galloped round and round. The five men in green ran in doing flips as they came, then climbed to the top of the tent and swung from the rafters, twisting and dropping and catching each other, making pyramids and loops. Cecily sat stock-still, mesmerized. The clowns came in again, and this time they brought the seal with them, and it balanced a lamp on its nose.

The brunette in the bright pink dress walked in with the two tigers, snapping a whip to get them to climb ladders and leap through hoops. One of the men in green climbed to the rafters again, this time with a lady in a sparkling dress of a lighter green hue, and they swung and dipped and twisted—they spun like tops, hanging just by their teeth—to the gasps and cheers of the crowd. Seven sleek black horses—"Liberty horses," Mr. Tebow announced them as—trotted into the ring and bowed and danced and maneuvered to the slight gestures of a man dressed all in white, his hair sleek and black like the horses. A lady in gauzy blue introduced as Catherine LeGrande climbed to the rafters and swung prettily on the trapeze, then dropped toward a man swinging violently opposite her, and he caught her by her feet and kept on swinging.

Then Mr. Tebow shouted into his megaphone: "And now, straight from her home in Paris, France, here she is, the incredible Isabelle DuMonde!" Curtains at the back of the tent parted, and the three white Percherons trotted past Cecily and into the ring in a majestic line, the tall red feathers on their elaborate headdresses bobbing in time to peppy music the band played. On the back of the rearmost horse stood the beautiful woman in the sparkly red dress. She seemed to have no trouble balancing—just stood there gracefully, arms out like wings, smiling like she was meeting a prince. She somersaulted to the ground, and, before Cecily could blink, leapt up onto the back of the next horse. The crowd roared. The woman hopped into the air and landed again on the trotting horse. She did a handstand on its back.

She flipped to the ground and vaulted up onto the first horse in line, as all three kept trotting in a regular rhythm around the ring, and the woman held out her arms again, basking in the cheers of the crowd.

"That's Isabelle," the man said, startling Cecily, who hadn't noticed that he'd come to stand beside her. "She's going to teach you to do that."

CHAPTER 10

Wednesday, February 18, 2015
Itasca, Minnesota

A fter Molly presented the details, Liz was quick to agree. By all means, Caden should do the project he wanted to do, and do it full-out, testing Cecily, Liz, Molly, and himself, so he could track Cecily's DNA as it traveled and diminished down the line: half of it would be present in Liz, a quarter in Molly, and an eighth in Caden. Liz even insisted on paying for the tests, so Molly wouldn't have to feel beholden to Evan—"It's *our* family, after all," she'd said—then sat back and smiled, swirling her black coffee in its paper cup. They were sitting by the window in the hospital cafeteria overlooking the icy river; Molly had taken her lunch hour to visit Cecily, but, after just a short chat, Cecily had needed to rest.

It was unnerving, to say the least, to see Cecily laid out this way, so Molly had been glad to have something practical to discuss with Liz, something she could at least pretend to be in control of. Though God knew it wasn't easy to want to help Caden right now, after the things he'd said last night. But, as she was always telling her clients, she had to take the long view. Yes, she was angry and hurt today, but: lab coat. Ph.D.

"Thank you, Mom," she told Liz now, "but it's too much. I could split it with you?"

Liz waved that off. "Listen, what if we made this a surprise for your grandma's ninety-fifth birthday? We'll have the results by June?"

Molly laughed, glad to see Liz seeming like herself again, as well as to think ahead to Cecily's birthday. Surely Cecily would be back to herself by then, too, right? "Yes, long before June." Molly had done some research this morning. "Six to eight weeks, the website said."

"Perfect! Wish I'd thought of this myself. How do we get started?"

Molly explained about ordering the kits online, and Liz dug into her purse for her phone and wallet. "You know, not that she's talked about it often, but your grandma's said a few times that she wished she knew more about her parents, where she came from. She doesn't even know what ethnicity she is—she thinks Irish and French, so that's what we've always said, but really: Can you imagine living almost ninety-five years like that? Never *really* knowing who you are?"

"And *we* don't know who *we* are, either, as a result."

"True! And I've never been able to get her to tell me one thing about her childhood. She says she doesn't remember! Only that she was in an orphanage and that her life really began when your grandpa and I came along. I stopped asking years ago. Even Dad wouldn't talk about his childhood, and he grew up right here! I mean, I know he had Norwegian ancestry, and his father was the doctor here in town, but that's about it. Mom said it was a sore subject for him, but I never understood why."

Molly nodded. "Grandpa never told me anything, either, and all Grandma ever mentioned was meeting Grandpa when he was her doctor at the sanatorium out in Rhode Island." Molly had always loved that story, though Cecily had never filled in enough details to satisfy her, no matter how she'd begged. When Molly had lived in Newport, she'd always meant to drive up to see the old sanatorium building, which, though long ago repurposed, was still standing in the far northwest corner of the state, on the Massachusetts border. Cecily's consistent reluctance to say anything about the time she'd spent there (and who could blame her, really?) had probably discouraged Molly from making the journey—or else, with the way life seemed to go, she'd simply never found the time.

Liz sighed. "I don't know any more than you do, Moll." She seemed to have something else on her mind, but, after a second, just gave her trademark decisive nod. "Yes, this project will be good for all of us. What's the website?"

A few clicks later, Liz was asking for Caden's email address. "I'll make him the administrator, so the results will go straight to him."

"Maybe you should make me the administrator, Mom," Molly said, "and I can help him."

Liz looked up. "It's his project. You've got to trust him with his own business at some point. Anyway, he's the one studying this—he probably knows more about genetics than you do, right?"

Molly sighed. Once again, the gap between her own instincts and what she'd advise a client was glaring. *Don't let your mother dominate you. Trust your teenager with more than you think you can.*

Don't let your ex-husband sleep on your couch.

Right. Though, actually, Liz, moments earlier, had offered a great solution to that problem: Evan could stay at Cecily's house, keep an eye on things, make sure the pipes didn't freeze—as long as Cecily approved. Liz was going to ask her about it later.

Molly didn't know why she hadn't thought of the idea herself, but it was certainly a relief to think Evan might not need to spend the weekend in the bungalow.

After a couple minutes, Liz was done. "Four kits, on the way! I expedited shipping, so they'll be here Friday." She smiled, tucked away her phone, and sipped her coffee again. She really did seem like the old Liz. Pre-widowhood Liz, even! Maybe it had taken a fresh crisis to jolt her out of her lingering grief? Molly had certainly seen all kinds of stranger things happen, when it came to grief. "Four hundred forty-five dollars seems a small price to pay for my mother to finally get some answers about where she came from. For *all* of us to get some answers."

Molly agreed, then remembered something. "I don't know how we'll be able to surprise Grandma, though. The test requires a saliva sample. It isn't just like a hair from a hairbrush, you know?"

"Oh!" Liz thought for a second, then smiled a little, wicked smile. "How about you ask your old friend Stacey to pretend it's something the doctors here need?"

"Mom!" Now, *this* seemed not like Liz at all, not Liz pre- or post-anything. But to see her seeming excited—even up to some mischief—was wonderful. Maybe this project of Caden's would do more good for all of them than Molly had even imagined. Molly grinned. "Okay, I'll ask her."

After work, Molly, warming up her car, found a new text from Liz, sent at 5:56 P.M.: *Grandma doing ok. Was awake for a while. They even had her get out of bed for a minute. She says Evan can stay in the house as long as he wants, lol. I think it's a great idea.:)*

Lol? A smiley face?

Uh oh. Despite the good show she'd put on earlier, Liz was clearly, seriously stressed.

Okay, so maybe it was good Evan was coming to town. Maybe it actually would be a help. Molly shot off a quick reply telling Liz she'd let Evan know, then opened a new text to him. *My mom wants you to stay at my grandma's house and keep an eye on it,* she wrote, before she could think twice. *So you can stay as long as you want. Lots of games coming up in the next week plus, at least unless they lose.* She wrinkled her nose and clicked Send.

He replied instantly: *Great!*

Molly rolled her eyes and put the car in gear. Caden was at George's house; they'd had practice after school, and George's parents, bless them, had offered supper again.

She was almost out of town when a new message from Evan came through the Bluetooth. She gave the command to read it, and through the stereo speakers came the electronic voice: *I should be able to stay a week. Maybe two? Will check with the guys and let you know.*

She laughed out loud and turned on the radio. *The guys*—his business partners in the brewery the three of them had started in Newport after college. How often had Tony and Matt seemed to be more in control of her life than she was?

Molly turned up Demi Lovato's "Skyscraper" and soon was hollering along, letting her whole range of post-divorce pent-up emotions rip—the grief and the fear, the hope and hopelessness, the anger and regret, relief and sorrow, memory and joy.

Then the song was over, and she turned down the radio, wiped her face with her glove, and composed herself, inwardly rehearsing the cool, chipper tone she'd use when she saw Caden.

Guess what? Your dad's going to get to stay a little longer!

CHAPTER 11

Thursday, February 19, 2015
Itasca, Minnesota

*C*ecily hated being stuck flat out in bed. Hated, hated, hated it. She'd hoped she'd die without this ever happening to her again. That she'd just scurry around keeping busy until the very minute she suddenly keeled over.

Lying flat out in bed, a person had too much time to think.

Though, in truth, any time Cecily opened her eyes, Liz hardly gave her a moment to compose herself. Nope, every single time, Liz was right there, wanting to know if Cecily needed her pillow fluffed, a drink of water, a little something extra from the cafeteria. "You've got to eat, Mom," she'd say.

Cecily would just look at her and blink. She loved the way Liz was wearing her hair these days, in light blond ringlets around her face. The resemblance to a latter-day Meg Ryan was uncanny. And all her pretty turtleneck sweaters and chunky silver jewelry. Jeans and practical snow boots. The exact picture of a devoted daughter, Cecily had to believe.

And Cecily would think, *I have to tell her.* Because she had never been so vividly aware of *"her age"* before, nor ever so clearly registered the looming reality of her demise.

She'd swallow, move her lips around to loosen them, working up to a real speech—but her throat always felt so dry. "Maybe a little water," she'd end up saying. And Liz would hop to, then invariably follow up the water by reading aloud another card that had arrived with another flower arrangement. "Isn't that nice?" she'd say. "The news has really gotten around town. Everyone's praying for you." And Cecily would nod, feeling that the moment for confession—for bringing up such long-ago things—had passed.

Well. Anyway. To whose benefit would the truth be, really?

Wouldn't it just upend everything?

If Cecily went to the grave with nobody knowing, would anyone truly be worse off?

Cecily hardly thought so. The secret couldn't bother her anymore if *she* was dead, and nobody else would ever have to know. That's what Sam had finally agreed would be best. After so long, he'd said, what would be the point? And wasn't he usually right about most things? Good old trusted Dr. Larson, yes, indeed. Everyone in this whole town had looked to him for advice on all matters, ranging from health to moral rightness to the cultivation of string beans.

He had told her again and again throughout their life that she had done "far more than enough" good to make up for whatever she'd done that had been questionable. But she never could quite believe him, and, after he was gone, there'd been no one left who knew the truth of her at all.

She was tired, drugged, in and out of dreams. The slight high of the initial shock of injury was gone; now she didn't have the wherewithal even to read. And this perky little "therapist" kept coming by, wanting her to sit up, and even, once, swing her legs off the bed and attempt to stand. "For heaven's sake," Cecily had said, though she'd done her best, after the "therapist" promised that the sooner she started moving, the quicker she'd recover.

This part was very different than the San, where they hadn't wanted you to get out of bed at all; where they'd said you wouldn't recover if you *did*.

Sometimes she thought she heard Sam's voice. Sometimes he said her name; other times, things like, *Turn down the TV, hon.* Even if the TV wasn't on! Maddening, really. She'd tell him—not out loud; she didn't want the nurses to think she'd lost her mind—*Dr. Larson, I don't want to stay in bed for one more second!*

You have to, he would say. *Longer hospital stays have been proven, in the event of hip fractures in the elderly, to reduce the chances of death.*

She wondered if until Monday qualified as a "longer stay." She didn't feel cheerful at the thought of dying. Not much better was the thought of extended weeks of "rehab," as they called it now.

Any way you cut it, she didn't have much time left—and she still had so much to do. Yes. So much atoning for her mistakes.

God doesn't keep a balance sheet, hon, Sam said, but she didn't think he knew that for a fact, even now.

CHAPTER 12

June 1939
Wallum Lake Sanatorium, Rhode Island

S am may have been fresh out of medical school and new to the staff at the sanatorium, but there were a few things he knew for sure. One: he wasn't supposed to play favorites.

But he couldn't help it. He already had a few. The eight-year-old boy, Patrick, who staged vast battles with toy soldiers across the hills and valleys his body made in the bed, ending each day with an earthquake that toppled both sides. The ten-year-old girl, Betty Drake, who had straightaway informed Sam that everybody who was anybody called her Tootsie and that she was going to be a doctor when she grew up. (He'd already started sneaking her back issues of *The Lancet*.)

And then there was the beautiful dark-haired girl-almost-woman— her chart said she'd just turned nineteen—who wouldn't stop crying.

She was on the women's ward, an open-air porch that ran the length of the front of the building. The beds—fifteen of them—were lined up with their headboards against the wall, so each patient had a view of the distant lake. The women stayed out here day and night year-round, even as the snow flew in and covered their blankets while they slept.

It was mid-June now, though. The Rhode Island weather was nearly perfect. Not too hot during the day, pleasantly cool at night. The maples and big copper beeches, the azalea and larkspur, were in full bloom; birds were singing. There weren't the terrible mosquitoes here like back in Sam's home of northern Minnesota. There could hardly have been a lovelier place to convalesce. Of course, there were disruptions to the quiet, due to the repairs that continued on the roof and the sawing of blown-down trees from last September's hurricane, and a lot of rules and things that patients weren't allowed to do, but those things—the absolute rest, the gradations of restrictions—were all for their own good.

So why was this girl-almost-woman crying so incessantly?

Every day, as Sam made his rounds up and down the porch, he couldn't help pausing to ask her what was wrong. Was her pain intolerable? Every day, she'd smile through her tears and make up something new. *The moon is so far away. I don't think Goldilocks really ever found the right-size chair. Bessie Smith will never sing again. Spiders die as soon as they lay their eggs. So many people are starved for love all their lives.*

Her dark eyelashes were always spiked with tears; her eyes were an extraordinary sapphire blue.

Sam knew it was true there were plenty of things to be sad about in this world. Especially here at the San, where most of the patients stayed for years to take the rest-and-fresh-air treatment; where many of them were released only by death. There was no cure for TB, not yet. Only the hope you might, inexplicably—by God's grace?—get better. Though God knew the doctors were always trying to figure out a way to help, trying for a cure. Sam had assisted Dr. Overholt on one artificial pneumothorax procedure so far, collapsing the patient's lung so that it could rest and heal. Dr. Overholt was also a pioneer in pneumonectomy, having been the first in the world, in 1933, to successfully remove a patient's right lung.

As interested as Sam was in seeing that revolutionary procedure performed and in assisting the legend—Dr. Overholt's mortality rate overall was just 22 percent, versus the 47 percent other surgeons worldwide averaged now on the pneumonectomy—he hoped things would not come to that, in this case.

The girl-woman's chart said she was five feet tall and ninety-two pounds and had been here at the San since last November; that she'd been ordered here by the health department off the hurricane-ravaged streets of Providence after her sputum test had come up positive. The police had been enlisted to bring her, and one of the officers got a black eye for his trouble.

Had she been crying ever since? There was no note in the chart. Sam asked one of the nurses, who frowned and told him it had started three weeks ago, and they had no idea what had brought it on.

The girl's name, the chart said, was Cecily DuMonde.

Sam decided that he would try to make her stop crying.

"Tulips," he said to her the next day. It was not exactly a direct refutation of "Percy Bysshe Shelley died before he was thirty, before he ever knew the impact his poetry would have." But close enough, he thought. He pretended to be studying her chart, but he was smiling a little, and, when he looked up, she was gazing at him with those sapphire eyes. Her tears had actually stopped. She folded her hands atop her blankets and pointed her chin.

"The nature of time," she said. "How you can never get it back, once it's gone."

"Molasses cookies."

"The great Boston molasses flood of 1919. Haven't you read about it? People drowned in the stuff."

She had a point. But. "Children," he said. He smiled, thinking of Patrick, Tootsie, the others he was doing his utmost to help.

But the girl-woman's mouth trembled. "Children," she said, and she was crying again.

"You can't rescue everyone, Sam," he heard his mother telling him.

Sam, who, at age five, had dashed into the street to scoop up a kitten who'd been hit by a car, run home with her in his hands, and demanded that his father—who was not one to be demanded upon, in normal circumstances—operate to save her. The operation was a success, and Tabby was part of the family from then on, always walking with a slight limp.

Sam, who, at seven, cared for a Northern saw-whet owl with a broken wing, splinting the fracture, then helping the bird exercise until it could fly again.

Sam, who, at eight, rescued a mouse from Tabby's mouth; then, realizing the mouse was pregnant, kept her safe and well fed in an aerated shoebox in the garage until she gave birth and for two weeks after that, until the six babies were big enough to release, along with their mother, into the woods at the edge of town.

"Not everyone *deserves* to be rescued," his mother said.

His mother wasn't one for intervention. Not in anything. "This too shall pass" was one of her favorite sayings. Or, "God's will," she'd say, and sigh.

Sam had decided early on that these were cop-outs.

Maybe he'd decided it the night he was seven and his mother barricaded him and his two older sisters, Margaret and Eleanor, in the girls' bedroom with her, enlisting all their help to push a dresser in front of the door. "He's brokenhearted, you understand," she whispered, while their father ranted outside and pounded on the door. Having received a bottle of whiskey for delivering a baby the night before, he'd poured glass after glass with supper, then gotten angry that the roast was tough. "This too shall pass."

"Answer me, goddamn it!" shouted their father, pounding again. Eleanor rose up slightly, her mouth opening, but their mother grabbed Eleanor's wrist. Eleanor, even more than the rest of them, could not stand to be in their father's bad graces, but their mother put a finger to her lips and shook her head swiftly, and Eleanor shrank down.

"Say it with me," their mother whispered. "This too shall pass, this too shall pass . . ." On and on they incanted it, until their whispers drowned out their father's rage and he went away.

They slept on the floor all together, and, in the morning, their mother went downstairs early to start breakfast. By the time the children had cleaned up and gone downstairs, their father was sitting at the head of the table reading the newspaper, as if nothing were out of the ordinary.

The approximate same thing happened again a month later. And again two months after that. The precipitating events were unpredictable. It always happened just when the children had almost convinced themselves that it wasn't going to happen again. That whatever monsters had been living inside their father—for that was how their mother explained it—were dead and gone.

Only, that was never true.

Their mother said their father was brokenhearted about their little sister, Abigail, who'd been only four when the Spanish flu took her life. They'd all had the sickness—it had walked in the door on the breath of some patient or other; the entire town was scourged by it, thirty-seven dead, in their town of just eight hundred—and their father had done his utmost for everyone, from the smallest infant to old Mrs. Swenson, who was ninety-two. All the same, he'd lost thirty-seven people, including little Abigail, who had simply turned a bright shade of blue one day and died. Sam's father, on his knees by her bedside, went on for half an hour, trying to breathe life back into her. And he could not. Sam, who was lying nearby—their father had lined up cots for his four sick children in the dining room, so he could keep an eye on all of them at once—saw the moment that their father's shoulders slumped; saw him creak from his knees to his feet like he was eighty years old, and hang his head.

"He loves you all so much, you see," said their mother. "He loves everybody in this town. He holds himself responsible. But not everybody can be saved."

Sam thought he'd rather be like his father, who tried, than like his mother, who watched her life go by like she was a spectator at a parade that slightly displeased her.

Still, though, his father frightened him. And he didn't want to be frightened of his father; he didn't think it was right. And one evening, when he was twelve years old, the monsters came out, and Sam refused to run upstairs after his sisters and mother. "Come *on*, Sam!" his mother implored him from the bottom of the back stairs, their usual escape route.

Sam was in the dining room. His father had stood up, overturning his plate, spilling gravy across the lace-rimmed cloth, and he was yelling in Sam's face so intensely that Sam felt his hair blowing back.

"Sam, *please!*"

Sam had ideas about justice, and that his father terrorized his family on random occasions did not seem just to him. It was 1924, and the newspapers were filled with tales of Johnny Torrio, Leopold and Loeb, the murderess Belva Gaertner, and a group of U.S. Army aviators trying to be the first to circumnavigate the globe by air. (Sam read the *Chicago Tribune* at the library almost daily; he was always in search of another Dave Fearless story or other novel to absorb him, transport him to other worlds, where boys had more power to change things.) Sam didn't know where his father was getting liquor these days. Obviously, there was some source from Canada. Sam wished briefly that he had a gun, or magical powers; that he knew how to stop everything.

But he didn't.

"Sam, for God's sake, please!" cried his mother, and this got his father's attention, so that his father marched four steps from the dining room through the swinging door into the kitchen and—the door was still swinging so that Sam could see—struck her across the face so hard that she was knocked off her feet. She landed on the floor with a soft "Oh!"

Sam's father looked back at Sam, horror in his eyes. "Look what you made me do!" He ran a hand over his hair, looking for his next target, then picked up a kitchen chair and smashed it against the wall. Sam, unfrozen by the noise, ran into the kitchen, his instinct to protect his mother uncontrollable. But his father was leaving through the back porch, letting in a blast of cold air. Sudden quiet came down. The broken chair parts seemed to tremble.

His mother was sprawled across the linoleum, leaning on one elbow.

It was a position he'd never seen her in. Her nose and mouth were bleeding. Her hair was falling from its pins. "Sam," she said. "Don't you see what I mean?"

"The sweet smell of a horse's breath," said Cecily DuMonde, when Sam stopped by her bed on a Wednesday. She actually wasn't crying.

He couldn't help it: his eyebrows shot up. "Is that a good thing or a bad thing? A source of sadness or happiness?"

"Don't you know?" She laughed, and the pretty sound arrested him. He could think of nothing to say.

She sighed. "You know, things can be both at once. That's called 'bittersweet.'" She looked up. Her deep eyes magnetized him, and his heart began to cartwheel in a dangerous-feeling way.

That night, in the single bed in his cabin at the edge of the sanatorium grounds, he woke from a dream in a cold sweat.

What if she didn't survive? What if she was one of the ones he could not save?

"Dr. Larson," she said the next day. She was wearing red lipstick. Had even painted her fingernails to match, he was thrilled to see. "I don't want to stay in bed for one more second!"

"You have to," he said, even as he noted on her chart: *Significant improvement in mood. Sudden belligerence = a strong will to live.* In his mind, he added, *Thank God.* "Your X-rays still show significant cavitation in your lungs. Rest and fresh air are required, you know that."

"And all these damn pills?"

He managed to keep a straight face. "Yes, and all the damn pills." Each patient was required to swallow thirty-two per day.

She folded her arms and looked off at the horizon, pouting. Her dark, wavy hair was swept back so he could see the tiny mole on the side of her neck. She had a rosebud mouth. The most perfect little earlobe.

He wasn't supposed to be noticing things like that.

"Dr. Larson," she said, training her gaze on him again. Those long lashes blinked a slow blink. "Do you have any idea who I am?"

Her chart said she was low-income, a ward of the state, had never had a visitor. "No," he said. "Why don't you tell me?"

She pointed a finger to her chin, playing at pondering. The red polish on her nail had an appealing sheen. "I don't think I will," she said. "I don't think you could handle it."

Sam laughed. And then he thought maybe she was right.

CHAPTER 13

Isabelle's feet were propped on an overturned half barrel, and the bottoms of her red stockings were filthy, with holes in them large enough to show the calluses and dirt on her feet. In the shadow of the costume tent, she was smoking a cigarette using an elegant jet-black holder that matched her wildly curly bobbed hair. Up close, Cecily could see that several glittering red sequins had been torn from the bodice of her short dress—tiny red threads hung loose—and her red lipstick was nearly worn off.

Mr. Tebow had brought Cecily here after the show and introduced her, then hurried off, promising to be back soon. The sun was sinking and the day cooling; there were still more than three hours till the evening show.

"So, kid," Isabelle said, blowing out smoke, "the act is that you're my little sister, and I'm teaching you to follow in my footsteps."

"Your *sister?*"

Isabelle shrugged. "Tebow thought you looked like me. I guess you do. And I don't have a say about any of it, so here you are. Anyway, I never had a sister. Could be fun. You ever been on a horse?"

"No! No, ma'am. Not until today, for the parade!"

Isabelle's laugh was throaty, like she'd been smoking cigarettes for a hundred years. "Don't call me 'ma'am,' kid. I'm nineteen. Not old enough to be your mother, *capiche?* Did you like the show?"

"Yes!"

"Did the horses scare you?"

In truth, Cecily had found many parts of the show so thrilling that they were frightening—or was it the other way around?—up to and including Isabelle's acrobatics with the horses. But, if she was to be Isabelle's little sister for the act—her whole heart had seized on to the idea—she wasn't about to let on. "No!"

"Good. Anything scare you?"

"No," Cecily said, then quickly realized that might not be believable. "Maybe the snake." It had been twined around the shoulders of that woman all day. She'd paraded around the ring between two of the final acts while Mr. Tebow advertised the allures of the sideshow.

"Smart girl. Want to come meet the horses? They don't like the snake, either."

Cecily nodded. Isabelle stubbed out her cigarette and tucked the holder behind her ear, slipping her feet into a pair of shoes unlike any Cecily had seen. They were flat, made of felt, and lined in what looked like rabbit fur. Isabelle noticed Cecily gawking, but didn't explain, just started limping away.

Cecily hurried to follow her.

The three white Percherons were lined up with a dozen grays, all munching hay from a sweet mound before them, along the edge of the stable tent behind a rope of canvas. "This is where they get a little breather between shows," Isabelle said. Here, the calliope was a distant whistle and hum, and the sideshow talkers' enticements mere murmurs, as they exhorted folks to step inside this tent or that one to view the fat lady, the snake charmer, the tattooed man.

A woman in pants with bobbed brown hair was scrubbing a tin bucket outside the stable tent. She looked up at the sound of Isabelle's voice and smiled.

"That's Janey, our groom," Isabelle said. "You ever have a question and I'm not around, ask her. She's married to one of the Robinsons." Those were the men in green who'd flown and twisted above the crowd. This woman did *not* seem glamorous enough to be the wife of one of them.

"Janey," Isabelle called. "This is Cecily. My new little sister for the act."

Janey frowned slightly. "Any experience?"

Isabelle laughed that throaty laugh. "We're making it up as we go."

"Typical. Well, welcome to the circus, Cecily." And Janey went back to the bucket.

Cecily had never been greeted by an adult as if she were an actual person, rather than an undesirable source of disruption and noise. Instantly, she saw why one of the glamorous Robinsons would've fallen for Janey hard enough to marry her; that it wasn't a mismatch, after all.

Isabelle made a clicking sound and reached out to one of the Percherons, gesturing for Cecily to hold out her hand, too. The horse was gigantic, taller than Cecily by three. He leaned down and nudged Isabelle's hand. Cecily thought she saw kindness in his eyes. Then, he leaned down a little farther to nudge *Cecily*. "This is Wyatt," Isabelle said. "You can pet him on the nose. There you go. He's a complete sweetheart. Give him carrots and he'll love you forever. Janey, got any carrots?"

Cecily, entranced by the wiry softness of Wyatt's nose, was only vaguely aware of Janey as she came over to give some carrots to Isabelle. Being high up on Blanco's back earlier today had been nothing compared to this: the intimacy of Wyatt's brown eyes, the sweet-smelling warmth of his breath.

Isabelle arranged a carrot on Cecily's palm and guided it toward Wyatt. The horse's lips tickled Cecily's palm as he nibbled the carrot away. She was too mesmerized to laugh.

The other two white Percherons, Isabelle introduced as Doc and Virgil. "Doc is laid-back, generally, but, once he gets in the ring, he loves the applause more than any of us." Virgil, she said, was high-spirited, the most apt to try to trick you with something unexpected, if you weren't paying attention. Cecily fed them each a carrot out of the palm of her hand. "Boys, this is my new sister," Isabelle told them, and Cecily's skin hummed with pleasure.

Then, the older girl's voice changed; she sounded far away and strange. "With horses, you can't cheat, and you can't lie. They know. They instantly know. They read your body language. If only humans had that skill." She laughed abruptly, reached up to scratch Doc behind the ears. "And you never ask them to do something they don't want to do, or that they're not ready to do. Or something you wouldn't want to do yourself, if you were a horse, if you know what I mean."

Cecily didn't know, not exactly. But she decided right then that she would pretend to understand everything that Isabelle said, until she did.

"We were thinking we'd call her Jacqueline," Isabelle told the tiger lady and a clown with a blue neck ruff, whom she'd introduced to Cecily as Mavis and Ron. The four were sitting at a square table inside the cook top, which buzzed with conversation and the clinking utensils of the performers. Cecily was focused on the incredible meal that was loaded on her tray: sliced ham, scalloped potatoes, sweet corn, more stewed tomatoes; chocolate pie for dessert. When she'd first gotten in line behind Isabelle and gotten a glimpse of what was in store, she'd tugged the older girl's sleeve and confessed in a whisper, "I ate at lunchtime." Isabelle had barked out a laugh and said she'd better get used to having three squares a day from now on.

"Jacqueline DuMonde," Isabelle said to her friends now.

"Oh, yes, that has a lovely ring, especially with your French pronunciation," Mavis said, and Ron, mouth full of potatoes, nodded in approval.

Isabelle turned to Cecily. "You like that, kid?"

Cecily stopped mid-bite on her corncob, realizing with a start what Isabelle meant. "But I'm Cecily McAvoy."

They all laughed, not unkindly, but Cecily felt bruised by it. She set down her corn, sat up straighter, pointed her chin.

"We've all got stage names here, kid," Isabelle said. "The better for running away."

"I'm not running away," Cecily said. "My mother's coming back for me. She said so on the form."

Isabelle had gray eyes, and they went soft as a kitten's fur. "Aw, kid," she said, and everyone at the table was quiet, until Mavis said something under her breath that made Isabelle laugh suddenly, and it seemed they forgot about Cecily.

Cecily hunched over her plate and started shoveling potatoes into her mouth, bite after bite until her stomach hurt, and then she kept right on going, because she honestly didn't trust, after all, that there'd be more tomorrow, or that they wouldn't send her right straight back to the Home.

Then it was time for Isabelle to get ready for the evening show, and Mr. Tebow hadn't come back yet. Isabelle said she couldn't have Cecily underfoot around the horses today—"You're so green, kid, you might get hurt"—so Cecily should find herself a place in the stands and watch the show, then find her way back to the caboose at the end of the night. "Can you do that, kid? You'd better not get lost, or Tebow will kill me."

Cecily had never been on her own—trusted with her own safekeeping—in her life. And in the middle of this crowd, plus all these tents and freaks and wild animals!

But, after a second, she saw the opportunity. "Sure!" she said, and grinned. Isabelle was already turning away.

Cecily wandered along the crowded midway, weaving through the crowd to examine the maze of small, dirty sideshow tents. Signs promised each held wonders inside, and men in tattered sequined jackets stood before each one shouting about them. Here was Madame Genevieve, the snake charmer. Lorraine LaPointe, the Bearded Lady. The World's Tallest Man, Henry Thompson. The sword swallower, Fredric

Roseau. Paul Leduc, the World's Most Tattooed Man. The Tiniest Man in the World, Little Red, and the Fat Lady, Ursula Eve. Cecily sneaked into the menagerie tent and examined the tigers in their wagon-cage, the lion in his, the chimpanzees, the camels, the zebras. All were too vivid to believe. The smell was as heavy as a real thing. Outside again, men swung hammers to try to ring a bell. A thin man in a green apron pulled taffy on a marble slab. Ladies and kids lined up for waxed paper bags of roasted peanuts and popcorn. Cecily sneaked a peek into the Hall of Mirrors and saw herself looking back, wide-eyed and freakishly tall.

That was enough for her. Anyway, she didn't have any money, plus she wanted to get a good seat for the show.

At the Big Top, she sneaked in the back, where Mr. Tebow had brought her in before. Inhaling the peculiar combination of smells— sawdust, manure, wax-coated canvas, scorched popcorn—she pushed through the crowd and climbed to the top of the rafters. She wanted to keep watch over everything and everybody; to be closer to the aerialists as they flew.

Nothing was less thrilling the second time. And even more thrilling was when Mr. Tebow bellowed, "The incredible Isabelle DuMonde!" and Doc and Virgil and Wyatt came thundering in, and there was Isabelle in red on the back of the last of them, arms splayed out, as if she could capture the world.

After the show, Cecily pretended to be part of a large family nearby. The mother had looked especially kind, doling out nickels for her older children to run for candy and peanuts. Even the father had held the littlest boy in his lap throughout the performance, pointing things out, explaining things, soothing him when he got scared of the lion. As Cecily made her way down the stands with them, one of the older boys gave her a puzzled look, but the parents didn't even notice her, and she split off once outside, as the family headed toward the field where cars were parked in long rows.

Leaving the lights of the Big Top behind, she saw the cook top had disappeared. So had the blacksmith shop, the stable tent, and, from what she could see craning her neck, all the sideshow tents and the menagerie tent, too. She heard the noises of people shouting and, soon, behind her, of poles and canvas falling.

She didn't like the shadows of the train yard. Down the line, she saw a man yanking two camels along by their ropes, a monkey riding on his shoulder. The horses were being loaded into a stock car. A clown was pulling the seal in a wagon, holding a herring just out of reach of its nose, and the tall man and the fat lady walked together toward one of the sleeper cars. Isabelle had explained that the Sax & Tebow Circus had no elephants. "Too small-time," she'd said, with a shrug. "We can dream."

Men Cecily didn't know were walking by; train men, maybe. She hurried for the caboose, though, once she got there and climbed up onto the vestibule, she had an equally bad feeling about opening the door.

She glanced back at the shadows and made her choice, grabbing the metal handle and shoving her way inside. A lantern was burning on the table, but nobody was there. Cecily walked through the small kitchen area, past the stove and tiny icebox and small booth of table and benches, and into the middle compartment. Here, on one side, were two seats facing each other, while the other side had been made over into a tall bunk for sleeping, complete with a thin mattress and a railing, plus thick cushions lining it all around. This bunk had been constructed just for Cecily, Isabelle had explained. "We thought you'd think it was fun. Just be sure to hold on tight! Anyway, the cushions should keep you safe." Isabelle's bunk was in the compartment on the far end. "They made the caboose over just for me, and now I'm going to share it with you. It's noisy and bumpy back here, but at least we've got a little privacy."

Cecily grabbed her suitcase from where Mr. Tebow had set it this afternoon, then struggled to haul it up with her as she climbed the ladder to her bunk. Dolores and Flip were not going to believe this—her bed was in a train caboose with a clown painted on its side! Right under the cupola, so she could look out!

She got on her knees to peer out the window, but all she could see was darkness, and all the sounds were odd and disconcerting: the clanking of chains and rolling of wheels, the crack of a whip, the bellow of some animal, the shout of a discontented man.

It was a jarring thing to go from one life to another all in one day.

Cecily sank back down to sit cross-legged on the bunk, then unlatched her suitcase and opened it to take inventory in the dim light cast by the distant lantern.

Her thin nightgown, two pairs of clean underwear, and a dress that Cecily had never seen before. That was all Mrs. H. had packed for her.

Unless she'd slid a book into the inside pocket? (Not likely—but maybe Miss Oversham would've insisted.) Cecily ran her hand through. No book. But she felt a small, thick piece of paper. She pulled it out: a card with a picture of a bearded man wearing a crown, plus the caption, *Hope begins with Saint Jude.* In smaller print was written, *The patron saint of lost causes.*

She remembered: Her mother had told her that this had belonged to her daddy. She didn't know how she could remember that, when she hadn't seen the card in all the years she'd been at the orphanage, but she did. It seemed amazing that it was here. Something from her daddy.

She flipped it over. It said to pray to Saint Jude in cases that were despaired of, impossible, hopeless.

She sighed. She certainly was feeling all those things now. Her daddy was dead for sure, and look how Isabelle had reacted when Cecily had said her mother was coming back for her. Like it could never, ever be true.

Cecily felt tears welling. *No,* she told herself. No, she wouldn't cry. She lay down, squirmed her way underneath the covers, then looked at the card again, into the eyes of Saint Jude. "What the blazes does prayer have to do with anything?" she asked him out loud. She'd never prayed to be adopted into the circus, and now here she was. She'd prayed and prayed for her mother to come back, and her mother never had.

On top of that, the people outside were tearing down the circus. By morning, Isabelle had said, they'd be in another town, with no trace of them left here. Every day was the same: another town, another pair of shows, another move on the train in the night. "Before you know it, we'll be a thousand miles away," Isabelle had explained.

"All the horses and people and tents and *everything*?" Cecily had asked, and Isabelle laughed and said yes, everything and everybody.

So how was Cecily's mother ever going to find her now? Now that she was going to be traveling with the circus as "Jacqueline DuMonde"?

She tried to blink back the tears that came at that thought, but she couldn't, not anymore, and her stomach was aching, too. Why would Isabelle and Mr. Tebow have such confidence that she could *be* "Jacqueline DuMonde," bareback rider extraordinaire, when today was the first time she'd ever even met a horse? And what would happen if she couldn't do what they expected? If she couldn't learn the tricks, or understand all that she was supposed to?

Would they trade her in for some other orphan girl?

Well, that could be all right, if only she'd end up back with Flip and Dolores—

But the odds of that were pretty clearly exactly none, since the circus was leaving here tonight and wouldn't be back for a year, according to Isabelle. Cecily would end up abandoned on the side of the tracks in Nebraska or Alabama or someplace she'd never even heard of.

All right, then.

She made herself stop crying. She wiped her face. She was just going to have to try. And try and try and try.

Anyway, Isabelle had proclaimed them sisters, and Cecily was not going to give up that chance.

She swallowed, imagining what Flip would say: *We've all got to grow up someday. Guess what? Today's your day.*

If only Dolores were here, too, to tell Cecily what might happen next.

Cecily sighed, closed her eyes, and tried to imagine Dolores poking her shoulder to whisper in her ear.

Your mother will find you in Iowa, she heard her saying. *She'll know you despite your name.*

Some time later, she struggled halfway out of sleep when she heard Isabelle's voice: "I told her to come back here—"

And the man's—Mr. Tebow's—voice: "I swear to God, Isabelle, I thought I could trust you."

Cecily didn't open her eyes, but felt Isabelle boosting herself up nearby to look in the bunk. "Aw," she said. "Out like a light. Poor kid must've been dead on her feet." There came a sweet adjustment, a tucking around her, of the blanket, then Isabelle was gone, and Cecily's face was wet with tears at the unexpected tenderness, and then she was asleep again.

And some time later, out of a different dream, she heard the train creak and rumble into motion.

And she was gone.

CHAPTER 14

Friday, February 20, 2015
Itasca, Minnesota

*C*aden's skates sent up a swoosh of ice crystals as he skidded to a stop amid the Rams defenders, then took off after the puck. "Go, Caden!" Molly shouted, pumping her fist toward the arena's rafters.

"That's my boy!" Evan shouted, beside her, gloves thudding as he clapped. The crowd roared as Caden took a shot. The puck bounced off the goal—the crowd moaned—and the Rams were all over it, slapping it toward the rink's other end. "That's okay, buddy! Next one!" Evan shouted.

The game was a great one, but, oh, *this* part was not good. Not good at all—how it felt to be standing beside Evan. That warm-blanket feeling of comfort, spiked with the old attraction like a too-sweet punch with Fireball whiskey. How could he feel so familiar, when she hadn't seen him in so long? His curly dark hair was a bit longer, starting to show a little gray. But his blue eyes, the scent of his aftershave, the bump on the bridge of his nose from when he'd broken it in a long-ago Maine pond hockey game, were the same. Just as he had told her: the same.

Of course, they must've attended a couple hundred of Caden's games together, before. Evan, who'd grown up playing hockey in Maine and played defense for Colby, had been the one to insist on getting Caden on skates almost before Caden could walk—and probably, in the end, the fact that Minnesota produced far more NHL players than any other state had influenced him to give up the fight about Caden moving to

Itasca. And now Caden was playing varsity—just a few minutes a game, but still—as a freshman for one of the top teams in the state.

Evan was already dreaming of the 2018 Olympics, Molly had found out since his arrival this afternoon. "And the moon is made of cheese, right?" she'd said. "A little pressure on the kid, maybe?"

Evan had shrugged. Grinned. Then, she'd learned that he'd followed every game—every play—online, and could recite their son's entire junior high and high school (so far) career, minute by minute, shot by shot.

She'd actually *been* there for every play—but she couldn't do that. Couldn't *remember*.

She'd met him first at Cecily's house, having canceled her three o'clock. He'd brought his suitcase inside, and she'd shown him where the thermostat was, the snow shovel, the coffee maker, the Wi-Fi password—all the essentials. Then, it was off to the hospital to visit Cecily. Liz, Cecily reported, had been there earlier, but "looked like death warmed over. I told her to go home, get some rest. It wouldn't do for her to get sick, too." As for Cecily herself, she'd been out of bed once each day, had even taken a couple of steps with a walker. *Thank God*, Molly thought.

"As good-looking as ever," Cecily pronounced Evan. "And remind me why the two of you split up?"

"Grandma, please." Yes, it was great to see the spark back in Cecily's eyes, but—seriously. Cecily *knew* every detail of what had gone wrong between Molly and Evan, because Molly had told her.

Evan shifted in his chair. "Well, it wasn't because I didn't love her, I promise you that," he said, which gave Molly a visceral start.

Cecily had laughed. "Ah, matters of the heart," she'd said, then leaned back in her pillows and sighed.

CHAPTER 15

April 1940
Wallum Lake Sanatorium, Rhode Island

*E*veryone had started to notice the way the handsome Dr. Larson lingered too long on his rounds at the bedside of Cecily Du-Monde.

Cecily didn't mind the talk. Being the center of attention had never bothered her. Anyway, it gave the women on the ward something diverting to think about—though the nurses did not, of course, approve.

But Cecily had done nothing to encourage the attentions of the man. In fact, she'd been borderline unfriendly for much of last summer and fall. She distrusted doctors, as a rule. Also, obviously, he only felt sorry for her. Once she was better—which she intended to be soon—he'd move on to try to fix the next broken thing.

But it was difficult to actively dislike a man who, after Cecily happened to mention that she missed hearing music, had set up a gramophone record player on the ward—"I told my supervisors we needed to experiment with the effect of cheerful music on recovery," he'd said, kneeling to plug it in—and continued to bring in new music for the women to listen to. Artie Shaw, Glenn Miller, Billie Holliday, Ella Fitzgerald, Benny Goodman—all her favorites, which she'd confessed when he'd pressed her, plus a few like The Andrews Sisters and Frank Sinatra to placate the other women. They were allowed to listen only after breakfast for one hour, and they were not allowed to dance, of course, and only Barbara, who had out-of-bed-two-hours privileges, was allowed to change the records. But still. Cecily knew he'd bought it with his own money.

And then there were the books.

The day he'd announced, with his secretive little smile—she did like that smile—that she was well enough to be allowed to read for an hour a day, she'd instantly started to cry.

He'd looked crestfallen. "What is it now?"

She'd tried to explain how much it meant to her—how lonely she'd been without books, which had been her most reliable companion in life.

"I know what you mean," he'd said, and, from that day on, he almost never failed to bring her a new book. "This is one of my favorites," he would always say. She had the idea that he spent part of every evening perusing his shelf to choose his next bestowal. Soon, she had a stack of them by her bedside. And she began to think that, even though he was a doctor, he had some redeeming qualities.

She could not get through the books in one hour a day; not even close, though she was a fast reader. She was better at following rules here than she had been at other points in her life—perhaps because the doctors had said it was a matter of life and death, and she understood, if nothing else, that she was at their mercy. Anyway, the nurses watched you like hawks here; you could get away with nothing.

She begged Dr. Larson for her privileges to be extended. "Even an hour and a half!"

He sadly told her no. "For your own good. I'm sorry." He always asked her for a report on what she was reading; that was the reason, she had to think, that he'd started lingering so long. He wanted to be told he was right, and admired for his good taste, that was all.

Then, she had to have another artificial pneumothorax, which meant a great deal of pain and absolute rest, flat on her back, for days.

When she was pronounced fit to be propped up on pillows and then, finally, to read, he brought her a beautiful first edition of Edna

St. Vincent Millay's *Renascence and Other Poems.* "For you to keep," he said,
quietly enough that no one else could hear, making notes on her chart.

Then, it was Christmas, and he brought her a box of candy.

"You just feel sorry for me because I never have visitors," she said,
twirling the red ribbon around her finger. The other women were forever
spending their Sunday and Thursday mornings getting ready for potential guests: setting their hair, applying their makeup, hoping someone
would come. Cecily just read. She thought it was better not to have
hope, the crucifying ups and the nauseating downs of it. Yvonne, for
example, spent hours each Sunday getting ready for the man she referred
to as her "fiancé"—Cecily wasn't so sure about that—and he showed up
maybe one Sunday of four, and stayed for half an hour at most, tapping
his foot, eyes darting around like he feared being arrested. After he left,
Yvonne invariably ended up in tears. If he didn't come at all, she'd also
cry, but more quietly, letting her mascara run, saying she just didn't care,
anyway. Or she'd blame the train schedule, or the fact that the San was
so out of the way that the nearest stop was miles away, and staff only
drove out to pick up visitors on Thursdays, and her fiancé worked then,
so if he couldn't borrow his father's car on any given Sunday to drive up,
there was no way for him to come. "It just isn't *fair,*" she'd wail.

"Me, sorry for you? No," Dr. Larson said, with that smile, and Cecily cocked her head and popped a chocolate into her mouth. She ate
them all that Christmas Day, savoring them slowly one by one, so they
wouldn't freeze overnight and break a tooth in the morning. She had
enough blankets to keep her warm out here on the porch, and wore a
wool cap day and night. Anyway, being cold wasn't the worst thing that
had ever happened to her.

"Listen to this," she told him, one day in late January. The daylight
hours were lengthening, and she loved watching the light play across the
snowy field, the shadowy skeletons of the trees at twilight. She read out
loud from the last page of the Millay book. "'I looked in my heart when
the wild swans went over. And what did I see that I had not seen before?
Only a question less or a question more.'" She looked up.

He swallowed visibly. "'Nothing to match the flight of wild birds flying,'" he answered her. "'Tiresome heart, forever living and dying—'"

He was gazing at her in a way that seemed full of some promise that she hoped he wouldn't try to make, because only disappointment could result.

Nurse Turner, one of the most senior nurses in the whole San, happened to be walking by. "You get that girl too excited," she muttered to the young doctor.

And Cecily wanted to say, *No, no, you've misunderstood,* as Dr. Larson quickly went back to making his notes.

"I'm not long for this place," Cecily said, after a moment, though she didn't know why.

He looked up again. "I know," he said, and he didn't smile.

He was transferred off the ward; she heard he was assisting in the surgery all the time now. It was a promotion for him, and she was glad about that. Nurse Sheridan brought new records, and Cecily worked her way through the stack of Dr. Larson's books, plus, of course, the library cart came around from time to time, and the girl with the newspapers. Cecily missed the doctor, a bit, but even that didn't bother her. She'd been around the sun enough to know that nothing—good or bad—ever truly lasted.

Yvonne had been moved off to isolation, and she didn't come back. "Discharged," was the official word, but everyone deep down knew that she had died.

Cecily wondered if that so-called fiancé felt heartbroken or simply released; she knew it had been wise not to become close with Yvonne.

Her utmost goal was self-preservation, now more than ever.

The new doctor on rounds, Dr. Redmond, authorized her to knit, if she wanted to—she didn't—and, more important, to attend movies in the new theater. She saw Jimmy Stewart in *Mr. Smith Goes to Washington* and *Destry Rides Again*; Judy Garland in *The Wizard of Oz* and *Listen, Darling;*

Clark Gable and Vivien Leigh in *Gone with the Wind*. Many of the women were motivated to go to the movies mostly because the male patients went, also—otherwise, the men and women weren't allowed to mix. Cecily, lost in the flickering images on the screen, couldn't have cared less about that. She hadn't been to a movie in over two years, so these were all brand-new to her, with their bright, beautiful, aching worlds. Yet, watching them made her feel strangely like life might be getting a little closer back to normal.

Whatever "normal" was.

Though she had no idea where she would go, if released from the San. (*When* released, she ought to say.) Maybe she'd find a way to get back to New York City, and really make a go of it, though she had less hope now that it would be all she'd dreamed of.

Maybe she was just getting older. Not so many stars in her eyes. At least she was getting better at not letting sadness or regret overwhelm her. The books from Dr. Larson helped, as did reading the newspapers about the war in Europe. She tried to keep in the know, to focus externally rather than internally, because that made her realize she didn't have it bad at all. In fact, being here in the San right now was quite preferable to many places she'd been in her life before.

"It's not often in life a human being achieves stasis," she told Dr. Redmond. "I'm looking at it like a tiny miracle, because when does change ever cease to happen in this world?"

Dr. Redmond just looked at her quizzically—Dr. Larson would've understood, she thought—then said he was authorizing her to walk about the grounds for an hour a day, or even work in the gardens, if she wanted to.

Ha! Just in time for spring!

Cecily's clothes, when pulled from storage, revealed themselves to be threadbare, torn, "ready for the rubbish bin," in the words of Nurse Sheridan, who whisked them away and the next day brought Cecily a paper-wrapped package containing a dress and sweater. "For you to keep," the nurse whispered, and Cecily didn't know if they had belonged to a patient who'd died or to Nurse Sheridan herself, who was about Cecily's size. Either way, she was not too proud to accept them. The dress was black with a subtle floral pattern of tiny mauve and pink roses; the sweater, a white cardigan embroidered with pink roses around the collar. "A perfect fit!" Nurse Sheridan pronounced, and Cecily wanted to hug her; just barely refrained. She'd worn only hospital gowns for nearly a year and a half. It had been a very long time since she'd felt the least bit pretty at all.

At the authorized hour, Saturday at two, she walked out alone across the expansive front lawn, feeling unsteady as a new lamb, giddy, set free. Everything amazed her. Daffodils were showing their yellow heads; the cloud-mottled sky was an extraordinary blue. The earth beneath her feet felt so inviting that she took off her scuffed brown T-strap pumps— they didn't go with the new dress, anyway—and carried them, not caring that the grass was cold and damp with muddy patches, or that the women on the ward had been scandalized by her lack of stockings. She'd painted her toenails red for this occasion, and they shone through the mud and pleased her.

"Miss DuMonde?"

She looked over, and there was Dr. Larson, approaching from the direction of the staff cabins, which were some distance away, up among the trees. She hardly recognized him at first, as he wasn't wearing his white coat, just a pair of belted gray slacks and a white shirt open at the collar, a pair of brown and white spectator shoes. He was thinner than she would have guessed, and looked younger without his usual doctor's coat and necktie.

"Miss DuMonde," he said again, and smiled. "Does this mean you're free to walk about?"

"No, I'm making a break for it."

He laughed. "I'm glad to see you. I was just up at my cabin, reading, and looked out and thought it was you. It's my day off."

Her eyes narrowed. "Don't you like to go to town?"

"My housemates do. I like the quiet. Most of the time."

"I'd go to town, if I could."

He laughed again. "I'm sure you would." He seemed to be sizing her up. He'd never seen her out of her hospital bed before. "May I walk with you?"

"If you think you can keep up."

He smiled at that, and they fell into step together. Cecily was pleased to think she was providing the hundred or more bedridden patients along the front porches with something to gossip about. But Dr. Larson seemed unaware of any watching eyes. He walked with his hands clasped behind his back and his head slightly bowed, listening carefully, it seemed, to her rave about the buds popping out on the trees, the squish of the mud between her toes.

The lake, which she'd been looking at for a year and a half across the rolling field, was, up close, magnificent, rippling with life. Ducks paddled near the rim. "Oh, God, they're fantastic," she said. "Look how you can see their feet at work, even when they seem to be so still!"

They neared a bench, which was half hidden from view by a willow tree. "Would you like to sit?" Dr. Larson asked. The bench wasn't so hidden that their reputations could be compromised, Cecily guessed, but enough so that their faraway observers would probably get bored, trying to glimpse them through the just-budding screen of branches. Maybe that was all right.

"What a lovely tree. Thank God it survived the storm," she said, and sat down. She didn't like thinking of that horrible day of the hurricane, a year and a half ago, two months before she'd landed here at the San, and she was tired. This was the longest she'd walked in all these months, and both the knowledge of that and the feeling satisfied her. She glanced over her shoulder at the long porch where she'd spent so many months, then leaned back, held out her arms, closed her eyes, and blurted the rest of the Millay poem: "'House without air, I leave you and lock your door. Wild swans, come over the town, come over the town again, trailing your legs and crying!'"

The doctor sat down beside her, not close. "You still have to be very careful, you know."

She laughed. "I know, Doctor."

"Call me Sam," he said. A slight breeze ruffled the branches of the willow, and Cecily felt the tremor of it.

No way, she said to God, and directed the conversation to books. He'd been reading *Don Quixote*; she, *A Room with a View*. He did not much care for the poetry of Whitman, while she had memorized three verses of "Song of Myself." Together, they recited "Annabel Lee," and Cecily felt a shiver again, and said she'd better be walking back. He probably thought she was a nice girl. Down on her luck, maybe, but from a good family. Respectable. Ha.

He was twenty-eight years old, and, when he'd started the job here last June, had just graduated from the medical school at Brown University. There, on its Providence campus, the hurricane had only knocked down some trees, though Dr. Larson had (of course) rushed to try to save the people who were drowning in their cars as the waters rose downtown. "I'm not a great swimmer, but I can keep my head above water, you know," he said, and Cecily didn't think the modesty was false. He had grown up in northern Minnesota and had two older sisters and a real live mother, and his father was a doctor, too.

Halfway back up the lawn was where they parted. In the distance up the hill were visible the massive piles of logs that had been harvested from the pines blown down by the storm. The noise had been incessant, Cecily's first winter here, but she'd never seen the resulting stacks before.

The doctor asked if she'd be out walking again tomorrow, or if she was going to church. "No to both," she said. "I don't do church, and I'm not allowed out walking again until Monday."

He frowned slightly. "I'll be working then."

"Well, nice seeing you!" she said cheerfully—her way of saying *goodbye forever*.

His eyes narrowed. "May I visit you sometime?"

"Oh, yes, of course, I have to return the books you loaned me!" How had she almost forgotten them?

"I'm not worried about the books," he said.

Ha. Once he got them, he'd be gone for good. "Well, I am," she said, and tossed her hair and began climbing the slight hill back toward the San, the mud chilly between her toes.

CHAPTER 16

*A*fter the game, Evan ruffled Caden's sweaty hair and pulled him into a bear hug. "Proud of you, son."

Caden pulled back, trying for cool in front of his teammates, who were whooping and shouting and high-fiving all around. They'd beaten the Rams 5 to 3, adding another notch to their belt in the rivalry and edging closer to State. "I was hoping I'd get a goal so you could see me." His cheeks were pink from exertion.

"Next time, Cade. Next game, or the game after that. I'll be here."

Caden smiled, shook his hair out of his eyes, and headed for the locker room with his teammates, the *chunk-chunk* sound of their skates filling the cinder-block hallway.

Standing beside Evan, Molly watched her son go, feeling strangely overwhelmed. The little-boy pride of Caden; the seeming *necessity* of the connection between father and son. Why did it surprise her so much?

Maybe she had gotten used to thinking her son was just *hers.*

As Caden disappeared around the corner, Molly glanced up at Evan, trying to think what to say—something constructive; oh, she was going to try!—but he just looked down at her, shook his head slightly, took a few steps away, and pulled out his phone to make a call. As if he hadn't been moved at all by the moment with his son.

She was ashamed at her relief; felt some aggravation, some sorrow.

And then she thought: Friday night, past ten on the East Coast. A girlfriend?

Well. Molly didn't care about that.

She took out her phone, too.

Nothing.

Odd that Liz hadn't texted to ask about the game. She'd sent a message earlier saying that, much as she wanted to come, she just didn't feel up to the drive into town tonight. *Give Caden a hug from me! Go, Hawks!* Very odd. Liz had missed only one other home game of Caden's all season, when she'd decided against driving into town in a snowstorm, and she'd texted Molly constantly throughout it, asking for reports.

Was she avoiding Evan? Or maybe—more likely—just exhausted from the week, from all the worry about Cecily. Molly wouldn't bother her anymore tonight, not even with a text. With Cecily in the hospital, no way would Liz have her phone turned off, and any slight noise could wake her.

Molly slid her phone back into her pocket, noticing that Evan was still some distance away, with his back turned; still on the phone with someone.

Yep. Definitely a girlfriend.

Later, back at the blue bungalow, Caden sliced open the box on the kitchen counter that had arrived that afternoon from Ancestry. They'd all gone out for pizza, Evan had driven them home, and Molly had been so enjoying watching and hearing Caden fill his father in on his life—she'd learned quite a few things, it was embarrassing to admit—that she'd invited Evan to come inside to watch the "ceremonial" package opening. He'd been fussing since he'd learned about Liz having paid for the test kits, swearing that, the minute he saw her, he was going to write her a check. And now he was going on about how maybe they'd learn something about *his* ancestors, too. Was his father really 100 percent French, as he'd liked to brag? Had his mom really had an ancestor who'd come over on the *Mayflower*?

Leave it to Evan, Molly thought, to make everything about him.

"What's it say, bud?" she asked, as Caden pulled out a brightly colored instruction sheet.

"It's just about how to do the samples and stuff."

"Oh, great! You know, I can probably get Grandma Cecily's tomorrow, when I go to the hospital to see her. And Mom's, too. Then we could get them shipped out on Monday. If it takes the full eight weeks to get the results, it's already going to be cutting it close, with your due date of April 24. I mean, hopefully they'll come sooner, but we'd better plan for worst-case, don't you think?"

A shrug.

Molly sighed, avoiding looking at Evan, though she felt his eyes on her like an old question. He probably thought she was overmanaging Caden—but he had no idea, *none*, what it took to be a single parent. The deadlines, schedules, meals, laundry. The little heartbreaks that happened every day and needed to be soothed.

"You guys want some ice cream?" she said, evading. Another tactic she would've told her clients was not effective, but, whatever, it was almost ten o'clock at night.

"Sounds great," Evan said, and she got out the bowls and spoons and the Cherry Garcia from the freezer and started dishing it up, while Evan and Caden talked about the game.

It was nice, actually. This little domestic scene. Hearing Evan give Caden little tidbits of advice on stick handling, defense, the importance of sharpening his skates—

But, no. Wait. She couldn't go down this road. Fall into a comfort she hadn't even realized she'd been missing. That was the last thing she wanted to do.

She put the bowls of ice cream in front of the two males she loved most in the world and told them to hurry up and eat. "It's late, bud, and your dad's got to get over to Grandma Cecily's house and get settled in. You two can spend the whole day together tomorrow, all right?"

Caden looked at his dad with a flash of uncertainty, but Evan was looking at Molly with an old familiar smile that said she'd just given him the world—and Molly's stomach started to hurt again at the sight of it, though she had no idea why.

CHAPTER 17

Spring 1928
Outside Sturgeon Bay, Wisconsin

*I*sabelle said you could be afraid of anything you wanted to, except the horses. "Imagine you're a tiny kitten, held in the palm of their hands. You have to trust them that much. And they have to trust you that much, too." Cecily didn't point out that horses didn't have hands; she just agreed. That was what she did, whenever Isabelle said anything at all.

Isabelle also said that the winter always seemed to last forever, but that this one might not last long enough. Cecily—whom Isabelle always called "Jacqueline"—didn't think that made any sense, but she accepted it as true, nonetheless. She was not yet eight years old.

They were spending the winter outside of Sturgeon Bay, Wisconsin, at the Sax & Tebow winter quarters, which was really a farm owned by Mr. Sax. Cecily had never even met Mr. Sax until the circus train arrived at Sturgeon Bay in November after the season, because Mr. Sax, besides being part-owner, was also the circus's advance man. All season long, he traveled one stop ahead of the show, making sure that the posters which had been plastered all over every town by the publicity men (who traveled two weeks ahead of him) still dominated every wall and billboard; confirming food and hay and ice deliveries for performance day; and laying out the route from the trainyard to the site he'd selected for the tents, plus the parade route, too, with his trademark red arrows.

On the farm were four enormous barns with stone foundations to house the animals, two big bunkhouses—one for women and one for men—a cookhouse with a dining room, and a huge equipment shed. Another building provided tiny apartments for married couples, including Janey and her aerialist, Ralph Robinson; the Bearded Lady, Lorraine LaPointe, and Little Red; the Fat Lady, Ursula Eve, and the lion tamer, Harrison West; the snake charmer, Madame Genevieve, and Vince, the clown who trained the seal; plus, the tiger tamer, Mavis, and her clown, Ron.

An uninsulated plank building approximated the Big Top. It was here that the Robinsons practiced their aerial routines, and Catherine LeGrande and her husband, Buck, who rented a house in town and came to the farm only to rehearse, practiced on the trapeze. Here, too, Mavis worked with her tigers, Harrison West with his lion, Vince with his seal, Geoffrey Jones with the camels, Paul Giacometti with the seven black liberty horses, and Isabelle with Wyatt, Doc, and Virgil. (The Arabian riders had scattered for the winter, and those horses, plus the gray and black Percheron teams, were allowed a winter of relaxation, with only a skeleton crew to care for them.)

Cecily would've liked to stay with Isabelle in the bunkhouse and take meals in the cookhouse with her and the other performers, too. Instead, she was assigned to stay in the white frame house with Mr. Sax and his family, which included a girl, Nonie, who, like Cecily, was seven, and a boy, Ted, who was nine. She and Nonie had become fast friends—Mrs. Sax was forever yelling up the stairs at them to quit giggling and go to sleep— and together the three children walked to school one mile each morning and one mile back in the afternoon, Ted tossing sticks and snowballs and making up stories about wolves while Nonie steadfastly ignored him and Cecily repeated that she wasn't afraid. Ted boasted he was going to be a ringmaster like Tebow, once he got old enough—"Because we *own* the circus, see, and I can do what I want"—and Nonie was secretly practicing on the trapeze, though her mother, who, as far as Cecily could tell, hated every last thing about the circus, would've killed her, if she'd found out.

Cecily loved school. There were eighteen kids in six grades in one room. The teacher, Miss Johnson, was harried but kind, and there were shelves and shelves of books to read whenever Cecily completed her assignments. She and Nonie together had made up the entire second-grade class until Miss Johnson promoted Cecily to third grade, then to the fourth, where Cecily and Ted made up the entire class. Cecily still finished her work long before Ted did, so she continued to get in plenty of her own reading.

Even more than she loved school, though, Cecily loved the afternoons, when she would find Isabelle on the farmyard and they would train together for their act. Isabelle said that Tebow, who was off traveling to set up next year's schedule, had written that they should plan to have Cecily standing on Isabelle's shoulders as Wyatt cantered them both around the ring.

Before they could so much as *try* that, Isabelle said, Cecily had a lot to learn.

At first, Isabelle had her practice on a balance beam. Within days, she was doing front flips off the end, like she'd modeled for Tebow at the Home. Next, she had to try to vault onto a barrel that was supposed to approximate a horse's back. She quickly got strong enough to do it, if the barrel was low enough. Once the barrel was placed at the height of the Percherons' backs, though, she failed and fell again and again, no matter how many times Isabelle demonstrated. Cecily was just too small. And, if she couldn't vault onto a stationary barrel, she was not going to be able to vault onto Wyatt's back when he was cantering around the ring.

And, if she couldn't do that, riding on Isabelle's shoulders was decidedly *out*.

Nonie said Cecily shouldn't worry that she was going to be exchanged for another orphan girl, but Cecily guessed Nonie had never been bought or sold, either.

And then, a beautiful white pony was delivered to the barn.

"His name is Prince," Isabelle said. "Tebow bought him for you, and he wants you two doing your own act by the time we set out in May."

"He's *mine*?"

Isabelle grinned and ruffled Cecily's hair. "Consider him your Christmas gift."

Prince was friendly, easygoing, and, with Isabelle's help, easy to train. Cecily got up before sunrise every icy morning to feed and water him and muck out his stall, snow crunching under her feet as she walked from house to barn. He was always awake, waiting for her. She went straight to him after school, too.

She learned from Isabelle the proper way to clean his hooves, curry his coat, comb his mane and tail, check and clean his eyes and ears and nose and dock area. She learned to halter him and lead him at a walk around the frozen yard.

Then, she learned to ride him without a saddle, without Isabelle even leading him. Round and round the ring they went, at a steady pace Isabelle had determined and which she timed with a small, strange device she called a metronome. If Cecily ever got excited and urged the pony faster, Isabelle would shout to slow down. They rode so long at this pace that Cecily felt it in her dreams, the rocking of her body in tandem with Prince's, the coarseness of his mane in her hands. Sometimes, overcome with love, she would lean in, hugging his neck, and he would toss his head and puff air out his nose, which she thought was his way of saying he loved her, too.

She could easily vault onto the barrel when it was positioned at the height of Prince's back—Isabelle still made her practice over and over—and soon she could do a front flip straight from standing on the balance beam. Isabelle showed her, also, how to hang off the side of the beam, using just one arm, the other extended for show. Cecily wasn't quite strong enough to hold the position, but she was working up to it. Isabelle hung from rings and pulled herself up; she hung by her legs and sat up into the air, the way the aerialists did. Cecily tried to do everything Isabelle did. Most of it, she couldn't, but she knew she was getting stronger.

Isabelle brought her to the costume designer, Margie, whose sewing room, piled high with costumes under construction and repair, was at one end of the women's bunkhouse. Margie measured Cecily and made notes in pencil in a tiny notebook while Isabelle talked. "Blue is her color. Look at those eyes. Sapphire. A lot of swing in the skirt. Plus, white trim and sequins. A tiara with fake sapphires. And a blue headdress for Prince to match."

Cecily grinned. She and Prince were going to look like a million bucks, and she told him so that night while she mucked out his stall. He stomped a foot and nodded; she was sure he understood. She just had to learn the tricks in time.

That night, Nonie whispered to Cecily in bed, "I wish I was a star like you."

Mrs. Sax appeared in the doorway. "Girls? Are you sleeping?"

"Yes, Mommy," Nonie said, feigning a yawn and snuggling deeper into the pillow.

Cecily's thrill at imagining how she'd look on Prince's back in her new blue costume cracked like an egg. She wished she could be a normal girl, with a mother who cared if she was sleeping.

The circus had been through Iowa last fall, but Madeline hadn't come.

"Now!" Isabelle said, holding Prince by the halter, and Cecily ran, focusing on his back, where she'd put her hands to vault up—

She crashed into him, fell back, and landed in the dirt. Prince shook his mane. He was used to standing still. Isabelle had had Cecily standing on his back for half an hour at a time, not letting either of them move. After days of this, she'd begun leading him around the ring at a slow walk as Cecily stood on him, balancing, wearing a safety harness that was suspended from the ceiling. Now out the big open door was the *drip, drip, drip* of melting snow, the sun at a late-afternoon angle. It was March; they had only two months to get ready for Cecily's first show.

Isabelle fed Prince a carrot. "Try again," she said.

Isabelle said that the premier bareback rider May Wirth didn't use a blanket on her horse's back, nor any handles to grab on to, so neither did Isabelle, and neither would Jacqueline DuMonde.

Cecily dreamed it, day and night: the feel of Prince's rippling muscles and coarse hair beneath her feet; the rhythm of the canter; circling her arms above her head, the way Isabelle had shown her. The front flip from standing, as Prince circled the ring.

She dreamed it, but she couldn't actually do any of it. Not yet.

She slid her Saint Jude card under her pillow and held it secretly in her hand while she slept. *Make me as good as Isabelle, please,* she prayed, *or I don't know if they'll keep me.*

"I don't like it, I'm telling you," Mrs. Sax told Isabelle. The sun was setting on another melty-muddy, late-March day, and she'd appeared in the doorway of the practice barn and called them over. She'd never come out to the circus yard before, that Cecily had seen, and she seemed to have come in a hurry, because she wasn't even wearing a sweater over her thin cotton dress. "I don't like it one bit. This girl is *smart.* And so young. And now I get a letter from Miss Johnson that you're pulling her out of school to make sure her *act* is ready in time?"

No more school? Cecily's stomach lurched. She looked to Isabelle to gauge how she should react, but Isabelle was just coolly lighting a cigarette.

"For God's sake, doesn't this circus have enough *acts*?" Mrs. Sax said. "Can't she be added later in the season?"

Isabelle blew out smoke. "All due respect, Mary, take it up with your husband and Tebow. They think she'll be a huge draw. Nobody's got a kid this young who can do stuff like this, not even Ringling."

"Oh, for heaven's sake." Mrs. Sax crouched in front of Cecily, the hem of her skirt brushing the mud, and grabbed Cecily's arms. "Cecily, what do *you* want? I thought you loved school!"

Cecily had no idea if Mrs. Sax knew about the money that Tebow had paid Mrs. H. for her. Would Mrs. Sax understand that Cecily felt obligated to prove she was worth it? That she still worried about getting left on the side of some railroad track in some place she'd never heard of?

She felt Prince coming up behind her. His breath was warm on her neck, like he knew she needed soothing.

"Mary, we both know it's not up to her," Isabelle said quietly, and Mrs. Sax stood and brushed off her skirt.

"Well. You can better believe I'm going to take this up with my husband," she said. Then, she frowned at Cecily like she was mad at *her*, too. "Supper is in one hour. Don't be late." She shot an extra-angry glare at Isabelle. "And, no, this child is not coming back out after supper. She needs to get some *sleep*."

"She needs to take care of her pony."

"That can be done *before* supper," Mrs. Sax said, and she turned and marched back toward the house.

Isabelle sighed and slumped back against the barn, smoking. Cecily stroked Prince's nose, which made her feel better, though she hated to be the cause of so much discord. But she felt her suspicions confirmed: that it was only Mrs. Sax who insisted Cecily live in the house and go to school; that, otherwise, she'd have been thrown in with the grown-up performers to spend all day training, with no objection from anyone. She didn't know what to think about that.

"You know, you're lucky, kid, to have her in your corner." Isabelle blew out smoke and pulled her sweater tighter. She dropped her cigarette into the mud and ground it out with her shoe. "All right, back to work."

After Cecily stopped going to school, her tenure in the house didn't last much longer. Mrs. Sax said that, if she was going to be out so late with Isabelle every night, she'd better stay in the bunkhouse. Nonie was losing sleep, she said.

There were pros and cons to all this, as far as Cecily was concerned.

She had lost Nonie and Mrs. Sax. But now she got to watch Isabelle rehearse in the mornings. Isabelle would line the horses up outside the barn, then vault easily onto Wyatt's back. At a slight click from her, they would thunder into the practice ring, Doc, Virgil, then Wyatt with Isabelle, her arms high, smiling like there was a whole crowd there, and not just Cecily, cheering.

Cecily never tired of seeing Isabelle's incredible flips and maneuvers, nor of being the small audience for other acts. She especially loved watching Mavis—who looked like an average woman these days, wearing pants and a heavy coat rather than the spectacle of her bright pink dress—put the tigers through their paces, the power of their limbs as they climbed ladders and leapt through hoops.

Another pro: nobody ever made her go to bed at night. After dark, if Cecily wasn't feeding popcorn to the monkey or sardines to the seal, she was watching Don and Vince and the other clowns walk on stilts or juggle, or listening to the grown-up talk and laughter around the bonfire. The World's Tallest Man, Henry Thompson, would fold himself into a too-small chair and play harmonica. Little Red would dance with his wife, the Bearded Lady Lorraine. Janey's husband, Ralph Robinson, teased Isabelle that she had a shadow, because Cecily barely made a sound, and, when Isabelle would yawn and stretch and say she was going in to bed, Cecily would just get up and follow. Isabelle had fixed it so that Cecily had the cot next to hers; she'd even had a man in the shop burn a wooden sign to read JACQUELINE DUMONDE, and hung it above the head of the cot, so it looked permanent. "Hey, she's my kid sister, what do you expect?" Isabelle would say, grinning and ruffling Cecily's hair. And Cecily felt the hum of a pleasure she'd never known.

The aches and bruises she had from falling would fade with time, Isabelle told her.

Then, Tebow came for a visit, and he wanted to see her act.

She'd put on her new blue costume, including the sparkling "sapphire" tiara, and, in the cool spring air, she was shivering, trembling with nerves. "Don't worry, kid," Isabelle said, stroking Prince's nose as they stood outside the barn. "Just do what you do."

So, Cecily vaulted onto Prince's back. He shifted his weight slightly as she gained her balance, and she was able to shift with him.

"Here we go," Isabelle said. Cecily circled her arms above her head and smiled the way she'd seen Isabelle do, and Isabelle led Prince over to the door. When Isabelle clicked, Prince trotted into the barn, into the ring, and Cecily stood smiling on his back as he ran round and round at the practiced pace, Cecily feeling his muscles as if they were an extension of her own, the way Isabelle had said to do. This was her first time working without the safety harness.

Tebow stood with his hands clasped in front of him, and, from what she could tell out the corner of her eye, was not as pleased with her as he once had been.

She geared up her mind and body for the front flip, letting Prince's steady movement ripple through her. She counted for herself: *One, two, three*—

She didn't do it.

All right, then.

One, two, three—

She flipped—landed on Prince's back—and kept her balance! She raised her arms, triumphant, but Tebow did not look pleased.

She heard him and Isabelle arguing afterward. She'd made her exit, leapt down from Prince, and led the pony back around to just outside the door, so she could listen. "That's *it?*" Tebow said.

"She's a little kid! She's doing amazing!"

"In *months*, this is all you've managed to teach her? She needs to be spectacular!"

"She *is*."

"Not nearly enough. Not nearly enough."

Cecily didn't make a sound. She stroked Prince's nose and leaned on him, knowing her heart would break if she had to leave him and Isabelle.

But there was no rule against her heart being broken. She knew that, too, from experience.

That night, Isabelle stayed out at the bonfire longer than she ever had. Tebow had left before supper, headed for Milwaukee, and, all night, Isabelle had been staring into the flames, looking so melancholy that Cecily had forgotten her own upset and only wished for Isabelle to talk and laugh as usual. Tonight, the older girl hardly glanced up, even as her friends began, one by one, to say good night.

Mavis and Ron were the last to go in. "You all right, Belle?" Mavis said. "You'll put the fire out?"

"Yes, fine," Isabelle said. Mavis and Ron exchanged looks, then walked off in the direction of their apartment.

Cecily watched the dancing flames, wishing she had done a better job today. She had done the best she could, but it wasn't enough, and she finally saw what Isabelle had meant when she'd said the winter might not be long enough. Cecily thought of her little suitcase, stowed under her cot. Would she be packing it soon? She remembered the prayer card, which she'd replaced inside the suitcase's pocket when she'd moved to the bunkhouse. *Please*, she prayed.

"Can you keep a secret, kid?" Isabelle said.

Cecily looked up. "Yes!"

"My name's Betsy Cahill," Isabelle all but whispered. "I'm from Providence, Rhode Island. Nobody else knows, so keep it quiet, all right? Don't ever call me by that name."

Cecily nodded quickly. "Where's Rhode Island? Did you have to take a boat to leave it?"

Isabelle smiled, shook her head, and put a finger to her lips. "It's way out east, and it's a state, not a real island. We'll get there someday, probably."

An island that was not an island didn't make sense, but Cecily believed Isabelle, anyway. "Why did you leave?"

Isabelle's lips pursed. "My mother died when I was eleven, and, when I was twelve, my father married a woman I couldn't stand, and who couldn't stand me. I didn't last a year in the same house with her. When the circus came to town, I stowed away on the train, and I didn't come out for three days. When I finally did, we were in Cleveland, and Tebow asked me what I could do. I said I was good with horses. Which was an utter lie. I'd ridden one once, at the home of a friend of my father's."

This was a lot to take in, but Cecily had picked up especially on the catch on the last word. "I never knew my father at all," she ventured. "What was yours like?"

Isabelle grabbed a stick and poked the dying fire, then dropped the stick in and let it burn. "He kept pennies in his pocket and would pretend to pull them out from behind my ear. Before my mother died. Then, afterward, he grew old overnight. I almost didn't recognize him, you know? It was as if he was driving a car and decided to give up on steering." She gave a short laugh. "And then the car went into a fast river and bobbed away on down it. The woman he married was only twenty-two. I knew she was just after his money. She didn't even bother to deny it to me. She was about to have a baby when I left. I guess she thought that would make her seem serious."

Cecily couldn't help feeling a bit wounded at that news. "You might have a real sister, then."

Isabelle waved that off. "Not really. Anyway, my father was hoping for a son and heir. He owns a mill that produces worsted wool. 'Cahill Woolen Mill.' Very high-quality stuff. For suits and things, you know? I guess he thought a baby boy would solve all his problems. William, Junior, I suppose." She pulled out her cigarettes and lit one. "I've never written to him once to tell him I'm alive. I think he would be fifty years old now."

Fifty years old! Near death! "Well, you should write to him right now! Don't you know how lucky you are? To have a *father*?"

Isabelle's eyes narrowed. She smoked, then shrugged. "He knew it was a choice between her and me, and he chose her." She brushed invisible dust off her pant leg. "Anyway, there was a rider here with the circus called Suzanne, and she taught me everything she knew, like I'm doing now with you. And then Suzanne left the show to get married." She smoked again. Cecily didn't know what to say. Would Isabelle leave *her* someday? To get married?

Then Isabelle smiled. "So, kid, you're the only family I've got. Don't you forget it."

"Oh, Isabelle!" Cecily had had no idea: Isabelle really needed her, just as much as Cecily needed Isabelle! "I'll learn any new tricks you show me, I swear I will, don't worry!"

Isabelle reached over and patted her hand. "It's a rough road, kid, this life, but you and me are going to be all right, aren't we? Sisters."

"Yes!" Cecily said, and she meant it as a promise, and she'd go over Niagara Falls in a barrel before she broke it. She hadn't kept her oath to Flip and Dolores, but that hadn't been her fault, exactly—they'd been just kids, without any choice in things. Now she was grown up, almost eight—and she was Isabelle's sister.

CHAPTER 18

Saturday, February 21, 2015
Itasca, Minnesota

O h, I don't know, Moll," Stacey Thorson said, hands in the pockets of her nurse's scrubs, when Molly asked her late Saturday morning at the hospital about taking the saliva sample from Cecily. "I could get in big trouble for doing that, you know."

"Oh, of course! I didn't even think!" Molly'd been up half the night ruminating, but evidently hadn't thought twice about making this outlandish request, though she and Stacey hadn't been close in years. She wanted to blame Evan. Not that last night had gone horribly—he'd said good night pleasantly enough, after they'd finished with ice cream and making arrangements for today. But, if he hadn't come to town, she could've probably continued avoiding thinking about the past. Instead, now, she kept hearing what Caden had said the other night: *It was probably your fault. You just need to accept it.*

But Molly had spent years—a decade!—trying to accept what had happened. Even as it had happened again and again! Trying not to blame herself for losing the babies. Trying to heal her grief, even heal her *body*, while her doctors, mystified, would only say "keep trying." She'd spent weekends at Kripalu doing primal scream therapy, workshops on detoxing after trauma, discovering your inner goddess, writing your way through grief. She'd studied and trained and traveled to get certified in Reiki, yoga therapy, Jin Shin Jyutsu, and craniosacral work.

And yet.

She'd kept on having miscarriages. Her marriage had broken apart.

Now, though, she wanted to believe there'd been a reason for all of this—even for her dad's dying long before it should've been his time. Because her journey had taught her more than she'd ever expected to need to learn about suffering—and about how to help people find their way through it—and it had brought her here, back home. In Rhode Island, she hadn't yet put together all she'd learned, but, here in Itasca, she'd managed to build the practice of her dreams, if she'd known enough to dream of things that, ten years ago, she'd had no knowledge of at all.

Sure, not everyone here believed in alternative modalities, but Molly was, slowly but surely, building a good reputation. She kept the two arms of her practice separate and was careful not to push her talk therapy clients into alternative services. But—for those who were open to it! She had clients, previously immobilized by grief, often for *years*, who were now launching businesses, creating online dating profiles, eating healthy, exercising, not drinking or smoking anymore. These were not small things! These were habits that created the framework for a life of possibility. And Molly was the only practitioner within a hundred miles offering these particular modalities.

She liked to think of the time when her grandpa Sam had been the only doctor in town. She liked to think he'd be proud of her.

Of course, it was a different thing entirely to try to convince Caden that all the suffering—hers, and Evan's; even Caden's own—had been for a *reason*: to bring Molly back home to Itasca, to help these people who needed help.

If only she could keep from getting so angry with him.

If only he didn't say such stupid-teenager things . . .

Even this morning, she'd snapped at him again, because, when she'd stuck her head in his door, intending to tell him goodbye and that she loved him, she'd spotted teetering stacks of dirty bowls on his desk, piles of sweaty T-shirts and filthy socks strewn across the floor. "Oh my God, we're going to get *cockroaches!*" she'd blurted. "Clean this place up *before* your father picks you up today, or you're grounded!" Which was ridiculous—cockroaches surely couldn't survive the subzero temps outside, right? Also—way to make herself look like the not-fun parent, at just the moment Evan was going to swoop in and probably treat Caden to one of the best days of his life.

Now Stacey was looking at her quizzically, seeming to want to help, and Molly was embarrassed. "I'm sorry, Stace. That was lame of me, to ask you that."

"Oh, no," Stacey said, brushing off the apology. Her eyes sparked. "Listen, though, I'll tell you what I *can* do." She leaned in to whisper her plan.

"How are we doing today, Mrs. Larson?" Stacey sang out, as she walked into Cecily's room, carrying a tray that held the Ancestry kit's test tube alongside a lemon slice on a small white hospital plate. ("To make it look official," she'd told Molly with a wink.) Molly had brought the lemon from home, because the Ancestry instructions said that older people sometimes had trouble creating enough saliva to fill the tube, and that a wedge of lemon would do the trick.

"Fine, thanks." Cecily's white hair gleamed in the sun that streamed through the window, reflecting off the snow outside.

"Just another little test," Stacey said. "Very painless. All you have to do is fill the tube to the line with saliva." She looked down at her pager, pressed a button. A *beep* sounded. "Oh, dear. An emergency! Listen, Molly, can you do me a favor and help with this?" She shoved the tray at Molly and hurried out.

Well, she wouldn't win an Academy Award, but it got the job done.

"Back in my day, that would not fly as nursing care," Cecily grumbled, hitching herself up to sit straighter against her pillows. "Now, this doesn't have to do with TB, does it? I am *not* going to be incarcerated again."

Molly felt a stab of guilt. Yet one more thing she hadn't put together today: that a spit test was what had landed Cecily in the sanatorium, long ago. "No, Grandma, not at all. Nothing like that."

"Hey, Mom! How are you feeling today?" Liz was walking in, still wearing her parka, her face flushed from the cold outside. "Oh, hi, Moll!" Liz hugged Molly, and the familiar comfort was a relief: this morning, when Molly had texted to ask if Liz would be at the hospital and if she needed anything, Liz had responded simply, *Yes, see you in a bit.* A long list of instructions and to-dos, specific arrival and departure times, would've been far more expected—not to mention questions about Caden's game, Evan's arrival.

Cecily was spitting into the tube. "I can't imagine what they need this for," she grumbled.

Liz gave Molly a secret thumbs-up and a wink. But, wait—was that a tear in her eye?

Yes, and now it was running down her face.

Molly thought of all the times she'd confided in her grandma Cecily rather than in her mom, all the times Cecily had listened to Molly's frustrations about Liz: how Liz so rarely showed emotion, how she was so distant and businesslike all the time, or else her head was in the clouds of her latest creations, not on the ground where Molly needed her. And Cecily had, time and again, dried Molly's tears and said, "Listen, your mom is who she is, and we love her for it, don't we?"

At the time, teenaged Molly wouldn't answer; she'd grudgingly, silently wish for a different mother, or, at least, that her mother could be different! Molly had actually often thought that the reason she'd become a therapist was because she was so hungry for *connection*, for people to talk about what they really *felt*.

Now, though, Molly saw that the answer to Cecily's question—*we love her for it, don't we?*—was *Yes!* Resoundingly! The unflappability, the dependability, the practicality, the unexpected bursts of creativity and laughter—Molly absolutely relied on all of it, and had, all her life.

And Liz did not seem like herself at all right now. As far off as she'd
been the other day, this was, like, a hundred times *more* off.

"Are you all right, Mom?" Molly ventured.

Liz waved Molly off, busily removing gloves, scarf, parka. "Oh, yah,
fine."

Molly exchanged a glance with Cecily, as Cecily handed over the tube
of saliva and Molly closed it up.

"Did you get some rest, honey?" Cecily asked Liz.

"Yah, yah," Liz said, piling her things on the chair by the window.
Molly saw her wipe her eye before she turned to ask Cecily with a smile,
"How are you feeling today, Mom?"

Neither Cecily nor Molly could pry a thing out of Liz, even when Molly
took her down to the café for a cup-of-soup lunch, while Cecily's therapist
came to work with her on getting out of bed and taking a couple more
steps with the walker. All Liz would admit to was feeling "a bit out of
sorts; probably just tired, you know?" Then she started asking how Evan
was faring in the house, if he'd noticed any problems, if he'd been sure to
open all the taps to make sure no pipes had the opportunity to freeze.

This was more like it—more like the Liz that Molly knew. Not
asking how things had gone with Evan, or between Evan and Caden,
but how Evan was finding the house. Aggravating, as always—but the
normalcy of it was a comfort today, too.

They finished up and walked back toward Cecily's room, Molly con-
scious of the tube of Cecily's saliva in the little package in her purse.
She should've gotten her mom's sample while they'd been out of view of
Cecily; she'd have to remember later, she thought, as they whooshed up
to the second floor in the elevator.

Just outside Cecily's room, Molly's phone buzzed with a text from
Caden. *Practice was great*—plus a picture of the left side of his face, his
eye bruised blue all around.

She gestured for Liz to go ahead, and, five seconds later, she had Evan on the phone. "What is going on? A black eye? Does he have a concussion? Does he need to come to the hospital? I'm here! I'll meet you at the ER!"

Evan was laughing. "Moll, calm down. He's fine. Just a normal day of hockey practice. He got elbowed, not hit with a puck. The trainer ran him through the concussion protocol, and he checked out fine. We're having lunch at the Thai Garden now."

Molly tried to unclench her jaw. "Only when you're left in charge is that a 'normal day of hockey practice.' Are you sure he's all right? Maybe I should come get him—"

"He's fine, Moll. I can handle it. How's your grandma today?"

Molly exhaled. "—Um, she's okay." Molly wasn't going to mention how off *Liz* seemed, or how weird it had been to fool Cecily into giving that saliva sample.

"Hey, Moll," Evan said, in a new, more serious tone. "Can we set a time to sit down together, just the two of us? Maybe tomorrow?"

He paused long enough that she had to answer. "Um, okay . . ."

"We need to talk about how I can spend more time with Caden. I mean, I haven't even gotten the time that was allotted to me by the court, and that wasn't nearly enough, to start."

Molly went light-headed. The world was suddenly tilted off-kilter. *Her son. Hers.* She was not going to let Evan take him from her. No way. *No way.* Oh, they were going to sit down and talk, all right.

She swallowed. Tried to sound like an adult. "Let me text you later, and we can set a time."

"Okay." He laughed a little, as if everything was just fine now that he was going to get his way. "And, hey," he added, "don't worry about our boy, okay? He's just inhaled about two pounds of pad Thai. I'm pretty sure that's a sign of good health."

After they said goodbye, Molly unclenched her teeth, took another deep breath, closed her eyes, and leaned back against the hall's handrail, trying to shake off her anger and fear with a little prayer of thanks:

that Caden was okay, that Cecily was well enough to grumble, that Liz seemed at least *halfway* normal—

She pocketed her phone and headed back into Cecily's room.

"Ah, there she is!" Cecily was sitting up in bed, bright-eyed in the sun, with Liz looking tired beside her. "The incredible Molly Anderson!"

"Oh, Grandma," Molly said, her face heating up like she was eight years old again.

CHAPTER 19

July 1930
Iowa City, Iowa

A nd now, the incredible child phenomenon, Jacqueline Du-
Monde!" Tebow's voice thundered from the loudspeakers, as
ten-year-old Cecily, standing on Prince's back, raised her arms,
pasted on a smile, and clicked to Prince. Stagehands pulled the tent flaps
back, and Prince was in motion, cantering for the ring, his ears perked
to the cheers of the crowd.

They were in Iowa City, and Cecily wanted to put on the best show
of her life so far, in this, her third season with Sax & Tebow—just in
case. Somewhere in the shadowy grandstands—she tried to see into
them, but could not—somewhere sitting watching, high in the rafters
or from the front row, could be her mother, Madeline.

The band played Cecily's number, "Five Foot Two, Eyes of Blue."
As Prince cantered to the rhythm, she flipped frontward and landed on
her feet on the rippling muscles of his back to the crash of a cymbal,
clutching his hair with her toes. The crowd whooped; she steadied herself.
Prince shook his mane, basking in the cheers as he continued round the
ring. Cecily counted to the music, then—at the exact planned moment—
jumped down into the dust and vaulted right up onto Prince's back again,
holding up her hands as the cymbal crashed once more. She loved the
smell of sawdust and popcorn, the shouts and gasps of the crowd, the
feel of Prince's body under her feet. Quickly, she sat sidesaddle, then hung
upside down off his side, hooked on with just her legs, the dust of the
ring inches above her sparkling tiara. She swung back up and posed again,

then did another flip to another cymbal crash, Prince's back moving under her feet. She heard the song's words in her mind as the band played: *Five foot two, eyes of blue, has anybody seen my girl?* The crowd roared. She held out her arms, then did a little curtsy, as Prince cantered round and round.

"Good job, boy," she said to him afterward, out back in his stall in the stable tent, rubbing his nose and feeding him a carrot. In the ring now was Isabelle, and Cecily, listening to the distant *oohs* and *ahhs* of the crowd, imagined her leaping from Doc to Wyatt to Virgil and back again. Tebow wanted Cecily and Isabelle to combine acts, but Isabelle had so far resisted. Cecily still wasn't tall enough to work with the big horses; at least, that was the reason Isabelle gave, though Cecily suspected Isabelle just didn't want to wonder, when she heard the crowd cheering, if it was really for *her*.

Cecily didn't blame her one bit. What else did they really have?

That and each other, anyway.

Cecily stood on Prince's back for the curtain call with all the performers— they marched out waving to the crowd, then processed around the ring and back out again. The instant Cecily was out from under the Big Top, she leaped down and asked Isabelle to take charge of Prince. "Sure, sure, go on!" Isabelle said, smiling and waving her away. Whenever they were in Iowa, she always let Cecily go out to watch the crowd exiting. Again, just in case.

Cecily ran around the Big Top, removing her tiara as she went, as if that alone might make her look like a normal girl, like Cecily McAvoy, a girl whose mother would know her. When she got to the corner, she peered around. The grounds were dark, the crowd a bit disoriented. The menagerie and sideshow tents had all been taken down while the big show was underway, the canvas and poles hauled back to the train on wagons by the roustabouts.

Cecily watched the backs of the dispersing crowd. How would her mother know she was waiting? Maybe this had been her trouble all along—keeping too far out of sight.

She squared her shoulders, tossed her hair, and stepped into view, striding out toward the crowd. Someone saw her. "It's Jacqueline Du-Monde!" A boy ran over, asking for her autograph. A dozen more people lined up behind him. Cecily smiled and signed for them all, even as she watched the crowd filing past.

Suddenly, a dark-haired, pretty woman stood before her. The woman had to be about the age that Cecily's mother would be! Was there a chance? Cecily had to think: yes!

The woman smiled. "My daughter would very much like your autograph. She admired you so much. She's just a little shy to ask."

The hope that had shot through Cecily at the first two words crashed down. Of course this woman had a daughter. Who was shy; who lived a normal life, with parents who brought her to the circus.

But that daughter was not Cecily.

She signed the woman's program, made hasty apologies to the rest who were waiting, and dashed back behind the Big Top.

She stopped, doubled over, trying to catch her breath, her chest aching like she'd been torn in two. Why hadn't she realized it before? It had been just a foolish dream, that she'd ever find her mother in Iowa. It was never even anything Dolores had really *said*—

"Hey, kid, get out of here!" a workman yelled. He must not have recognized Cecily in the darkness. The Big Top was going dark, the side poles being removed. Another man shouted, "Let her go!" Cries came as a few stragglers ran out from inside. Tears stung Cecily's eyes, as she backed away into deeper shadows.

Another shout: "Now!" Immediately, the bale rings slid down the poles, and fifty thousand square feet of paraffin-treated canvas settled toward the ground, swelling and billowing on the air underneath. Pole-riggers grabbed the bale rings and swiftly unlashed the canvas, while the men at the stakes all around pounced onto the mountain of collapsing canvas, climbing up the seams, unlacing the leather cord that bound the sections as they went.

Cecily felt the collapse like it was her own hope—a thing she'd been carrying all these years without even realizing the weight of it.

She looked at the tiara in her hands and wanted to throw it into a ditch. To run away forever.

But where would she run *to*? She had nowhere. She had no one.

She wiped her face, put the tiara back on her head, and began walking toward the train. Cecily McAvoy was dead. She was Jacqueline DuMonde forever now.

The horses were stashed away in the stock cars by the time Cecily got to the train, and she hated that she'd missed her usual nightly routine with Prince: helping Janey groom him, giving him carrots and apples, leading him to the train, bidding him good night. Now, Janey had already led him up the ramp and into the car, where he was wedged in with twenty-six other horses, all standing so close together that they couldn't move, so they couldn't fall over in transit and get hurt.

In the distance, the front part of the train was still busy, as the wagons full of canvas and poles were being loaded onto the flatcars. At the back, though, at Cecily and Isabelle's caboose and the real caboose behind it, where the conductor rode, all was quiet and dark. Only Isabelle and Cecily stayed to the rear of Tebow's private car. The other performers stayed in bunk cars up ahead, and the roustabouts and grooms stayed far out in front of that. Some workers even slept out on the flatcars, if the weather was nice enough, because a hundred of them were assigned to sleep in a car with only fifty bunks in it.

The rear door to her caboose was open. Cecily bounded up onto the vestibule, but froze outside the door when she heard Tebow shouting: "We've got to do *something*, Belle!" Cecily crouched so she wouldn't be seen, though the two of them were on the opposite end of the car, in the compartment where Isabelle's bunk was. Cecily could see them through the passageway, in the light of Isabelle's lantern. Isabelle was still in her red costume, eyeliner smeared, red lipstick chewed away.

"We're losing money hand over fist," Tebow said. "Gate sales keep going down. Nobody's got the money to go to the circus. But they'll find money for things they really want. I've had more than one man talk to me about it. They said they'd pay up to a dollar to see her dance."

"No! No, no, no! She's a child! What is wrong with you, even to think of it? It won't be three days before someone grabs her out back and rapes her! You know that as well as I do."

Tebow ran a hand over his hair, seeming almost ashamed, which Cecily had never seen him be. "I'm desperate," he said, as if that made up for something.

"There are a thousand things you can think of! Or I'll do it! If you've got to have a peep show, for God's sake, take me and not her. This place is my life. She's still got a chance at a different one." Isabelle turned her back on him and leaned on the doorframe of her compartment, arms folded.

"Isabelle." Tebow sighed. He moved close up behind her and put his mouth against her hair. "You know I'd never share you. Bad enough to watch them all ogling you in the ring." He slipped his arms around her waist.

Cecily covered her mouth with her hand.

Isabelle stayed standing with her arms folded, looking at the floor. "You like to pretend you're not unscrupulous," she said. "But you're so very willing to do unscrupulous things."

Tebow sighed. He nuzzled her neck. "Belle, you want to blame me for things that aren't my fault. I'm trying to feed people. Keep them employed. It's getting rougher and rougher out there."

"You know that kid's like a sister to me. And she's only ten! Four years younger than I was when you started with me. A *child*. You've got to promise me you'll let her alone!"

Another sigh. "All right, Belle. I don't want to argue." Tebow's hand cupped Isabelle's breast.

Isabelle flinched, but, after a second, leaned back into him, letting her eyes drift closed. Cecily stayed frozen, afraid they would hear her in the overpowering quiet.

"You'd better be extra good to me, though," Tebow added, pulling Isabelle closer. "She'll be fourteen before you know it, and you'll be old by that time, Belle."

Isabelle's eyes snapped open. Her face went pale, and Cecily thought for an instant that she might've whirled and stabbed him, if only she had a knife in her hand.

Then, her expression shifted to a strange grimace. She seemed to be deciding something.

She freed herself from Tebow's grip, wriggled her red pantalets and attached stockings down. She turned to unbuckle Tebow's belt. "I'm the one you want. Don't forget it," she said. She about-faced again and braced her hands on the doorframe, while he let his pants fall down.

Cecily felt frozen in place, still afraid to make a sound. Isabelle's skirt hid what they were doing, but Cecily knew, because she'd seen animals, and she could see Tebow's and Isabelle's faces. Tebow, with his eyes closed as his body moved behind Isabelle's. Isabelle, who seemed to be smiling, grimacing, and crying at once; Cecily could see tears glistening on her face, and it was all she could do to keep from screaming and running to tackle Tebow to try to get him *off* her—but some part of her must have known that that wasn't something she should do.

Tebow, eyes squeezed shut, made a deep *Oh!* sound. Isabelle smiled, opened her eyes—and saw Cecily.

Her eyes got huge. Tebow moaned again and sighed, his eyes still closed.

Cecily jumped up and ran into the darkness, her breath pounding in her ears.

"So," Isabelle said much later, standing in the doorway between her and Cecily's compartments. Cecily had run straight for the front of the train, but Prince was already wedged into the stock car, and all she could do was try to talk to him through the slats. She imagined she heard him huff in response, but, for all she knew, she might've been talking to any horse at all. She'd wandered the shadows of the trainyard for a while, but, with the train unmistakably leaving soon, she'd slinked back to the caboose. Hoping to avoid Isabelle altogether, she'd washed her face and brushed her teeth as quietly as possible, then crept up into her bunk and stretched out like a corpse. But Isabelle had come out, long black cigarette holder dangling from her hand. "Now you know."

Cecily said nothing.

"Look, I'm sorry you had to see that. You probably were scared. But there's no need to be scared, all right? Do you have any questions?"

Cecily bit down hard on her lip. She supposed Isabelle meant about the mechanics of things. But Cecily had no interest in that. Flip had shown her his boy parts once, and she had not found them impressive.

Other worries were top of mind now. She didn't want to judge Isabelle. She'd spent so long believing Isabelle was always right. But, no matter how she wanted to, and though she told herself it was childish to care so much about everything—even to be clutching her old Saint Jude card like she was right this minute!—she could not hold in a: "How *could* you?"

Isabelle gave a short laugh. "Listen, he's not so bad. Sure, I didn't like it much, at first. I was pretty young then. Now, I guess I love him, in a way. I think he loves me, too." She blew out smoke. "In a way."

Cecily had always dreamed that one of the glamorous aerialists would fall in love with Isabelle; that it was only a matter of time. Now she knew that Isabelle was fooling herself about what love was; that Isabelle seemed to feel she didn't even have a choice.

"Listen, kid," Isabelle said. "How do you think we got the caboose? Why do you think we don't have to stay in the bunk car with the other girls? He pays a whole fee for this car every single leg we travel. We've got our own private bathroom with water, for God's sake!" She paused, and her tone went lower. "How do you think you got Prince?"

Cecily bit down harder on her lip. She bit until she tasted blood. She hated being mad at Isabelle—and what right did she have to be mad at her for *this*? She knew Isabelle was only trying to protect her.

And she knew, without Isabelle, she'd be lost, she'd be nothing.

She thought again of her mother and started to cry.

"Oh, kid!" Isabelle said, though Cecily hadn't thought she'd made a sound. "Listen, will you come down here, please?" She stubbed out her cigarette, and Cecily, feeling helpless, climbed down and let herself be gathered into Isabelle's arms. The older girl was too thin to really sink into, but Cecily tried, leaning on her shoulder, letting go of all her stored-up tears of the years without her mother, as Isabelle rubbed her back and whispered, "You're going to be all right, kid, I promise you. You're gonna have a better life than I do, okay? I'm gonna see to it," and Cecily tried and tried to believe her.

CHAPTER 20

> ›

Sunday, February 22, 2015
Itasca, Minnesota

W e're afraid Cecily may be taking a turn for the worse," Dr. Olson told Liz and Molly at noon on Sunday. They'd ended up pulling into the parking lot at the same time and walking in together, without having exactly planned it, and Dr. Olson had just been coming out of Cecily's room. Now he adjusted his glasses. "Her body is healing fine, but, as of this morning, she's beginning to show signs of delirium. And agitation, which can be a sign of developing depression. This isn't uncommon in older patients after major surgery, especially just coming out of anesthesia. We were hopeful it wouldn't turn up at this stage. And she seemed fine yesterday. But, this morning, one of the nurses said Cecily was talking to her mother, as if her mother was in the room, and then she got very agitated when the nurse questioned her."

Molly glanced at Liz and quickly saw: nope, they were not going to mention how Cecily had never actually known her mother. "What's the plan, going forward?" Liz asked. Thank God, at least *she* was acting more normal today. Molly, even after two large cups of coffee, did not feel like herself at all. Last night, when Evan had dropped off Caden, as Molly had fussed over their son's awful-looking black eye, Evan had insisted on scheduling a conversation. For today! Caden was spending the day with Evan again, then they would all meet back at the bungalow at five, so Evan and Molly could talk while Molly made supper, trying to keep on track for an early night, so Caden would get plenty of rest before tomorrow's game.

Naturally, Molly had stayed up till 2 A.M., reviewing her court papers and googling things like "reasons a judge will change custody agreement." What she'd found had not been encouraging. What if some judge actually believed she'd acted in bad faith by not letting Caden travel to see his dad at Christmas, despite the weather and the fact that he'd had hockey games on either side of the planned dates, or by not rescheduling another trip? (As if there'd been time, with hockey!)

Now her stomach was hurting, too, over Cecily, as Dr. Olson went on about adjustments to medication, adverse effects on her recovery, possible delay of her transfer to The Pines.

"I'm sorry," he finished. "I know, after getting through surgery and the last few days, it's tempting to think you're through the worst, but, with a person this old, this is where it gets really hard, unfortunately."

Liz and Molly thanked him, glanced at each other—Liz looked as stunned as Molly felt—then squared their shoulders and walked into Cecily's room.

Cecily was lying back with her eyes closed, her white hair frizzing out across her pillows. She looked exhausted—and incredibly, undeniably *old*.

"Mom?" Liz said, going straight to Cecily's bedside. "Mom!"

Cecily's eyes fluttered open. Molly waited by the door, hoping for the usual joke or sarcastic comment.

Nothing. A couple of blinks.

Liz was frowning, her face flushed. "Mom, Dr. Olson said you seem to be getting depressed. Are you? Are you feeling confused at all? Listen, I'm not going to have you give up on me. I'm not going to have you leave me."

Slowly, Cecily smiled. "Now, that isn't up to either of us, is it?" She patted Liz's hand. "Though I've tried so hard, all these years, to keep you."

Liz looked at Molly, and Molly could tell she was thinking the same thing: what an odd thing for Cecily to say.

Liz regrouped. "Mom, the doctor said you were talking to your mother."

"I never knew my mother," Cecily snapped. "You know that. When I was four years old, she left me at the Home! I never knew her at all. I don't remember, I mean!"

"She *left* you?" Liz said. This was new information, and a fresh shock, almost more than the shock of Cecily's appearance or aggravated tone. Molly—and Liz, too, she knew—had always assumed that Cecily's parents had died, that that was how she'd ended up in the orphanage.

"Yes! She checked it on the form that she was going to come back for me, but she never did!"

"Oh, Mom." Liz reached for Cecily's hand. Tears were in both their eyes.

"I really can't think of anything," Liz said later, when Molly asked again what she could do to help. They'd spent an hour trying to get Cecily to tell them more, learning only that she remembered, as a child, seeing on some form that her father was dead and there was no known address for her mother. The subject did obviously agitate her—little wonder—so they'd finally given up and tried to engage Cecily in small talk instead. They'd had no more luck with that, ending up talking more to each other across the bed about Evan's demands and Caden's black eye and the predictions people were making about tomorrow's game—that it was going to be tough, that the defense was really going to have to step up. Cecily stared at the wall, seeming barely to be listening, then finally said she was tired and they should go. Liz and Molly had looked at each other in alarm: Normally, Cecily would have been the most up-in-arms of anyone about any hint of a threat to Molly, the most excited about Caden's team making the next round of playoffs. "We can only hope tomorrow will be better, and that she'll be able to go over to The Pines," Liz had murmured as they'd walked out.

Now they were in the visitors' lounge, and Liz was finishing spitting into her own Ancestry test tube. Molly, in the end, had forgotten to have her do it yesterday. As Liz handed over the tube, yesterday's same strange sheen was back in her eye.

"Is something wrong, Mom?" Molly said, trying to sound offhand, as she twisted on the cap to release the stabilizing fluid, shook the tube for the required five seconds, then slid it into its plastic sleeve and sealed it up. "On top of what's wrong with Grandma, I mean. You don't seem like yourself."

"No, no. I'm fine," Liz said, sounding distracted, as she searched her purse for her gloves, her keys. "Think I'll go to SuperValu. I'm running low on things, and I need to bake a cake for Harold and Bess, to thank them, you know?"

"Right now? You seem exhausted. And you need to keep your strength up, for Grandma. Hopefully the transfer *will* go through tomorrow, right?" Molly refused to believe that Cecily's turn for the worse wasn't going to turn right back around, and quickly.

"No, no, they need a cake," Liz said absently, as she stood to wind her scarf around her neck. "It won't be fancy like one of Mom's fifteen-layer jobs." She laughed a little. "Maybe an applesauce spice."

"Let me make it, then. I can do it tonight. You need to get some rest, because you're coming to Duluth for the game tomorrow with me, right? As long as Grandma's okay, I mean, and you can get the transfer done early in the day? Caden would be so disappointed if you weren't there."

"Oh, no. I want to make the cake. I'll be fine for the game. Anyway, you've got that talk with Evan tonight." Liz shrugged into her parka, then hugged Molly briefly. "Good luck. Don't let him rattle you. Now, when do we expect those DNA results, again?"

That odd light was still in Liz's eyes. "I'll get them sent out tomorrow," Molly said, then remembered: with the game, tomorrow was going to be nuts. They'd have to leave by three thirty at the latest to drive to Duluth, and Molly hadn't even checked the forecast yet to see if they'd need to add extra time for weather. "Or Tuesday, at the latest. Then it'll be six to eight weeks."

"Okay, then." Liz gave her trademark nod, like she'd just decided something. Molly just had no idea what.

Six to eight weeks, Liz thought, as she walked out of the hospital into the breathtaking cold of the sunny afternoon. *I'll live that long, won't I?*

Then, she had to laugh, and scold herself for being overdramatic.

It was just a biopsy. Having to have a biopsy didn't necessarily mean you had cancer.

It had all happened so fast. Just Friday morning, in the shower, she'd felt the lump. It was tiny, hard, like a pebble, just under the skin of the lower portion of her right breast. Probably a cyst. She'd had one of those ten years ago. Nothing to worry about. Still—she heard her father's voice—it was always best to be sure; to get an exact diagnosis. "Nothing can be assumed," Sam had always said.

So, on arrival at the hospital that morning to visit Cecily, she'd headed first to the office of Dr. Hokannen, who was head of oncology and an old friend of her father's. Sam had been one of his mentors, in fact, when Dr. Hokannen had first arrived as a young resident, right around the time Molly was born—almost forty years ago. He'd been taken in as part of the extended Larson family, attending Fourth of July picnics and Thanksgiving dinners, watching Liz's little family grow, even golfing with Dean and Sam from time to time. Then he'd married Nancy Carlson and had a family of his own. Dean had sold them their house—a modest Victorian not far from the hospital—and Molly had babysat for his two kids, who'd now be in their late twenties. Five or so years ago, Nancy had divorced him and gone off to Florida. Official gossip was that she just couldn't stand Itasca winters anymore, but Liz remembered Dean laughing about that as he took off his socks one night before bed, saying there had to be more to any divorce than that.

Dr. Hokannen was, luckily, in the hallway outside his office, and he grinned at the sight of Liz and hugged her. "I was just thinking about you and your parents! I meant to call you!" he said. He'd heard about

Cecily, had even stopped by her room to visit. "She seemed mostly like herself, I was glad to see. I know you must be concerned." He wanted to know if there was anything he could do. "Well, actually," Liz had said, and asked to speak with him privately. It wasn't like her to ask for special treatment, but, in the middle of everything going on with Cecily, and the long road of recovery ahead, she hadn't wanted to be worrying about this little cyst of hers, not even at the back of her mind.

A quick examination made Dr. Hokannen frown. He said there was no need to waste time; an ultrasound would tell them everything they needed to know. With one phone call, he was able to slip her in for one within an hour.

Two hours after that, she was back in his office, and his frown had deepened. "There's no fluid, so it's not a cyst," he said bluntly. "I'm going to schedule a biopsy."

He was able to wedge her into Monday morning's schedule—early, 8 a.m., before Cecily's scheduled transfer to The Pines. He didn't want to waste time, he said again, though this time with a new gravity.

"Even if it's cancer, in all likelihood, it's treatable," he said, his gentle seriousness reminding Liz of her father. She had to think that Sam must have schooled him in how to deliver such news. "At least we know your mom hasn't had any trouble with this, so there's no genetic suggestion that it would be cancer."

"We'll wait for the evidence, then," she'd said.

Now she got into the cold Grand Cherokee and started it up. She clutched the steering wheel and looked out at the snow-crusted river. It had been hard to spend hours with her mother and daughter yesterday and today and not say a word, not scream out, *I'm having a biopsy tomorrow!*

But how could she have, really, even if she'd wanted to—especially today, between Molly's upset over Evan and Dr. Olson's bad news about Cecily?

Liz took a deep breath. "Dad," she said out loud. "I'm scared."

A crow cawed. A nurse hurried past, headed for her car, post-shift, parka open over her scrubs, sneakers avoiding ice patches.

"I'm really scared!"

It wasn't as if she heard a voice, not exactly. But she got a sense: *Tell your mother.*

What?

She sensed it again: *Tell your mother.*

"No way. I can't tell Mom. You heard the doctor. She's getting weaker. More confused. She needs to focus on her own recovery, not start worrying about me."

She's stronger than you know.

Liz shook her head. Hearing her father's voice? Talking back to him? Impossible. She clearly needed rest. She'd slept hardly at all Friday night, instead watching eight straight episodes of *Law & Order* on cable—winking in and out of dreams on the last three, admittedly—after opting out of Caden's game out of simple fear that Molly would be able to tell something was wrong. Last night, she'd slept a little longer, more at ease with her secret, and she'd felt more optimistic today. It was just a biopsy. Not the end of the world. Only 20 percent of all biopsies turned out to be cancerous, a quick Google search yesterday had told her.

No, she did not want to burden Molly with this. Nor her poor mother, certainly. Telling Eric wasn't an option; she hadn't even heard back from him since the message she'd left on his voicemail last week about Cecily. Chances were good that all this meant was that he hadn't come down off the mountain yet—although there was that same old chance he'd been buried in some avalanche.

But she'd had twenty years now to practice the art of surrender on that score, while Eric financed annual "big climbs" with camp counseling in Utah, fishing in Alaska, climbing-guide jobs in Patagonia, Switzerland, Tanzania. Liz still (and, yes, maybe it was delusional) hoped he'd settle down, have a family, even move back to Itasca. She'd had a moment of hope at Dean's wake, when, rushing to bring a stack of dirty plates to the kitchen, she'd spotted him and the recently divorced Tori Amundson—his old high school flame—in the Adirondack chairs overlooking the lake, obviously deep in conversation despite the cold air, the snow dusting the ground. But, two days later, he'd hugged Liz goodbye in the driveway, climbed into his rental car with a flash of his devil-may-care grin, driven to Minneapolis, and boarded an airplane. She hadn't seen him in the three years since.

So, no: it wasn't as if she could call him up to chat about her biopsy.

Anyway, maybe there'd be nothing to tell.

All these years tending to my family, she thought, and, yes, she was feeling sorry for herself, *and I'm left so alone.*

She heard her father: *One step at a time. We wait for the test results.*

"Thanks, Dad," she said out loud. Who cared if she was off her rocker? It consoled her to think he might be watching over her.

Why, she wondered briefly, did she so rarely try to talk to Dean? Just because she was still so mad at him for leaving her?

Well, that was one more thing she couldn't think about now. Wouldn't, anyway.

She shifted into reverse and headed for SuperValu.

Hours later, with the applesauce cake in the oven and the kitchen cleaned up, Liz stood in the doorway to her pottery studio, the three-hundred-square-foot building she'd had built to her exacting specifications when they'd bought the house. Dean had insisted that there'd be no more frustrations with a too-small space, like the one she'd fashioned off their garage at the house in town. Here at their dream lake house, she'd have everything just the way she wanted it.

Last night, she'd turned up the heat, and this morning she'd switched on the water line. Now the late afternoon sun, setting over the snow-covered lake, streamed in, showing dusty surfaces too long unused. Liz flipped on the lights, pulled a piece of clay from a bag she'd nearly used up last fall. A little dry. She wrapped it in a moist towel and let it sit while she slid a rag over the worktable and shelving. Last fall, she'd fired everything she'd made, and sold a lot of it, so there was a feeling of empty space, of starting over. That seemed good.

The clay was ready to be wedged. She patted and dragged it along the table until it was brick-shaped. Then she pushed it away and down; lifted it up and pulled it back toward her. Down, away, up, back; pressing with her hands to get any air out. Down, away, up, back, over and over again.

The sun was level with the horizon when she sat down at the wheel.

A piece of the clay brick. Water on the hands.

She flipped on the motor, and there was the familiar whir, the clay beginning to turn.

Her wet hands slid along it, shaping it; being shaped. Waiting to see what would emerge.

PART TWO

Lucky

CHAPTER 21

Sunday, February 22, 2015
West Palm Beach, Florida

K ate," said Dr. Alvarez, "we've talked about this before, but I really would like you to acknowledge the worst-case scenarios you've thought of *out loud*, before you leave us tomorrow."

Kate bit her pinkie nail. She was fifty-seven years old—too old to be spoken to like a child. Though maybe she'd been acting like one, in this latest chapter of her life. Gunning Mark's Porsche convertible to 110 on A1A just before midnight Christmas Eve—God, the sweetness of the wind on her face!—then braking and veering so suddenly and violently—she would've sworn there was a turtle in the road—that the Porsche ended up (unaccountably; she could not reconstruct it, no matter how she tried) across the bike path on the opposite side of the road, facing the way she had not been going, nosed into a crisply trimmed hedge. She'd been naked under her white Prada coat, and barefoot, and, when she'd seen the flashing lights come up behind her—had she blacked out for a moment? She didn't remember any time passing between the hard stop and this—she had, unfortunately, stumbled out and opened her coat for the cop. It might've worked when she was younger.

She'd blown a 0.12 percent on the Breathalyzer and spent most of Christmas Day in jail, before her friend Marie bailed her out and brought her straight here to the rehab center. Humiliated as Kate was to make Marie Harrington her one phone call, she knew Marie would fix everything: somehow guarantee the incident was kept out of the news; call in a favor to her friend, the director of the center, to get Kate right in. It had taken every ounce of humility that Kate possessed to ask for these things. "Anything for you, baby," Marie had said, hugging Kate goodbye under the center's portico, her white BMW idling in the circular drive. "Now, swear you're gonna be okay?"

Kate had a long history of needing people when she didn't want to; of swearing she was going to be okay.

She'd been in rehab for three months ten years ago, back in California, just before she'd met Mark. And fifteen years ago, for six months, after the catastrophe that had ended her TV career. Probably a dozen other times in her earlier life, she *should've* been in rehab.

To say she didn't trust herself was an understatement.

Mark's lawyer had arranged everything beyond Marie's purview: paid the fine, exchanged jail time for the time in rehab, even gotten the sentence reduced since Kate had checked herself in so willingly and instantly. Her license was suspended for six months. This was, by some miracle, her first DUI.

Born under a lucky star, her mother had always told her.

Not that Kate bought that for an instant, not really.

"I know you've said you didn't intend to harm anyone except perhaps yourself, correct?" Dr. Alvarez prodded. "But we've been talking about admitting that your addiction had escalated to the point where you had no control over *who* you might have harmed. I want you to consider this only because modifying your behavior for these reasons is a bridge to beginning to care for and love *yourself* as much as you care for and love *others.*"

"I understand," said Kate—ever the girl who tried to please.

But worst-case scenarios were tiresome, and, honestly, too terrible to acknowledge. A late-night bicyclist whirring down the path (the bicyclist: dead). The power pole four feet closer (Kate: dead). A car in the oncoming lane (perhaps a whole family on their way home from a Christmas Eve service: dead). Kate ruminated on all these possibilities—constantly, in truth. But she couldn't list them out loud, not even to Dr. Alvarez, because that would make them real.

Which was exactly what Dr. Alvarez wanted, she guessed.

How did rubbing Kate's nose in the face of the damage she might've done—if only she weren't so damn "lucky"—*help* her? Wasn't she here to be *helped*?

Sobriety, she thought, was tiresome, too.

"It's a way I used to be," she said, plucking at a loose thread on the cuff of her long-sleeved white T-shirt. "Reckless. I'm not that way any-more." She had been being extremely careful for a long time, in fact—up until a couple months ago, at least.

Dr. Alvarez raised an eyebrow, made a note. "Let's talk about your strategies going forward. Now, your sister's coming to get you tomorrow to bring you to your mother's in North Carolina. You and I will have phone sessions three times a week, and I can meet with you in person as often as you like, once you come back home. Have you decided how long you're going to stay at your mother's?"

"We'll see how it goes."

"I'd advise that you create a plan, Kate."

Kate shrugged. "My mother and my sister don't trust me to be alone."

Dr. Alvarez cocked her head. "Do you trust yourself to be alone?"

Kate laughed. "I've done a fine job of it so far, haven't I? Two months a widow and I land myself in jail." Some days, ever since the call had come about Mark, Kate had found it hard to care what happened to her at all. That her mother and sister were going to bat for her—still, after all these years—was her saving grace, honestly, but also struck her as just plain exhausting. Her flare-ups of largesse and I-can-conquer-the-world; her low points of drunken despair. Why did they even bother? Weren't they exhausted, too?

What was going to make this time any different?

Dr. Alvarez made a note. Then she looked up and, behind her glasses, blinked. "Kate, you've been sober for fifty-nine days now. Sixty, by the time today's over. Do you realize what an accomplishment that is?"

Kate shrugged. "Not so hard, in here," she said, though she instantly realized that wasn't true. Every day was hard. Every day, not drinking was hard. Out in the world, it would be that much harder. Even though she was clean now, that didn't mean her body and mind didn't remember the joy and release they got from drinking.

Oh, how she *hoped* this time would be different—

She was trying to have faith, the way everyone in here talked about, but that wasn't so easy to do, either.

Plus, once she left, she wouldn't have Ransom, her therapy horse, and whether she'd be able to keep from losing her mind to grief and her same mad furies again without him, she wasn't sure. Though she hadn't had much to do with horses since she was six years old, when visits to her grandparents' farm had ended, finding Ransom had felt like coming home. For all his moods and persnickety (she would swear) opinions, he had really *saved* her, these last two months. A beautiful chestnut with a white blaze, he'd shown her that she could be reliable, just because he needed her to be.

It was something, at least. And not a little thing.

Unfortunately, the trouble with bonding with him the way she had—currying him, feeding him, riding him every day on the beach—was that he, too, would soon be gone. Assigned to the next arrival who needed him. And this was undoubtedly the right thing. What was Kate going to do, take him home?

Dr. Alvarez blinked again. "Do you think that your mother's will be a nurturing place for you as you reenter your life—and I really want to encourage you to think of yourself this way—as a sober individual?"

"I think she'll keep me in line," Kate said, then gave a short laugh, though nothing was actually funny.

Mark had up and died on her, that was the entire problem, Kate thought, as she headed for the stable and Ransom along the palm-shrouded trail. How was she supposed to deal with *that* and stay sober?

Mark, who'd shown up in her life by literally bumping into her as she was heading into the Gower Café on the Sony lot after an audition, and he was walking out. "Excuse me!" he'd said, then blinked and added, in a way that actually seemed involuntary, "May I buy you a cup of coffee?"

She was so used to the double take—people still recognized her from her five years as Rosetta on *Love and Yearning*, if not from her cameos on *The Love Boat, Charlie's Angels, Dynasty, Hart to Hart*—that it wasn't really flattering anymore, except that she'd been forty-eight at the time. Why she'd let her guard down and said yes, then yes to dinner that same night, she had no idea. Maybe her therapist then had been encouraging her to try behaving differently for different results.

She'd only ever had bad experiences with men. Men who'd loved her as arm candy—in the early days, her agent had billed her as the next Raquel Welch, "a luscious brunette you won't be able to take your eyes off of!"—but, in private, belittled her, laughed at her, pinched or slapped her, so she'd know who was in charge, who mattered and who didn't.

If they bruised her so it showed, she always left—but a lot of the ways they bruised her didn't show. One of them had mentioned casually, when they were cuddled on the couch watching TV one night, how easy it would be to break her neck, with the proper grip and just a slight flick of his wrist, and she'd come to assume, without precisely realizing it, that that was a desire and skill they all shared.

She had never been married before. Mark was five-eight, cue-ball bald with a gray goatee, ten years older than her. Ordinarily, she'd have never given him a second glance. "It almost seems you *like* this man, Kate," she remembered her therapist observing, with surprise, after the second date or so. And she had to admit: she did. He'd been divorced a few years and had three college-age children whom he spoke of fondly. He did not badmouth his ex-wife, Carin; nor did he speak of her often. All Kate knew, really, was that Carin had never remarried and had been "a wonderful mom." He did his own landscaping—his backyard was a haven—spoke ardently of his California asters, and was a devoted viewer of the *PBS NewsHour.* He averaged a bike-a-thon a month for charity. He lost track of the story in any movie they watched, because he was so focused on the musical score; he could transpose any piece he heard into written notes on the page, which astonished her. He'd been raised on a farm in southern Minnesota, though he'd been in California for forty years, ever since moving there at eighteen to start at USC.

And he was kind to her. At first, she'd laughed at him for it. Then, she'd started to like it. And then she'd tried to push him away. He wouldn't let her. "You're the love of my life, you must know that," he said, which was surprising, given that he'd been married to Carin for twenty-four years. (What had gone wrong between them, Kate didn't know, nor did she ask.)

A year after Kate and Mark met, they were married in his backyard, with the asters in bloom. A year after that, she was bemoaning another failed audition—despite her stints in rehab, nobody was willing to take a chance on her after what had happened that last time—when he blurted that he thought they should move to Florida. His younger son, Ryan, had gone there for a job in yacht sales; his daughter, Hannah, was starting as a medical resident in Miami; and his older brother, Walt, had retired to Vero Beach after a lifetime in Minnesota, having had his fill of frigid winters. In Florida, Mark said, their California money would go further; last the rest of their lives, even. Kate could retire, just enjoy life. Mark could do some work remotely, and commute to L.A. when he had to, for a couple years. Then he'd retire, too—the minute he turned sixty-two, he promised.

Kate didn't want to give up on her career; on her *self*, it felt like. She knew she was far better than her looks had ever allowed her to be. Plus, now that she was older, her emotional range was greater. Maybe people would finally begin to see her talent.

Mark finally got exasperated, said that wasn't realistic, not for Hollywood. She was fifty years old. "What are you trying to prove? I'm offering you the chance to be happy. Not to have any cares. For the first time in your life!"

His exasperation was so out of character that it took her aback, and made her feel she must be in the wrong, somehow.

Then, she realized: he'd never believed she would succeed at breaking back into the business. He'd just been humoring her—since day one, probably.

Also, he didn't seem to notice or care that her mother, at that time, still lived in Laguna Beach.

Of course, Kate almost never made it down to see Clarissa. With traffic, the drive each way was at least two hours. Anyway, Clarissa was invariably busy with her work at the domestic violence shelter, though she'd supposedly retired.

"Let's not hang on to the past!" Mark said, with, again, uncharacteristic enthusiasm, fanning out on the table in front of her a stack of real estate listings he'd printed in color, tiny photos showing swimming pools of cerulean blue, kitchens with stainless Sub-Zero freezers, spotless glass tile. "Let's have a new adventure!"

Finally, Kate ran the idea past her mother on the phone. Clarissa responded with a distracted-sounding, "You have to do what's best for you and Mark," as if Kate's proximity made no difference to her whatsoever.

So Kate told Mark she would move to Florida.

And they'd been happy there! He hadn't retired on schedule—"Just one more" project always came his way—but usually he was gone only a week or two each month. He'd hung on to his house in California, to make the back-and-forth lifestyle easier; Kate imagined he enjoyed the time there by himself, and the pleasures of their time together in Vero Beach were heightened by the time apart, too.

Their house on the barrier island overlooked a long stretch of empty sand beach. They slept with the curtains open so the sunrise would wake them. They drank fresh-squeezed orange juice every morning and ate dinner at the club most nights. A Bose sound system pumped music throughout the house and out to the courtyard and the pool. On winter mornings, when they wanted to wake before sunrise, Mark set it to play the *Star Wars* theme as their alarm. Once a month or so, Ryan would come up from West Palm, or Hannah from Miami, to join them for dinner or the weekend. Walt and his wife, Linda, who lived in a modest bungalow just across the bridge on the mainland, would come out to spend the occasional Sunday afternoon sipping piña coladas by the pool.

Kate had decided against complete sobriety—it was just so *not fun*, socially; not to mention embarrassing, to have to admit you might've had a problem in the past. The New Kate had her drinking under control: one piña colada by the pool, one glass of wine with dinner—or, if she was at a party, two of champagne. She'd promised herself and Mark that she'd stick to these limits, and she did (for the most part). The New Kate had a walk-in closet full of DVF wrap dresses, Christian Louboutin pumps, swimsuits, straw hats, Tory Burch flip-flops, beach cover-ups. And, as it turned out, a knack for planning events; it wasn't long before she was chair and emcee of four annual galas. She starred in a local production of *The Sound of Music* as the Mother Superior, which she hoped would prove, at least, that she had a sense of humor about herself. For the first time in decades, she had women friends—lunch dates, shopping buddies—to the point that Mark, when he was around, good-naturedly complained.

If she'd been walking a high wire, an instant from disaster with every move she made, she hadn't exactly realized it.

Except, some nights, after Mark had gone to sleep, or nights when he was away in California, she would sneak downstairs and have an extra glass of wine. Or two. Sometimes three. There was no harm in it that she could see. She'd flip on the big TV, get sucked into episodes of *Dallas Cowboy Cheerleaders: Making the Team*. The girls who'd gained a little weight in the offseason: God, the poor things.

And then, one early afternoon last October—she'd been bracing for hurricanes, believing it her worst nightmare that one would strike while Mark was away—she'd gotten a call from a California number. For one soap-bubble moment, she'd thought maybe her agent had put in a word somewhere—

It was an ER doctor at Hollywood Presbyterian. Mark had had a heart attack, which had killed him instantly.

The first thing Kate did was call his oldest child, Ben, who was in medical school out in L.A. By some miracle, he answered. He stammered that, yes, he'd call his brother and sister and mom and let them know, then added that he'd go to the hospital to "claim the body" and begin to "make arrangements," which stunned her. "I'll be there by tomorrow!" she blurted, but Ben just said thank you and hung up. She looked blankly at the phone, wondering what he'd been thanking her for.

The second thing she did was to set the phone on the kitchen counter and pour herself a glass of Pinot Gris. She drank it in three swallows, booked her ticket out of Orlando for that night, then poured a second glass, which she brought upstairs to drink while she packed. Her DVF wrap dress in black. Her black Louboutin pumps.

By the time she saw the children and Carin, late the next morning at Mark's house—they walked in as a mob without knocking (and how had Ryan and Hannah made it from Florida so quickly, ahead of Kate, it seemed?)—the four of them had the service planned. Mark was to be buried in a plot in North Hollywood that he and Carin had purchased together in 1985, the year that Ben was born.

They might as well have taken a baseball bat—each one of them in succession—to Kate's knees.

Though none of them seemed to have a glimmer of a thought that anything was amiss. Mark had evidently never brought up any possible alternative arrangements; Kate, of course, had never thought to ask. Maybe she'd imagined they were too happy to die—certainly, at least, right *now*.

The force of his children and his ex-wife, all together, was too much for her to overcome. Anyway, she knew Mark would've wanted his children to be soothed in any way they could be.

So, she didn't say a word. She went through motions and tried to smile, to not be a bother, in this place and with these people where and with whom she so clearly did not fit. (Her mother wasn't there; Clarissa had—to Kate, this was inexplicable—moved to North Carolina the year before and didn't "feel up to" travel, even for her daughter's husband's funeral.)

Only days later, after the whole thing was done and Kate had had four glasses of wine at the backyard reception—the same backyard where Kate and Mark had been married; now the house would be sold, the proceeds divided among the children—did Carin come up to Kate and say quietly, "I'm sorry, Kate. It's just that we were a family for so long."

Ransom seemed to sense it was their last ride together. He walked out carefully toward the beach with the group of six, as usual, through the canopy of palms, but, once his hooves hit the long stretch of sand, he started to edge ahead, tossing his head impatiently.

Did he finally trust Kate enough to carry her at the speed he wanted to go?

Kate had been told that this was why they'd been assigned to each other: they both had a reckless side that the other would help assuage. And, so far, they had.

But it was their last day. Kate looked back at the group leader, Dr. Jill, who waved and grinned and shouted, "Just this once!"

Kate laughed with delight. "Okay, buddy, go," she whispered, giving Ransom a little squeeze, as warm wind rustled her hair. The horse's muscles rippled to life, and she held on tight, letting her body move with his steady rhythm. Empty beach stretched as far as she could see.

She leaned in.

"Look, you know I'm right," Lana said, just as if she were the older sister, as she merged onto I-95 heading north. Behind her sunglasses, Kate was squinting. The outside world seemed terribly bright. Lana had picked her up at 8 A.M. sharp—way too early, as far as Kate was concerned, but the center and Lana had both required it.

"Can you just give me five minutes to adjust to being out here?" Kate said.

Waiting wasn't Lana's style. She pushed her voluminous dark curls out of her eyes, flipped on her turn signal, moved into the middle lane, and pushed her Honda CR-V to eighty. Cars in the lanes to either side sped past, one after another after another.

If Lana had ever had an agent, Kate had always thought, that agent would've compared her to Halle Berry, and not been far off. But Lana had gotten a Ph.D. in American Studies instead, and now was a professor at the University of North Carolina. She'd written and published five, six, maybe seven, books on racial identity; Kate had somehow lost track.

"I'm just saying, the more I think about it, the more I think your . . . your feelings of ungroundedness, shall we say, go back to our—to *your*—father and his literal abandonment of you. You felt it more than I did, because you were *six*. You *remember* it. You *witnessed* it. You took it *personally*. This looms large in your pain body. I mean, you can't escape it, can you? Isn't that what your drinking is all about? About this gaping wound you're trying to fill?"

Kate had also always thought it unfortunate that Lana had minored in psychology. "*You* felt it, too. You've been pissed about it all your life."

"Well, I was the obvious *problem!* The *reason* he abandoned us. But you—you had done nothing wrong, you had *been* nothing wrong, and yet, you were abandoned all the same. You've been *hurt* all your life."

Kate rubbed her temple. They were going to be in the car for almost ten hours. Lana had insisted on driving all the way down from Raleigh to pick up Kate straight from the door of the rehab center, as if Kate couldn't be trusted to get herself onto an airplane and up to Wilmington and their mother's Kure Beach condo without taking a drink. Well, maybe that was a safe bet. And it was generous of Lana, for sure, to drive all the way here and back, cancel her classes for a couple days, and all the rest.

But why did she always have to leap right into the deep end? And why had she not brought Kate home, at least to grab some different clothes and *see* the place—something about how Dr. Alvarez had thought it would be better not to be reminded of the old life, just yet, as long as Kate had the option? Only no one really *had* given Kate the option. "I just don't see how a DNA test is going to help," Kate said, and she had more reasons than her sister knew for being frightened of one; for questioning whether it might not be best to leave certain stones unturned. "Anyway, what if it proves that Mom's been lying to us all these years? You really want to put her through that? Put all of us through that?"

"Why do *you* want so badly to protect her? At your own expense? Do I need to remind you? I have features that would suggest I am at least part Black. And I have had experiences all my life based on my appearance that tell me I am 'less than,' due to the systemic racism inherent in American society, while *your* appearance has been lauded, rewarded, because *you* look very much like pictures I've seen of Clayburn Montgomery, the white man who is our reputed father."

Kate remembered—both too well and as a sort of general blur—what had happened shortly after Lana was born. She remembered, somehow, standing outside the back door of the brick house in Kentucky, gripping her mother's skirt, as Clarissa held baby Lana. She remembered her father, shutting that door in their faces.

Kate never saw him again. She had no wish to.

Lana, on the other hand, had tracked him down. Twenty years ago, then again ten years ago, and five years ago. How she'd stood it, over and over again, him hanging up on her each time she proudly announced her name, *Lana Montgomery*, Kate had no idea.

Then again, Lana swore that, despite their mother's unwavering insistence all these years, she was 90 percent sure Clayburn wasn't her father at all. *It's just that ten percent chance—I just want that to be acknowledged.*

"Remember," Kate said, "Mom said her mother told her, that same day Clayburn kicked us out, that Mom had been adopted at birth; that her biological mother was Sicilian. That has to be where you got your features. From our biological grandmother. Right?"

"Right. Yes. And Mom recently got some news about that."

Kate's stomach fluttered. "What do you mean?"

"I should leave it to her to tell you." Lana pushed up her sunglasses and switched lanes to pass a Subaru that was going only seventy-five. "Listen, though, a colleague of mine did her DNA recently, and it got me thinking. The tests are affordable now, and really easy. Everything I've written and studied so far has been about *not* knowing. Imagining, *perceiving*. But now I could actually write the next chapter! About *knowing*. I think I'm ready for that. And, see, if I just sent my own test in, I'd find out if I was Sicilian or whatever—but, if you did it, too, we'd find out for sure if Clayburn is my father. And if *Mom* did it, she'd find out where *she* comes from. She always says we should leave the past in the past, but I think it would help us *all* if we knew the truth."

Kate spun her corded bracelet around her wrist. It used to be that Kate was the one calling the shots, protecting Lana from hard truths, deciding what was what. But that had been a long time ago. "I'd rather just say I believe Mom that Clayburn *is* your father. Not put her through this."

Lana shook her head. "Whatever Mom's reasons for keeping it hidden all these years, it's time. You're in crisis, and *I* need to know who I am."

"I'm not in crisis right *now*," Kate grumbled, thinking again of that moment standing at the bottom of the back stoop, her little six-year-old self clutching her mother's skirt and looking up at her larger-than-life father. Lana's birthday was in September 1963, and she'd been brand-new when their father had kicked them out, so this moment had to have taken place a couple months before Kennedy was shot—but, in Kate's memory, it had all happened the same day, the same instant, even: everything destroyed. She wished suddenly for a glass of wine. She could almost taste it: a lush Sancerre. "Anyway, you said Clayburn has a whole new family now—four grown daughters, eight lovely grandchildren. You said you saw them on Facebook. You don't really think he'd welcome you as his daughter after all these years, do you? Is that what you're hoping for, if the test proved you were his?"

"That might be your hope," Lana said, in a clipped tone. "It is not mine."

Kate guessed her sister wanted to be asked to elaborate, but what would follow would be a list of a hundred reasons why Lana, with her "lifelong feelings of *difference/different-ness*," as she'd written in one of her early books, just *knew* Clayburn wasn't her father, along with her dreams of the man ("probably Black, probably ignorant of my very existence") who was.

Kate didn't take the bait, instead squinting out the window at the swampy forests zipping by.

Obviously, she did not like thinking that Lana might not be her "full" sister, not least for the fact that it would mean their mother had been lying to them all their lives. And she did not like thinking about her father, whom she had loved, as much as she had feared him.

Why was Lana insisting on it now?

Come to think of it, Kate did remember Clayburn setting her on the back of a horse, likely more than once, leading her around at a slow walk . . .

Why hadn't she thought of that before? Not even in all this time with Ransom, not till right this very moment. Memory was so fickle.

If anyone ever asked, Kate always said her father had been dead a long time.

Clarissa's whole day felt like one of "waiting"—for the girls to arrive; to see how Kate would seem—though, in fact, she was in motion nonstop, doing a huge shop at the Food Lion, carting everything up the three flights to her condo, putting everything away and cutting the roses and finding the right vase and making up the guest room bed with fresh sheets, then cleaning everything again that she'd already cleaned yesterday. She hadn't heard from her daughters, but there was no point trying to call; Lana would have let her know if there was any problem or delay. And at least cleanliness was one thing Clarissa could control, in the middle of so many things that she could not.

Finally, she stashed away the vacuum and Swiffer and Windex and set out for her usual beach walk, tacking on an extra half mile to pass more time—she averaged two miles a day, which she didn't think was too bad, given that she was almost seventy-nine years old—keeping her eye out for leaping dolphins in the vast, sparkling blue. Her downstairs neighbor, Sally, claimed they were out there every day this time of year, though Clarissa, her eyesight being what it was, rarely spotted them.

Back home again, she poured herself an iced tea and got to work making a salad and prepping stuffed zucchini—"zuccanoes," the Moosewood recipe called them—to go into the oven. Lana was a "pescatarian," while Kate, off and on, had tried out being vegetarian. Clarissa didn't know, now, what she was. The knife kept slipping in her hands as she minced the garlic and mushrooms; she was more nervous than she'd realized.

She was trying not to think that this was the last chance she had to get it right with Kate. With Lana, even.

But it might be. It really might be.

Her condo was a two-bedroom, third floor, facing the ocean. Her bedroom and the living room had sliders to the deck, which overlooked the beach and the crashing waves, and the dining area was open between the kitchen and the living room, so she could see the ocean from every room, except, of course, for the two bathrooms—since when had Americans decided that every last one of them deserved the immense luxury of their own private bathroom, Clarissa wondered—and the back bedroom, where Kate would stay. Clarissa had considered giving up the master suite to her daughter—Kate was so used to a posh life; the guest room here would no doubt be a letdown—then decided against it. Not that she wanted to punish Kate for being "in recovery" once again. Not at all. Clarissa understood: It was a disease. Not Kate's *fault*.

Years ago, a therapist had told Clarissa that Kate's difficulties weren't Clarissa's fault, either. Clarissa had been trying all this time to believe it.

She cued up Ella Fitzgerald on Pandora and set the table while she sang along with "It's Only a Paper Moon": blue goblets for water, her white Pottery Barn plates and woven blue and white napkins, silver seashell napkin rings. She set the dozen yellow roses in their blue glass vase in the empty, fourth place, so she and Lana at either end would be able to see each other around them. She would seat Kate facing the ocean view, the roses.

She'd given all the alcohol she'd had on hand—not much, just three dusty bottles of Chardonnay—to Sally, who'd sworn she'd keep them "under lock and key."

Clarissa did wish she had a glass from one right now, though.

"Mom," Lana said, from her end of the table an hour later, "I just think it would help Kate and me both, to get definitive answers." The girls had arrived on time, looking worn thin but, even after their long drive, still on speaking terms and smelling of their expensive shampoos and perfumes when Clarissa hugged them, and Kate had seemed happy enough with the back bedroom when she'd brought her suitcase in. "Nice place, Mom!" she'd said, which had made Clarissa's heart go soft—just the normalcy of it, maybe; as if she'd been expecting a stranger to arrive and now saw it was her *daughter*, after all. She hated that this was Kate's first time seeing the condo—Clarissa had lived here a year and a half—and that they hadn't seen each other at all in more than three years. She still felt terrible that she hadn't gone to Mark's funeral, or even to visit Kate in Florida afterward. She'd thought the travel would be too taxing, but that had more likely been a cover for the real reason—her fear that *Kate* would be too much for her, that she wouldn't know how to help her; that she'd only lose her own hard-earned peace of mind in trying.

Somehow, she heard what Monty, the piano player in her jazz band, would have said: *Lame excuse, Clare.*

"Not to mention *you*, Mom," Lana said now. "If what you say is true about us having the same father, wouldn't it feel good to have it proven, once and for all?"

"Of course what I say is true. And I made my peace with all that a long time ago." But Clarissa's hands were trembling as she sliced through her zucchini. She did not like to think about the past. Especially, she did not like to think about Clayburn Montgomery. "Anyway, this is a bit much for Kate's first day, Lana, honey."

"But, Mom, you can't avoid this forever. It's the questions and unknowns that have led to . . . to Kate's difficulties!"

"My husband died," Kate put in. "*That* was difficult. Stop pestering Mom." Kate's eyes flashed to meet Clarissa's, and Clarissa saw in them (*oh, God, of course—DNA*): the rape, the baby. Kate and Clarissa's "little" secret. 1973. Kate had been only fifteen. Nobody knew, not even Lana.

Lana tossed her hair. "The two of you would sweep the whole world under the rug, if you could! And where does it get you? Meanwhile, *I* don't know who I am. I *could* just send in my own DNA, but I thought a little *support* would be nice. A little *solidarity*. Not to mention support for my *work*. I should've known the two of you wouldn't be in favor of the truth."

"That isn't fair," Clarissa said. "I've always told you the truth." In fact, starting when the girls were small, Clarissa, to explain their differing characteristics, had told them what her own mother, Lola, had said, that last, awful day when her parents had disowned her: that Clarissa was adopted, that her birth mother was Italian. Clarissa—who hadn't known for years whether to believe Lola at all, or been able to figure out whether believing or *not* believing her was more painful—had, for the girls' sake, tried to make it a fun curiosity. *We don't know who our family is! We might be Italian! We might be anyone!* Maybe it hadn't been the right strategy, but it was all she could think of, at the time. "Clayburn Montgomery is definitely your father, both of you."

"I just don't *believe* you, Mom," Lana snapped. "Look at me! Anyway, don't you understand that it would be far better for me to think I had a father who never knew about me than one who turned me away at the first sight of me?"

Clarissa swallowed. Whenever she allowed a thought of it to enter her mind, Clayburn's heartlessness still shocked and pierced her like a stab wound—and, if it felt this way to her, how must it feel to Lana?

Maybe this was why Clarissa had been so resolute about not looking back. She had wanted to protect her daughter—and herself—from the pain.

But this had probably done Lana no favors, in truth. Lana, who'd been zeroed in from an early age on her "differences": her skin, shades darker than Kate's; her curly black hair; her deep brown eyes, when Clarissa's and Kate's were blue. Then, around the time Lana was a teenager, a friend had brought her to a high-end salon in L.A., where the stylist had told her, laughing, "Girl, you may be white, but this is Black hair you've got here!" Lana had come home demanding to know if she was Black, and Clarissa, startled, had said, "No! Italian, I think! As I've told you, I don't really know!" But Lana, for a while, had ended up experimenting with identifying as Black, then ultimately made it her life's work to study cultural assumptions around the formation of racial identity in the U.S. Her third book, *Passing?: Awakening to Being the Darker Sister,* had cemented her place as an expert on "evolving racial 'identities' and colli/usions," as her website bio put it.

And Clarissa was achingly proud of Lana, of course—of her prodigious intellect, and of her yearning, wide-open heart. Also, Clarissa had to admit, if one *believed* Lana was Black, Lana could certainly be perceived that way. ("Especially in cases where a person's lineage is unknown," Lana's website explained, "identity can be, in large part, about *perception.* Perception of the self. Perception by others.")

Clarissa did not believe Lana was Black—how could she be, when neither Clayburn nor Clarissa were? But Clarissa also had to admit that the reason she'd driven the girls all the way across the plains and mountains to California, almost without stopping, after that awful last day with Clayburn and her parents, was because she had not wanted Lana growing up in the South, or even in the North, where the color of her skin—whatever its origins—might get her beaten or killed, or certainly, as had already been proven, ostracized. Clarissa'd had the idea that California would be more open, accepting. To go there had been instinct, almost—but instinct about *what*?

She sighed. "Lana, as I've explained, we don't know where your characteristics come from, because I might be adopted, or, for all I know, my mother was trying to cover up some affair *she'd* had. The only birth certificate I have—from here in North Carolina—states that Jack and Lola Duncan are my parents. My mother once told me that I was born here when they were on vacation. She also told me that I was born upstairs in the house in Lexington, which was obviously a lie. So, the long and the short of it is, I just don't know what's true."

Lana's mouth thinned. "Should we tell Kate about what Marlys sent you?"

"Well, I don't know if that's even *real*," Clarissa snapped, because she still couldn't swallow the idea that it might be—though she'd had three months, now, to try. Her cousin Marlys, to whom she hadn't spoken in fifty years, had found her on Facebook and messaged asking for her mailing address. Three days later, the old, yellowed letter had arrived, with a sticky note from Marlys explaining that, after Marlys's father's death, she'd found it inside the back of a painting he'd inherited from his sister, Lola, years earlier.

"Can I show it to Kate?" Lana asked. "Is it still in the sideboard?"

Clarissa pursed her lips and gave a brief nod, because with Lana there was only one possible answer, but she did wish Lana would just let them eat one meal in peace. She tried shooting Kate a look of apology, but Kate was focused on her plate, and Lana was already up, digging in the sideboard drawer, pulling out the envelope.

Clarissa did not like mysteries. She did not like surprises. But secrets, she understood. There were reasons to keep secrets.

She went back to cutting her zucchini, though she'd lost her appetite.

Lana sat back down, extracted the yellowed paper, unfolded it, and read out loud:

May 15, 1936. Dear Mr. and Mrs. Duncan, Congratulations. You are now the parents of a beautiful little girl, CLARISSA ANN DUNCAN, born May 8, 1936. The McNaughton Children's Home guarantees the

*quality of this child and knows you will be entirely satisfied with her. The
biological mother was at least partly of Italian (possibly Sicilian) descent,
though her family had been long in this country and was well educated and
wholly Americanized, and she was extremely young (19) and beautiful. The
classically handsome father, from an old English family long in the U.S., was
studying to become a doctor and is on scholarship, barely making ends meet.
Though the couple were engaged and deeply in love, they did not feel, to their
regret, capable at this time of caring for a child, and they wanted more than
anything for her to have all the advantages that any child could hope for. We
are glad to have played a role in finding that home for her, and wish you the
happiest of futures with her. Sincerely, Dr. Joseph Addington, Director.*

Lana looked up. "It's on stationery from this place, the McNaughton Children's Home, but there's no address, which makes it hard to
verify. I tried googling the name and nothing came up."

Kate had stopped eating a full minute earlier; her fork dangled from
her hand. "Wow. So this verifies what Lola told you, Mom. You're adopted."

Clarissa shook her head quickly. "But Lola was always making things
up! She could've written this herself, for me to find after she was gone.
To make me *think* she'd told the truth."

Kate looked at her quizzically. "Why would Lola have bothered to
forge something like this when she'd already disowned you?"

"I don't know. But that woman was always beyond my ability to
explain."

"Also," Kate said, "if it *is* true, if Grandma and Grandpa knew you
were Sicilian, why would they have disowned you for having a baby
whose skin was a little darker? They would've known where the trait
came from."

Clarissa set down her fork and knife, giving up on trying to eat. She
took a deep breath and spoke carefully, as if to pretend this whole story
had nothing to do with *her*. "Well, people were incredibly bigoted back

in those days, you have to remember, Kate. Jack and Lola wouldn't have wanted people to know they had a grandchild with darker skin, no matter where that darker skin came from. If they blamed me, if they said the wrong man had fathered my baby, they could disown me and have their own reputations remain intact. You know, my father, being in the horse business, was all about bloodlines."

"But they could've just admitted you were adopted!" Lana said.

Clarissa shook her head. "In those times, that would've been more shameful than disowning me. They wouldn't have wanted people to know that they couldn't have children of their own. And all Clayburn was probably thinking about was running for office. It's hideous, really. It's all just hideous. I'm just so sorry that it was the environment you girls were born into. Honestly, as horrible as it seemed at the time, I have to think that all of us were lucky to get out."

"But, Mom, don't you want *answers*?" Lana blurted. "If we do this test, it will connect you to anyone you're biologically related to, anyone who's submitted their DNA to the database. Assuming this letter is true, you might even find your biological parents! Doesn't it *bother* you, not knowing?"

Clarissa swallowed. Blinked against a sudden burning in her eyes. She looked at Kate, thinking of that baby, born on the first of June, 1973.

Would *he* be in the database?

Then, she thought: disowned once already. She wouldn't be able to handle it again. To find out she hadn't been wanted, even before she was born? Or, equally painful, that she *had* been wanted, but time and death meant she'd lost the chance of being claimed? No, she would not be able to stand it.

She blinked again and tried to sound calm. "Lana, honey, I'm almost seventy-nine. Any biological parent of mine is long dead."

"A sibling, then! Maybe! Maybe we have whole scores of relatives we don't know about."

And in Lana's eyes, then, Clarissa saw not just the usual mix of fury and curiosity, but simple, straight-out pain. That, coupled with the anguish in Kate's, made Clarissa realize suddenly how dead wrong she had been, and for how long.

She had spent her life hoping that, if she loved her daughters *enough*, *well* enough, she could make up for the absence of their father. She'd probably known it was a foolish hope—especially since Clayburn's absence had not been mere absence, but a violent disavowal.

Though, together, the three of them—Clarissa, Kate, and Lana—*had* made a family. And Clarissa had been proud of how she'd overcome the odds, proven she didn't need anyone, despite her debutante/Duncan past, which had raised her to believe in her weakness more than in her strength. (Though she'd always been confident atop a horse; maybe it was the memory of that that had gotten her through.) Sure, she'd struggled for those first several years, first at the commune, then in this or that secretarial job. Her two years at Sweet Briar premarriage had meant little in California.

But then, after what had happened to Kate at fifteen, Clarissa, spurred not so much by her past experience with Clayburn as by a sudden fury with the injustices of the world, had founded a domestic violence center in Orange County. She'd served as its director for nearly twenty years, coordinating everything from shelter and education to legal services and counseling for more than four thousand women and children who would've had nowhere else to turn.

She knew she'd saved more than one life. Maybe, in fact, she'd saved hundreds.

But now, all these years later, here were her daughters in front of her, struggling. Needing, themselves, to be saved. Clearly, her avoidances had taken a toll. Her unwillingness to talk about things.

She remembered Dr. Phil saying that doing the same thing over and over again and expecting different results was the definition of insanity.

She did not want the same results: Kate, drunk, crashing up her car; Lana, alone in the world and seemingly unable to stop battering her head against the wall of these questions of identity. (Clarissa couldn't help it: much as she was proud of Lana's career and fierce independence, much as she knew that *aloneness* was what she herself had modeled for Lana, a mother still wanted her daughter to *have someone.*)

Could a DNA test actually help Lana and Kate *move forward?*

But—no. It was wild even to think of. The ways it might rock the boat! When Kate's recovery was the most important thing now.

Clarissa had to be practical. Keep her feet on the ground. That had been the job of her life, after all—giving her daughters a steady base, because she knew so vividly what it was like not to have one; or, at any age, to have it ripped away. If she'd failed at times in the past, that didn't mean she could give up trying now.

"Hey, what's that?" Kate said, pointing to the little card that was peeking out from the envelope in front of Lana.

"It was enclosed with the letter," Lana said. "But we have no idea why, or what it means."

Kate reached for the envelope and took out the prayer card illustrated with a picture of a crowned, bearded man. As much as Clarissa had not wanted to see or think about that letter, she quite liked the card; had even been back-of-mind thinking of having it framed. "'Hope begins with Saint Jude. The patron saint of lost causes,'" Kate read, then laughed. "Fitting for us, I guess."

To Clarissa, it looked as if a dark cloud had lifted off Kate with that laugh. Could hope be switched on like a light? Just from some small feeling of connection? Of new possibility?

Then, she saw. Her daughters *needed* this. Her daughters needed *family.* To know who they were. And what they needed, at this point in life, needed to outweigh Clarissa's need *not* to know. Needed to outweigh Clarissa's fear of looking back, of upsetting the delicate balance of her life.

Besides, Kate's painful secret—the one Clarissa had been so insistent on keeping—well, what if the truth coming out could help put Kate's broken pieces back together again? *Help* her recovery, instead of hurt it?

"I think we should do the tests," Clarissa blurted. "If it's okay with you, Katie? I think Lana's right. It would be good for us to do. All of us together."

Kate's eyes crinkled slightly; Clarissa wasn't sure what that meant.

Lana looked at her sister. "What do you say, Kate?"

Kate looked at Lana. Then back at Clarissa. Her eyes filled with sudden tears. "Okay."

Lana shrieked, getting to her feet, running to hug them each in turn. "I have the kits in my suitcase! I'll go get them!"

"Oh, of course you do," Kate said, and she gave Clarissa a wry look that made Clarissa laugh and hope suddenly: Yes, they were going to be okay. They were all going to be okay.

Well. Hope was a thin thread to hang on to, but sometimes it was all you had.

CHAPTER 22

Spring 1935
On tour with Sax & Tebow

*T*he first time Cecily saw him, she was nearly fifteen years old, and she was up in her bunk in the cupola of the rattling caboose late one April moonlit night as the Sax & Tebow train began groaning slowly out of the yard at Clarksville, Tennessee. She didn't know what had made her sit up—as suddenly as if she'd heard a mystery sound, though she hadn't—toss off the blanket, and get on her knees to look out the cupola window, which she had cracked open to let in the spring air, despite the layer of soot that would form on her blanket by morning.

He was running out of the woods, a heavy-looking knapsack slung over his shoulder. Along the length of the train, a dozen ragged men were emerging like fleas off a dog in a bath, but this one, young and tall and wearing a newsboy cap, was the closest to Cecily, and he'd caught her eye, besides. His long legs stretched as he ran. His worn boots kicked up dust. He was clearly aiming for the flatcar loaded with wagons, several cars ahead of Cecily's caboose. Would he make it?

She held her breath, hoping so. The train was picking up speed. Another man trying for it was grabbed by a cop and yanked to the ground; another bull chased after two more, shouting.

The young man flung his knapsack onto the flatcar. His arms and legs pumped. He leaped for the side, grabbed the upper rail—a split second passed where he was likely to be killed—and then he was on! He pulled himself up and disappeared, probably crawling underneath a wagon to hide.

Cecily let out her breath and, after a moment, lay back down, feeling oddly satisfied, as if she'd had some investment in the outcome, though why she'd imagine that, she did not understand.

Tebow's hair and mustache had gone gray, though Isabelle said he was "only" forty years old. (*Ancient, in other words,* thought Cecily.) Isabelle said he was trying everything to keep the circus "afloat." That was why they'd gone on tour earlier than ever this year—Tebow and Sax had added fifty stops to the usual schedule. Though, so far, Cecily had overheard, operating costs were still outstripping what they took in at the gate. Circuses all over the country had shut down in recent years, what with the hard times, and those that were still in business had mostly transitioned to traveling by truck rather than train. It was said to be the modern way, but Tebow said the very idea was "inglorious" and "stank of desperation," and he didn't think it would save money, besides.

It was a "miracle," Isabelle said, that he'd managed to keep them all going this long. But they'd been out on the road just three weeks so far, and the workers hadn't been paid in two, and the performers had gotten only half their salaries in cash, the rest written up as IOUs.

Some folks were disgruntled, muttering at meals (which, admittedly, were far less extravagant than they'd been even last year) that this couldn't go on much longer. Cecily, though, wasn't bothered, at least not in the short term. Her entire time with the circus, she'd only ever taken two or three dollars per week of her fifteen-dollar, then twenty-dollar, weekly salary. It wasn't as if she had any time or place to spend more than that. Besides, money had always been a bit meaningless to her, since she'd always had a place to stay and three squares a day guaranteed. At the end of each season, when the IOU column was added up and Tebow paid it out, Isabelle had always taken the bulk of Cecily's earnings and put them into an account in the Bank of Sturgeon Bay near Sax's farm in Wisconsin. "Think of it as your trust fund, kid," Isabelle said, whenever she showed Cecily the handwritten bank book with the numbers filled in. Of course, what Cecily had earned in her first years with the circus had been lost when the bank failed, early on in the Depression, but she'd accumulated quite a lot more since then. And this year, so far, in the IOU column next to her name in the ledger was written *$51*.

It crossed her mind for the first time to wonder—would Tebow ever be able to pay that, much less what would accrue in the coming weeks? What would she do if the circus failed and the IOUs were rendered meaningless, the way the bank had failed and lost her earnings before?

She decided there was no point in worrying about things she couldn't control. Anyway, she had maybe two thousand dollars in the Bank of Sturgeon Bay, and she was pretty sure she could live on that for a long while. Also, it was insured now, so couldn't be lost, thanks to FDR—or so Isabelle had explained and Cecily had accepted as true.

Of course, she had no idea how she'd live on her own if the circus failed—where she'd go, what she'd do. It was too disconcerting even to think of her circus family falling apart and scattering to the winds, so she stopped allowing herself to imagine it. Sax & Tebow couldn't possibly fail, and that was that.

In Lexington, a photographer came to take new publicity shots of Isabelle with Doc, Virgil, and Wyatt, Mavis with the tigers, Cecily with Prince. "Show more leg!" Tebow yelled, pacing. The forty-four Arabian horses and their riders were gone—too expensive—and the seal and the orangutan had died last winter. Two zebras, both camels, and Tebow's beloved Blanco had been sold. The dream of getting an elephant was long gone. Harrison West and his lion, plus his Fat Lady wife, Ursula Eve, had gone to work for Seils-Sterling, Paul Giacometti and his liberty horses for Al G. Barnes. The brass band had been let go to save on salaries, the bandwagon sold to a collector; Buzz Gerberding at the calliope provided all the music now. Two years ago, Catherine LeGrande had been dropped from the sky by her husband, Buck, breaking both legs and a collarbone, and in the aftermath of

the accident Buck had, by all accounts, lost his mind. All in all, Sax &
Tebow traveled with ten fewer railcars than in the past, which saved
on per-mile charges, but also meant they were that much less of a
spectacle on arrival. ("Still better than arriving by *truck*," Tebow would
spit, when questioned.) Cecily and Prince always brought up the rear
of the parade, and she'd see the people who lined the streets standing
on tiptoe, peering into the distance behind her, as if asking, *That's it?*

"It's up to you now!" Tebow shouted, as Cecily smiled and posed,
smiled and posed.

Afterward, the photographer, who'd taken a liking to "Jacqueline
DuMonde," presented Cecily with a Brownie box camera. "It's just an
amateur thing. Cost a buck, is all," he said. "Take it and have fun." As
Cecily turned the heavy thing over in her hands, she was relieved to stop
worrying for a moment about money, or the dead orangutan or the
absent lion or the ghost of Catherine LeGrande twirling above in gauzy
blue, or all the things that people had seen slip through their fingers in
recent years, like sand.

Three mornings later, Cecily hopped down from her bunk the minute the
train came clanking to a halt in Evansville, Indiana, and soon went out (in-
cognito: slacks, a cardigan, a cap and kerchief) into the rising day with her
camera. Tebow, who'd seen the gift of the Brownie being presented, had
given her the assignment, suddenly envisioning selling her snapshots to
Life magazine. "'A girl's-eye view of the circus!'" he'd proclaimed. "'Inside
the mind of a girl bareback rider!' Brilliant!" A feature on Sax & Tebow
would change the direction of all their fortunes, he'd said, promising he'd
pay to have her photos developed, then select the best ones to send to *Life*.

So, as daylight rose and men hauled the wagons down off the train
and hitched up the work horses, while others paced out the tent sites
in the field near the great bend in the Ohio River and pounded stakes
coded with colored streamers to mark where each tent would be raised,
and unloaded giant rolls of canvas and began spreading them across the

damp ground, Cecily skulked around, trying to capture the activity in the low light of the rising dawn. She found she didn't mind not being in the spotlight, at least for a few minutes, for a change.

And then she saw the young man.

It had been at least two weeks since she'd watched him jump the train—how she recognized him, she wasn't sure, except there was an unmistakable grace to the way he moved his long limbs—and at least four years since she'd heard Tebow tell Isabelle that he was going to fire all the white roustabouts and hire only Black men from then on, because he could pay them half what he had to pay whites, and the two wouldn't work together, anyway. Isabelle had raged, saying Black men traveling with the circus would make them seem low-class, not to mention put all the women in danger. None of this made sense to Cecily, and Tebow had held firm, citing economics.

The young man's skin was the color of an old penny, and he was pounding in a tent stake with a crew, seven men wielding huge sledge-hammers in a choreographed dance, creating a song of wood on metal. She guessed he was no more than seventeen, and that he was bigger and stronger already than he'd been two weeks ago, and that he'd had to learn quickly the rhythm and flow of the pounding.

Had he jumped the train in search of a job, or just in search of a ride out of Clarksville? If the latter, then events had overtaken him—but that was true for many of the people who traveled with Sax & Tebow, Cecily knew.

She snapped a picture of him with the crew. And then another—just of him in profile, his long legs still for a moment, the hammer at rest in his hand. And then the crew hurried on to the next stake, and none of them noticed her at all.

The third time Cecily saw him, she was leading Prince through the maze of tents in the back lot to line up for the parade. It was the eighth of May, and the circus was in Springfield, Ohio. She was wearing her short

sapphire costume, tiara, and satin slippers. All around was the typical
bustle of the performers gathering, straightening costumes and headdresses and getting the animals ready to go, and Prince was walking with
his usual careful dignity, letting nothing bother him.

Suddenly, he reared up, whinnying, jerking back from Cecily. She
cried his name, but he reared again, now yanking the lead from her hand.
Oh, God, if he ran away—

There was a flash of motion in front of her, low to the ground. It
was the young man, lunging to pluck a snake from the grass and hurl it
far away, out toward where there was no one. Quick as that, he was up
again and had hold of Prince's lead and was pulling gently to get Prince
to settle down, saying in a calm, deep voice, "Hey, boy. Hey. It's all right.
I got you."

Prince shook his head and ran a small circle three times around Cecily and the young man, who calmly raised the rope over Cecily's head
each time, as if the three of them were in some strange dance. Then,
Prince stomped his foot, blew out air, shimmied out a bit more nerves,
and leaned toward the young man, who began stroking Prince's chest
with a gentle force that seemed to settle the pony further. "That's right,
boy. Just a little-bitty ole grass snake. He wasn't gonna harm no one.
That's right."

Cecily's fear and alarm were shifting to jealousy and anger: the young
man had seemingly stolen Prince's affection and absolute trust in one
fell swoop. "Thank you," she snapped, heart still pounding. She held
out her hand for Prince's lead.

The young man handed her the rope, tugged his cap brim, and
smiled. It was an extraordinary smile, bright and yet mysterious, that
both arrested her and made her want to run. There was a look in his eyes
of knowing things he would never tell her. "You're welcome," he said.

As he turned away, he pulled a handkerchief from his back pocket to
wipe his forehead, and a tiny, folded piece of paper fell out.

She watched him walking away, glanced around at the people passing, and, when she was sure she wouldn't be noticed, she led Prince

forward, snatched the paper out of the mud, and stuffed it down the front of her dress.

She waited till she could sneak back to the caboose after the parade to pull it out and unfold it.

On it, written in pencil—the handwriting was crooked, unmistakably (Cecily thought) a young man's—was:

Medicine show Blues / Hot Snoot sandwich
Aunt Mary Orr, 330 Beale St, Memphis
What is the feeling you feel when you finally belong somewhere /
how do you
Recognize it?

It made little sense, but sounded important. And he probably needed his aunt's address, besides. Cecily would have to figure out a way to get this little paper back to him.

She had never paid much attention to the lives of the roustabouts, but now she carefully observed their routines. They ate after the performers and other staff, except at breakfast, when they ate first, having been up working since 3:30 or 4 A.M., while the performers slept in. They lived in a bunk car near the middle of the train, just behind the flatcars that carried the wagons. They worked all morning, setting up, and slept during the afternoon show, if they could find a quiet spot among the hay bales. Then they worked late into the night to tear everything down and get it back onto the train. There were more than fifty of them, and they tended to stick together with their crews, traveling in small groups of six or seven.

The circus made stops in Cincinnati, Versailles, Seymour, Bedford, Bloomington, Odon, and Robinson, and Tebow sent Cecily's film off to

Kodak for developing, ordering two copies of each print with instructions for them to be sent to him in Cedar Rapids, Iowa, fourteen stops down the line. "You've got to spend money to make money," Tebow said, but he didn't buy Cecily any new film. Maybe taking pictures was just another thing that was going to slip through her fingers.

Meanwhile, she was no closer to getting the young man's note back to him. She asked Isabelle, "If you had to get a message to a roustabout, how would you do it?" Isabelle lifted an eyebrow and said Cecily had better *not* have a message for a roustabout.

So Cecily was on her own. It was that way more and more these days, seemed like. Isabelle had grown increasingly peevish in recent years, after Tebow had put her in charge of managing a peep show that played in a back-row tent, off the midway and behind the tents of Madame Genevieve, the snake charmer, and Fredric Roseau, the sword swallower, unadvertised except by "whisper of mouth," as Isabelle liked to describe it. Ticket sellers would search out men roaming alone in the crowd "with a certain look in their eye" and tell them in secret tones of the wonders on offer for the low, low price of fifty cents, "just over yonder, just back of beyond."

Isabelle was always complaining about "the girls," arguing with them and Margie about their tearaway costumes—just how much could or should be torn away was constantly in debate—plus keeping a hawk-eye out for new "talent" in every town they went to, because rarely did a peep-show girl last more than three months, and Isabelle tried to keep at least five on hand at all times, or it didn't make for much of a show, she said. "At least their job doesn't require the amount of training that *yours* did," she told Cecily, with a short, humorless laugh. Then she shook her head. "Though, God, what I wouldn't give for one true *professional*."

Effingham, Mattoon, Champaign. Isabelle wasn't staying overnight in the caboose these days; it was just three short steps through the vestibule to Tebow's private car, and the two had stopped any pretense of secrecy in recent years. Anyway, it wasn't as if they were the only pair in the circus living together without benefit of a legal marriage. The older

Cecily got, the more she'd discovered that almost everybody had someone they paired up with, at least from time to time. And some who'd been living as married couples throughout Cecily's tenure with Sax & Tebow, like Little Red and Lorraine LaPointe, weren't actually married at all.

Cecily found it lonely to travel through the nights in the caboose by herself, and she had no idea why Tebow continued to pay for it. "You're my special little star; I've got to have you well rested," Tebow had said with a grin, earning a glare from Isabelle, but Cecily could hardly believe that was the whole story. The circus had a lot of stars. She guessed Isabelle must have simply put her foot down about keeping it, but why? It just made the other girls think that Cecily believed herself important, when Cecily would've been glad to live in the bunk car with them, because maybe then she'd have found at least one friend.

Besides, when she was with other people, she was invariably Jacqueline DuMonde: savvy, sassy, on top of the world. When she was alone, she was just Cecily again, as lonely and small as she'd ever been.

She took to leaving her few things—books, cardigan, satin slippers, empty Brownie box camera—scattered about the caboose, even in the kitchen area, which always before she and Isabelle had kept impeccably tidy. She did not exactly realize: this was simply to get Isabelle's attention; to try to get Isabelle *back*. "If things aren't a hundred percent shipshape, that's the first sign everything's about to go to hell," Isabelle had always said.

Now, though, Isabelle would raise an eyebrow at the clutter if she came in, but not say a word. It was as if she'd stopped caring altogether, or at least had more important things on her mind. Then, on a pretty May morning in Decatur, Cecily was sitting on the step of the caboose putting on her shoes when the newest peep-show girl, who couldn't have been more than a year older than Cecily, came out of Tebow's car, dark hair mussed, wearing last night's sparkling costume, carrying her high-heeled shoes. She moved in a way that said she did not want to be seen or heard, and she was evidently so focused on achieving that goal that she didn't look up to notice Cecily at all.

Cecily—puzzled, at first, and then alarmed—was watching the girl walk away across the open field when Isabelle came out onto the vestibule in her robe with a cigarette. She narrowed her eyes when she saw Cecily; when she saw that Cecily had seen the girl.

"Don't look at me like that," Isabelle snapped. "You have no idea what all I've had to do to save you. The sacrifices I've made."

Cecily blinked back tears. It seemed as if Isabelle had decided to hate her for things that Cecily had never asked for or done; to blame her for everything that had ever gone wrong, or was about to—whatever that was.

And Cecily grew lonelier still, as the days heated up across the rolling green land.

In her bunk, years before, Cecily had constructed a bookshelf with a gate fixture across it that kept the books from falling out while the train was in motion. She ordered books throughout the winter from the Sears, Roebuck catalog, and, before the circus set out in the spring, carefully selected those she'd bring along for the season. Her shelf was only two feet long, so she had to pick ones she wouldn't mind reading again and again. She was currently rereading *The Red Pony*, and she'd been using the young man's note as a bookmark. Every night, before she extinguished the lantern and went to sleep in the lonesome caboose, she read it like a prayer.

She began to wonder: What *was* the feeling you felt when you belonged somewhere?

Whatever it was, she was sure she had never felt it. Would she recognize it?

She pulled out her Saint Jude card and asked for help finding a way to return the young man's note to him. If anything had ever seemed impossible, it was that.

She lay awake nights, trying to think of a way. She could not, of course, go anywhere near the bunk car where the roustabouts slept. Besides, even if she hoped to slide the note under his pillow when the car was unoccupied, she'd have no way of knowing which bunk was his, and, even then, it could go to the wrong person, because the men were assigned two to a bunk. She could not go near the young man in sight of other people—it simply wasn't done—and she couldn't go anywhere where she might find him alone, even if she knew where such a place might be.

Just in case, she carried the note with her everywhere. But two weeks passed, and she was no closer to solving the problem of how to get it back to him. Her little bunk was getting hotter and hotter as the summer warmed. She kicked off her blanket and slept fitfully, waking with a thin film of soot covering her nightgown and skin.

Then, the same day that the Sax & Tebow train crossed the broad Mississippi to arrive in Hannibal, Missouri, two things happened. First, Janey, while leading Doc down the ramp out of the train, tripped and fell and broke her ankle. Later that same morning, as Cecily left the cook top after lunch by herself, intending to go check on Prince, she saw the young man. He was alone, too, by some miracle, and stepping into a thick line of trees alongside the field. Probably going to try to catch a nap. She looked to make sure no one was watching, then hurried after him.

In the cool shade of the trees and brush—overhead was thick with the sounds of birds singing, insects buzzing, the rustling of leaves—she couldn't see where he'd gone. She took another step in, and a branch cracked under her foot.

His head poked out from behind a tree. When he saw her, his mouth went sideways; his eyes narrowed with suspicion.

She unfolded the note and held it out so he could see. "I just wanted to give this back to you," she whispered. "It fell out of your pocket when you helped me with Prince."

At that, he frowned. "That was weeks ago. Miles and miles ago. You been hanging on to it all this time?"

"Yes. I couldn't figure out how to get it back to you."

He smiled, then—that bright, mysterious smile. "Guess you're not as hoity-toity as you pretend to be." He came over in three long strides and took the note from her hand. He was at least ten inches taller than she was.

"I'm not hoity-toity at all!"

He laughed and held up the note, and she liked the curves of his mouth and the soft, knowing brown of his almond-shaped eyes. "Thanks for this," he said, turning to go back behind his tree.

"Wait! Wait, please."

He turned.

"What do you think *is* the feeling you feel when you finally belong somewhere?"

He blinked slowly, as if he was recognizing her actual existence for the first time. "If I knew," he said, "I guess I wouldn't have written it as a question." His slight Southern accent was not a Tennessee one, Cecily knew that much for sure, and it made her wonder how he'd ended up in Clarksville; where he was really from.

"What's your name?" she asked.

"Well, Miss Jacqueline DuMonde." He said the name in a way that made her almost ashamed of it; at least, she was ashamed that he knew who she was, when she hadn't known him. "My name's Moses Washington Green. But most folks call me Lucky."

Somehow that all made perfect sense to her. Anyway, she liked the sound of it. "My real name's Cecily," she blurted, then felt her face heat up. She couldn't believe she'd said it out loud. "Almost nobody knows that," she cautioned.

He cocked his head, as if wondering, just as she was, why on earth she would've told him such a thing. This, oddly, made her just rush on. "But you can call me Cecily, if you want. Just don't let anyone hear!"

He nodded. "Well, good," he said, like none of that made sense to him at all.

"I saw you when you first hopped the train, back in Clarksville," she said, as if that could explain.

His eyes widened for an instant, but he quickly composed his face, cocked his head a little again. "Well, it is good to meet you, Miss Cecily DuMonde." She had never thought of merging those two names, and she liked the sound of them together, as, again, he turned to go.

But she had so much more to talk to him about—she knew that for sure, too, even if it also made no sense.

"I know you're good with horses," she blurted.

He stopped and turned to look at her, and she saw then that he was even better with horses than she'd understood, just from the patient way he held his head.

"I don't know if you heard, but our groom, Janey, she just broke her ankle this morning, and Isabelle's beside herself saying what're we gonna do without her. If you go to Tebow and tell him you'll do the job for the same price as you're working now, or even just a little bit more, I bet he'll put you in it, at least till she's better. It's for Prince and Doc and Virgil and Wyatt. Tebow won't want to hire anybody extra because of the money, but we're really going to need the help. You should go right now, before someone else thinks of it."

A pause, with him just looking at her. She felt strangely out of breath.

"You gonna try to get me into trouble?" he said.

"No! No, I just—I don't have many people I can talk to. I'm an orphan and, well, I've been here such a long time now—more than half my life, almost—and I've almost forgotten I was ever anything *but* Jacqueline DuMonde, and I think the story of my life has got to be so much more than this, this on-and-off-the-train without ever actually *getting* anywhere, and I used to almost think it was fun, but maybe I'm tired of it, or else I just wish there was someone who really *saw* me, all the questions I have and my dreams, like the things you wrote in your note, you know? *Destinations.* Not my *sequins* that make me look as if I'm 'hoity-toity' or a 'star,' which I'm not—" She stopped herself, again unsure why she'd told him all of that, or even where it had come from.

"I don't much have anyone I can talk to, either," he said, and, when he turned and walked back deeper into the woods, she thought it would be the last time they ever talked, that he was gone for good.

But, half an hour before the evening show, Tebow brought him to the stable tent and introduced him to Isabelle as the substitute groom. The young man—*Moses Washington Green*, Cecily thought, with a secret little thrill she did not understand; and then she thought, *Lucky*—quickly took over fitting the horses with their headdresses. Isabelle fussed and fumed that he wasn't doing it right, that he couldn't *possibly* be *capable*, but Doc and Virgil and Wyatt warmed to him right away, and Isabelle noticed a rip in the hem of her red sequined skirt that required Margie's immediate attention, so she had no choice but to leave Lucky to it.

Cecily, in her sparkling blue costume and readying Prince for the show, privately thanked Saint Jude for Lucky's presence in the stall beside her, though she had to wonder if Janey's broken ankle had truly been necessary.

But, then again, who was she to question God's plan?

She'd had to pretend she didn't know Lucky, of course. And that Isabelle was so up-in-arms about him certainly wasn't good, when Cecily had been hoping to get back into Isabelle's good graces somehow.

Still, when no one was looking, Cecily walked by and winked at Lucky. He was filling a water bucket from a hose and gave a slow nod back, in acknowledgment, without changing the unreadable expression on his face. If anyone had been watching, they wouldn't have noticed a thing. But Cecily felt the earth tip slightly on its axis—though, again, it was hard to understand why.

CHAPTER 23

Friday, March 6, 2015
Itasca, Minnesota

I hope caramel macchiato is still your favorite," Evan said, holding
out a paper cup from Jean's Beans to Molly. He'd come into her
office reception room with a blast of frigid air, looking very East
Coast in his striped scarf, heavy Burberry coat, dark jeans, and new-
looking lace-up boots.

"Yes, thank you!" she said, and, though he was the primary reason
she'd been losing sleep these last two weeks—their conversations about
custody had been both fruitless and excruciating, and they had another
planned for right now and had to get *something* worked out, because Evan
would be driving out of town at 4 A.M. tomorrow to catch his flight
out of Minneapolis—she was oddly happy to see him, and oddly glad
he'd stayed as long as he had.

But then, custody arguments aside, he'd actually been helpful to have
around. He'd driven Molly and Liz to the game in Duluth—an especially
big help because Liz had still seemed so out of sorts, even sleeping in
the back seat the whole ride home—celebrated the victory with Caden,
then been at the home game two days later when Itasca was eliminated
in the last round of sectionals. For Caden, hearing "there's always next
season, bud" from his dad had probably helped take the sting out of the
loss more than anything Molly ever could've done or said, and there was
no point resenting that. Evan had also helped when it was time to move
Cecily over to The Pines, cheerfully loading flower arrangements into
the back of Molly's Mazda, running back and forth to Cecily's house

six times to make sure she had every particular book and pair of socks she wanted, and fending off a dozen Prayer and Action ladies who'd arrived bearing cookies and cakes and cross-stitch projects, wanting "just a peek" at Cecily "to make sure she's all right!" If not for Evan, their good intentions might just have been the death of Cecily.

And, in the days since, he'd been spending every possible moment with their son, whenever Caden wasn't in school: taking him out for meals, playing hours of hockey at the town rink in a pair of used skates he'd picked up at Play It Again Sports. Molly didn't know what they talked about, but Caden, whose black eye had faded to a sickly shade of yellow, simply seemed happy to have Evan *around*. Plus, Evan had been keeping the walks shoveled and the lights and heat burning at Cecily's house, which was a huge relief to Liz, and thus to Molly.

Of course, now he was leaving with his fun-parent status intact, and Molly would be left to the rest on her own, whatever came—including whatever mess he created with possibly suing her for more time with Caden. She straightened her spine. "Well, Mr. Bouchard. Shall we go into my office?"

He nodded, and she led him into the talk therapy room. He looked around at the arrangement—a comfortable love seat, two Danish Modern armchairs, her clean, light wood desk, a pair of tall bamboo plants, colorful art on the walls—and said, "Nice."

"Thanks." She sat down behind her desk—she never sat here when she was with a client, but she needed *some* barrier in place right now— and took one blissful sip of macchiato. Evan, removing his coat and scarf, settled into the chair across from her and gave her a look she almost remembered—a mix of a question and a statement, neither of which she'd ever truly been able to decipher. He sipped his coffee. A cinnamon cappuccino, she'd bet anything.

Then, he said, "I'm just wondering what we're really going to do here, Moll."

Ah, so the macchiato had been meant to weaken her. "Evan, as I've said. He loves it here, and he's on track to be a starter next year in hockey, on a team with a great chance at the state championship. You can't uproot him. At age fourteen? Take him away from his friends, his classes, his team? He probably barely remembers his old friends, and I know the hockey program in Newport isn't nearly as good as this one. You'd be sabotaging him." She'd been saying pretty much the same thing since their first conversation, almost two weeks ago.

Evan sipped his coffee. "Hockey's important—"

"Yes, what about the Olympics? Staying here is his best shot at that, if you're serious."

"But family's more important."

"Well, then, he should stay here for that, too!"

Evan cocked his head with a look as if to say, *Bullshit*. His parents were in Maine, his sister and her kids in Seattle. Himself in Newport.

"Look," he said. "I'm not an idiot, contrary to your opinion. I know the Olympics is basically a pipe dream. What I also know is that he needs me. He's mine as much as he's yours, Moll. And he needs his dad. I'm just not going to let a long absence like the last one happen again. That was a real fuckup on my part, and I'm not going stand for it again. Not from me, and not from you. So, I don't know. Maybe he lives with you for the hockey season, and me for the rest of the school year."

"Are you insane? Break apart his school year every year? Just from that idea alone, it's clear you don't have his best interests at heart. Anyway, you don't even know what it takes to be solely responsible for him at this stage."

Evan let out a breath of frustration. "You've got to at least consent to July and August for now. I told you, my parents want me to bring him up to Maine, and I want to get him back out surfing, before he forgets how. I'm trying to be reasonable here, Moll. Maybe we can talk about the school year later."

"July and August was not our agreement at all. And I've already paid for him to go to hockey camp in Brainerd for two weeks at the end of July. He *wants* to go."

"But the agreement we had in place hasn't been—"

He stopped himself. Took another sip of his coffee. When he lowered the cup, his mouth was thin. "Molly Bouchard, this is fucking ridiculous, and you know it." His eyes flashed to her, and in them was a look she didn't recognize at all.

She set down her coffee, stomach whirling. She tried to remember the principles of Nonviolent Communication, but, under the weight of his gaze, she was coming up blank. "Okay, maybe we should take a step back—"

"No, I'm being serious. How did we get here, anyway? *Here*, arguing about our *son*?"

She swallowed and sat back. She did not want to revisit the pain. Not the old pain, nor the pain of the present moment. "You know how we got here," she said quietly.

"I refuse to accept that. Your father died, and you freaked out. I don't think *I* did anything wrong at all. But I got defensive and hurt and stuck in one way of thinking, and I just stopped fighting you, and you left, and you took me to court and took my son."

She swallowed again. "That is not how I recall it."

Evan set down his coffee. "Have you grieved your father, Molly? Or helped your mother? Really?"

She looked at him. *Damn it.* How was it still true that he knew her better than anyone? She'd shown up here in Itasca two years ago thinking she'd grieve with her mother; instead, she'd ended up buttoning herself up just as tightly as Liz herself was. They'd never talked about Dean. Not two words.

"Your father wouldn't want this for us, Moll," Evan said. "This . . . split. This arguing."

That was true, too: Dean had been a believer in happy families. That was his stake in the ground, his number one priority. He'd been the most successful residential real estate agent Itasca had ever known, not because he cared about properties or profits, but because he cared about families and happy homes. And, as buttoned up as Liz was around everyone else, with Dean she'd let her hair down. In Molly's memories of her parents together, they were always laughing, joking, having a grand time, even just day-to-day with the small, inane details of life.

She and Evan had lost that, somewhere along the way.

"You've been threatening to get a lawyer," she said.

"I'm not talking about that now. I'm talking about you. About our son."

"What do you want me to do, Evan? I'm not going to let him go back to live in Newport without me. And I'm not leaving Itasca. My practice is thriving. I'm doing some *good* here. And my grandma and my mom need me. I *do* help them. Just by being here, I do."

"Well, I can't leave Newport. I own the brewery, which we're just in the process of expanding, not that you care, and I own the house, which, I'll remind you, we love—"

"Believe me, I know all about how you've built your empire. All the *effort* you've put in. And I remember the house." A tiny antique Cape in the oldest part of town, built before 1800, which they'd gently restored, room by room, together. "It was mine, too, you know." It was odd to think, but, though she'd lived in Maine for college, and for a short while in Boston afterward, Newport was really the only place, other than Itasca, where Molly had ever felt at home.

Evan looked at her for a long moment, then his eyes softened, for no discernible reason. "Moll, listen," he said. "I know you never believe this. But I lost our babies, too. It wasn't just you. We should've been able to grieve together. Not let it divide us the way it did."

Tears sprang to her eyes. His tender gaze was cracking through every inch of protective shell she had. "How," she managed, "how, *how* do you expect we would've managed that?"

"I don't know, Moll, but we're adults. We should've tried harder." He swallowed visibly. "We have a living son we should've tried harder for."

She'd never felt so accused. Worse, she didn't even disagree. "It's all done now, Evan," she said, even as her entire body was reverberating with dismay—that this was how he saw things. Saw *her*. "We can't change it. Even if we're sorry. Even if we regret *everything*. We can't change it."

"*Are* you sorry, Moll? You took my son away from me. I don't want to live fifteen hundred miles from him anymore. I've had enough."

Molly wiped away a tear with her fingertip. Swallowed again. She truly hated this. *How did we get here?* "What does that mean, Evan?"

His jaw hardened. "It means I think we really messed this up, Moll. *You* did. This was a bad, bad mistake. And you need to fix it."

Liz was sitting next to Cecily's bedside, flipping through an old copy of *House Beautiful* without registering what she was seeing. Cecily's eyes were closed, an issue of *People* sprawled open across her lap. Liz had grabbed the magazines from The Pines' library for diversion when Cecily had said she didn't feel "up to" reading books. Nor had she felt "up to" seeing anyone except family, the last few days. Unmistakably bad signs—though her therapists had reported that rehab was going "just fine, considering her age."

Not incredibly reassuring, after all, but Liz would take what she could get.

Her cell phone rang. She flinched when she saw the local number, but quickly hid her nerves. "Excuse me, Mom," she said, and Cecily gave a wan smile before letting her eyes drift closed again. Another decidedly *not good* sign.

Liz clicked to answer the phone as she walked out to the hallway. "Hello?"

"Hi, Liz," said Dr. Hokannen, and she couldn't read his tone to know if the news was bad or good. After a few brief pleasantries, he said, "Listen, I'm not going to beat around the bush, okay? Your biopsy shows it's cancer."

Liz felt as if all her blood dropped to her feet. She was suddenly dizzy, cold.

"The good thing is we caught it early. Why don't you come in on Monday and we'll talk about your options, okay?"

She hugged herself tight with her free arm, but that did little to help steady her. It was Friday today; she'd have to wait out the weekend. But what was there to say? "Okay," she managed, and they set the time.

Liz didn't look quite right when she came back in after her phone call, Cecily noticed. A little unsteady and pale. Cecily worked her mouth— every part of her was just so tired—then managed, "Everything all right, hon?"

Liz blinked. Gave a sudden, weak smile. "Fine, Mom."

Cecily sat up slightly, made her voice stronger than she felt. "Now, don't start trying to *shelter* me from things. Did something happen?"

"No, Mom. Everything's fine." Liz picked up *House Beautiful* and flipped it open again.

Cecily sighed and sank back into her pillows. It was a strange thing about getting old: everyone imagined you knew nothing about anything, or that you couldn't "handle" it—as if you hadn't handled a thousand things they had no idea about before they were even born. She imagined Sam would say she ought to just relax and enjoy that other people were taking care of her, for once, instead of the other way around, but she was not of a mind to enjoy it. Not one bit. In pain and exhausted as she was, she was itching to get back to work, to bake a fifteen-layer cake and sit down with it and a cup of black coffee across her kitchen table from Molly. The poor girl was a wreck at the thought of losing Caden for even a few weeks a year, and Cecily had a few things she could tell her about that.

About luck. About loss.

But. Would Cecily ever have the chance to sit at her kitchen table with Molly again? Or do anything halfway normal? Was she going to make it out of this "rehab" place alive?

She knit her hands together over the blanket. Another perky thera- pist would be coming along soon to make her get out of bed and walk, and God knew it felt like too much to Cecily, having to learn to walk again, this far (nearly ninety-five years!) into life.

God knew, in a way, she'd been through enough to make up the entirety of a life.

Finito, as Isabelle would've said. *Capiche?*

But Isabelle also would've said, *A person has to make her own luck,* and so Cecily repeated these words out loud to her daughter, and Liz looked up from *House Beautiful* to give her a cock-eyed look.

With effort, Cecily smiled. Sudden tears filled Liz's eyes. "Oh, honey," Cecily said. "Whatever it is, it's going to be all right."

But Liz, typically so unflappable, looked suddenly—this was without precedent!—on the verge of becoming unhinged. Cecily wondered with a start if she'd been *found out.* Had Liz learned the truth?

But how? No one knew.

Unless Cecily herself had let something slip when she'd been drugged or not in her right mind, these last couple of weeks? Oh, she hoped not—that would be an awful way for Liz to find out. The worst. In fact, maybe part of the reason why Cecily had started declining visits from everyone except family was out of fear she might inadvertently divulge something to the wrong person and, within hours, that same something would be all over town. It wasn't easy to keep secrets in Itasca, and it certainly hadn't been easy to never once speak the truth out loud in almost seventy years.

What would everyone think? The Prayer and Action ladies? The book clubs and committees?

But, most of all, Liz. Liz and Molly. What they thought was all that would matter to Cecily, in the end.

Cecily had always told herself that she was *sparing* Liz from knowing painful things; that she was protecting her out of pure *love.* But now, Cecily felt a pang of regret that she'd kept so much from her.

But for Liz to learn the truth was unthinkable. She would be so angry. Molly, too.

Cecily could die hated by those she loved most.

But it was cowardly, wasn't it, not to tell them?

Cecily hadn't felt afraid of anything in a long time, but she was afraid now. Of the truth itself?

Or was it of the possibility—she felt it edging ever closer—that she would leave the earth with no one remaining who knew her whole story, or about the dreams she'd once had?

CHAPTER 24

Summer 1935
On tour with Sax & Tebow

I sabelle hated Lucky from the start. She tried everything to prove he didn't know what he was doing with the horses, but she couldn't trip him up. She swore that she, Doc, Virgil, and Wyatt could "hardly *function*" without Janey, who'd gone to recuperate at her parents' in Milwaukee. She railed that it was inappropriate ("if not *unacceptable*") to have a Black groom for the prize show horses.

Tebow, though, said it made perfect sense from a budgetary standpoint, and that she ought to be happy. The roustabout crew could function a man short for a couple months—anyway, Lucky was still getting up early to help with setup, so his old crew wasn't even *fully* a man short—and did Isabelle really want to do all the work of caring for Doc, Virgil, and Wyatt by herself, including mucking out their stalls, their section of the railcar?

Finally, Tebow said, if Isabelle didn't stop fussing, he was going to change the billing and possibly the order and content of the acts to make Jacqueline DuMonde the headliner, and Isabelle merely Jacqueline's "older sister." No more would Cecily simply warm up the crowd for Isabelle. "I'll bet little Jackie could even handle the big horses now," Tebow told Isabelle, implying that maybe Isabelle wasn't needed anymore, maybe "Isabelle DuMonde" was passé, washed up at the age of twenty-seven.

Someone other than Cecily must've overheard him, because Cecily didn't say a word, but rumors started to fly. "A miracle she's lasted this long, really," people started to whisper, about Isabelle. Of course, no one truly believed Tebow would do it: take his darling Isabelle off the headline, even if, in what seemed to be developing as the general view, she deserved it.

The circus made three more stops in Missouri, then crossed into Iowa—Ottumwa, Oskaloosa, Iowa City, Cedar Rapids, Waterloo. In Waterloo, Tebow came to Cecily with a yellow envelope full of the snapshots she'd taken, freshly returned from Kodak. He'd already chosen the best ones, he said, and sent them off to *Life* with a letter telling all about Jacqueline DuMonde and the Sax & Tebow Spectacular (a moniker he'd just invented). "Hang on to these copies," he told her. "We may need them." He didn't say for what.

Privately, in her bunk, on the night of her fifteenth birthday, which went unremarked by anyone, Cecily studied the images she'd managed to capture. Madame Genevieve with her snake twined around her shoulders; a laughing clown; Wyatt looking handsome in his feather headdress. Maybe there was a chance *Life* would like them, she thought.

Then, without admitting even to herself that she was doing it, she sneaked the one of Lucky—serious-looking in profile, gazing into the distance, sledgehammer in hand—out of the stack and slid it into *Pride and Prejudice*, along with her Saint Jude prayer card.

A lot of things seemed impossible, more so even than usual, of late.

Cecily would've sworn she'd come to terms, years ago, with never finding her mother. But, still—it was reflex, really, in Iowa—at the sight of any pretty, dark-haired young woman, she'd feel a tiny leap in her heart, a surge of hope, which she'd just as quickly slam down, reminding herself ruthlessly each time: Madeline would probably look much older now, and the chance of ever finding her was a seed pearl swirling down the drain of a huge town swimming pool, if it wasn't already long gone.

Anyway, this season, Cecily had other things on her mind, things she preferred to think of—or, at least, felt helpless *not* to think of. Primarily: there were two times a day when she could hope to have a short stretch of minutes alone with Lucky. This was during the performances, when she'd lead Prince back to the stable tent after their act, at the same time that Isabelle was leading Doc, Wyatt, and Virgil toward the Big Top and the ring. Prince expected a great deal of attention, love, grooming, and carrots in reward for his performance, which Cecily, in the past, had typically administered on her own, as Janey had always gone to help Isabelle.

Fortunately, Isabelle had announced that she didn't need or want Lucky's help, so Lucky stayed with Prince and Cecily. It was a quiet time in the tent, with hardly anyone around, especially during the evening show, with the draught horses and their handlers out tearing down the menagerie and sideshow tops and hauling them back to the train. Anyway, with the Arabians all sold off, their riders and grooms long gone, the stable tent was half empty all the time.

"Where are you from?" Cecily asked Lucky.

"Around," he said. "You?"

"Same." She grinned.

He laughed. "All right, then. Little farm in Alabama. Left out on my own when I was eleven, though."

"Oh!" She told him about the orphanage in Chicago, Tebow coming to buy her when she was seven years old; the box her mother had checked on the form.

"Are you joking me?" Lucky said.

"No, are you?"

He shook his head.

"Why did you leave home when you were only eleven?"

"Stepdaddy trouble," he said. "Anyway, no way was I gonna get stuck in that sharecropping life. My mother had sent me to school to make sure I wouldn't, but my chances were looking doubtful to me."

"Oh," Cecily said, as if she understood about all that, which she didn't. "Where did you go?" She imagined he would say to his aunt's house in Memphis.

"Rode around awhile. Ended up in New York City. Harlem. Then, when it got bad there, five years ago, I left out. Been traveling ever since."

Cecily took this in, currying Prince. She felt she wanted to know everything about Lucky, every little detail of everything he'd seen or thought or done in all the years leading up till right now, and the feeling left her tongue-tied, as if she had too many questions to choose only one to ask. Finally, she said, "I've never been to New York City. What's it like?"

He gave a quick grin. "Music coming out of every door. People dressed to the nines, you know? Sharp suits, white hats. And the poets—man." His smile faded. "But that was before. Before people got desperate and things got dingy and mean."

Cecily understood, then. "You're a poet, aren't you? That's what that little note I found was?"

He shrugged and took a carrot out of the bucket to feed to Prince. "My grandma back in Alabama," he said, and it was as if he was telling a secret. "Every year, on my birthday, she would make me a cake fifteen layers high. Fifteen thin little layers, you know? Cookin' each layer separate on top of the stove in her little old hoecake pan. Now I don't know how she came up with the money to do it. She must've saved all year."

Cecily's heart squeezed, hearing the homesickness in his voice, and imagining how much his grandma must have loved him, to save her money all year for a special cake for him. The wonder of a cake fifteen layers high was hard to imagine, and, again, she couldn't seem to find the right words—not to convey the sweet pain in her heart at the thought of it, nor of all the birthdays he'd missed since leaving home at eleven, nor of the fact that no one had made her a birthday cake in all her life, at least not that she could recall. "What kind of icing?" she asked.

That quick grin again. "Chocolate. Spread on the layers warm." The words themselves, staccato at first and then drawn out in his gentle accent, sounded like poetry, to Cecily.

L

As the weather warmed and the Sax & Tebow Spectacular crisscrossed the cool green hills of southern Wisconsin, stopping in any town that had a flat field big enough to contain them, Tebow announced it was time to become more spectacular, to better fit the new name. "It's all our necks on the line here," he said. There'd been no response from *Life*; he was starting to think the package had been lost in the mail. "We may have to send in those copies!" he told Cecily. Her stomach lurched slightly, because she knew she could not (*would* not) part with the picture of Lucky. Would Tebow notice it was missing? Maybe not; he was so distraught lately.

Then, one morning in the stable tent, he said he wanted Cecily to join Isabelle's act; to stand on Isabelle's shoulders as the Percherons cantered round the ring.

Cecily exchanged a glance with Isabelle. Sure, they'd talked about this back at the start, when Cecily was about half as tall, but—was he actually losing his mind now?

Isabelle was clearly wondering the same thing. "We can't add something like that mid-season," she snapped. "That would require weeks of practice. Months! *With* safety equipment, which we don't have here. And the boys won't like it, anyway." By *the boys*, she meant the horses. "When would we even find time to rehearse?"

"We've got to give the people something they can't stop talking about," Tebow insisted. He turned to Cecily. "You willing, kid?"

She glanced at Isabelle, who cocked her head. Cecily swallowed. Her mouth felt dry. "Sure!" she said, because, ever since Tebow had paid Mrs. H. for her, she never had gotten over thinking he might someday decide she just plain wasn't worth it.

Cecily stood on her right foot, wobbling atop Isabelle's left shoulder. Isabelle, with iron grips on Cecily's ankle and right arm, stood wobbling atop Wyatt's back.

"That's right!" Tebow shouted, clapping once loudly. Wyatt, fortunately, did not startle. "Now pose!" Slowly, Cecily lifted her left leg like a railroad crossing arm out to the side, then raised her left arm. Her standing leg trembled with strain.

Isabelle was trembling, too, pulling on Cecily's arm to counterbalance Cecily's lean. "Goddamn it, you're heavy!" she spat from below. "Count of three, down!" She counted, then pushed Cecily off. Cecily landed, jarring her knees, her feet sending up a tiny cloud of dust.

"We've got a long way to go!" Tebow said, and Isabelle shot Cecily a weary look, gave a tiny shake of her head, as she slid down off Wyatt.

"Let's take five," she said, massaging her shoulder as she walked away. Cecily rubbed her arm, which hurt where Isabelle had been grabbing her. She saw Lucky, then, standing in Prince's stall, watching her with his brow furrowed. She shot him a glance, trying to tell him not to worry, but his frown deepened, and he shook his head, almost imperceptibly.

"You think I'm crazy, don't you?" she asked him later, during the afternoon show, when they were alone in the tent.

A tiny smile, as he curried Prince. "Suppose it's not up to me to decide."

She moved closer to him, her hand on Prince's warm flank. "The circus is in bad trouble. We've got to save it." She put a finger to her lips, to indicate he should tell no one. He gave her a skeptical look. Everyone knew that nobody was getting paid; that, if it wasn't for the promise of three squares a day and the knowledge that, out on the road, pickings were slimmer than slim these days, half the workers would just plain walk away.

Cecily felt vaguely chastised; on the defensive. She took another step closer. "Anyway, I have to do what Tebow tells me. Besides, Isabelle's my sister. I mean . . ." She looked up into Lucky's eyes. Why did she want to trust him with all her secrets? She didn't know. "Not *really*, but she's more like a sister than most real sisters could ever be, I'm pretty sure."

He cocked an eyebrow at that, which made her laugh, made her want to forget every trouble.

"Are you going to write me a poem?" she ventured.

He stopped the motion of currying and looked at her in a way she couldn't decipher, then smiled slightly and picked up the motion again. "Huh. Let's see."

"Or maybe we could write it together! I don't know much about poetry, but I read a lot. I love words. Maybe you could teach me how to use them to write a poem."

A few strokes of the curry comb, her heart in her throat, and then he asked, "What do you want it to be about?"

She laughed. "A boy who's inscrutable?"

He gave her his smile, at that. "No, I think it's about a girl."

She pointed her chin and smiled back. "What's this girl like?"

"Well, headstrong," he said slowly, currying. "Pretty much fearless. You'd call her a fool, if she weren't so smart." He shot Cecily a grin to tell her he meant no offense, and she put her fists on her hips to say there was some taken.

"A fool?"

He nodded. "Sure. But, if you thought that, you'd be the fool. See, she gets devoted to the wrong people, people that don't deserve it, but that's just because her heart's wide open enough to swallow the whole world."

Cecily took a slight step back, feeling accused.

Lucky went on calmly. "And she's so fearless, it makes other people scared for her. They start thinking they want to protect her, put her in their pocket and carry her around, 'cause she seems so small. Truth is, though, she doesn't really need anybody. She's doing just fine on her own."

Cecily wasn't sure anymore that this was a story about her, but Isabelle was leading Doc, Wyatt, and Virgil into the tent, so Cecily went quiet. Prince nudged her, wanting a carrot, and she whispered to him,

"Patience, love," though her eyes were still on Lucky, who was filling a bucket from the hose and not looking at her at all.

"The first thing you gotta think about when you're writing a poem is the way each word sounds," he said, in their quiet time during the evening show. She'd insisted she was serious about learning how, and even that he let her take notes in the little notebook she knew he carried around in his shirt pocket. (He said he never let anybody touch his notebook, and she said, "But I'm not just anybody, am I?" He rolled his eyes, fished it out, and handed it over, along with a stubby pencil.)

"What do you mean?" she said now.

"Listen," he said, then carefully pronounced: "Exquisite."

She smiled. "Are we talking about the same girl we were talking about this afternoon?"

He grinned. "Write it down," he said, and, as she did, he added, "Sanguine."

"How do you spell that?"

He told her, then said, after a beat, "Oblivious."

She looked up. "Oblivious!"

He grinned. "Has a nice sound, doesn't it?"

She pointed her chin. "Incandescent," she said, in opposition.

He shook his head slowly and gave a low whistle. "Good one."

"Applies, too, doesn't it?"

He laughed, as she added it to the list.

Then, she said, "But how do we put them all together, into a poem that describes this girl?"

"The first line's always the hardest."

"I think it should have a boy in it, too." She glanced up. "One who isn't afraid to sleep out on a flatcar underneath a cage of pacing tigers just so nobody will bother him, and who's carried four particular books with him for a thousand miles."

He'd told her these things about himself, and he was grinning. "Maybe more like three thousand."

"Tell me the name of your books again. Maybe they need to go into the poem."

He shook his head a little, but ticked them off on his fingers. "*The Weary Blues, Home to Harlem, Harlem Shadows, As I Lay Dying.*"

"They all sound so sad!" she said, as she wrote the titles down. When she looked up, something in the soft way he was looking at her made her say, "About this girl." She swallowed, gathering her courage. "What if it turned out that she did need somebody?"

He cocked his head.

"I mean, what if there's somebody she's devoted to who does deserve it?"

He took a step back. The look on his face was very serious, but she couldn't tell what it meant. "I'd say she'd best start learning how to be careful," he said, and turned away.

She felt a prick of sadness, watching the square of his shoulders from behind as he grabbed a pitchfork and started moving hay. She glanced down at the notebook in her hands, deliberating for only a second before she flipped a few pages back. In his familiar handwriting, she saw:

Exquisite
Bittersweet
Would I give my life to reach you?

CHAPTER 25

March 2015
Kure Beach, North Carolina

larissa had wanted literally to kill the boy who'd raped Kate a month after her fifteenth birthday, in late August 1972—actually hunt him down and kill him (*with a knife;* Clarissa had imagined it more than once, watching him bleed).

But Kate hadn't even known his last name, or where he lived. He was just some nineteen-year-old blond surfer (*nineteen!*) Kate had met on the beach one afternoon, and she'd gotten into his old Corvair with him that evening and ended up bruised and scratched, with a black eye and ripped bikini, and still everyone—yes, Clarissa and Kate both knew this to be true—would say it was all Kate's fault, because she'd gotten into his car wearing only that bikini. (What had she *imagined* he wanted? her friends had asked, even as they were driving her home, watching her bruises purple while she shivered.)

Now, with the saliva samples shipped off to Ancestry and Lana back in Raleigh, Clarissa found herself lying awake nights wondering not what the DNA tests might reveal about her own past, her parentage, but whether they might find her grandchild—and if that might just be a big mistake.

Clarissa, who did not like thinking about the past, now could not *stop* thinking about it. All her life, she had tried so hard to do "the right thing." But it had not always been easy to know what the right thing was. (Almost never had it been easy, in fact.)

She'd been convinced, for example, that she was doing the right thing when Kate had come to her just before Christmas 1972, four months after the rape, to confirm the worst. And, no, Kate did *not* want an abortion; she'd actually looked horrified, when Clarissa asked. Kate imagined she could already feel the baby fluttering around in there (it was really still too early for that, but Clarissa kept quiet, realizing that to say so would've broken Kate's heart a little bit more) and none of this was *his* fault, Kate insisted, cradling her tiny belly protectively, in a way that made Clarissa proud, confirming what she'd always known: Kate was *stalwart*, brave, Clarissa's right-hand man, Clarissa would've never made it anywhere without Kate, Clarissa wouldn't have made it ten miles out of Lexington.

So Clarissa, coming up (*somehow!*) with the money for a one-way plane ticket, had arranged to send Kate to Oregon to stay with Clarissa's sister-friend Gloria from the commune. Gloria had been like a second mom to little Kate, those first years in California—or maybe a *first* mom, given how overtaken Clarissa had been by baby Lana then—and, in the years since, had acquired a goat farm of her own twenty miles outside Portland, along with her partner, Jill. Kate was going to Oregon, Clarissa explained to Lana, nine, "for the educational experience of learning all about a goat farm!" Lana bought it (Clarissa had always touted belief in the "school of life") and, furthermore, decided she wasn't jealous, nor even truly curious, because, well: goat farm. While she'd be playing at the beach with her friends.

In other words, Clarissa had arranged it so nobody would ever have to know. And Gloria and Jill, true to their word, had never told a soul. (Not even after Kate got famous, when the tabloids would've paid a pretty penny for the story.)

And Clarissa and Kate had never, ever discussed it—the rape, the baby—not in all the years since, though Clarissa, leaving Lana with friends in Laguna, had been there at Good Samaritan in Portland for the birth of the little boy. While Gloria and Jill spent the entire twenty-four hours of Kate's labor making sure Kate didn't suffer any guff for being unmarried, Clarissa had stayed squeezing Kate's hand. And, afterward,

Clarissa had *held* the baby; his little fingers had gripped her thumb! Her grandchild! With his little eyes squeezed shut; the perfect little gums in the open mouth as he cried. As Kate had said: not his *fault*, his origins! And Clarissa had felt (to her shock) her own heart being ripped out, too, when Kate, glassy-eyed, two days after the birth, two days she'd spent holding and whispering to the baby—Clarissa had been unable to discern one word—had signed the papers and, sobbing so hard Clarissa felt the shaking of it in her bones, kissed his forehead and handed him over to the woman from the adoption agency.

Three days after that, Clarissa drove Kate back home to California, with Kate stretched across the back seat, crying, the entire eighteen-hour trip. Or so Clarissa recalled. But they must have stopped overnight? Clarissa couldn't remember. In any case, when they arrived home—it was very late at night; Clarissa did remember that—Clarissa told Kate stiffly that she would have to pull herself together, so no one would know. Maybe Clarissa had been speaking, also, to herself. *Pull yourself together. Stop thinking about that little fist around your thumb! Those perfect little gums!* "I am not about to stand by and see your life ruined," Clarissa had told Kate, there in the driveway of their Laguna Beach bungalow.

And Kate had blinked and straightened.

And Kate, who had always been a "good girl"—straight A's, a dozen sweet friends, plans of applying to law school—had become a girl who ran around with boys and smoked weed and drank way too much and barely graduated from high school.

And then she had become an actress.

And she had become an addict. Hollow as a bone from lost love.

All Clarissa's fault? That old therapist had said no. Clarissa wasn't so sure. Also, she did *not* want to talk about it. (Not with Kate, not with anyone.) What it would mean if this child came to light. Kate's child. Child of the surfer-rapist. Everyone would learn what Clarissa had done; how cold she'd been. How intractable. There was a moment (in the hospital? back at the goat farm afterward?) she'd actually shouted at poor, broken-in-two Kate: *No, you cannot keep the baby! You cannot change your mind!*

And what would it do to Lana, always such a stickler for the truth, to find out her mother and sister had kept such a secret from her? She'd be sorry for Kate, maybe, but furious with Clarissa (the lies she'd told!). She would think Clarissa should've known better, done better (and, oh, she'd be right!)—or, at the very least, *told* her.

And Kate! Kate who'd been ripped wide open in more ways than one; who'd done her best to sew herself back up, the way her mother had told her to. It was no wonder, the way her life had gone afterward. What would it do to her now, if that baby turned up? ("Baby"! He'd be nearly forty-two years old. What was he *like*? Clarissa couldn't help wondering.)

What if, instead of helping Kate's recovery, as Clarissa had at first imagined, the DNA results set in motion something that made her spiral down? Traumatic memories, or some kind of rejection from the child if he *did* turn up—perhaps he would be angry, perhaps he would not want to meet Kate!

It was little wonder Clarissa tossed and turned for nights in a row, wishing she'd never let Lana talk her into sending in those tests. That foolish gust of optimism Clarissa had felt!

When, honestly, some things were *meant* to be swept under rugs—weren't they?

In the absence of being able to drink, Kate took up counting things. *One . . . two . . . three . . .* On and on, in a steady rhythm. She would sit on her mother's deck, wearing her big hat and sunglasses, counting the waves breaking on the shore. She made it up to five hundred one day.

At five hundred and two, Clarissa came out and set a book on the table. "Have you read this? I think it might be helpful." *The Seat of the Soul* by Gary Zukav. Kate had heard of it—what viewer of *Oprah* hadn't?

"Okay," Kate said. Still the girl who tried to please—plus, now, a houseguest, and a demonstrated delinquent, trying to prove herself redeemable.

Clarissa pretended to be adrift, distracted, even absentminded—and anyone might be, waiting for test results that were about to tell them who their parents were! But Kate knew from experience that Clarissa was never actually these things; that she was watching every move Kate made. But Kate was being so careful; she never even ventured downstairs in the late afternoons alone, on the chance she'd meet a neighbor, unaware of Kate's circumstances, who'd offer a gin and tonic with a cool wedge of lime.

She was really hoping she would be different this time. She almost—almost—felt she had a reason to be.

So she joined Clarissa on her beach walks, the two of them strolling in silence, Kate trying hard not to wonder about her baby, her *son*—where he was, what he was doing; some days she pictured him a chef, other days an airline pilot, a pediatrician, maybe an actor, like her!—and what would happen if the DNA test turned him up. Harder to think: it could also turn up her baby's father, "Rick," whose last name Kate had never learned; whom she'd known for a total of six hours, and who had changed her life forever. Of course, she despised the man—she'd count herself lucky if he was dead by now—and yet, she found she couldn't hate him entirely, because she had grown, in the seventh, eighth, ninth months of her pregnancy, to love her baby with the entire depth and width of her cavernous heart, and the thought of her son's existence now was a beacon of light for her at the end of the long dark tunnel of her recent life.

Walking beside her mother, Kate said none of this out loud. Clarissa, who claimed to be on the lookout for dolphins, seemed instead mostly to watch her feet, as if afraid of tripping, of losing her footing in the sand. Both women wore their hats, plenty of sunscreen and loose, long-sleeved clothes, so they did not get burned.

Kate liked Kure Beach—was really growing fond of it, in fact—though she had no idea why her mother had chosen to retire here. When Kate asked, Clarissa just said she'd somehow felt called, having visited an old friend here ten years earlier and fallen in love with the place. "Anyway, I'd never have been able to afford a waterfront place in California, or even to stop working, really. And I never truly felt at home there, not in all those years. Plus, this way, I get to be closer to you girls. I missed you after you left, you know. Just knowing you were nearby."

"Aw, thanks, Mom. I missed you, too!" Kate said, surprised, though she wondered. Kure Beach wasn't *that* close to Raleigh, and certainly not to Vero Beach. There had to be more to it, didn't there? "Do you think you were born near here? I mean, North Carolina's a big place. We don't have any idea where the McNaughton Home was?"

"No. None." And Clarissa's mouth zipped closed. It was almost a visible thing.

Kate couldn't stop herself. "Didn't your birth certificate say? Place of birth? I mean, assuming it's true you were adopted, and they changed the parents' names to Jack and Lola's, wouldn't the place have been the same?"

"That part was left blank," Clarissa said, and kept walking.

So, they weren't going to talk about it. Of course.

In the bathroom brushing her teeth that night, Kate suddenly noticed her father's face in the mirror. His nose, cheekbones, eyebrows. She did remember him to that degree—though she tried not to think of it, *not* to remember him. She didn't have a single photograph of him, so there could be no maudlin moments of wishful gazing at the image of his face, as the writers of *Love and Yearning* would've surely scripted.

But now, with her mother's origins so undeniably mysterious (and why did this seem *sudden*, like a *revelation*, to Kate?) she found herself—to her surprise—in search of something else to root her down. She'd never realized how much solace she'd taken in "knowing where she came from." Regardless of how horribly her grandparents had acted when Lana was born, Kate's happiest early memories were with them at their beautiful horse farm: Jack Duncan had taught little Kate to ride; Lola had hosted elaborate tea parties, trusting Kate with her finest Limoges. And Kate had imagined that she shared their blood, "belonged" to their "line," knowing as she did in some vague, childish, yet somehow utterly ontologically satisfying way that Grandpa Jack Duncan had been a Son of the American Revolution; that Grandma Lola's people were proud descendants of an Englishman who'd come to America as an indentured servant and made himself into a well-respected cobbler in Norfolk before 1800.

Now Kate had to face it: none of those people might actually be her people! The DNA test would tell them, once and for all. And then—what would be left? Would the test results actually connect Kate, Lana, and Clarissa meaningfully to anyone on Clarissa's side?

And, meanwhile, the Montgomery line—could Kate claim it? Did she even want to?

What she knew for sure was that she remembered the feeling of floating in the wind from when she was six years old, and maybe for the rest of her life after that, and for the feeling to intensify right now was exactly the opposite of what she needed.

She got into bed and, seemingly without thinking, clicked open Facebook on her phone. Lana had previously told Kate the names of Clayburn's four daughters. All were married, and none had kept the last name Montgomery, but Kate remembered the oldest's. She had never looked her up, but now typed in the name: *Tricia Montgomery Robinson.* There. Kate selected her profile from the list of options. They did not share any mutual friends. Tricia had just turned forty-nine and lived in Columbus, Ohio. She liked *Friends* and Def Leppard and bichon frises, had kind brown eyes and bright blond hair with expensive highlights, a husband who surprised her with roses on their anniversary, and two nearly handsome teenaged boys who played soccer.

Scrolling through Tricia's feed, Kate thought, *I can find no reason to hate this woman.*

And then, there it was. A photo from last October captioned *Family Reunion for Dad's 80th! All the Montgomery girls together again!*

They were posed around a picnic table under a sheltering maple, its leaves on fire with the autumn: Clayburn and his wife, Roberta, seated in the center, their four daughters surrounding them, the eight grand-kids seated in front: five boys, three girls. (The husbands had evidently been deemed nonessential for the photograph.) They all looked happy. Wholesome. Problem-free.

Kate blinked away tears. Gary Zukav said that a father could feel his daughter's energy, could feel when she started to try to heal any wounds that existed between them, even if there was no communication. That could hardly be true, could it?

Kate zoomed in on her father's face. (All right, yes, the writers of *Love and Yearning* were right—she had to do it.) Clayburn Montgomery: nearly fifty-two years older than when she'd last seen him. Face still razor-sharp and handsome, his hair silver, his smile slight and almost bitter-looking. He wore glasses now.

Did he ever think about her? About Kate, his firstborn? Had he ever watched her on TV? Seen her that time she'd been on the cover of *TV Guide?*

God, was that what she'd been trying for, all along, by trying for the shows that had the broadest distributions possible? To *reach* him?

(Or—it flashed through her mind now—to reach her son?)

In fact, when she was thirty years old, she'd been offered a shot at an exceedingly good role on Broadway. And she'd turned it down, hadn't even taken the audition, because she'd thought, *Who would ever see me there?*

A hundred thousand theatergoers, that was who. But probably not Clayburn Montgomery. Or a baby boy born June 1, 1973, in Portland, Oregon.

Kate took a deep breath, badly wanting a drink. She set her phone aside, picked up *The Seat of the Soul* and skipped ahead to the chapter titled "Addiction." She had a session tomorrow morning with Dr. Alvarez. She would make it through till then.

"Gary Zukav says my soul wants to heal," she told Dr. Alvarez on the phone. She was sitting cross-legged on her bed, keeping her voice low, feeling like a teenager trying to keep her mother from hearing. She could hear Clarissa puttering in the kitchen, unloading the dishwasher, making a fresh pitcher of iced tea.

"Do you think it does, Kate? Does your soul want to heal?"

Kate had never told Dr. Alvarez about her son. She didn't know how to broach the subject now.

Anyway, there were no guarantees that the DNA test would turn him up. And, if she started telling everyone how much she suddenly was hoping to find him (the hope was shining so brightly right now, like a sunbeam hitting a mirror, that it could blind her, start a fire), there'd be no way to put that particular genie back into the bottle.

"—I looked up my father's family on Facebook," she whispered into the phone instead. "The family he kept, I mean."

Dr. Alvarez didn't say anything. A moment passed.

And Kate burst into tears.

Dr. Alvarez advised keeping busy; Kate decided to take up cooking. She'd always looked at food as somewhat the enemy. A necessary evil, at best. Now, who cared if she put on a few pounds? It wasn't as if she was ever going to get back on TV.

She subscribed via email to *NYT Cooking* and relied on Clarissa to bring back cookbooks from the library, plus the ingredients she wanted: a dozen tomatoes and a handful of basil from a local farmstand; cabbage, white beans, spinach greens, sweet corn, crabmeat, bread crumbs, garlic, sweet onion. Gaining confidence, she googled the recipe for monkey bread, which she'd tasted once, years ago, and never forgotten. After two days' assurance from her mother that baking with yeast truly wasn't *that* hard, she finally tackled the project, kneading the dough, letting it rise, shaping little balls to dunk in butter and roll in cinnamon and sugar, then arranging these in her mother's Bundt pan and drizzling the whole concoction with a melted butter–brown sugar sauce. Once the pan was out of the oven and the bread only slightly cooled, she tore off a piece and, as the first bite melted in her mouth, thought: *Yes*—it was definitely worth it to go on living.

And then one night in the back bedroom, the sound of the waves muted and distant, Kate woke up sobbing. She didn't remember what she'd been dreaming, but her body was racked with an anguish that she could not rein in. Her mother came into the room. "Kate? Kate! Katie, honey, you're okay!" A cool hand came to rest on Kate's forehead.

Kate was sobbing. "Mom, I was so scared!"

The cool hand stroked Kate's hair. "I know, honey, but you're safe now. You're safe."

In the morning, Kate wondered if that part had been a dream, too, but she didn't think so, and coffee on the deck with the rising sun had never tasted so rich, so entirely validating. "I think, when I go back to Florida, I'm going to buy a horse," she told her mother, tearing off another piece of monkey bread, which, it turned out, made as excellent a breakfast as it did a dessert.

"That's a great idea, honey!" Clarissa said, and, for the first time in days that Kate had seen, smiled.

"Maybe you'll want to come riding," Kate said. Clarissa rarely mentioned it, but Kate remembered: Clarissa had been a skilled equestrienne, as a girl. Jack Duncan had owned thirty thoroughbreds, give or take.

The smile broadened. "I think I'm too old for that now, honey."

"Never say never," Kate said, feeling, at the sight of her mother's smile, a jolt of hope.

And, for a second, she wondered—where did that smile come from? It didn't look like Jack's or Lola's. Would they find it had come from Clarissa's biological mother? Father?

Well, they would know soon—to that level of detail, maybe. Lana had said sometimes people shared pictures of their forebears on the Ancestry website. Whether or not Clarissa ever agreed to talk about it, they would know.

Kate picked up a huge piece of monkey bread and tore off a bite with her teeth, and Clarissa—who was still, deep down, a Sweet Briar girl—blushed slightly at the bad manners and looked into her coffee cup, moving it to swirl the liquid inside. Kate chewed with relish and watched her mother, suddenly hoping—defiantly!—that they would find out everything. Everything that had never been spoken; she hoped it would all spill out like a vase full of marbles strewn noisily across a concrete floor. Kate was so tired of secrets, tired of all the things she'd kept inside plus all the things she'd never known and had to guess at. (In treatment, they'd talked about the connection between secrets and addiction, but Kate hadn't even realized—and would not have been able to name—all the secrets she'd been keeping, all her life. Nor had she ever realized till now: how exhausting!) She could no longer keep tidy all she knew and all she wondered about, when, taken together, it was enough to make her explode. Her son. Her father (was he her sister's father, too?). Her *grandparents*, for God's sake—who *were* they?

Soon. They would know. Soon.

CHAPTER 26

July 1935
Northern Wisconsin

On the third of July, in Ashland, Wisconsin, Cecily found a tiny note tucked under Prince's bridle with a single word on it: *Conspiracy!* She had no idea what it could refer to, but she knew it was from Lucky, because she recognized his handwriting, the thick strokes of his pencil. But *conspiracy* was definitely a five-dollar word, and sounded nice, besides, so maybe he was starting a word game, or another poem. They hadn't had a chance to talk at all yesterday—someone had always been around—so maybe he was trying to say he was sorry for turning his back on her the other day, to start up the conversation again.

She tracked down a pencil, flipped the little note over, and wrote a word that had always been one of her favorites: *Delicious!* Sure, it wasn't that unusual, but, when you really *listened* to it, it sounded so nice. She slid the note back under Prince's bridle and went over to practice with Isabelle.

"No, no, no!" Tebow said, and Isabelle, standing on Wyatt's back, where Cecily had failed to land, said, "Come on, try again."

Cecily limped back to her starting point. She had tweaked her knee just now, as Wyatt had shifted just as she was about to leap onto his back, and she'd stopped herself short to avoid a larger disaster.

But the pain in her knee was going to make the whole day, her two performances, almost impossible, she could already tell.

She saw that Lucky, over in Prince's stall, was peering around Prince's neck, watching her, looking worried. She wondered if he'd found her note, the word *delicious*. She liked thinking about that little note far more than she liked thinking about her knee, or the storm that threatened in great, haunting swaths out over Lake Superior, or Isabelle's peevishness, or the look on Tebow's face, which was of a man watching everything he owned dissolve before his eyes like a pile of sugar in a pounding, warm rain.

"Go!" said Isabelle from Wyatt's back, and Cecily ran, leaping as her hands met Wyatt's sturdy flank behind where Isabelle stood—and Wyatt stepped aside.

Cecily fell, hand then hip slamming the ground, raising dust that burned her eyes. Quickly, she scootched out of range of Wyatt's hooves. "Oh, *Wyatt*, sweetheart!" said Isabelle.

Cecily scooted over to lean against a hay bale, trying to catch her breath. She knew she was supposed to bounce right back up after any fall, but her knee was screaming—she'd twisted it much worse than last time—and her wrist was, too.

"What is wrong with that horse?" Tebow yelled.

"There's nothing wrong with the *horse*," Isabelle said, sliding down off Wyatt's back and going for the carrots.

Cecily's knee was swelling. She held her aching wrist, struggling not to cry. Why didn't Isabelle seem to care that she was hurt? And how was she going to do her act today at all now? The hay bale behind her back poked and scratched her through her costume, but that was the least of her pains.

"Goddamn it!" Tebow said.

Lucky came out of the stall. "Want me to get some ice for her knee, sir? I believe it would help."

Tebow frowned. "Oh, are you a doctor now?"

"Saw my grandma fix up plenty of injured folks."

"Fine, fine," Tebow said, making a brush-off gesture, and Lucky ran.

"I told you we shouldn't have tried this without safety equipment,"

Isabelle said primly, holding out a carrot in the flat of her palm for Wyatt, and Cecily started to cry, just a little, though she tried to hide it.

When Lucky got back carrying a pie pan containing three large shards of ice from the cookhouse, he crouched beside Cecily, wrapped one in the handkerchief from his back pocket, and held it out to her. She pressed it to her knee, using the wrist that was injured, too, to hold it in place. It did help lessen the pain, almost instantly.

"Tried to warn you," Lucky whispered, which made no sense to Cecily, but, when she cocked her head, he just shook his in return, pressed his lips together, and got to his feet. He stood beside her with his arms folded, his attitude that of a soldier guarding a castle door.

Tebow came over from where he'd been arguing with Isabelle. "You're in charge of Jackie," Tebow told Lucky. "We need her in the parade, she needs to get to her meals, she needs to rest between shows. She needs to be on Prince's back for those two shows today. I'm going to try to get a doctor for her. Meanwhile, if she can't walk, you carry her. Got it? Can you do that and take care of the horses, too?"

Lucky's mouth thinned, but he said, "Yes, sir."

"Good. I'm counting on you."

In the distance, thunder boomed. The sky opened. Rain fell in fat drops outside the stable tent, faster, faster, till they poured like a bucket overturned. "Goddamn it!" Tebow yelled, and ran out into it, fading away into the blur as he rushed toward the Big Top. Cecily didn't know what he imagined he could do about any of it, and, when she looked over at Isabelle, she wondered why Isabelle had such a look of satisfaction on her face, and an almost hatred, as she watched Tebow disappearing.

Lucky led Prince out into the rain to line up for the parade when it was time, then came back and helped Cecily up from where she sat on the ground. "Don't put any weight on that knee," he advised. "Want me to carry you, or do you want to hop?"

Her face heated up. "I'll just lean on you." She should've ridden Prince out, but she never did that—Lucky always led him out, and Cecily walked out behind them—so it was just stupid old habit that had caused her not to.

Lucky's expression was impassive. He nodded and moved beside her. His hand was warm on her waist; he crouched so she could lean on his shoulder.

But, out in the cold rain, her satin slipper sank into the mud with each pathetic hop she made.

"You're gonna slip and fall," he said.

She blinked up at him. She didn't mind seeming helpless, just this once. "Then carry me."

He gave another stern nod. As he bent, she looped her arms around his neck. He lifted her easily, cradling her, and began to walk. His face was smooth and handsome, dappled with raindrops, and very serious, his eyes narrowed, his mouth thin. She had never been so close to any boy before, at least not in a way that had made her take notice like this. The rain was making his shirt stick to her leg, his arm stick to her costume behind her back, so that it almost seemed she was melting into him, or the other way around. He was warm, and the side of her that wasn't touching him was cold—

She caught herself. She should be thinking about the show. Her livelihood; her whole life. This rain was a disaster. If it kept up, few Ashlanders would come out to the parade, even fewer to the show. The rain would make hands and feet, trapezes and ropes and animals, slippery—make everything the performers did even more dangerous than usual—but to cancel would mean losing an entire day's ticket sales, which Tebow clearly couldn't afford. Also, with her knee, Cecily wasn't going to be able to put on a good performance, if any at all, and she could hurt herself worse by trying—

So why was she so unaccountably . . . happy?

Her side was warm against Lucky's shirtfront, his arms warm around her. She could feel the rise and fall of his breathing as he carried her along the line of the parade, the other performers exclaiming and swearing over her swollen knee.

Reaching Prince's side, Lucky set Cecily down on her good foot. Mud engulfed her slipper. He circled her waist with his hands and lifted her quickly onto Prince's back. Prince shifted underneath her; he did not like the rain. She stroked his wet mane and tried to straighten his headdress. Without Lucky's heat pressed against her, she was suddenly so cold that her teeth began to chatter. Her hair was plastered to her head, and she'd have to sit sidesaddle on Prince's back, not stand, as she usually did in the parade. She wasn't going to be too impressive, in other words, nor much of an advertisement for the show.

Lucky frowned, looking hard at her swollen knee, rain-soaked with the rest of her. "You should keep ice on that."

Despite everything, this (the seriousness of his concern? his investment in her experience of her pain?) made her so happy that she laughed. "Now, that wouldn't look right at all! In the parade?"

A sudden smile broke across his face. He tugged his cap brim, wiped the raindrops from his cheek. "I'll be here when you get back," he said.

That night, after the show, the rain had finally stopped, leaving cool, steaming mud behind. Most of the animals and wagons had been loaded, and those folks not already aboard the train were drifting toward it. At the bottom of the caboose's vestibule steps, Cecily was in Lucky's arms, one hand at the back of his neck. Over her other arm was looped a pair of wooden crutches the doctor had given her that afternoon.

She'd used the crutches all day for short distances, but they hurt her under her arms, and were the wrong height, and slipped in the mud. So, after the show, while the circus was taken down around her, she'd sat on a hay bale, waiting for Lucky to get the horses put up in their railcar and come back for her. Her knee was swollen to twice the size it had been this morning, despite how the doctor had wrapped it.

But she had done her entire act, and done it without falling—both shows, and despite the wet mess of the rain. She didn't know, really, how she'd managed it, and now her teeth were chattering, and she couldn't tell if she was just cold or in shock of some kind after the long day in pain.

Lucky looked around, as if to see if anyone was coming—no one was—then looked down at her. "Can you use the crutches to climb up?"

She bit her lip and blinked. Her knee was screaming. "I don't think so. Can you carry me up?" He'd done so this afternoon, setting her gently down on the vestibule. She didn't know why he was hesitating now.

Slowly, he nodded. He took the crutches from her and reached to slide them up onto the vestibule. Then, turning sideways so as not to bump her feet or head, he carefully stretched his leg to reach the bottom step. He got his footing with one foot, then hoisted up the other, jostling her as they landed. He shot a grin down at Cecily, like he was surprised he'd made it, and she beamed back up at him.

Up one more step, then another, and they were on the vestibule. She wished he didn't have to set her down.

Of course he did, though—and soon she was situated on her crutches, looking up at him.

"You gonna be all right?" he said.

She tried to smile. "I think so. Will you come for me in the morning? To help me to breakfast?" They would be in the next town by then.

"Sure thing." He touched his cap brim.

"Thank you," she said, wishing she could think of something more, but the pain in her knee seemed to drown out thought.

Down the line came the shouts of men boarding the train. The whistle blew, and Lucky glanced in the direction of the noise. "'Night," he said, then bounded down the steps and ran toward the flatcars. She watched as he disappeared into the darkness.

The next night, in Superior, Wisconsin, when Lucky set Cecily down on the vestibule of the caboose, her head was full of images of the day. Sitting sidesaddle on Prince's back at the tail end of the usual Sax & Tebow parade, which today had trailed behind the town Fourth of July parade, the fire engines with their blaring sirens, the marching band playing "Yankee Doodle" and "Over There," the decorated floats and tractors. Many in the crowd had been waving tiny flags, as larger flags fluttered from front porches and banners from streetlamps, everyone trying to shake off the dust of the hard times and get in the spirit of the holiday. There'd been two sold-out shows. Cecily had managed again, during her act, not to fall, and to keep smiling through excruciating pain, and perhaps the day's ticket sales had been enough to make up for yesterday's near-rainout. At least, Tebow had seemed in a much better mood, as if something had suddenly lightened his load. A thick morning fog had burned off to picture-perfect blue skies.

Now the night was clear and warm, and Cecily's knee was swollen to the size of a melon. It hurt so badly that she almost couldn't feel it; she had turned off that part of her brain. She had also—almost—succeeded in turning off the memory of Isabelle glaring daggers at her all day, as if Cecily were doing something bad just by *existing*.

"I tried to get you some ice, but they won't have any till morning," Lucky said. He had been with her for almost every step, these last two days. He had lifted her on and off of Prince, on and off the train. He had followed her to meals, watching to be sure she was managing her crutches all right, filled her plate for her and brought it to the table, then followed her away again when she was done eating. Little Red had joked that the two of them could have their own sideshow tent: "The Black-White Boy-Girl: One Body, Two Heads!" Isabelle had shot another glare, while Cecily blushed.

Now, in the distance, a red firework exploded across the sky. "Oh, look, it's started!" Cecily pointed, and Lucky turned, smiling as the bloom faded down.

Tonight, the Sax & Tebow train had only to cross the bridge over the big St. Louis River to Duluth, Minnesota, and that wouldn't take longer than an hour, so the train (though of course they could never plan exactly, traveling fourth-class freight and having to fit in among the other trains) would likely not leave until past two in the morning. There was plenty of time to enjoy the evening. A lot of the circus folks had even gone into town.

Another firework burst. "You know where we could see best from?" Cecily pointed to the ladder that led to the roof of the caboose.

Lucky raised an eyebrow. "How are you gonna climb that thing?"

She scoffed. "If I can do a somersault on the back of a cantering pony, I can certainly climb a ladder."

Not that it was easy. She couldn't bend her leg, so she had to mostly pull herself up with her arms, swinging out her rear end at each rung to hop her good foot up to the next. Lucky waited at the bottom, pretending not to watch, but startling slightly each time she made a sudden move. When she got to the top, she scooted backward across the red roof to lean against the cupola, and Lucky climbed up after her, staying low, looking around to make sure no one was watching. Some folks were on top of the bunk cars in the distance, beyond Tebow's private car, but they were focused on the fireworks, *oohing* and *ahhing* as explosions lit the sky. Besides, people had gotten used to seeing Cecily and Lucky together, these last couple days. And, if Isabelle saw them—well. Cecily, in a private fit of rebellion, told herself she plain didn't care.

"Guess there's no stopping you from *anything*," Lucky said, and she smiled and gestured for him to come sit next to her. He considered the idea for a moment, then did it.

With him beside her, she felt the world had a new clarity; that all the parts of her had been rearranged to an order they had always been meant to go in. He gave a big sigh, and seemed to relax, and only then did she realize she had never seen him relax before. That he'd always been worried and watchful about who might be watching *him*.

In the distance, the fireworks bloomed. She settled back to watch, happy that he felt he could be at ease with her.

Shifting her position slightly, she drew in her breath at the pain in her knee.

Lucky looked down at it, and his gaze had a weight that was almost a touch. "Wish I could make it better."

You do, she wanted to say. Instead, she laughed and said, "It's ridiculous."

He frowned. "What is?"

"Being injured! I hope you aren't going to put *this* in our poem."

He smiled, then sighed again, leaning back against the cupola and lacing his hands together over drawn-up knees. For a moment, they watched the fireworks exploding, then he said, "I've got to tell you something." He turned to her with serious eyes, as the worst possibilities—he hated her, he was going to tell Tebow tomorrow he wanted nothing to do with her!—ran through her mind. "Listen," he said, "you know those boys'll do anything she tells them to, right?"

It took Cecily a second to set aside her fears and catch on. "Isabelle?" she blurted. "You think Isabelle told Wyatt to step aside so I'd fall? That's impossible. She'd never do that."

Lucky spoke in a low tone. "I heard them talking, day before yesterday. Her and Tebow. They don't notice me when I'm around. He told her Cole Brothers made an offer to buy us, and he's haggling with them for better terms, but right now they want you and not her. Said they don't need two bareback acts. And she was *angry.*"

"What? That doesn't even make sense. Tebow would never sell to Cole Brothers! And Isabelle wouldn't—! Anyway, even if all that was true, why would Cole Brothers want me and not her? Her act is much more impressive!"

Lucky's mouth was thin. "I'm telling you the truth."

"I don't doubt *you,* Lucky. But . . . you must have misunderstood! Isabelle would never try to hurt me. And I don't think Tebow would ever sell! Especially not to Cole Brothers!" Cecily shook her head quickly, dismissing the whole impossible notion, then smiled and changed to a far more pleasant subject. "Anyway, I'm just glad he assigned you to look after me. I don't know what I'd do without you."

Instantly, she bit her lip; there'd been more longing in her voice than she'd intended to reveal.

He gave a quick, fleeting smile, though his eyes were more serious than ever. "Cecily," he said, drawing out the last syllable, as if she were in some kind of trouble, or as if he were asking a question.

She couldn't help smiling, embarrassed as she was. Anyway, whatever the question, she thought her answer was yes, and she realized that the fact of that didn't frighten her; it made her feel brave. Slowly, she reached out and brushed her fingertip against the back of his hand. He glanced at her sideways, almost suspiciously, then looked back down at their hands. Slowly, he turned his hand over, and she folded her fingers inside his palm. It was as if there was nothing else she could do. He kept his fingers stretched out flat, and, after a moment, she traced one finger along his palm like Annie Sullivan passing a message to Helen Keller, and she thought he would know what it meant, and perhaps he did: She heard him breathe in sharply once, then, after a second, sigh. When she looked up at him, he was gazing at her the way you'd look at a newborn lamb.

"Cecily DuMonde," he said gently, and it was as if now he'd decided to answer everything *she* might ever ask.

"Moses Washington Green," she answered, pronouncing each syllable carefully, and the pleasing sound of his name, and the soft way he was looking at her—as if she were a place he'd like to live in—made a tear well in her eye. It trailed down her cheek, and Lucky watched it for a moment, then, with his thumb, brushed it gently away. At the sweetness of his touch, another tear fell. As he brushed this one away, she noticed, as if for the first time, the beauty of the details of his face—the sweet slope of his upper lip, the width of his handsome nose, the short dark lashes over his eyes—and she knew then that she loved him, and that it was the first real thing that had ever happened to her in her life. She felt a rush of exhilaration, then of sudden terror: What if she could never make him hers? What if he didn't love her back? She'd be shattered. Lost.

"You're going to be all right," he said softly, as if he could read her mind, as if her face were as transparent as glass straight all the way through.

"Do you know that feeling," she said, and it was both difficult to breathe and the easiest and most satisfying it had ever been, "the one where you know you've found where you belong?"

He drew back, and her heart squeezed in on itself. He folded his arms and shrank from her. In the distance, another firework boomed, followed by the sounds of cheering. "You shouldn't say that, Cecily." He was watchful, tense, again. "Anyway, you know it isn't true."

She blinked. She remembered Tebow watching her walk the rail at the Home. The trick to not falling was to move fast. "Moses Washington Green," she said. "You know it *is* true."

He was looking off into the distance, where fireworks were exploding, one after another after another in a grand finale, and the circus workers' cheers grew louder, their relief at not being the spectacle making them boisterous and almost drunk on the high of the release of all expectation, and Cecily touched Lucky's arm. "Please," she said.

He turned to her. "You're a fool, Cecily."

"But you know it's true as well as I do. I know you do."

He looked at her another moment, then sighed and relaxed again, with a slight shake of his head, and he leaned in and cupped her face in his hand, and his breath was warm and sweet in the second before his lips touched hers.

And with the warmth of that touch, all the possibilities of the world tumbled and strained and broke open, and Cecily's tears flowed freely and were a relief and a joy, because in this moment she finally knew what it meant to be a human girl—not a performer, not an orphan, not someone trying desperately to prove her worth. She was just a human girl, full of frailty and doubt and hope and striving, and if all the forces of this same world would be stacked against her soon, she didn't care; just right now, she didn't care at all.

"Yes, I know it's true," Lucky whispered, his lips brushing hers, the warmth of his hand on her face a comfort she had never known. "God help me, Cecily, I do."

CHAPTER 27

May 1946
Providence, Rhode Island

S o, you see, I really loved him," Cecily told Sam, and she was crying. They were sitting in a booth at the café where she'd worked before the war, and his coffee was growing cold in front of him. "I had no idea it could cause so much harm. I really didn't."

Sam was desperate to make her stop crying. He knew now that she had cried enough for a lifetime, and he hadn't waited out the entire excruciating war—his time in France and Belgium, her time working at the Providence Shipyard—to give up on her now.

Or had he?

"No idea whatsoever!" she continued. "And I was naive back then, I know, but I was so young. And I'm sorry! I wish I could change it, but I can't. I can't." She stopped, sat back and blinked. Her eyes softened, and she gazed at him as if he had the power to redeem her. If only he had the will.

Did he?

And why would she ask this of him now, after all this time—and what could this redemption, if bestowed, even mean—when, always, she had had some reason why not?

He'd asked her first when she was discharged from the San in the summer of '41. He was worried about her, honestly—she talked about getting a job! Was she truly strong enough? (He had not examined her himself; he wanted to trust his colleagues' judgment, but couldn't, not entirely, not when it came to her.)

What it came down to was that he wanted to take care of her. If they got married, she could live with him in married housing at the San. She could read all day by the lake.

"You don't want some sick wife on your hands, when all you do is take care of sick people all day," she said, and she went up to Providence, rented a small apartment, and started working at this very café, serving pie and coffee, ham and eggs, to strangers. Every time Sam had a day off, he'd drive down to the city, take her to the movies, and ask her again to consider it. (She looked so awfully pale; he missed her—just having her *nearby*—as much as he'd have missed his right arm.)

Then, it was the attack on Pearl Harbor; his enlistment. "We can't possibly get married now, when the future is so unknown," she said, though most people they knew *were* getting married in a rush, as if trying to set something in stone to hang on to in the face of the unknowable. Sam would've preferred that, himself. But Cecily wouldn't even accept an engagement ring. "Don't be silly," she said. "You're going to change your mind about me, I guarantee it. There's a whole big world out there, you'll see."

During the war, there'd been no fewer than four letters telling him she'd "misbehaved." It was a sailor on leave, a welder at the shipyard, a clamdigger, another welder. *I am so sorry,* she wrote, each time. *But, obviously, I am no one you should want to marry. I hope you'll forget about me. It's the only way you have a chance at happiness, my darling.*

Each time, it was like she'd ripped his heart from his chest.

He tried to forget her. There'd been several nurses who'd been willing to help him try.

He couldn't forget her. *Why do you do this?* he wrote to her, after her confession about the second welder. *When you know you are so entirely loved? When you know I want to give you the whole world?*

I don't know any such thing, she wrote back.

Now, finally, Sam knew the real reason why. He had seen and treated men with their guts shot out who'd probably felt better than he did right now. He gestured to the waitress for more coffee. "Pour out the cold stuff, would you?" he asked, when she came over. "Life's too short for cold coffee." Truth was, after the war, he had much less patience for anything the slightest bit physically uncomfortable—for less than perfect circumstances in anything—than he'd once had. Wouldn't you have thought the opposite? That, after weeks out in the ice and snow with injured and dying men, bombs falling all around and the constant threat of imminent attack, he should be able to tolerate anything now?

And yet, he could tolerate almost nothing. He'd gone back to his old job at the San just for the peace and quiet, the old routine.

He and Cecily both watched the waitress—*Ruth*, said her name tag—take his coffee cup over to the sink behind the counter, pour it out, and fill it with fresh from the pot. They watched as if she held the key to the secrets of God. Her hips switched in her pink dress. She brought the cup on its saucer back, set it down in front of Sam, and said, "This time, why don't you drink it, and stop making your girlfriend cry."

Sam flinched, and Cecily reached out to Ruth like a supplicant to the Virgin Mary. "Oh, no, he isn't—it isn't his f—"

Ruth was already gone.

Cecily sighed, gave Sam a weak, half-apologetic smile, and took a tiny sip of her coffee, which had to be as cold as his had been. She wiped the tears from her face with the flat of her hand.

He took a sip of his coffee, too. It was so hot it burned his tongue, and his despair at this was so instant and outsize that he actually wanted to cry.

But he didn't. He swallowed and set the cup down to cool.

"But do you see now?" she said, blinking wet lashes over sapphire eyes. Her quiet voice raked through him like metal. "Do you see now why I can never marry you?"

CHAPTER 28

Summer 1935
Wisconsin

The second week of July, everybody got paid. It was like a miracle. No one could explain it, anyway, because it wasn't as if crowds had increased substantially, or costs decreased at all. Mrs. Sax had come down on the train from Sturgeon Bay to Manitowoc—another small miracle, as Mrs. Sax hadn't been to a show in years—and right away there was cash for everyone, which Tebow handed out joyfully from a table he'd set up next to the bunk car in the railyard, drawing thick black lines through old IOUs in the ledger and writing in the new amounts. He asked everyone to take only as much as they truly needed, so Cecily took just five dollars out of the two-hundred-plus she was owed. Had the Saxes—again, it would have to be by some miracle, in these hard times—sold their farm? No, that couldn't be the answer: Where would the circus stay during the winter? What would everyone eat, without the mountains of vegetables Mrs. Sax grew and canned?

But no one knew what the answer *was*. (It certainly wasn't *Life* magazine. Tebow had plain stopped talking about that, without ever even asking Cecily for her set of copies of the snapshots.) And so, for a couple wild hours, it was said "for sure" Sax & Tebow had been sold to Cole Brothers—the rumor'd been flying far more than Cecily knew—and the announcement would come any minute. Cecily's stomach whirred as she wondered—was she going to be let go? Was Isabelle?

But, before the matinee, Tebow announced instead that there had "absolutely not" been such a sale, and there was not going to be, if he had things his way.

He still wouldn't explain where the cash had come from. A new silent partner, people agreed—it was the only possibility. Cecily decided that might as well be true; she'd lost any sense of being in the know, as Isabelle hadn't spoken to her since the third of July, since Cecily's injury.

Ever since Lucky had kissed Cecily, that night in Superior, he'd been distant, blank-faced, and wouldn't talk to her at all, apart from the barest exchanges of necessary information. He still helped her at meals, and helped her on and off the train, and on and off of Prince. Still, Cecily had been beside herself, thinking she might never reach him again, not even from inches away.

So it was that, on the day of Mrs. Sax's arrival, Cecily was balancing on her crutches outside the cooktop, bereft, watching him walk away, when Mrs. Sax came up and said, "Cecily, I admire you for what you're doing, but I do *worry* about you." This was the first time in at least three years that Mrs. Sax had said a word to Cecily, having long ago pegged her as an influence on Nonie and Ted that could not be abided. (It was true that Mrs. Sax considered the entire circus an influence on her children that could not be abided; she had forbidden Nonie and Ted from traveling with it even during their summers off from school, insisting she needed their help at home.)

Cecily figured Mrs. Sax was talking about the new tricks Cecily had been trying to learn with Isabelle to save Sax & Tebow. Or else the fact that she was continuing to perform on her injured knee. "Oh, well, it's important to so many people!"

Mrs. Sax's mouth was thin. "I just hope you know what you're doing," she said.

The next night, in Sheboygan, Lucky set Cecily down on the vestibule of the caboose and stepped back from her. It was late, and dark—not a lamp burning, even, in the caboose. "You all right now?" he said.

She blinked at the impassiveness in his eyes, which settled on her in a way that made her hopelessness feel heavier than ever. "I'm fine," she said. She situated her crutches under her arms and turned to go inside, opening the door.

"Cecily," he said quietly, and she stopped and turned to look at him. She could see the seriousness of his face in the shadows. "You know I'm trying to protect you, right?"

"I don't need protection," she snapped.

"You *do* need it. You don't understand."

She tossed her hair. "I don't *want* to understand. Why would I?"

He leaned in, speaking through clenched teeth. "Could get us *killed*."

She cocked her head. She didn't really believe that was true—at least, if the world was the way she wanted it, it wouldn't be. And she thought that vision of the world was an ideal worth standing up for. Anyway, if she'd learned anything in her fifteen years on earth, it was that all of life was a high-wire act regardless. The way she'd felt when Lucky kissed her—like nothing had ever been so real—was a feeling she'd risk anything to have again, to hold on to.

That night in Superior, she'd thought he felt the same. But seeing his tense face now, she realized—maybe not. Maybe he didn't actually love her enough to stand up for anything with her. To step out onto the wire.

She looked up, searching for the truth in his eyes, but she could see nothing in them beyond the screen of his caution, his nobility. She hated to think he would let his pragmatism rule; that he would hide from her, from possibility, when he had said he knew they belonged together. "What's life *for*, Lucky, if all you ever try to do is *survive* it?" she snapped, and she crutched her way inside, shutting the door behind her, starting to cry.

If it was really true that he didn't love her enough, she was doomed to be Jacqueline DuMonde forever, inhuman and sparkling, riding in circles in the dust.

The next morning, in Port Washington, as she dressed, she tried to keep her spirits up. He could still come to his senses! She knew she'd been unfair not to appreciate that he was trying to protect her—maybe he just needed a little more time!

But when he didn't arrive at the usual hour to fetch her for breakfast, she knew he was gone for good. She struggled to hop down the caboose steps, unable to keep her tears at bay, knowing that he would never kiss her again; that she would never again in her life feel the way she'd felt when he did. She crutched straight over to the stable tent and Prince, not wanting anyone to see her crying.

At least Prince was happy to see her, nuzzling her hand, seeming to understand she needed comfort. Only to confirm the worst—that Lucky was really gone—she slid her hand under Prince's bridle.

There was a note! She brushed away her tears, yanked it out and unfolded it. In familiar thick strokes of pencil, it said:

Bring me all of your
Heart melodies
That I may wrap them
In a blue cloud-cloth
Away from the too-rough fingers
Of the world.

(Langston Hughes)

Her joy was instant, soaring. In the sand of Prince's stall, where no one but Lucky would see it, she used a stick to draw a heart with a musical note inside, knowing he would know that it meant, *Yes. Please. Thank you.*

"Someday, I want to go back to Harlem." They were in Prince's stall in Racine two days later during the matinee, and Lucky was speaking in low tones as he curried Prince. He'd said nothing to her about the Langston Hughes poem, but had simply gone back to talking to her the way they'd talked before, and Cecily's relief at having this particular order restored to the world was immense. Also, strangely, absent the pain of Lucky's defection, she was far more bothered by the pain in her swollen knee, which she was icing now, sitting off to the side on a hay bale. She had managed again not to fall during her act, but, truth was, it all took a toll: the trying, the pretending, the hurting. "And I'm going to build me an empire."

Sudden delight washed out Cecily's pain, and she found herself craving, more than ever, to know everything he knew, to feel everything he felt. She grinned. "What kind of an empire?"

He laughed. "'The only emperor is the emperor of ice-cream.'"

"*What?*"

"That's a poem by Wallace Stevens. Do you know it?"

"No!" She laughed.

Cecily did not know much about sex. She had seen Isabelle and Tebow doing it that one time, and Isabelle had, much later, said she guessed it was a nice thing to do with someone you loved, but that Cecily should never, ever be casual or mercenary about it, the way the peep-show girls were, or let any boy pressure her into it. "Remember, you don't need them. They'll try to make you think you do, and they'll try to make you do all kinds of things on account of it. But. You *don't* need them. You've got me and Tebow and your circus family looking after you, and if you ever start to feel like there's some boy you *need*, I want you to tell me about it, and I'll remind you that you don't. *Capiche?*"

But this had been two years ago or more, and, given the way Isabelle hated Lucky already, not to mention how she wasn't currently speaking to Cecily, Cecily was not about to confess that she was beginning to feel she needed him. She and Isabelle had, of course, on account of Cecily's injury, stopped rehearsing their tandem act, and Isabelle didn't even keep her things in the caboose anymore; didn't even step foot inside.

Cecily lay awake nights—her knee hooked over a pillow to elevate it at Lucky's recommendation, though that didn't really seem to lessen the pain—wondering about all this. What had she done that was so wrong? What could she have done differently?

More important, though—what was *need*? (And why couldn't she shake this maddening feeling that she needed Lucky? Even when, regardless of what he might have felt or desired when he'd kissed her weeks ago, he seemed to want only her friendship now! She thought of what he'd written in his notebook: *Bittersweet. Would I give my life to reach you?* Was it really true that loving each other could get them killed? But it made no sense to her that such a pure, good thing could lead to harm! Everything in her railed against the notion, even as she fought against lingering desires that she could not seem to control.)

It was driving her crazy, too, that everyone in the circus seemed to understand about these things, except her. (Was need one and the same with love? Or simply with desire?) Janey with Ralph Robinson. Mavis with Ron. Little Red with the Bearded Lady, Lorraine LaPointe. ("Love'll make you do crazy things," Little Red had said sadly one day at lunch, after Lorraine had climbed to the highest aerial platform in the center of the ring and threatened to jump, on account of something Little Red had said to her; he'd had to kneel in the dust shouting apologies for ten whole minutes and finally ask her to "make it official" before she would come down.)

Whatever the particulars that Cecily didn't understand, what she did know was that all these people had made things *happen* in their lives, hearts and bodies tumbling. It was true she didn't know of any performers who'd fallen in love with a roustabout, but, in the circus, everything was bound to happen sooner or later, even if it hadn't happened already.

Besides, every couple in the circus was an odd one. A trapeze artist and a horse groom; a bearded lady and a three-foot-tall man; a tiger tamer and a clown. She had to think, in the end, she and Lucky could be the same.

Under the sheet in her bunk, her knee propped up, she gazed at the snapshot of Lucky that she'd moved from inside *Pride and Prejudice* to the book she was reading now, *A Farewell to Arms*. She traced the lines of his face and prayed to her Saint Jude card, without knowing exactly what she was asking for. (*More*, she would think, in a prayer that was almost wordless. *Please. Love.*)

She had only had ice cream three times in all her life, and, even if she didn't have the experience to know exactly what it was she was asking for, or hoping to receive, she did know that it was Lucky who'd made her realize she was tired of being denied the sweet, human things about living—and that they all seemed to reside now in him; that he was the one with the power to bestow them.

In Kenosha, when Lucky set Cecily down on the vestibule of the caboose, she said, "Tell me about your empire again."

He grinned. "'Let be be finale of seem. The only emperor is the emperor of ice-cream.'"

She grinned back. Couldn't help it; the feeling she got when he smiled was a happiness as sheer as a cliff face. "What does that mean?" she said. "'Let be be finale of seem'?"

He thought for a moment, looking at her with soft eyes that turned her inside out. "I think it means that you make up your mind how things are, and then that's how they are."

"Oh," she said, and, without thinking, she reached for his hand and caught it.

He flinched at first, but quickly gripped her hand in return, even took a step closer. But when he spoke her name, it was with his teeth clenched. "Cecily."

She shook her head, rejecting the rebuke. "I know you think I'm a fool, Lucky, but I don't care. If loving you makes me a fool, then I'll be a fool my whole life."

He blinked, then, and his whole body seemed to relax. To surrender like a sigh. For a moment, they swam in each other's eyes.

"Let be be finale of seem, Lucky," she whispered, squeezing his hand tighter. "If things could be exactly the way you wanted them to be, how would you have them be?"

He swallowed, blinked again. He squared his shoulders, his jaw. He seemed to be making up his mind. "I love you," he blurted, surprising her in a way that warmed her all through, and his voice was steady, though she could feel him trembling. "You drive me crazy, and there's never a minute I'm not thinking about you, there's never a minute when I don't want to be beside you. I think you're the only light in this whole dim, forsaken world."

Her heart thudded. She remembered the fireworks on the Fourth of July, the blooms of brightness raining in the dark sky. She moved closer to him. "I think the same things about you. I love you, too, Lucky. I've been lonely my whole life, and now I'm not lonely anymore. Not when you're here, I'm not. Loving you means more to me than anything."

A slow smile broke across his face. He gazed into the distance for a moment, gripping her hand firmly in his, then looked down into her eyes. "'Let be be finale of seem,' huh?"

"'The only emperor is the emperor of ice-cream,'" she said, then reached with her free hand to click open the door to the caboose. She looked up at him with a question.

He glanced at the cracked-open door, then back into her eyes. "What's life for, Cecily?"

"You," she said.

He nodded in his quiet, serious way and said, "You," then followed her inside.

CHAPTER 29

Friday, March 13, 2015
Itasca, Minnesota

"Caden, a little help, please?" Molly said, as she wrestled two heavy sacks of groceries out of the back of the Mazda. But he was already going inside the bungalow, the front door swinging shut behind him.

Well, he was mad at her. Again. Still.

She could've killed Evan when she'd found out he'd told Caden it was "almost a sure thing" that Caden would be spending July and August in Newport and Maine, the Brainerd hockey camp notwithstanding. "Maybe we can get a refund, Cade, or find some other time you can go," he'd told him. Molly, of course, had not yet agreed to this—but how could she refuse now? And damn Evan, anyway, for making her doubt all she'd managed to build here, not to mention doubt her conviction that everything in the years leading up to now had happened for a reason. That here in Itasca was exactly where she was supposed to be, right now.

No, he just thought she'd made a "bad, bad" mistake!

And what had she done? Said? That day? Just agreed to keep talking, basically; to keep trying to come to some arrangement. This even as she'd found herself back-of-mind wondering—did he think they'd made a mistake *divorcing*?

Surely not. She'd seen him on the phone late at night after each of the hockey games. A girlfriend back east seemed the only possible explanation.

And so, after dinner at the Thai Garden that Friday night (the three of them; it was Caden-focused, peaceful, *fun*), Evan had hit the road at 4 A.M. on Saturday—the weather was clear; a near-miracle, in early March, blizzard season—to catch his flight back to Providence. *After* he'd told Molly, on his way out the door of the bungalow on Friday, "We're going to figure this out, Moll. I swear, taking you to court would be my very last resort."

Her mind had not exactly been at ease in the week since his departure—to say the least.

And, for some reason, she hadn't told her mother about any of this. Maybe because she still had the feeling Liz was keeping some secret from *her*, or else just because Liz obviously had enough on her plate already. Molly *had* tried telling Cecily, but Cecily got overwhelmed so easily now. When Molly got emotional in the telling ("And then he . . . and then he . . . !"), Cecily just closed her eyes and asked Molly to turn on *Jeopardy!* "These *exercises* make me so tired," she said. "Three times a day, can you imagine?"

Molly'd had a constant lump in her throat, this entire past week. (Cecily had not been putting on her makeup, though Liz had left the cosmetics bag right there on her bedside table, and for Cecily not to "put on her face" was clearly not a good sign.) And now—Molly was realizing—she'd just asked Caden in the car if he knew if any of his friends were going to the hockey camp in Brainerd in July.

So that was why he was extra pissed off. And, yes, maybe she'd been trying to sway him to her side—she didn't want him to leave her for two months, not during the summer, not any time at all. *Damn Evan, anyway,* she thought again, wrestling the bags up the icy concrete steps, balancing one bag on her hip to open the door. *Getting Caden's hopes up that way.*

Evan had been gone almost a week and hadn't called. (Hadn't called *Molly.* He'd been calling Caden twice a day.)

What did that mean, the not calling? She thought he'd said he'd wanted to keep talking. *Taking you to court would be a last resort, Moll.*

She really should call him, in case he was out there interviewing attorneys or something. She should be proactive.

She didn't want to. Just couldn't face it. Not right now.

"Caden, would you *please* come help me put the groceries away?" she called into the quiet house, pulling the door shut behind her to keep out the cold, struggling to balance while she pried off her boots, using the edge of the mat for leverage.

No answer.

Mastectomy. Lumpectomy. Radiation. Tamoxifen. Herceptin. Chemo.

Words that Liz had never, ever thought would apply to her.

Cancer.

Dr. Hokannen had taken her through her options on Monday, and ordered a bunch of blood tests. On Wednesday, results in hand, he'd called to say he was going to refer her to a breast cancer specialist in Duluth, adding that he would "hazard a guess" that they'd recommend a lumpectomy rather than a full mastectomy. Before seeing the specialist, he said, she should have an MRI—to be sure the cancer hadn't spread. "That way, they'll have all the information they need to proceed with your treatment plan, all right?"

Liz wished she could ask Dr. Hokannen to go with her to her appointments in Duluth, but she guessed that would be inappropriate.

She just felt so alone.

She knew she was going to have to tell Molly eventually—obviously—but she was holding off, hoping to limit the amount of time Molly had to spend worrying before Liz's treatment got underway. (Not to mention Eric—should Liz tell him at all? Expect him to come jetting home from South America? Certainly not! And if she told him and he *didn't* come, how would that feel to Liz? Awful! Yes, this was what the kids would call a "no-win," for sure.)

The MRI was scheduled for eleven days from now, which was good—Liz would be able to see Cecily through that much more rehab before needing to decide about or schedule a surgery for herself—and also, bad, because Liz was obsessing about it. At her wheel out in the studio, throwing bowl after bowl, she'd find herself going down an imaginary checklist of what might have caused the cancer. The chemicals in the glazes she'd been using for almost fifty years? Too many McDonald's french fries during the '80s? The short amount of time she'd breastfed her kids? (It had been the '70s; her doctor, and her father, had both said formula was just fine, if not actually *better*.)

She'd find herself wondering, despite herself, not *if* the cancer had spread, but—*how far?*

In the end, what felt like the only thing she knew for sure about her cancer: she did not want to tell her mother she had it.

She'd always been fearful of hurting Cecily—maybe due to the scar down Cecily's midline. (Maybe this was why Liz had never truly rebelled; why she'd left it at bell-bottoms and becoming a potter.) Liz had seen the scar just once, when she was about eight—Cecily wasn't one to show off her midsection for any reason—and, when asked, Cecily had explained it was where Liz had been born out of. *So, you see, I always love this scar, because it's from you!* Cecily had said, and Liz had felt the pang of regret—she'd *hurt* Cecily—the sting of pride, and the solace of knowing exactly where she belonged.

There was a delicacy to Cecily underneath her hard-charging ways. Most people didn't see it, but Liz did.

So, no, Liz was not going to tell Cecily she had cancer—no matter what her father might try to tell her from the other side.

"Mom, why don't you tell me some stories from when you were young? Before I was born?" It was Saturday and, out the window of The Pines, snow was pouring down. Liz would need to head out soon, get over to check on Cecily's house, get to the store, get home.

But she didn't like how pale Cecily looked. How out of sorts. Shouldn't she be getting *better* by now, not worse? *Another reason not to tell her,* Liz thought, deep down.

Cecily licked her lips. "Did some magazine tell you to ask me that?"

Cecily had sharp edges now that she'd never exhibited before. From the pain? Had to be, Liz thought. "Is it supposed to increase my chances of survival? Make me remember what it was like to be happy and young?"

"No!" Liz lied. "I'm just curious. You've never told me much about your life before."

"Oh, honey." Cecily sighed. "Young and happy don't always happen at the same time."

CHAPTER 30

August 1935
On tour with Sax & Tebow

To Cecily, love was like a faucet turning on. A miracle; a release of pressure; gratitude; flow.

She didn't know if Lucky experienced it the same way. All he would say was that he hoped he didn't draw attention for bathing so frequently of late, which she thought had to be a joke, so she laughed and kissed him.

They had plenty of privacy now. Her knee was still swollen, and everyone was used to Lucky helping her at meals and walking with her—slowly, as she crutched along—to and from the caboose so he could help her up the stairs. Whenever anyone was around, she'd struggle with her crutches, and wince or gasp each time she even slightly bent her knee, trying to ensure that no one would begin to think it was time for her to start climbing steps on her own.

Lucky insisted on being careful not to act too friendly within anyone's view. ("We aren't a tiger tamer and a clown," he insisted. "We aren't the same thing at all.") But, after the evening show, when he walked with her back to the caboose, the cover of darkness let him slip inside. Nobody knew he wasn't where he was supposed to be. His bunkmates, he said, would figure he was out under the tiger wagon, while those who were used to seeing him sleeping under the wagon would figure he was in the bunk car, if they thought about him at all.

Of one thing, Cecily was certain: Once Lucky made it the four long steps in darkness through the caboose and up the ladder into her bunk, no one would ever find him. The only other person who'd ever come inside the caboose was Isabelle, and she had forsaken it—and Cecily—months ago. (Cecily imagined the scene, if anyone did find him: she would stand before him, shielding him from any possible harm.)

Pressed against his body was the first place she had ever felt at home. She supposed he wasn't perfect—no one was—but she couldn't see how. His every muscle and tendon, the soft brown of his eyes, the strong beat of his pounding heart.

Miracle, release, gratitude, flow.

She would fall asleep with her head on his shoulder, and, when she woke up in the morning, he was always gone, out working with his crew. He assured her there was no way he'd be caught sneaking from the caboose in the dead of night as the train groaned into its next stop. All he had to do, he said, was crawl past Tebow's private car, then stand up in the darkness and walk toward the front of the train like a man who had nothing to hide.

They had three weeks of bliss, and Cecily did not stop to think it couldn't go on forever. She did not stop to think of the future at all, nor of the fact that the circus was moving in the wrong direction: south.

For three weeks, all she knew was, for the first time in her life, she was loved.

Then, one day, without warning, Tebow came into the stable tent and told Lucky that Janey, broken ankle healed, was returning to the circus from Milwaukee. Lucky's services as a groom would no longer be needed; he was back on the roustabout crew full-time "starting tomorrow." Tebow also announced that Isabelle had said that Cecily's knee was much better, so there was no need for Lucky to help her around anymore. "She's got her crutches," Tebow said. "She can manage on her own, starting now."

"But—But I don't—" Cecily said, but Tebow was already turning away, and Lucky gave her a quick shake of his head.

After Tebow was gone, Cecily went over to Lucky and whispered, "How are we even going to see each other now?"

He glanced away, then looked down at the hay-covered dust, shaking his head slightly in a way that made her stomach hurt.

"What is it?" she whispered.

He looked up at her with the saddest eyes she'd ever seen, gave one more tiny shake of his head, then turned away.

That night after the show—her stomach had ached all day; Lucky hadn't even met her eyes again—she crutched her way back toward the caboose, hoping that, if she looked pathetic enough, Tebow might change his mind and reassign Lucky to helping her. Should she stage a fall down the caboose stairs, let out a scream to make sure everyone saw?

But there was no one even around.

All night, she tossed and turned alone in her bunk as the train clattered and clanked toward its next stop. She didn't allow herself to think of the worst possibilities.

In the morning, Janey was in the stable tent, and, under Prince's bridle, Cecily found a tiny note which said:

Animosity.
Perspicacity
Preemptive
Bittersweet.

She had no idea what the list of words was supposed to mean, and, if she suspected, she wouldn't admit it, not even to herself.

She told herself he would find some way to see her. He'd gotten practiced at sneaking away from the caboose. Surely, he would sneak to it, as well. He had to.

But he didn't come, nor even leave another note for her, and she didn't catch the slightest glimpse of him anywhere, for three entire, excruciating days.

Finally, in Bowling Green, against all manner and protocol, she got up early, crutched her way over to where the roustabouts were pounding stakes, and found the crew she recognized as his. The dawn was steamy, dripping. The day would be miserably hot.

Seeing that he was not with the men made her stomach hurt worse than ever; she knew then what she still could not admit. She crutched her way closer, interrupting them. "I'm missing one of Prince's silver brushes," she said. A complete fabrication. Prince didn't even have silver brushes. "Where's Lucky?"

The men glanced at each other. One took off his cap, pressed it to his chest. "Lucky left out, ma'am. We ain't seen him since Eddyville."

"Guess he didn't like the reassignment," added another.

If Cecily hadn't had the crutches under her arms, she would've collapsed. Screamed. Cried. As it was, she just stood there blinking, a moment too long.

"Somethin' else we can help you with, ma'am?"

"No."

"Then we ought to get back to work."

"Yes, of course. Of course," Cecily said, and turned away, as the *ting, ting, ting* of the hammers started up again behind her.

She somehow scraped her way back to the caboose, crawled up into her bunk and curled onto her side. She remembered watching as Catherine LeGrande twirled on the trapeze in gauzy blue, swung toward Buck, then slipped from his hands and was free, flailing as she fell, fell, fell, then smashed and crumpled in the dust.

Cecily could still smell Lucky on her pillow. She thought: *How could he?*

Why?

She could not show she was bereft, of course. Or, she tried not to. "What's the matter with you?" Little Red asked in line at supper that night. Cecily was limping through, struggling with her crutches as she tried to manage loading her plate, too. "You look like you been unplugged."

"A wilted flower," added Lorraine, wispy beard wobbling as she scooped potatoes onto her plate. She noticed the tiny portions on Cecily's. "Aren't you hungry, kid?"

Cecily gave a wan smile. "Not really."

Lorraine's bushy eyebrows came together; the long hairs around her mouth twitched. "You haven't got the flu, do you?"

"No. My knee hurts."

Lorraine's eyes shifted, softened. "Aw, you poor kid."

"What happened to your other half?" said Little Red. He was the one who'd suggested Cecily and Lucky make themselves into a sideshow act. Cecily resented that now.

But all she could do was square her shoulders, point her chin. "Reassigned," she said, as if it didn't matter. As if she didn't know the whole truth of how gone Lucky really was.

She thought of him out there with his old knapsack, the four precious books inside, as she cried herself to sleep. ("We aren't a tiger tamer and a clown," she heard him say, to which she cried, *But don't you love me?*)

She sneaked off to the library early one morning in Hopkinsville, Kentucky, to look up *perspicacity*. She wrote down the meaning: *The quality of having a ready insight into things; shrewdness.*

That was certainly not true of her. Was he referring to himself?

And—*preemptive: Serving or intended to preempt or forestall something, especially to prevent attack by disabling the enemy.*

He had left to protect her, then? Or—to protect himself?

She was almost sure that was what this meant. Someone must have seen them together and warned him (animosity)? He *did* love her; he hadn't wanted to leave (bittersweet)?

But what she couldn't even begin to understand was why he hadn't asked her first. She would have told him she'd stand up to anything, or she'd run away with him, if worse came to worst!

She was sure he knew as well as she did that they were each the only place where the other belonged.

So, then, she had to wonder: Would he come back?

She began to think: Yes! He surely knew the Sax & Tebow schedule. It was posted inside every car of the train. He was probably following along, just lying low for a while.

She decided to pack her little suitcase. She would run away with him. If there was danger in that, she didn't care. All she'd need was *Anne of Green Gables, Wuthering Heights,* a nightgown, street clothes, money. Lucky had been making only a dollar a week, he'd said, so she started taking ten dollars each week of her twenty-dollar salary from Tebow. It wouldn't do to draw suspicion by asking for the hundreds she was owed—at least not until Lucky had made contact.

Tebow complained about handing over the money, but he did have it, thank goodness. Cecily filed the cash inside *Anne of Green Gables* and stashed the book inside the suitcase under her bunk, where it would be easy to grab.

And, somehow, she managed to go on smiling and performing. Her knee, by some miracle, healed, and Tebow didn't bring up her and Isabelle combining acts, and the circus moved from town to town to town and wasn't bankrupt yet—again, by some miracle, had to be, everyone said.

In Huntsville, on the same day the summer heat and humidity finally broke, leaving blessedly cool air snaking in the windows of the caboose, Cecily thought maybe she did have the flu. She woke up later than usual, and was so nauseous that she barely made it down to the toilet before she vomited. She closed the lid, disgusted—the toilet opened onto the track, so the vomit would sit below the caboose all day and stink up the place—and rinsed her mouth at the sink, then crawled back up into her bunk. Maybe Lucky had come home to Alabama to wait for her, she thought. Maybe today he would come and find her. Though she had no idea if Huntsville was near Lucky's old homeplace, or if it made any sense at all to think he might've returned there, when he'd been gone nearly seven years—or even to imagine he was coming for her at all.

Still, she had to think: maybe. And thinking so gave her the pep to get up and get herself into costume for the parade.

By lunchtime, she was feeling better. Ravenous, even. She piled her plate high with ham and biscuits, stewed okra, collard greens. She went back for a second piece of chocolate pie.

Isabelle, watching Cecily scrape her second dessert plate clean, lifted a sculpted brow. "Better watch you don't start packing on the pounds."

It was the first time Isabelle had spoken to her in weeks, and Cecily had the unprecedented impulse to throw the plate straight at her head.

The next morning, she was sicker'n a dog, as the expression went, here in the South.

"Jackie, where are you? What's going on in here?" Isabelle poked her head in the door of the caboose. "You're late! We're lining up!" She stepped inside. "God, what is that smell?"

Up in her bunk, Cecily moaned.

Isabelle was unimpressed. "Everybody gets sick sometimes," she said, as if she'd never forsaken Cecily, never given her that weeks-long silent treatment; as if they were "sisters" again. "You can't miss the parade."

Cecily rode sidesaddle on Prince, waving and smiling at the crowd through her queasiness. By lunchtime, she was starving again. This was one strange flu, indeed.

And, still, Lucky had not returned.

When this had gone on for a little more than two weeks, Isabelle came to the caboose one afternoon in Spartanburg, South Carolina, before supper. Cecily was trying to sleep. She was more exhausted than she'd ever been; she felt about eighty years old. And, weirdly, despite that she was throwing up nearly everything she ate, Isabelle was right that she'd put on a pound or two, and her costume was getting a little tight around the middle. She would have to stop eating so much. Yet, every time she made up her mind to do so, she only felt hungrier and hungrier.

Isabelle shut the door behind her, looked up at Cecily in her bunk, put her fists to her hips, and said, "Jackie, I want you to tell me the truth."

"No!" Cecily said, as her mind reeled. *Was there any chance she could be expecting a baby?*

No!

But Isabelle listed the symptoms, ticking them off on her fingers.

"No!"

"Let me put this another way," Isabelle said. "Did some man stick his thing in you?"

Cecily was shocked speechless.

"Goddamn it, Jackie! I thought I explained all this to you. I thought I told you that under no circumstances were you to allow that to happen! I told you that was how you'd get into trouble!"

"I—I—" Cecily could not remember Isabelle ever saying such a thing, not exactly.

"Who was it? Did he force you? Was it Tebow? God, if it was—"

"Isabelle! No!"

"I'll kill him. Whoever it was. Or did you think you were *in love?*" She said the words like they were poison.

Cecily wanted to throw up again. If Isabelle had ever told her outright what she was saying now, Cecily clearly hadn't understood (*into trouble* could mean all kinds of things!). Isabelle had never had a baby, and Tebow stuck his thing in her all the time! And all the other people in the circus, and the peep-show girls: Cecily had never seen any of them turn up about to have a baby!

But, if what Isabelle said was true—and Isabelle's starkness convinced Cecily it was—then she and Lucky had certainly done it enough times that "trouble" could be the result.

And Cecily suddenly knew that, about three seconds from now, Isabelle was going to realize that Lucky was the only boy who'd been around Cecily in recent weeks at all. "It was just a boy who came to a show up in Wisconsin!" she blurted. "It was just a mistake! He surprised me!"

"He *surprised* you? What does *that* mean?"

"He—he was kissing me, I let him kiss me, because he was nice and good-looking and everything, and then suddenly he was doing things I didn't understand! And it felt nice at first, and then, and then it just surprised me! And then he left and I never saw him again, because we were off to the next town! I never—never thought—this!"

"Goddamn it, Jackie, I explained all this to you! What did you need, illustrations? Signposts?"

"I'm sorry. I'm sorry!"

Isabelle scowled. "Listen, you sit tight. I'll be right back. I'm going to help you, goddamn it. *Capiche?*" And she was gone.

Cecily instantly started to cry, out of relief and fear. Isabelle had bought her story! (*Pregnant!* Cecily was *pregnant?* She wanted to scream!) But Lucky would be safe! And everything was going to be all right now, wasn't it? Isabelle was going to help her.

Isabelle would help. The thought calmed Cecily. No matter how nasty Isabelle had been in recent weeks, they were sisters—sworn always to help each other.

A tiny thrill began to whir within her. *Lucky.* Lucky hadn't left her, after all. A part of Lucky was growing inside her right now.

She rubbed her belly in a slow circle. She couldn't feel anything inside there, but there could be no doubt that Isabelle was right.

Could there?

No. Her whole body felt warm, sparkling. For the first time since Lucky'd been gone, she didn't feel the least bit sick.

"Hello," Cecily whispered to her belly. "I love you. I love you. Can you hear me? I love you. Hello!"

Ten minutes later, Isabelle was back, slamming the door behind her and holding up a long knitting needle like a conductor's baton. Cecily scooted backward, shrinking into the corner of her bunk, and every cell of her body was screaming in alarm, without her even quite knowing why.

"I'll explain to you what to do," Isabelle said. "I had to do it once a long time ago, to myself. It hurt and bled like hell, but it made it so I never had a problem again, so that's good, right?" She tried to laugh.

Cecily worked her mouth. "What do you mean?"

Isabelle rolled her eyes. "Do I have spell out everything for you, kid? A. B. C. You stick this up in there and make it so the baby can't grow, all right?"

Tears sprang to Cecily's eyes.

"Oh, Jesus," Isabelle said. "Don't get sentimental on me."

Cecily began to cry in earnest. She put her hands over her belly. "No."

Isabelle stepped closer. The knitting needle in her hand was long and thin and terrifying. "You want to let this ruin your life? Am I going to have to tie you down and do it for you? Save you from yourself?"

"No!"

"You've got to do it right away, or it'll just hurt worse and worse."

"Isabelle, no!"

"You can't be a bareback rider and be pregnant, kid." At that, Isabelle stopped. "I don't know why I'm trying to help you."

"You're my sister!" Cecily screamed. She was backed as far into the corner of the bunk as she could go. "Why would you want to hurt me?"

Isabelle's face changed, then, and she staggered back on her heels. She covered her mouth with her hand. "Oh, Christ. Christ! You didn't meet some kid in Wisconsin, did you?"

Cecily's throat closed up. *No! God!* She prayed: *Don't let her know, please, please don't let her know—*

But Isabelle's eyes were fire. "I saw you with him! I saw the way you looked at him. The way he looked at you. I told Tebow he'd better start keeping the two of you apart! But I never in a thousand years thought you would've actually crossed that line. For God's sake, you little fucking idiot—do you know what they'll *do* to you, if you have a baby that looks like *him*, especially down *here*—after everything I've done for you, trying to keep you safe, keep you fucking *virtuous*, God! I should've let Tebow have you the first time he wanted you! You don't know the gyrations I went through—and now to think you gave it away to some—"

"I told you, it was a kid in Wisconsin!" Cecily broke in.

"Don't you lie to me. You disgust me. You *disgust* me! And you had this caboose to yourself all these weeks—did you let him *in* here? You did, didn't you? Oh, Christ. Christ. I can't believe I was going to help you. I can't believe I felt *sorry* for you. You knew exactly what you were doing! And you *lied* to me. You are dead to me, Jackie. *D-E-A-D*. Dead. You goddamn whore."

And Isabelle whirled and was gone, slamming the door behind her.

It took a long time for Cecily to stop crying. But, once she did, she had to think: Surely, no matter what Isabelle had said in anger, the fact that they'd been sisters for so long would mean she was still on Cecily's side. She would come around. Apologize. Help. Cecily loved Isabelle; she had loved her for a very long time.

But Isabelle didn't speak to Cecily that night during the show—not to apologize, not to say anything at all.

Janey didn't speak to Cecily either, which was unusual, but not necessarily alarming in itself. Because nor was there any disruption to the usual routine, no call to come and talk to Tebow, nothing.

So, Cecily thought, *Well, maybe she's just going to keep it to herself? Let me figure out what to do when the season's over?* They had only three more weeks on the schedule.

Maybe Lucky would still come back.

He had to, now, didn't he?

The next morning, in Asheville, there was a loud knock on the door of the caboose. Cecily was feeling queasy, but she hadn't thrown up yet. In fact, she was dressed and ready to go to breakfast, for the first time in almost three weeks. It was as if knowing the truth about what was happening inside her body had set her free. (She was thinking: she could get through the rest of the season, have the baby in the spring, and come back to work again right after.) She had her copy of *Sense and Sensibility* in the deep pocket of her cardigan, and tucked inside it were the snapshot of Lucky and her Saint Jude card, which she had decided, from now on, she would carry with her everywhere.

Please, she said, imagining somehow it would be Lucky at the door.

But, as she moved to answer it, she heard Isabelle call out, "She's in there, I know she's in there, just go in."

And the door opened and a big police officer filled the doorway, and he grabbed Cecily's arm and dragged her out the door and down off the vestibule, where Isabelle and Tebow stood. Tebow, at least, had the grace to look regretful, wiping his brow with his handkerchief. Isabelle sneered, "You made your bed, you dirty little cunt, now go lie in it."

Cecily was shoved into the back of a police sedan that smelled of sour sweat, and they drove her through the downtown streets to jail.

To *jail!* It was in the back of a gigantic tower of a courthouse, all marble and stone and cold tile.

"We've got a place we send no-good girls like you," the sheriff said, as he turned the big key to lock her inside a damp cell. "Don't think we don't. The ole judge'll fix you up *good* with a sentence, you better believe."

"There must be some mistake," Cecily said, gripping the cold iron bars. She could almost feel the baby, swimming nervous circles in her belly. "I am Jacqueline DuMonde."

"Frenchie," sneered the sheriff. "Figures." He ambled away, keys on his belt jingling.

Alone in the cell, Cecily stood listening until she couldn't hear the sound of him anymore, then sighed and went to sit down on the hard wooden bench in the corner. She was too dismayed to cry. *Isabelle. Tebow. Prince.* Her circus family. All the vows Isabelle had made—

Cecily blinked. She couldn't think about any of that. If she did, she'd start to cry and never stop.

Anyway, she had always deep down believed that Sax & Tebow wouldn't keep her, so to find herself here didn't surprise her as much as it might have.

She squared her shoulders and decided: She would only look ahead and not back. She would be strong for the baby. Stewing in anger and heartbreak would surely be bad for him, so she would not do it. (Suddenly, she was certain: the baby was a boy. She would name him Thomas Moses, for her father, and his. *Tommy.*)

The sheriff hadn't bothered to search her pockets. She took out *Sense and Sensibility*, flipping through till she found the snapshot of Lucky, the prayer card.

Please, she prayed, staring at Saint Jude, her vision blurring.

She knew what she was asking for was maybe the most impossible thing Saint Jude had ever been asked for, but she wasn't going to stop believing. Even if he had never brought her mother to her. No, she would still not stop believing. She would not stop asking, she would not stop praying, she would not stop.

Please help me and Tommy find Lucky. Please keep us all safe. I don't know how. But please. Make us a family. Help us be a family.

Please!

PART THREE

Bittersweet

CHAPTER 31

November–December 1935
North Carolina Reformatory for Wayward Girls

C ecily was given a scratchy gray wool uniform and assigned to a cot in the dormitory of a massive, cold stone building called Rathbone Hall, which was on the huge campus of rolling hills blanketed with tall trees of the North Carolina Reformatory for Wayward Girls.

She'd spent three weeks in the county jail, then the judge had sentenced her to Wayward, as it was commonly known, until she was "at least" twenty-one years old, at which point her case would be "reevaluated." A social worker who'd claimed to be "familiar with the case," citing an interview with Cecily's "heartbroken, desperate older sister," had testified it was clear that (despite the older sister's "countless, selfless efforts") Cecily was incorrigible, a transient, a sex delinquent, certainly feebleminded and a danger to herself and others. That she had reputedly "(*whisper whisper*) with a Negro" and refused either to confirm or deny it ("a sure sign of confirmation"), the social worker said, showed she was past the point of no return, a complete psychopath of a type rarely seen in girls native to North Carolina. "We have a certain prostitute and potential murderess on our hands; a clear and present danger to society," said the social worker. "She cannot be allowed to roam free in our state."

As the judge handed down her sentence, he told Cecily sternly that he hoped six years at Wayward would be enough to set her straight, but he wasn't confident.

Cecily had held tightly to the Saint Jude card in her pocket, teeth clenched, knowing this was not the turn that her life had been meant to take, not at all.

"Oh, yeah, they say we're all feebleminded," said her new friend, Alice, who had the next cot over in Rathbone. Alice's thick blond hair, cut bluntly short, looked like a bad mistake, and she picked at her scalp and face almost constantly, leaving behind angry pink welts. She looked to be about fourteen; she'd been at Wayward since she was ten. She'd warned Cecily already that, if you tried to run away, they never failed to catch you, and you'd get whipped.

"Whipped?" Cecily said.

"Hickory switch. They make the other girls hold you down. The more times you try to run, the worse the switchin's get." Alice spoke as if she knew this from experience. "But, if they decide you're good, they move you on over to an honor cottage and you get to go on picnics." She gave Cecily a swift up-and-down look. "I doubt that'll happen for you."

Cecily didn't know if the other girls were aware that Cecily was expecting a baby. Tommy didn't show much yet, at least not in the baggy uniform, though he was definitely a part of her permanent record. When Cecily had first arrived, she'd been sent to the office of the superintendent, Miss Peters, who'd sat behind her desk, peering through the metal-framed glasses perched on the tip of her long nose, scanning the notes from Cecily's trial. When she looked up, her eyebrows were furrowed. "What it doesn't say here is what a *pretty* thing you are. Your eyes are just stunning. Was the father of your child handsome?"

Cecily didn't stop to think what an odd question that was. "Yes, very."

Miss Peters sniffed. "A Negro?"

"No," Cecily lied, crossing her fingers in her lap, down behind the desk where Miss Peters wouldn't see. At her trial, Cecily had said nothing; had let Isabelle's version of events stand as the truth. She was proud to love Lucky, and she didn't want to take it back, not even in any small way. But now she was beginning to see that she needed to do anything she could to protect their baby, and that, right here and now, to protect him was to lie. She had not realized there were actual laws against her and Lucky being together; that he had been right to think it would make some people angry enough to kill them.

Miss Peters cocked her head. "Now, child, why wouldn't you have said that in your trial? Your sentence might have been reduced."

"Oh, I tried to tell them," Cecily lied again.

Miss Peters sighed. "I tell you, this is a relief to me. I did not want to believe all that had been said of you, a pretty little thing like you. You were a transient?"

Cecily sat up straighter. "I was the star of a well-known traveling circus with an excellent reputation."

Miss Peters laughed, made a note, then looked up again. "Did the father of your child have blue eyes, by chance?"

Cecily could tell Miss Peters wanted the answer to be yes. So, fingers still crossed, she nodded.

Miss Peters nodded crisply in return. "Very good. It may be that we can make some special arrangements for you and your baby. It may be that this may all turn out very well for all of us, indeed."

Miss Peters then sent Cecily over to the reformatory infirmary for a "standard" two-week quarantine. A week or so in, the nurse told her that Miss Peters had made arrangements so that, when Cecily's time came closer, she would be sent to a "home," to stay until the baby arrived. "Lucky you! Not many girls get to do that. Now, don't you worry, they'll take good care of you there, and then you'll come right straight back to us!" The nurse, whose name was Miss Everett, had said this cheerfully, as if it was good news. Cecily wondered what kind of home it was (with a nice family? she could dream), and where the reformatory planned to house her and baby Tommy upon return. Not in the dormitory with the other girls, certainly? She hadn't seen any other babies here at all, and one thing she'd learned, starting when Isabelle had threatened her with the knitting needle, was that she wasn't the first girl ever to have a baby before she was married.

Better to keep quiet than to ask too many questions, though. Questions would draw attention, and she was already dead set on running away, never mind Alice's warnings. She just needed to get the lay of the land, so she could make a foolproof plan. She was determined to find Lucky before the baby was born, though how she'd manage it, she had no idea. The first step was to escape—soon, before Tommy made travel too hard. She was going to have to act quickly and decisively, same as turning a flip on Prince's back while he was running, then figure out the rest after that.

"What did you do to get in here?" Cecily asked Alice, but Alice just shrugged, her eyes darting back and forth, before she looked at her shoes, began picking her scalp again.

Cecily had aced every single mental acuity test Miss Everett had given her, and Miss Everett had noted everything in a thick file, which she said with a smile would go to "the board" for "review." Moreover, Miss Everett, showing she believed the results, had given Cecily an actual medical book to read, so that Cecily could learn all about how the baby was growing inside her. Miss Everett had also respectfully, even cheerfully, answered all Cecily's questions on the finer points of the matter.

Alice said none of that made one bit of difference. "They're still gonna call you feebleminded, 'cause they say only feebleminded girls do it."

The girls were shoveling manure out of the hogpen. Cecily's hands were cold on the rough handle of the shovel; her uniform itched her skin. But, Alice had said, better to be cold than to be in the heat of summer, when the manure stunk to high heaven.

"Do what?" Cecily said.

Alice laughed.

The food at Wayward was nothing like in the circus. Dried beans, mostly. Grits without butter. Cornbread, hoecakes. Canned tomatoes and green beans the girls had grown in the garden. Eggs from the chickens they kept. Alice said butchering season was coming soon, and then there'd be bacon and sausage. Certain girls were assigned to kitchen duty—cooking, cleaning, canning, sausage-making—and others to the farm. "We'll do the butcherin'," Alice explained. "And we deal with the shit, as you know." She laughed.

Cecily, still a "new arrival," on probation, had to make it through three months before she'd be considered for an honor cottage or a kitchen job, either one. Already she'd decided that escaping would be easier after she was assigned to an honor cottage, even taking into account that, three months from now, it would be the dead of winter, and she'd be more than six months pregnant. According to the book Miss Everett had let her read, that would mean she and Tommy both would be getting pretty big.

Still, she was convinced that waiting was the right plan. One, after she was in an honor cottage, the staff, having labeled her a "good girl," wouldn't be watching her so closely. Two, the honor cottages housed only twelve girls each, and they backed up close to the forest. All Cecily would have to do was not wake up eleven other girls while she sneaked out a back window and dashed for the woods. In Rathbone, 150 girls slept in wards of fifty each, and the slightest cough of one never failed to disturb at least a dozen others. Plus, six staff matrons were always keeping a strict eye over everything, and it was a long break over a wide lawn before you'd make it to any woods.

Everybody said there'd never been a girl who'd attempted escape and not been caught. But a lot of the girls in here weren't the brightest bulbs, Cecily had noticed. The ones who'd tried probably hadn't had a foolproof plan, or they'd blabbed to someone who'd ended up tattling.

So, Cecily didn't say a word to anyone, not even Alice. She bided her time. She still did her best to look only ahead, never back. She tried not to think about Isabelle or Tebow, or even Prince—not even when she woke in the night to the coughing of some other girl.

She tried to think not about the brief time she'd had with Lucky, nor about the pain of his being gone, but only of finding him again. She would go to Harlem, she'd decided. He had spoken of a librarian there who had been his friend.

For now, for her plan to work, all she had to do was behave herself and be polite, so as not to get demerits.

She was feeding the chickens on a muddy, cold day just after Christmas when Fern Aiken walked by and said, "Heard you got a baby growing in you," then added something insulting about what sort of baby she'd heard it was.

For fighting, Cecily was hauled to the office of Miss Peters, where she was given fifteen demerits, extra barnyard duty, and official notice that she would not possibly be considered for an honor cottage until the first of April—provided she didn't cause any more trouble in the meantime.

Then Miss Peters consulted her notes. "And yet, I've scheduled you to go to the Home in the early part of March, because I'd thought you were a better class of girl." She looked up, her mouth a placid line, her eyes pinpricks of mean. "I hope you won't make me regret making these *very special* arrangements for you. It's not one girl in two years who gets to go to the Home, you realize!"

Cecily flinched, cradling her belly in her hands. She was almost sure she felt Tommy kick. Her face ached where Fern had slugged her. Fern had gotten off scot-free, blaming Cecily for starting the fight.

"If we *do* have any more trouble with you between now and then," Miss Peters added, "the state prison is also an option. I hear it isn't so pleasant, giving birth there." She sniffed, adjusted her glasses, straightened her sheaf of papers. "That's all, Jacqueline."

Since the moment Cecily had been hauled off the train in Asheville by the police, she had never told anyone her real name. Somehow, it made all of this easier to bear.

Anyway, savvy, sassy Jackie DuMonde could handle anything—even things that might break Cecily in two.

CHAPTER 32

March–April 2015
Itasca, Minnesota

Liz did not like the feeling of waiting on things she could not control. And yet, nearly everything in her life was that way right now. Her MRI had been pushed back a week, and Cecily's recovery had been slow enough that her return home from The Pines was being delayed indefinitely. (Liz had started trying to find at-home twenty-four-hour care for her, but, even when it was for Cecily Larson, the old grande dame of Itasca's medical community, good luck, especially without a known start date—and, Lord, the cost! Liz had not come close to imagining it, and Cecily didn't have much money saved, after all her contributions to this and that community drive.)

And then, for some reason, these damn DNA results were niggling at Liz—as if she couldn't *stand* to wait for them another day.

Caden had shown her on his laptop the family tree he was building on Ancestry.com—so far, just for his father, Evan's, side. A sepia-toned photo of his great-great-grandfather Bouchard as a young man— uploaded by some other relative—had appeared. Incredible! Was it too much to hope that the Anderson/Larson side of Caden's tree could be filled in to such a degree? Would there be a photo of one of Liz's great-great-grandfathers or -grandmothers? Maybe Sam's father's father, who Liz understood had emigrated from Norway, or even—it was a stretch—a far-back ancestor on Cecily's side? (If the DNA revealed who her parents were, Caden said, Ancestry would probably know who her grandparents were, too.)

As much as all this was on Liz's mind, it was hard not to ask Cecily what else she might know, but Liz mostly held back, not wanting to tax Cecily. Besides, the couple times Liz tried, Cecily only said things like, "Oh, your father didn't like to talk about his family, so I don't really know, hon." Or, "I barely remember anything that happened before I met your father at the San. Maybe the TB destroyed my memory!" (At this, Cecily laughed.)

It made Liz think, in a way that hadn't ever occurred to her before, that her mother could be hiding something.

Well. Hiding something. Cecily wasn't well, Liz had to remember. And, Cecily was nearly ninety-five—even if she'd never acted her age before, maybe it was catching up with her.

And maybe Liz just had too much time to think, after all, spending so many hours in her studio, turning piece after piece for the Empty Bowl. She'd managed two kiln firings and was completing the work for the third. It was in the evenings, mostly, that she could get to the studio, and, even when she felt so tired that it was difficult to keep working, let alone keep standing, she loved watching the sunsets splashing pink across the frozen lake—or, some nights, the snow sprinkling down—as she worked at the wheel or set the turned pieces in exact rows to dry. For each bowl she got trimmed and ready for firing, she made a satisfying pencil tally mark on the white-painted wall, which made her feel permanent in a way that she knew she was not. Her shoulders and back were stiff (*not the cancer, spreading?* she thought, with an alarm that simply could not be sustained, so she set the thought aside) from the work. She was experimenting with bolder glazes: reds and blues, rather than her usual earthen tones.

It was consoling to think that, at least when it came to making bowls, she had some control over the outcome.

Then, they were done. And none too soon. The first of April. The fundraiser was tomorrow, and Liz's MRI in Duluth was the day after that. (The timing of everything was working out with a satisfying symmetry, after all.)

Molly came out to the lake house to help Liz wrap and pack the bowls, bringing cardboard boxes and brown wrapping paper, carting them through the slush down to the studio, and she couldn't seem to stop talking about Evan.

"He's had Caden on the phone *every* night, putting together this ridiculous Bouchard family tree. I guess they're, like, Skyping, sharing the screen or something, I don't know. They're getting deep into all these records, going back, like, seven generations, and, meanwhile, Caden's falling behind on other schoolwork. I texted Evan to say there needs to be more balance, especially with track season starting next week, and he just texted me back a thumbs-up emoji." She rolled her eyes, shaking her head.

Liz knew Molly wasn't over the divorce yet—wasn't over *Evan* yet; that much had been clear when he was in town—and that these were serious, grown-up problems, but somehow, just to hear Molly prattling on made Liz so happy that she couldn't help but laugh. "You know, if Caden was pursuing *your* side of the family tree like this, you'd say it showed his absolute wisdom, maturity, and devotion."

"—Mom!" Then Molly brushed her platinum hair out of her eyes and laughed, too.

"One of our featured contributing artists today, Liz Larson Anderson, comes from a long line of community philanthropists, her parents being none other than Dr. Sam and Cecily Larson." Vivvy Bengtson had always liked the sound of her own voice, ever since she and Liz had been in high school together, and today at the Empty Bowl, she had a captive audience of a size rarely gathered in Itasca: three hundred, all seated at long tables set up in the high school gym. Heaven, for Vivvy. She'd been talking for ten minutes already about the artists who'd contributed, the amazing arts community in Itasca, the need for everyone to be aware of food insecurity in the region, and the beauty of how it all came together, life sustaining life. Her thesis hadn't exactly all made sense, but she'd made it sound—clearly to her own ears, at least—like poetry. Somewhere in the middle of it all, Liz had quietly rolled her eyes at Molly, seated across from her, who'd hidden a sly smile behind her napkin.

"Now, you all probably know," Vivvy continued, "that Cecily Larson almost single-handedly raised the funds for both the new hospital and the performing arts center, and that hardly an event in Itasca these last sixty years hasn't been graced by one of her spectacular fifteen-layer cakes." Murmurs of appreciation. "And that Dr. Sam Larson—who was the son of Dr. Henrik Larson before him, who was the town doctor starting way back in 1910—now, Dr. *Sam* Larson, Liz's father, cared for pretty much this whole town through the fifties, sixties, and seventies! And many of us of a certain age were delivered by him! Did you know, it's a documented fact that he delivered five hundred and sixty-two babies over his career in Itasca!" Applause. Vivvy bowed her head and blushed modestly, as if she'd accomplished the feat herself.

Then she went on: "Now, for those of you who didn't know, our Cecily suffered a broken hip a couple months ago and is in recovery at The Pines." Murmurs of dismay, concern. *Oh, Lord,* Liz thought, *here come the hotdishes.* But that was just her high school self talking, out of habit resenting Vivvy and the small kindnesses of this town that could feel to Liz like burdens. Maybe some fresh flower arrangements would arrive for Cecily; maybe Cecily would allow some visitors again. That would be good. That could *help* Cecily. "So, let's give Liz Larson Anderson a *big* hand for continuing to make good after all these years on her family's legacy, and for fulfilling her commitment to make and donate *a hundred and fourteen bowls* today, even as she's been caring for our Cecily!" There was a warm round of applause, a whistle or two. Liz gave a slight wave, uncomfortable with the attention.

Her mother, though, would've loved it—would've probably jumped up and made a speech, telling everyone her next big idea for Itasca, where their next contribution should go. Liz smiled to imagine it.

"Mom, I can't believe you didn't tell me this before," Molly said, pulling into her parking spot behind her office. Yesterday out at the house, they'd loaded the bowls into the back of Molly's car; this morning, they'd ridden together to the high school to unload them. Now, with the event over, goodbyes and thank-yous and get-well-soons (to pass on to Cecily) all said, Liz, for reasons she could not explain, had finally broken the news about her MRI.

"You've had so much on your mind. I didn't want you to worry."

"Well, that's nice, Mom, but, also, ridiculous! You have a *lump*, it's *cancerous*, and you're having an MRI tomorrow to see if the cancer's spread. That's the kind of thing you tell your daughter as it's *happening*. Does Grandma know?"

"No! No, I didn't want to tell her. She's not well enough for news like this. I want her focused on her own recovery."

Molly's face crumpled. She shook her head slightly. "Well, I'm going with you to Duluth tomorrow. I can reschedule my clients. I just wish you'd told me sooner."

I have spared you weeks of worrying, Liz wanted to say. *I didn't have to tell you at all.* "I'll be fine on my own," she said, though she wasn't precisely sure. Maybe the suspicion that she might not be was what had made her finally speak up.

"We're *family*, Mom," Molly scolded. "Honestly."

And Liz, for reasons she could not explain, just laughed out loud. Maybe it was all too much. Her son on the other side of the world. Her husband gone. Her dad gone. Her mom "in recovery," but so very, very old. Liz would be the oldest generation soon—and its only representative. And how long would *she* last? It was *all* ridiculous, when you thought of it. The way time and life skated by. "I am aware of that, Molly. I was there when you were born, remember?"

Molly laughed. "Mom," she chided good-naturedly—but there was a tear shining in her eye.

And suddenly Liz did something she almost never did—leaned over and fiercely hugged Molly. She wanted to say how sorry she was, for all her shortcomings and failures, all the ways she'd been disconnected and strange. *Lost in her art,* was how people in Itasca described her, she knew. *She does beautiful work—have you seen?*

No excuse, when you came right down to it.

"Oh, Molly," she said, holding her daughter tight. "I'm sorry. Everything's going to be okay."

And this was the job of a mother, wasn't it? To try to spare her children pain—even if it meant telling a lie.

And Liz realized suddenly: Cecily *was* hiding something.

She thought about their sending in Cecily's DNA without Cecily's knowledge or consent. The bad feeling she'd had since then. Oh, the feeling of general foreboding could be about the cancer, yes. But—what if it was a knowing, deep inside, that Cecily had been keeping something from her all these years?

Oh, honestly, she scolded herself. Probably everyone in the world had this feeling while waiting for DNA results, right? And when the results arrived and showed that all was as expected, you'd just laugh to think of the foolish things you'd imagined, in the back, dark recesses of your mind.

Yet. Liz remembered something. Back when she was about eleven, a young woman—a teenager, really—Marcy, had come to stay in the guest room at Liz's parents' house, arriving just after Christmas and staying until spring. She'd helped out a little around the house, but mostly stayed in her room and listened to records—"Rockin' Robin," "All I Have to Do Is Dream"; sometimes she'd let Liz inside and the two of them would dance—as the baby inside her belly grew and grew. When it was time for the birth, Liz's father had delivered the baby in his office downstairs. Highly unusual. Liz still remembered Marcy's screams.

But what she remembered most of all now was, the day her father got back from bringing Marcy and the baby to Minneapolis, Liz, who was walking down the back stairs because she'd heard his car pull into the driveway and wanted to greet him, overheard her parents in the kitchen, and the grave tones of their voices had made her stop to listen. Her father was saying something about how Marcy was brokenhearted, but it was for the best, as her parents would take her back, this way, and he had met the couple adopting the baby and they seemed like fine people, and Cecily was crying, saying, "I can't do this again, Sam. I want to help them, but it's just too hard!"

And Sam had said softly, "You know we're not doing what was done to you."

Liz had crept back up the stairs so they wouldn't know she'd overheard, and, not having been able to make sense of what had been said, never thought much about it again. And Marcy was the only girl who'd ever stayed with them in order to have a baby, so there was no reason to think of it, really. But now she heard her father saying it: *what was done to you.*

What had been done to Cecily?

Was this DNA test going to turn up some baby she'd given up for adoption, before Liz was born? Some past trauma that, as the truth emerged and the memories resurfaced, could hurt Cecily—even *kill* her, at this stage? Yes, shocking news of any kind could probably actually kill her!

Oh, God, Liz thought, even as she stroked Molly's hair. *What have I done?*

CHAPTER 33

Spring 1936
North Carolina Reformatory for Wayward Girls

Alice tried to run away. Cecily had no idea she was planning it. And maybe she hadn't been planning it, exactly—rumor was that a group of high school boys lurking around the periphery of the grounds had been involved, perhaps as inspiration—but, either way, Alice ended up back at Rathbone, and all the girls were called in to the library to watch her be whipped.

Miss Peters pointed, then crooked her finger, at one uniformed girl after another, and each stepped forward for the job of holding Alice down. Alice was already lying facedown, spread-eagled, on the threadbare rug, dressed in only a thin cotton shift, and Miss Peters had the hickory switch in her hand. Cecily tried to hide behind Eleanor Kelly, who was a good six inches taller, but Miss Peters saw her and pointed, said, "Jacqueline. Come now."

Cecily's feet were lead, as she walked over to kneel beside Alice's shoulder. Tommy was big enough now that kneeling was awkward, even painful. Other girls held each of Alice's feet, her legs. The girl stationed across from Cecily, at Alice's other shoulder, looked up at Cecily and grinned, scraggly hair falling over gleaming eyes.

Cecily put one hand on Alice's upper arm. Alice's skin was hot. She was already crying softly. Cecily, moving her body so that Miss Peters wouldn't see, gripped Alice's hand.

"This is Alice Beene's *fourth* attempt at running away," Miss Peters announced to the room. "So she will receive forty lashes. You all will count aloud with me."

Miss Peters turned toward where Alice lay and looked at her a long moment, then raised her arm.

The switch flew, made contact. Alice cried out; Cecily flinched. "One!" said the room.

Switch, cry, flinch. "Two!"

By ten, Alice was writhing, sobbing. Tears streamed down Cecily's face, too.

By twenty, stripes of blood showed through Alice's gown.

The girls chanted on: "Twenty-one!"

Cecily cowered, feeling the intermittent breeze of the flying switch, holding Alice's hand tight enough to crush the bones. She imagined herself on Prince's back, cantering around the ring, her arms circled above her, the cheering of the crowd; Prince nuzzling her afterward, nibbling a carrot out of her hand. She thought of Lucky, running his hand sweetly over her hair. His body curled around hers, his strong arms holding her. *Let be be finale of seem.* Somewhere in this world, there was love. There was. There was.

That night, long after lights out, Cecily heard Alice sniffling. She'd been taken directly to the infirmary after the whipping—Eleanor Kelly and another of the taller girls had had to half carry, half drag her between them—and Cecily had been certain Miss Everett would keep her there at least a week. But no. She'd come limping back just before lights out, not meeting anyone's eyes. She'd creaked her way down onto the bed, lying facedown, of course.

Cecily herself was still trembling, and she said nothing to her friend—they'd get in trouble if she did. She thought of her old friend Dolores at the orphanage, late at night in the next cot over. *Something bad's gonna happen; I don't know yet just what.*

Cecily cradled her growing belly. It was ten lashes for each attempt at running away.

Ten lashes had seemed pretty bad. To lie on her stomach and take it? Ten lashes would hurt Tommy, no question. Besides, there was the threat of the state prison.

Was she going to have to wait until she got to the Home, *then* figure out a way to escape?

Waiting seemed as impossible as not waiting—but she had to do one or the other.

It was a week before Alice would speak to Cecily again, and Cecily didn't blame her one bit. Finally, though, with things seemingly back to normal, on a snow-coated morning in the hogpen, Cecily asked in a whisper, "Why do you do it, Alice? Why do you run?"

Alice shrugged, then winced from the motion. "Just can't stop myself, sometimes."

"But what are you running *to?*"

"Nothin'. Just running *away*. Been doing it all my life."

"Is that why you were sent here?" It was a common reason girls ended up at Wayward: "incorrigible" running.

"Sure, I ran away from my daddy. Every time I could. He always caught me, too. And then my stepma caught him in my bed with me. That's when I got sent here. He said he'd kill me if I didn't get out of his sight. She like to kill me, too. Only I bet he's been doing it to my little sister ever since I been gone. She was just gettin' to the age he liked." Her mouth worked for a moment, then she spat: "Seven."

Cecily felt this settling into her bones. Seven. Like she'd been when Tebow had come and bought her from the orphanage. "Oh, Alice," was all she could say.

Alice grimaced, shrugged, scratched hard at her head, then went back to shoveling manure, drawing in a sharp breath with each motion.

And whatever part of Cecily had still been considering running settled down, like a coin falling into a slot. Things were not as they had been for her before. She wasn't alone in the world now. She was loved; if she ran, she would be running to find Lucky, not just running away. That meant she had to be smart. Keep herself and Tommy safe, first and foremost. It was just her fate to be here now. She didn't have to like it. But she would wait it out, for Tommy.

The McNaughton Children's Home was on a tree-shrouded lot in the city of Wilmington. (Cecily, who'd assumed she'd be sent somewhere near Wayward, had been surprised to be told she was being taken on the train by Miss Peters; the rattling and clanking that were the sounds of home had lulled her to sleep so instantly and thoroughly that she'd had no time to plot escape. Anyway, she figured, better to wait till Miss Peters was long gone, back to Wayward.) The Home had a wide front porch with wicker furniture, where the girls—there were five others, all just as pregnant as Cecily—were not allowed to sit, because they were not to be seen. But they were allowed to go into the back garden and wander the winding brick paths. There was a bench among the shrubbery where Cecily could sit and read, and, when she arrived, the dogwoods were in bloom.

"Your only concern now is to grow a healthy baby," said Mrs. Oglethorpe, the house matron, looking over the thick file that Miss Peters had brought from Wayward. After a moment, Mrs. Oglethorpe slapped the file shut, locked it into her desk drawer, and smiled up at Cecily, as if she'd decided to pay it no mind. Cecily was wearing a white dress, which Miss Peters had given her, and Mrs. Oglethorpe had said Cecily would be provided with more pretty clothing, with everything she could possibly need. "You need not tell anyone that you've come to us from Wayward," she said. "In fact, it's best if you don't."

Dr. Addington, who came twice a week to check on the girls and who'd examined Cecily immediately upon her arrival, said the same things, plus, "What a pretty little momma you'll make." He had sparkling blue eyes and a thick white mustache. "Miss Peters did not exaggerate your charms. We'll just hope you don't have any trouble on account of being so small."

Cecily blinked nervously at that. The part she'd read in Miss Everett's book about how the baby was actually born had struck her as literally impossible. She had been too afraid even to ask Miss Everett to explain.

"And you won't give *us* any trouble, will you?" the doctor added, with a slight frown. "We don't take many scholarship girls, you understand. It's a considerable risk for us."

"No, sir, I won't be any trouble," Cecily promised. She wished she could get a look at Miss Peters's file, so she'd know for sure what all they really thought of her.

Meals were served at a long table in a formal dining room, where Mrs. Oglethorpe enforced manners that Evelyn Danner, who was from Virginia, swore were stricter than what she'd learned at finishing school. Cecily tried her best, at first, but soon—not wanting to stand out as a scholarship girl—joined the others in rolling her eyes about the extended instruction in the finer points of finger bowls, melon spoons, butter knives. Mrs. Oglethorpe remained undiscouraged. "You girls are going to make lives for yourselves after this, I promise you," she would say, and she was not unkind about it. "That's why we don't let you out to be seen within the community. So that you'll have some prayer of leaving here and building a new life afterward, with no one the wiser of the way your reputations have been compromised."

To such statements, the other girls nodded mutely, gave little smiles. Cecily just put her hands over her belly. She was still trying to get the lay of the land; some days it felt like that was all she'd ever done, all her life, wherever in the world she was, and that she'd never once fully comprehended it.

For one example, right now it was hard times all over the country—desperate times, really. But Louise Gibson had asked Cecily where *her* father had gotten the two hundred dollars a month it cost to keep her at the Home. "Mine writes me every month with the tally of what he's spent, and it'll be a thousand by the end. He's making me marry his biggest business rival when I get back, because he says he's not spending another dime on me and my bad decisions after this, and it'll serve Henry right for being a thorn in his side the last twenty years." She laughed. "They've told him I'm on a six-month European tour, and I'm supposed to be studying, so, if he asks me about it later, I'll be able to describe the Parthenon, the Louvre, all of that. Train trips across the glorious countryside, and the one time my trunks got lost, I guess. My father has my aunt mailing poor old Henry postcards from her travels, pretending they're from me."

But that all had to be a joke. Didn't it? (*Two hundred dollars a month?*)

Cecily was also dismayed to learn that the other girls were all planning to give up their babies for adoption. "It's in the best interest of the child," Mrs. Oglethorpe said, to which the girls gave their small smiles and nods and even echoed her—some sadly, some with relief (and Louise Gibson seemingly with relish). One girl, Harriet, chattered on about how she'd been promised that the McNaughton Home only adopted babies out to families that had an indoor toilet, plus a bathtub with faucets and running water. She was seventeen, and—maybe she hadn't had as easy a life as Louise and Evelyn had—to her, indoor plumbing seemed to be all that mattered. "He'll grow up in the lap of luxury. He'll take as many baths as he likes! Maybe even every day!"

When Cecily said there was no way she was giving up her baby, indoor plumbing or not, she was called into Mrs. Oglethorpe's office. She told Mrs. Oglethorpe that the baby was the only family she'd ever had, that her own mother had given her up and she would never, ever do that to her child, because she knew exactly how it felt.

Mrs. Oglethorpe frowned, folding her hands atop her desk. "Jacqueline, you're fifteen years old, and, though we've been doing our best not to mention this point, you've been sentenced to stay at Wayward until you're twenty-one."

Cecily pointed her chin, not about to say that she had no plans whatsoever of seeing that sentence through. "That doesn't mean I don't love my baby."

Mrs. Oglethorpe looked surprised at first, then just sat back and smiled slightly. "Well. You have some time to think about it," she said.

A woman named Millie came in to cook; another (Josephine) to clean and do laundry; an old, silent man to work in the garden. The sheets on Cecily's bed were crisp and clean, and she had a private room. It took her some time to believe it, but the girls honestly only had to do light work: make their beds each morning; keep their rooms tidy and themselves clean and well dressed; dry and put away the dishes (Millie always washed) after meals.

A handwritten, framed placard next to a portrait of Susanna McNaughton in the front foyer explained that the old, childless widow, upon her death in 1925, had bequeathed not just her house to the cause of "unfortunate girls," but also a large sum of money. So maybe that (not to mention, if it was really true, the two hundred dollars per month the other girls were paying) could explain why and how the girls were being so lavishly cared for. Mrs. Oglethorpe, at every meal when she said grace, always thanked the late Mrs. McNaughton for her "unparalleled generosity."

Still, Cecily just plain had a bad feeling about things—a sense that it would take just one wrong move to get in the bad graces of the doctor and Mrs. Oglethorpe, and that the punishment would be swift, severe.

Though—all appearances were to the contrary! Whenever the doctor came to look in on the girls, he was nothing but cheerful and kind, exclaiming over how well they were doing, almost fatherly in his pride, as if they were accomplishing notable things. The girls were good-hearted, for the most part, so there was only the occasional squabble, nothing like the fight Cecily'd had with Fern, and so no cause to get on Mrs. Oglethorpe's bad side (assuming the lady had a bad side, which, in Cecily's experience, everybody did).

Cecily had deduced that she could probably walk straight out the front door and down the street to the train station any time she wanted, at least if she knew just where the train station was. The pull was in-tense, unquestionably. She figured she could find it. And she had started to hear Isabelle: *Do you know what they'll do to you down here, if you have a baby that looks like him?*

Yet, she had also begun to think: What would it be like out on the road? What would she find to eat? Would people try to hurt her? Where would she end up giving birth? Would there be a doctor, much less one as seemingly kind as Dr. Addington? And how would she pay for it? While it probably wouldn't cost her two hundred dollars (a month!) to have this baby out in the world, anything at all would be more than she had. Her cash had been left behind when she was taken by the police; all she'd managed to save were the snapshot of Lucky and the Saint Jude card, because they'd been tucked inside the copy of *Sense and Sensibility* that she'd had in her pocket that morning. She'd kept the book, the snapshot, and the card all carefully hidden ever since. (At Wayward, it was behind a loose board in the hog barn, and, no matter how much she'd wanted to, she'd never once taken them out, not until it was time to leave for the Home, when she'd kept them from being detected by Miss Peters by stashing them down the front of her underwear.)

Alone in her room now, she would pull them out and consider them. The book, mud-stained now. Inside its pages, the snapshot of handsome Lucky. The card showing the bearded saint. *Where are you?* she would ask them. *What am I supposed to do?*

They never answered.

She knew Harlem was a long, long way away. And, even if she could manage to find Lucky, what if that, rather than marking the end of her troubles, was just the start of a whole new kind? Where could they go to get married? *Would* she get him killed, just by loving him?

What if he didn't actually love her back?

In the months since he'd been gone, she'd seen a lot of the world, and seen it much more clearly than she'd ever had cause to before. Nothing she'd seen had left her optimistic.

It wasn't that she was thinking of giving up. She would always love Lucky. But she was seven months pregnant, penniless, and being cared for in fine style—for no reason at all, that she could see. And she thought maybe it wasn't wise to question her good fortune in this, even if she did still fear that somehow she would get on the bad side of the doctor and Mrs. Oglethorpe, and they would make her pay.

Then, one night, Harriet began screaming. Dr. Addington was called and quickly came, squealing to a halt at the curb in his Lincoln, running inside with his black bag in hand, his wife trailing behind. (Mrs. Addington, Louise whispered to Cecily, was a trained nurse who came to the Home only for births.) There was a room downstairs off the kitchen—a former pantry—where all the babies were born. It was kept very, very clean, and the doctor had all the equipment he needed in there, lined up in the glass-fronted cupboards and on the shelves.

Still, Harriet had a hard time. Her screams could be heard for twenty-four hours straight. The doctor and his wife came out for only the briefest breaks and didn't say a word to anyone, or even smile, which was very unlike the doctor. The girls exchanged nervous looks at the breakfast, lunch, and dinner table. "Buck up, girls," Mrs. Oglethorpe said. "You probably won't have this hard a time, and, even if you do, Dr. Addington will take good care of you."

Finally—finally!—they heard the sound of a baby's cry. It was past 9 P.M. on the second day, and the girls, waiting nervously in the parlor, hugged each other and laughed, pregnant bellies bumping.

After breakfast the following morning, a shiny black car pulled into the rear driveway, and an older couple in expensive-looking hats and coats—the woman's was the most beautiful royal blue, with a mink collar—stepped out. They came to the back door, and the girls watched as Dr. Addington handed over Harriet's baby, swaddled tightly in a blue blanket, to the lady, who looked stunned in a happy kind of way. Her husband handed the doctor a thick yellow envelope, then laid his hand gently atop the baby's tiny head and smiled.

Harriet limped out some hours later, and the girls helped her upstairs to her room. She was pale, her face tearstained. She said the baby had been breech. Thank God for Dr. Addington, she said, or she and the baby both would've died. "The couple who came for him—did they look like they had indoor plumbing?"

"Oh, yes! Yes, yes!" the girls assured her, telling her about the shiny car, the woman's royal-blue coat, and Harriet dissolved into fresh tears, as she crawled back into her freshly made-up bed.

Late that night in her room, Cecily cried, too, flat on her back in her own bed. For the first time, she was frightened, so frightened that the hair on her arms was standing on end, because she had realized finally that she was out of options. She was not going anywhere, not running away, not finding Lucky. She was going to give birth to Tommy right here, where Dr. Addington was, because she had to be sure that Tommy was going to live. As his mother, that was her first and most important job, and Dr. Addington had already said she might have a hard time on account of being so small.

So, no, she had no options. None at all. And if they tried to punish her more on account of the baby looking like Lucky, she would stand up to them. She would bear whatever came—and protect Tommy at any cost.

But how was she going to keep them from taking him away? From actually *giving* him away—and sending Cecily back to Wayward to finish out her six-year sentence?

Even today, Mrs. Oglethorpe had asked her again if she wouldn't follow Harriet's excellent example and consider that her baby would be much better off with the wealthy family the Home had already found for him. "No," Cecily had said. "I will not consider it."

Mrs. Oglethorpe had looked so gravely disappointed at this that Cecily started to tremble, even as she said again, "No. My baby is mine. I am not giving my baby up."

CHAPTER 34

Friday, April 3, 2015
Duluth, Minnesota

In the waiting room at St. Luke's in Duluth on Friday, Molly couldn't focus on her magazine.

She hadn't wanted to tell Caden that his grandma Liz had cancer (*his grandma Liz had cancer!*), so had told him instead that, as she'd "just happened not to have any clients scheduled," she and Liz were going to Duluth for an impromptu "girls' day" of shopping.

In retrospect: a pack of cowardly little lies—but meant to protect him from worrying, give herself time to process the news, and figure out the right way to deliver it to him. Thinking of it this way, she guessed she could begin to understand why her mom hadn't told her sooner. Still, though—she wished Liz had.

She took out her phone. No messages.

After a second, she clicked on Evan's name. That stupid thumbs-up emoji was the last thing he'd texted her. He still hadn't called since he'd left Itasca on March 7. Four weeks ago.

Maybe he was over his head with the expansion project at the brewery. Maybe he even thought July and August were a done deal.

She really *could* let sleeping dogs lie. She had enough on her plate—

But, suddenly, she didn't want to. Maybe it was the shock of her mom being sick, but something in her now was saying life was too short to keep avoiding and evading the difficult conversations. She would've told a client: *Avoidance and evasion are the things that will keep you stuck.*

Hey, she typed. *Can you talk?*

Inside the tube of the MRI machine, Liz stayed stock-still, as ordered, while the machine whirred and buzzed and beeped all around. *It's going to be loud,* the technician had told her with a smile that seemed out of place; placative, at best. *Be prepared.*

But how could you prepare for your body becoming a foreign thing, for the disconnection from self, the odd sensation of the daughter—once a part of your own body, after all—waiting in the waiting room?

How could you prepare for the sense of separation that came when a part of your body was diseased? And you said, *No, not me, that is not me. That is my breast. (My bones? Another organ? The MRI will show me.) No, it is not me. It is not me at all. I am an artist, I am my dreams, I am my creations, I am not my body at all, the cells of my body may be diseased but my body is not me.*

Or is it?

And she realized, *This is real. This is happening. This is me.*

And she heard her father, Sam, plainly: *Tell your mother. She's stronger than you know.*

"I don't want to argue anymore," Molly said into the phone. "Let's just decide something."

"What's wrong?" Evan said. "Your voice sounds funny. Is your grandma okay? Why did you want to talk all of a sudden?"

"Why haven't you called me? I thought we were going to get this figured out."

"I thought maybe we needed a break. Anyway, it's the summer and fall we're talking about, so it seemed like there was a little time."

"So, you're not out there lining up a lawyer?"

"No, Moll. I told you. Last resort."

Molly sighed. Unclenched her fist, which she hadn't realized she'd been clenching. "My grandma's doing okay," she said. "It's my mom, this time."

Liz insisted afterward that they had to eat. "You look pale," she told Molly, and Molly laughed and made the bad joke that *she* wasn't the one with cancer. They drove down to Canal Park and had lunch at Taste of Saigon. The piled-high plates—cream cheese wontons, shrimp with pea pods, sesame chicken—were quick to come out, the food was hot and delicious, and refills on hot tea were endless. They talked about nothing—the fundraiser yesterday, the support groups Molly hoped to start offering this spring, Caden's need for new shoes again, as his feet never seemed to stop growing. They did not talk about cancer, DNA, Cecily, Evan. Their fortune cookies indicated prosperity and health, and they laughed and said, "Here's hoping!" Afterward, they walked together in the blustery wind and mist over to the ship canal and Aerial Lift Bridge, pulling wool hats down low over their ears, shoving hands deep into parka pockets. "I don't know why Mom hates to come here so much!" Liz said, like a joke, almost shouting to be heard over the wind, and Molly laughed, because it was true: every single trip Molly had gone on as a kid with her parents to Duluth, Cecily would all but rage about how she couldn't *stand* the thought of going over there, and Itasca was where life *was*, and why did they need to go there to "shop" and "dine out," anyway, and, no, do not *think* of bringing her back a T-shirt!

Now piles of dirty snow littered the walkways. Icy, gray water lapped the canal's concrete walls. As they reached the bridge, Molly squinted up at the web of steel girders through the mist, remembering how, much as she had loved those family trips, she'd always, at a certain point—like, standing right here—worried that this mass of steel would crash down on top of her as it was raised to let the colossal freighters pass through.

She found herself remembering how her dad had always reassured her that it wouldn't, and, just like that, she was thinking of Evan. "Call me anytime, Moll," he'd said, in that voice that still made her insides zing. "If you need anything." And, oh, again—the familiar comfort. She did *not* want to fall into it.

Yet—she kind of *did* want to.

Suddenly, Liz blurted, "I think I'm going to have to keep your grandma in The Pines for a few more months."

Molly was instantly back to the present, alarmed—as if some giant object *had* crashed down. "Months?"

"I don't know what I've been thinking, to imagine she could actually go home, even with at-home care. She's doing okay with PT, but it's still slow, you know? She's not strong—I mean, she doesn't seem strong mentally. And she can't do stairs! I guess we could set up a bedroom in Dad's old office for her, but, even then, I'd worry about her being alone, and you know she'd end up trying to do the stairs, anyway, and all kinds of things she shouldn't, and twenty-four-hour care is seemingly impossible to find, not to mention out of sight financially, and I'm going to be going through my treatments, so I'll be of no use for a while—"

"I can help, Mom. That's what I moved back home for."

"But you can't stay with her twenty-four hours a day, any more than I can. You have your clients. You have Caden. And, even if you *could* stay with her twenty-four hours a day, even if you *moved in*, you're not a nurse, and your grandma is going to need a lot of actual nursing care. And I may need help, too, unfortunately. We just need to face facts, you know. Be realistic."

"We'll figure something out, Mom," Molly said, trying to retain the optimism she'd felt in the restaurant, though Liz had made it seem suddenly unfounded.

Her phone dinged, and, out of reflex—it could be a client—she pulled it out of her pocket. Saw a new text from Evan: *I don't want you to worry about this stuff with Cade for right now. We've got time to figure it out. Tell your mom to give Cancer hell.* Plus an emoji of a fist. And a heart.

In her head, Molly said to him: *Stop trying to convince me I made a mistake. Just* stop *it!*

Not that he really was, but—seriously.

She texted him back: *Thx.*

And a heart.

She gave her mom the message. And Liz gave a far-off-seeming smile, her hair whipping in the wind.

"Don't be ridiculous," Cecily said, on Saturday at The Pines. She was half sitting up in bed atop straightened covers; she'd had her hair set and was wearing a bright purple track suit, plus red lipstick, applied crookedly. Perhaps these small improvements could be attributed to the five new flower arrangements that lined the windowsill, a sure result of Vivvy Bengtson's announcement at the Empty Bowl the other day. "I've been in here long enough already. Almost two months! I walked the length of the entire hall yesterday!"

"Hanging on to the rail, right?" Liz said. "Need I remind you there are no rails in your house? And there are stairs, which you can't do at all!"

Cecily frowned. "But I'm miserable here. And misery leads to death, I'm sure you know."

Liz wished for her father, who had always known how to calm Cecily, how to make the drama tone down. She also wished she didn't have to tell her about the cancer, but it seemed inevitable, suddenly. "Mom, listen, I haven't wanted to tell you this. But I need you to understand." And Liz began describing, in calm, clinical language, about her lump, her biopsy, her MRI. "Now we're just waiting for the results," she finished, "to see if it's spread. I'll know in about ten days."

Cecily blinked, looking puzzled. "But I have taken the best care of you since you were the tiniest little baby. How can this be?"

Liz wiped a sudden tear from her eye. They seemed to spring from nowhere lately. "I think it just happens, Mom. I don't think anything you could've done would've stopped it."

Now Cecily looked brokenhearted. She reached for Liz's hand and squeezed it. "Oh, but honey, you know I *would* have, if I could!"

Liz laughed away more tears. "Oh, Mom. I know."

They went back and forth a few more times—Cecily didn't believe it, wanted to know exactly how and when everything had unfolded, and "why on earth" she hadn't been informed. She seemed the most like herself that Liz had seen her in weeks—

Liz reminded herself: she had to be *realistic*. "Mom, listen, the important point here is that I'm not going to be in any shape to take care of you. Not even to visit you every day, for a while, probably. As much as I hate to say that. And Molly has said she'll help, but she's already got her hands full."

"Well, I don't accept this," Cecily snapped. "If you're going to be having cancer treatments, I want to be there with you. I'm not going to stand for being cooped up in here. You're going to stay at home with me, and I'm going to go with you to your treatments, I'm going to make you soup, I'm going to keep your spirits up, just like you've been doing for me."

"Mom, I appreciate that, but we have to face facts. You're in no shape to do that."

"I am your mother, and it's my job to take care of you!"

"Mom, please." Yet, Liz began to think: maybe Cecily could come stay at the lake house for a while. It was all one level, so it would be safer, and Liz could get one of those hire-a-nurse services to stop in and help out. Twenty-four-hour care wouldn't be needed, because Liz, even as she dealt with her own treatments, would be there to keep an eye on Cecily, to make sure she didn't take any unnecessary risks.

Obviously, Cecily would prefer being in her own home, but maybe this could be a stopgap measure, a stepping stone. Probably she'd be well enough in a couple weeks to make such a move, right, based on how improved she seemed today?

Of course, she and Liz would drive each other crazy. But even that thought cheered Liz, and, in her enthusiasm, she proposed the idea to Cecily.

Cecily frowned. "No. I only have a short time left on this earth, and I want to be in my own home. In town. With my books, and near my committee work. You'll stay with me. It's your home, too. I'll be better able to take care of you there."

"Mom, I'm sorry, but that just isn't realistic. You can't climb stairs, and that's that. And I don't think you're going to be in shape to do much committee work, let alone take care of me. Now, I will do anything for you, you know that. As I know you would do for me. But we have some limitations we have to work within right now. Remember how the doctor said that one in three people who break their hips end up being in a nursing home for at least a year afterward? We're talking about a significantly shorter time than that, even if you stay here a few more months, until I can get through my treatments. Or you can think about coming to stay with me, if you continue to improve over the next couple weeks. Those are really our only options, as far as I can see."

Cecily sighed. She looked very tired, suddenly. Almost defeated. "I don't *like* this."

Liz's stomach twisted. She didn't often allow herself to think: What if Cecily *didn't* improve? What if she simply spiraled down? "I know, Mom," she said, and her heart felt squeezed in a fist of love, duty, impossibility. "I know you don't like it. I don't, either. I'm sorry." But she simply did not know what else she could do.

CHAPTER 35

Saturday, April 4, 2015
Kure Beach, North Carolina

Lana called Kate's cell phone late Saturday night. Kate was half asleep, *The Seat of the Soul* splayed open on her chest. She'd taken to opening to random pages day by day, reading tiny, digestible bits at a time. "So," Lana announced, "I've been trying for weeks to find something online on the McNaughton Children's Home. And I finally did. Turns out, it was a place that *sold* babies."

"*What?*" Kate struggled to sit up, wide awake now, shoving the book off herself.

"Yeah. All kinds of circumstances, but the article I found said it was basically a home for upper-class unwed mothers. They'd pay a pretty penny to hide out there during their pregnancies, and the Home would sell the babies very shortly after they were born. And most of what the adoptive parents were told about a child's origins were lies—to keep things from being traced, I guess. So that bit about Mom's bio mom being Sicilian, that might not even be true. But, anyway, I would think this proves Lola was telling the truth—about Mom being 'adopted,' I mean."

"Oh. God," Kate said. "How much did they sell them for?" The instant the question left her mouth, it seemed inappropriate.

But Lana was unperturbed. "Thousands. Like, five thousand dollars, back in the 1930s. That would be like eighty-five thousand today. No one was ever prosecuted. They covered their tracks really well. I guess the doctor who ran the place had a stellar reputation. It was only after he died that what he'd been doing came out. Falsifying records and selling babies to rich, desperate couples. Like Jack and Lola, I guess."

Kate's stomach had started to hurt. "Lana, that can't be true."

"God, I don't know. It's online, so . . ." Lana stopped. Sighed. "Anyway, I don't know what the DNA test is going to reveal. Maybe we'll never know the whole truth. But you'd better tell Mom about this. I'd call her, but I think it's better if you tell her in person."

That was BS. Lana was simply reverting to being the little sister, hiding behind Kate, letting Kate do the explaining and make the excuses and the requests. Which, actually, wasn't so bad—it felt like Lana had cracked open a door, in some way, by trusting Kate like this.

But wasn't Lana worried that news like this could make Kate start drinking again? *Kate* was worried it could.

Apparently not; Lana just went on. "Oh, and, get this: The place was in Wilmington! Like, thirty minutes from Mom's condo. I'll send you the article; it has the address. Maybe the two of you can go see the place. I checked Google Earth, and the house itself still exists. Of course, the McNaughton Home is long gone."

Kate lifted her hair off her neck. "This is a can of worms, Lana."

"You think everything's a can of worms, Kate. When, in actuality, getting to the truth is what's going to set us free."

"And get you your new book."

A pause, then Lana's clipped I'm-above-fighting-you tone: "I don't think I'm being selfish, trying to get to the bottom of this for all of us. I really think it's going to *help*."

Kate tried to think what it must've been like for Lana: rejected at the moment of her birth. No wonder she'd had to develop a thick line of defense. No wonder she'd spent her life trying to *figure it out*, pin down some reason *why*, so there was some other explanation than *herself*—some other explanation than that she was irrevocably flawed, unacceptable before she'd taken her first breath, almost. Kate sighed. "I hope you're right about that."

"Listen, are you going to be all right with this? Do you need me to come down?"

Kate was already envisioning a fresh batch of monkey bread. Yes, there were ways to get through. "We'll be all right."

"Good, Katie. I trust you. Talk to Mom." Lana hung up.

I trust you. Kate was crying again.

"How are you liking the book?" Clarissa said, coming out to sit at the patio table with Kate late the next morning. The day was overcast and breezy, a pleasant-enough seventy degrees; in the distance was the constant roll of the waves.

Kate sat up straighter, startled out of the trance of wondering what was planned for her soul and if she was achieving it. "Good! It's great."

"Good." Clarissa put on her sunglasses and gazed out at the water.

"No dolphins so far," Kate said. She didn't want to tell Clarissa about what Lana had found out. Nor had Kate told her mother the stirrings she'd had regarding Clayburn Montgomery, or about looking Tricia up on Facebook, though Dr. Alvarez had said she should. Dr. Alvarez had said this not-talking thing, this simple *coexisting* that Clarissa and Kate had settled on, couldn't go on much longer, that it was actually a passive-aggressive form of "nonconstructive conflict." (Kate had described the habit they'd fallen into of eating supper on the couch, watching *Jeopardy!*, competing to see who could shout out the answer first, before the contestants even buzzed in.) "Are you angry with your mother, Kate?" Dr. Alvarez asked.

Kate didn't think she was. "Why would I be angry? She's taking care of me."

"Maybe this is an older anger," Dr. Alvarez suggested, and into Kate's mind had popped the image of Clarissa, long ago, shouting: *No, you cannot change your mind, you cannot keep him!*

She had almost fessed up to Dr. Alvarez—but not quite. Maybe next session. Maybe.

Now it was as if Clarissa could read her mind. "Kate," she said tentatively, taking off her sunglasses again, squinting slightly, her eyes very blue in this particular light. "I know we haven't talked about this, but I'm wondering how you're doing in regard to the DNA test. To what it might reveal, I mean."

Kate knew what her mother meant. But she couldn't go there. Just couldn't.

She wondered if Lana suspected the utterly colossal amount of not-talking Kate and Clarissa were doing—if that was why she'd tasked Kate with telling their mother what she'd found online.

I guess we have to start somewhere, Kate thought, even as she wished for a glass of wine. A bottle.

But. No. She was going to be better. Do better. She was.

"Mom, listen, about that. There's something I have to tell you. Lana called me late last night."

As Kate began describing what Lana had learned, Clarissa sat up straighter and straighter, as if someone was turning a big screw at her back, winding her up like a doll. Still, Kate didn't stop till she'd gotten it all out.

"Well, that is unacceptable," Clarissa snapped, then, and she was pale; barely breathing, it seemed. Kate wanted to reach for her—but didn't. "I simply cannot accept that," Clarissa said. "Being adopted, okay. I guess I've probably known that for a long time. But *bought? Sold?*"

"I know, Mom. I'm sorry. It's awful." Kate wished she hadn't told her; that there'd been no such news to tell. "But, listen, we don't really know what will end up being true. And, well, I just—I just have this really strong feeling that you were always, always loved."

Clarissa sniffed. "You don't know that."

"Yes, I do. It said so in the letter, remember? Your parents were young and they wanted the best for you. They probably didn't even know you were being sold. They evidently paid for the best possible care for your mother, right? And then they trusted this doctor to place you in a good home where you'd have everything you could possibly need. They probably didn't even know it wasn't a legal adoption."

Clarissa shook her head. "You just said the Home falsified every-thing. So that letter probably isn't true—just like I knew it wasn't!"

"Oh, Mom." Kate held up the Zukav book. "Remember? There are ways of knowing beyond knowing. Even if it doesn't make sense right now, I *know* that you were wanted. That it was only a matter of the circumstances." She swallowed, set the book down. "Just like with my son."

Clarissa's face crumpled.

Kate hadn't meant that the way it had come out: like she blamed Clarissa, like Clarissa *was* "the circumstances." "Mom, wait, I didn't mean—"

But Clarissa had popped up and was opening the slider back into the condo. Kate watched from outside as Clarissa grabbed her hat off the sideboard and headed out the front door, slamming it behind her.

Kate swallowed. Maybe Gary Zukav and Dr. Alvarez would say this first stab at actually talking marked some kind of progress, but Kate did not feel, in this moment, that it was measurable.

She stood and went inside to the kitchen. She looked in all the cupboards, one after another after another. She got out the stepstool to look above the refrigerator. She searched the linen closet, underneath the towels and extra sheets. Nothing. Her mother had left nothing. Just as Kate had promised Dr. Alvarez, Clarissa would keep Kate in line.

In the kitchen again, she got out a tall blue glass, pressed it to the ice maker, watched the ice crumble down, poured herself some iced tea, and went back out onto the deck. Phone in hand, she scrolled through Tricia Montgomery Robinson's Facebook page again. *All the Montgomery girls together again!*

Dr. Alvarez had said that some days would be harder than others. Had promised her, in fact.

Kate clicked to open her email. Sure enough, Lana had sent a message—subject *!!!!*—with a link to the article about the McNaughton Children's Home. Kate's finger hovered over the underlined blue text. And then she clicked it.

L

"Well, that doesn't make any sense at all," Molly said, peering at the screen of Caden's laptop, where he had it sitting on the kitchen counter. It was Tuesday evening, and Caden had told her when she'd picked him up from track practice that he had something he *had* to talk to her about. His urgency was so unusual that she thought for a second: *Did he get some girl pregnant?* (She hadn't even had a sex talk with him yet! Had Evan? Was she officially the worst single mom on the *planet?*) So, she was relieved, at first, to find it was just something about the DNA results he'd received in his email this afternoon.

He pointed to the line in the Ancestry family tree. "But, see, they don't share any DNA. There's no way Grandma Cecily and Grandma Liz are biologically related. Like, no way at all."

"Well, that must be a mistake," Molly said. "That's my grandma and my mom."

"I asked my teacher and everything. He said this shows you have about half of Grandma Liz's DNA. See here? So she's definitely your mother. And I have about a quarter of it, so your mother is definitely my grandmother. But none of us share any DNA with Grandma Cecily at all."

Why did Molly feel suddenly that he was the adult, and she the child? "Caden, seriously. That is just impossible."

"My teacher said it's definitive."

Molly shook her head. "They must have mixed up the samples or something. I'm going to call. Right now. Where's the customer service number?"

CHAPTER 36

May 8, 1936
Wilmington, North Carolina

L uck-eeee!" Cecily screamed, feeling like she was being torn in half. Her labor had been going on for hours, each pain worse than the last. She didn't know how much more she could take, and Dr. Addington had said the birth was still hours away, that she was still too small, the baby could not get out. "Lucky!"

His head down between her drawn-up knees, Dr. Addington laughed. "That's the most unusual choice of word at this moment, Miss DuMonde," he said, and his wife, at Cecily's side, patted her shoulder. "But, yes, you are lucky, because I'm going to give you something to help with the pain, and then, in just a few hours, you'll wake up, and your baby will be here."

Cecily was sobbing. The pain was so bad. "Oh, please, yes."

Mrs. Addington stroked her hair. "You're doing just beautifully, little girl," the doctor said, and he fit a mask over Cecily's nose and mouth. As she breathed in the gas, the pain began to lessen. Her spread-open legs seemed to detach from her body. Her head began to float away. "Let's just keep up the good work now," she heard the doctor say, as if through a cotton cloud, and then she was gone.

When she woke up, all was quiet, and she felt as if she'd been run through by the cowcatcher of a locomotive. The inside of her mouth was coated in fuzz.

As her eyes began to focus on the ceiling of the pantry, everything came back to her. The lights, which had been bright, now were dim. There'd been equipment lined up nearby her on the countertop—the doctor's metal tools, frightening at the time—and now there was nothing, which was even more frightening.

Where was Tommy?

It struck Cecily, then: Harriet had screamed for twenty-four hours straight. Had never been given anything for the pain. Her baby had been positioned entirely wrong, and yet the doctor had just had her push on through.

She realized: there was a thick cotton bandage taped over her entire belly. That wasn't normal.

That wasn't normal.

She began to cry. She had to know. *Where was Tommy?*

"Help, please," she said, but her voice was weak.

She balled her fists. She felt like a shipwreck. "Help!" she managed to yell. "Help me!"

She kept on yelling until Mrs. Oglethorpe came in, followed by the doctor. "Hush now, dear," said Mrs. Oglethorpe, patting Cecily's shoulder the same way Mrs. Addington had done.

"My dear, you gave us quite a time," said Dr. Addington.

Cecily could not stop crying. Somehow, she knew. She just knew. Nothing was all right. Nothing was ever going to be all right again.

"Your baby did not want to come, Jacqueline. We had to perform what is called a cesarean section."

They'd cut her open! Cecily had read about this!

"Where is he? Where is he?"

"I'm so sorry, Jacqueline." The doctor folded his hands, bowed his head. "Your baby, unfortunately, did not survive."

Cecily screamed. Screamed. Screamed.

She could not stop. She writhed, hurting herself where they'd cut her open. She tore at her hair. Mrs. Oglethorpe tried to grab her by the shoulders, but could not hold her down.

"Now, my dear," said the doctor, fitting the mask over Cecily's nose and mouth again, "you promised you wouldn't give us any trouble."

When Cecily came to this time, she could tell by the light coming in the window behind her that it was morning. The doctor was sitting beside her on a stool, making notes in her file. He was wearing fresh clothes, was newly shaved, and smelled of strong soap and coffee. "Ah, good," he said. "You're back."

She narrowed her eyes.

He sighed. "Don't blame me, little girl. It's a cruel world. And, when some time passes by, you're going to see that this is for the best. You're going to have a chance at life now."

"Where is he? Where is my baby? I want to see him." Back of mind, she wondered: Had they taken him? Harmed him? Because he looked like Lucky?

But Dr. Addington showed no sign of this. "We've removed your baby, to spare you the sight," he said calmly. "We've taken care of everything. You're not to worry about any of that, all right, little girl? Just focus on getting yourself better."

"I need to see him," she insisted, but a rap came at the door, and Mrs. Oglethorpe poked her head in. "Dr. Addington? One of the other girls has had her water break."

His face brightened. "A busy day!" He stood, setting Cecily's file on the counter, and was gone.

She lay catching her breath. A tear squeezed out of each eye. *Tommy.* She had not known anything except that he was hers, and that they were going to be together. A family. With or without Lucky, they would've been a family, no matter what.

Now she knew nothing at all.

It occurred to her to want to see what the doctor had written in her file. To make sure the doctor was telling the truth about Tommy dying.

If so, in the file would be the story of Tommy's whole life.

She struggled to half sit up—the pain was excruciating—and managed to stretch her arm far enough to reach the file. She couldn't hope to lift the whole thing, so she just snagged the first page off the top of the stack inside.

She lay back down and had to catch her breath again, but, when her eyes focused, there it was: the story, in the doctor's jagged handwriting. The story of "Jacqueline's" slow and difficult labor, of the doctor's decision to put her under and perform a C-section. He had listed many reasons why.

But, he wrote, the outcome had been a foregone conclusion. Tragically, in its attempts to be born, the baby had already been deprived of oxygen, and, by the time it was removed from the womb, could not be resuscitated. *The mother, petite and only age 15, simply was not equipped to give birth properly.*

Cecily wiped her eyes, trying to clear her vision. So, it was she who had failed Tommy; she whose body could not do the simple task of delivering him into life. It was she who had deprived him of oxygen, the first and most vital of his needs.

She, who had wanted, wanted, wanted him, as she'd never wanted anything in her life.

She felt the knowledge of her failure sinking into her every cell like lead.

And then she read, in the doctor's handwriting: *Due to the pt's status as a feebleminded inmate of the N.C. Wayward Girls Reformatory, tubal ligation was performed to prevent any future pregnancies, as ordered by the State Eugenics Board of North Carolina.*

CHAPTER 37

Saturday, April 11, 2015
Itasca, Minnesota

W hat's going on, Moll?" Evan said, on the phone on Saturday. "Cade said there's some issue with the family tree project, with the DNA?" Molly, at her desk in her office, wasn't entirely surprised he'd called. In fact, she'd thought he would call sooner— that Caden would've sent up some alarm—because, admittedly, she'd been obsessed: calling Ancestry, studying every online article she could find, researching and reading till her vision swam. She'd asked Caden not to go ahead with writing his paper until she got some answers; she'd spoken to Mr. Rasmussen about granting an extension. Last night, Caden had actually yelled at her—*How am I supposed to build my family tree when it's all . . . all fucked up?*—and she hadn't even chastised him for his language, because it had seemed about right to her.

DNA doesn't lie, she'd read, over and over again. As for Ancestry? *They don't make mistakes.*

Even Caden was on the side of the science. Molly hadn't realized how linear his mind was, how much he needed data to add up. That it might *not* was what seemed to upset him more than any ramifications of what it meant if these results actually *were* true.

"The tests are saying that Grandma Cecily's not biologically related to any of us," Molly told Evan. Even saying the words again made her queasy.

"Well, thank God they're not saying Cade's not my son," Evan joked.

"Evan, for God's sake."

"Just trying to lighten the mood, Moll. Sorry. I'm sure this must be hard."

Molly swallowed. "You have no idea."

"But, Moll, even if that's true, even if she's not biologically related, it doesn't really change anything, does it? She's been actively your grandma for your whole life, almost forty years. And actively your mom's mom for almost seventy years. I think she's earned the titles, don't you?"

Molly would've liked to see him maintain his equilibrium in the face of such news about *his* family. "It's just to think that she may have been lying to my mom—to all of us—all these years. I mean, it doesn't seem possible."

"Have you asked her about it? If she lied, maybe she had a good reason."

"You actually think there'd be a good enough reason to justify such a huge lie?"

A pause, then: "I don't know, Moll. It's just—I mean, your grandma's one of the best people I know. A lot of people don't tell their kids if they're adopted, right?"

Molly sighed. "It's just hard thinking she might not really be *ours*, you know?"

He was quiet a moment, then told her he was sitting on the bench near the old Trinity Church on Queen Anne Square in downtown Newport, where they'd often brought Caden when he was a toddler, and that everything was in bloom—magnolia blossoms in gradations of pink, a carpet of a thousand daffodils. She looked out the window at the gray sky, the spitting snow, and blinked back tears.

"—Listen, Moll," he said, "I was thinking maybe I should come out there again. You're going through so much. The construction here's in a good place, so I should be able to get away. Moral support for you and Cade, and whatever else I can do?"

Her heart had sped up; she willed it to slow down. This was exactly the comfort she'd told herself she'd better not fall into. "I don't think that's a good idea."

"Why not?" His tone was mild, but underneath was a tightness that sounded like anger.

"—Well, there's just so much going on."

"That's what I'm saying. I could help you."

It hit her like a hammer, then: she was still in love with him.

Well, *duh*. Of course she was. The signs had been there all along. She just hadn't wanted to admit it. Not to herself—and certainly not to him.

She didn't want to admit it now, either. Because she *certainly* didn't want to be the only one of the two of them who still had these feelings. Nor did she want to admit to her many mistakes of these past several years; her misinterpretations, misperceptions. Her failing to see him for who he really was—or even to see herself.

All her work to become enlightened, and it turned out she'd been blind to one of the most important truths of all. Evan's asking for more time with Caden wasn't what had caused her world to go off-kilter. *More* off-kilter, yes—but the original shift had happened when they'd divorced. And realizing that now—well, it was too late. Whatever mistakes she'd made, they were done. She was just going to have to live with the world tilted wrong, from now on.

"Evan, I just don't think it's a good idea. I mean, what would your girlfriend think? It's one thing to come out here for Cade—"

"What girlfriend?" he said.

Her heart gave a thud. "The one I saw you calling late at night, after the hockey games."

He laughed. "I was calling my *sister*, Moll. In Seattle. West Coast time? She wanted to hear firsthand how the games went. She knew how excited I was to be there."

Molly blinked. Right. He'd always been close with his sister. Amelie had been a great sister-in-law, too. Molly missed her. "Oh," she said. "I see."

There was a pause. "Hey, Moll," Evan said then. "Have you looked at Cade's family tree? Apparently, I'm on it. Next to you. Which is, I guess, in a way, why I'm offering to come out. Because we're family, in a way."

"Too bad we're divorced," she blurted, then could've kicked herself. *It's natural,* she would've told a client, *when we're feeling uncomfortable with our strong emotions, to fend them off with humor.* But—of all the stupid things to say.

But all he said, after a second, was, "Yeah. It is too bad." She felt the weight of the tenderness in his voice land on her shoulders like a cloak, and somehow the presence of their lost children, and then she thought, *Wait.* Did he mean—?

No, not possible. Was it? Should she say something? Ask him—?

No, it was ridiculous to think—

But, wait, yes, she *should* say something, just in *case*—

"Okay!" he said, his tone light now, and it was too late. "So, think about my offer, okay? I need more time with Cade, anyway, and maybe this is a good way to do it, until we can iron out something else. Your grandma's house is still sitting empty, right? Still needing a little TLC?"

She told him yes, she'd think about it, and, when she hung up, her hands were shaking.

She was getting nowhere with Ancestry or her research, and, by the following Tuesday, finally thought she'd better tell her mom. She asked Liz to meet her at Deep Woods Park near downtown—Molly had always loved the steep drive down to the river, the secret-feeling cove of tall pines—and brought two macchiatos from Jean's Beans. They sat across from each other in their heavy coats at a beat-up picnic table, as the weak springtime sun sparkled on the river and the melting mounds of snow, and Molly reluctantly, slowly, told Liz about the DNA results.

She hadn't realized how much she'd been hoping for reassurance, concern, advice on how to proceed, until Liz simply laughed and said, "Well, that's impossible! Obviously a mistake! Let's just forget about it. Caden can finish up his project without including Mom's sample, right?"

"But, Mom, they're really careful with the samples—I've called five times and checked—and I think we have to consider the possibility—"

"I disagree!" Liz said. She stood, brushing melted snow off the back of her coat. "I'll see you later, okay?"

Molly thought, *Seriously?*, and watched Liz walk to her Jeep and drive away. She sat alone to finish her macchiato, and the sun was strong enough that she finally took off her hat, leaned back and closed her eyes, relishing the first warmth of the season on her skin.

Later that night—it was nearly ten—Liz called in tears. "What do you mean my mother might not be my mother? And I'm not even Norwegian? I need to see the evidence, Molly!"

Molly realized: This afternoon, the news must have simply been too much to comprehend. So Liz had responded reflexively, with standard-issue Minnesota calm.

Now that the news had sunk in, the fallout was evidently going to be bad.

Caden, on his way to bed, snapped that he'd be fine home alone for a little while ("Yeah, sure, I'll just be sure I don't burn the house down, right?") and Molly, hugging him briefly, though he did not yield—why was he taking this DNA snafu out on *her*, for heaven's sake?—rushed out the door and sped out to the lake. On the way, she called Evan, waking him, she was pretty sure. He denied it, but she could almost see him stretched out on the sofa, "watching the news," pretending later that he'd heard every headline.

"Is your offer still on the table?" she said. "I think it would be good if you came out. I just told my mom about the DNA, and she is *not* taking it well. If you were here for Caden, to just be *with* him through all this, that would be amazing." She was going to set her own feelings aside; do what was best for her family, for her son. Caden *did* need his father. Caden *was* Evan's as much as he was hers. That was another reality she was just going to have to accept.

"Yeah!" Evan said. "Of course. It may take me a couple days to put it together, but I'll make it work. I'll get there as soon as I can."

"Good. Thank you. Thank you."

Liz answered the door looking as upset as Molly had ever seen her, and they sat together in the dim lamplight of the living room to look at Molly's laptop. "Black-and-white and lab results," Liz murmured, finally, seeming oddly consoled by the earth-shattering information in front of her. She sat back and sighed, and a strange light was in her eyes again. "Well, even science has to be wrong sometimes. They must have mixed up the samples, right?"

So that was why she seemed consoled; she'd decided not to believe it.

"Sure, Mom, that's probably what happened," Molly agreed, though she couldn't really buy that, not anymore. Still, she added, "I'll call them again tomorrow," because she thought, between this and the cancer and trying to care for Cecily, Liz's well-being was in serious danger, and Molly plain didn't know what she'd do if it turned out Ancestry was right that there was no mistake.

CHAPTER 38

Wednesday, April 15, 2015
Kure Beach, North Carolina

C larissa felt like she was losing her mind. The closer the day came that the DNA results were expected, the worse the feeling got. Walking the length of the beach, up and down, up and down (where were the goddamned dolphins?), day after day—by herself, since Kate had taken to going on her own—she could not stop thinking about it.

Because Lana had found, in some article online, the address of the McNaughton Children's Home. In Wilmington! Just thirty minutes away! And Clarissa and Kate had driven over there, and Clarissa had parked her Civic at the curb in front of the big old Victorian, now a private home. *That's where you were born, Mom,* Kate had said, in a tone of awe, but Clarissa couldn't fully believe it. The article (published in 1990 in *North Carolina Yesterdays*) seemed such scant evidence. What if it was wrong? Was the publication even reputable?

But she had to admit: adopted. Yes, almost certainly. But— *purchased*—by Jack and Lola? From—whom?

Clarissa could not imagine having given up her children for anything in the world. Any *price.* (And, yes, Clarissa had made Kate give up *her* baby, but this was different, surely—wasn't it?) Who had her biological parents—her *mother*—been? Greedy? Desperate? Selfish? Just plain too young to know any better? (Or to have any say in the matter?)

The possibilities seemed endless, whirling. Clarissa walked and walked, wondering what it all meant about who *she* was. Could it explain the course her life had run?

"Clare? Hey, Clare!"

She focused. A clear blue day, the sun shining; a tall, trim silver-haired man in a pink polo and white shorts standing in front of her, smiling. She recognized Monty, the piano player in her band. "Oh, hey, Monty!" She shifted her sunglasses to the top of her head; she didn't feel it was polite to talk with them on, though their absence left her squinting.

"We've been missing you at practice," he said. "You doing all right?"

"Oh, yes! Fine. You know, it's just that my daughter is staying with me."

There was some small talk; she was surprised she could manage it. Then, he astonished her: "Hey, you free for dinner tonight? Sounds like you could use a break, and I'd like to take you to McGillicuddy's. Can your daughter fend for herself one night?" He grinned.

Oh, God, no, she thought. She was seventy-eight years old; had thought "dating"—not that she'd done much of it, in the whole of her life—was entirely in the rearview. And she'd been glad to think so; had been turning down every offer for years. She could turn to ice in an instant, if she sensed some man getting his hopes up. "It's not really a good time," she said. "Not at all—with my daughter, you know."

"Well, that's fine." He was still smiling. "Maybe I'll text you and ask again."

She felt the familiar old discomfort brewing, and yet—she knew Monty. Liked him, from what she'd seen of him at their practices this past year. What would be the harm in having dinner? They were too old, weren't they, for disaster to result? There simply wasn't enough time for it to brew.

He had her phone number from the band info sheet, she knew, just as she had his, though they'd never used them to connect outside of practice.

"Well, you can *ask*," she said, with a little laugh. She lowered her sunglasses and started walking again, and, for an instant, hearing him laugh behind her and promise *I will,* she felt young again, and pretty—as if the things that had happened to her had never happened at all.

But, oh, this was foolish. Especially because, as her footsteps sank in the sand, she began to see it all unfolding again: the young lawyer Clayburn asking her father, Jack Duncan, for permission to call, when she was home for the summer after her freshman year at Sweet Briar; the front-page announcement in the *Leader*; the wasp-waist white dress and long veil; the mute loss of her virginity on her wedding night and Clayburn's seeming relief (*We made it, babe,* he'd said, rolling off her); the modern brick house in the suburbs with the electric refrigerator, the washing machine, the tree swing; baby Kate on a handmaid quilt.

In the early days, he'd said she looked like Elizabeth Taylor, only her sapphire eyes were more beautiful than Liz's violet ones, and— Clarissa was ashamed of this now—she had fallen for it, had actually *believed* it.

He hadn't hit her until after the first miscarriage; hadn't even given any sign that he might. (It had greatly surprised her, the first time. After that, she'd gotten good with makeup, with rearranging her hair, with creating fictional tales of how accident-prone she was.)

He said, if only she'd give him a son, he would be satisfied with her.

And what *joy* there'd been in the Montgomery household, in those weeks leading up to Lana's birth—once they'd been confident this baby was going to *make it*—little Kate thrilled to help with the layette, to anticipate a little sister or brother; a dozen red roses every Friday night. "Finally, you're giving me a son!" Clayburn said, again and again.

Then, Clarissa had given birth to a daughter who was three shades too dark.

She could still hear his voice that last day, the day he'd refused to pick her up at the hospital and she had to take a taxi home: *Slut. Thought you could fool me, huh?*

She could still feel his fist, slamming her tender middle. Could see him standing over where she was doubled on the floor, saying he'd give her the old Ford Ranch Wagon, but, as for money, that wasn't his problem.

And she could see her hands, clenched on the steering wheel as she drove out to her parents'—baby Lana on a blanket on the bench seat between Clarissa and little Kate—for what she'd imagined would be refuge. But when she got there, Lola had sent her straight to her father's office. Jack Duncan had been behind his desk, counting out a thousand dollars in cash, and he'd told Clarissa that she had brought shame upon him and upon her mother and she ought never darken his doorstep again.

And Lola, standing in the great hall under the portraits of the Duncan ancestors, her mouth thin, had said, "You may want to get some of your childhood things."

Even now, Clarissa's heart galloped in fury at the memory, and she walked faster through the sand, forgetting to fear tripping, forgetting everything but that she'd been a *good girl* all her life, done *everything* she was supposed to, day in and day out, the large things and the small, and *that* was her reward?

She remembered running up the sweeping staircase (God, how she'd hurt!), her vision blurring as she yanked things out of the drawers and closet of the room where she'd spent so many hours of her childhood, gazing out toward the horses in the rolling green pasture, dreaming of riding away. (Then, in reality, trudging downstairs for another lesson in comportment under Lola, another lecture on the importance of marrying well.)

She didn't have much space in the car—no, she couldn't bring her equestrian trophies (how ridiculous that thought was); she couldn't bring her old dolls—

She'd looked up to see Lola, standing in the doorway, smoking a cigarette, eyes darting nervously until they locked with Clarissa's. "We were never going to tell you this." Her voice was odd, croaking. "But you were adopted, anyway."

The floor fell out from underneath Clarissa; the sky started to spin.

"They told us your real mother was Sicilian, so maybe that explains why your baby came out so dark." Lola arched an eyebrow. "Unless you *did* go to bed with some gardener?"

"—Mother! God! No!"

Lola nodded, took one step into the room. Wobbled slightly back on her heels. "I'm sorry," she whispered. "I'd choose you if I could, but I have to stay with him." She stepped back, took one last drag on her cigarette, eyeing Clarissa up and down as if taking the measure of her, then turned away. And was gone forever.

Fifty-two years later, Clarissa was left with this stretch of white sand before her, wondering what on earth it all added up to. Her life. She'd thought she'd left the past behind, she'd thought she'd made her peace with it, but now it was all so vivid in her memory, and she was not at peace with it. No, she was not at peace at all.

She had realized almost immediately—even as she was driving Kate and baby Lana back down the tunnel of her father's trees and out to the highway that 1963 day—that what Lola had said about her being adopted might be true. Because it had not made sense to Clarissa when, right before her wedding, the first time she'd seen her birth certificate—she'd needed it for the marriage license—Lola had explained that it was from the state of North Carolina because Clarissa had arrived earlier than expected, while Lola and Jack were on vacation down there. Even at the time, distracted as she'd been with her wedding, Clarissa had thought, *Vacation?* Jack Duncan did not take vacations. He simply was not a believer. Any man who owned thirty thoroughbreds couldn't be, he said.

Anyway, what nine-months-pregnant woman heads off heedlessly on vacation? Not even Lola would be so foolish, Clarissa'd had to think. And Lola had, many times, told Clarissa that she'd been born right there, upstairs in the Lexington house!

Now, fifty-two years later, Clarissa walked and walked, not knowing who her parents were; who *she* was, after all this time. Nor did she feel consoled by the idea that, within days, the DNA test would likely tell her.

What if she learned the truth of where she came from—and it only made everything worse?

CHAPTER 39

May 1936
Wilmington, North Carolina

*B*y the time a week had passed, Cecily was made of lead entirely. "Jesus, Jackie, *you're* not dead," Louise told her. "You might as well smile and get on with it."

Cecily didn't think she would ever smile again.

Evelyn's baby had arrived safely, and the infant girl had gone off with another well-dressed couple in a fancy car, leaving Evelyn behind in a pool of tears. ("I'm just relieved!" she wailed, but Cecily could not imagine that was entirely true.) Two more pregnant girls were arriving tomorrow to move into Evelyn's and Cecily's rooms. Evelyn's mother was coming to fetch her, and Miss Peters would be coming for Cecily at 10 A.M. "sharp," after taking the early train from Wayward.

"You're hardly well enough to be up and about, Jacqueline," Mrs. Oglethorpe fussed, when she saw Cecily limping out the back door to the garden with *Sense and Sensibility*.

Cecily thought, if Mrs. Oglethorpe and Dr. Addington were truly concerned with her recovery, with how she was still bleeding and could hardly stand up straight, let alone walk, they wouldn't be sending her back to Wayward tomorrow to work in the hogpen.

But she had not complained, she had not said a word, she had not let on even the tiniest bit that she'd read her file and knew what they'd done to her, how they'd failed to save her baby, then butchered her to be sure she'd never have another.

It was a matter of simple pragmatism: She needed the bed, the clean sheets, the food, for her recovery. She needed the clothes they'd given her, including the maternity dress made of blue cotton flour sacks printed with tiny red flowers that she was wearing now.

But she was not going to let these people have the run of her any longer than she absolutely had to. She was done trusting anyone to have her best interests at heart. She was done trusting anyone to take care of her, even in any small way.

"It's my last day. Please," Cecily said. "I just want to sit among the flowers."

Mrs. Oglethorpe pursed her lips, then nodded. "*Sit*, though. No walking, except straight to the bench."

"Yes, of course," Cecily said.

At the stone bench, she sat and caught her breath. She opened *Sense and Sensibility* to the middle and pulled out the snapshot of Lucky, reading a line she'd underlined yesterday on the page the snapshot marked: *I will be calm. I will be mistress of myself.* She found the Saint Jude card among the pages.

But she was done praying for impossible things. She was done praying at all.

She watched a goldfinch hop from path to bush then flutter out beyond till it disappeared among the flowering trees.

She figured long enough had passed that Mrs. Oglethorpe would have moved on from watching her.

She filed Saint Jude back inside *Sense and Sensibility*, set the book on the bench. She slid Lucky's picture inside her bra, inside the thick strap under her arm, where the drops of useless milk leaking from her breasts wouldn't harm it, and she stood and walked out the back of the garden, into the alleyway.

And she was gone.

CHAPTER 40

Friday, April 17, 2015
Kure Beach, North Carolina

Lana called at 3 P.M. on Friday and said she'd gotten the DNA results, she had big news, and she was driving down to Kure Beach right away.

"Right now?" Clarissa said.

"Right now!"

Had Lana learned about Kate's baby? But wouldn't she be angry, if so? And what about Clayburn? The test had to have proven he was Lana's father, right? (*Had Lana learned who Clarissa's parents were?*)

"I'll be there by seven," Lana said, and she sounded more excited than angry.

"—Okay," Clarissa managed, and her hand was trembling as she clicked off the call.

"Kate?" she called, looking around, for an instant unable to quite make sense of her surroundings. Then she spotted her: out on the deck, reading. Clarissa went and opened the slider. "Katie, honey?"

Kate looked over her shoulder, and Clarissa felt love crash through her. Kate. Her Katie. *Thank God for Katie.* Clarissa remembered, that awful first day in the Ford Ranch Wagon, after she had explained that they wouldn't be going home again, how six-year-old Katie had asked, after a moment, *Does God have another plan for us, then?* And when Clarissa, startled—it had not occurred to her to think any such thing—had finally said, *Yes, yes, He must!,* Katie had nodded solemnly, then reached for Clarissa's hand, as if to say, *Then, here we go.*

Together, now, they would get through this. Whatever came, they would get through it.

"Katie, your sister got the DNA results. She said she has big news, and she's driving down tonight."

Kate's face shifted: surprise, nerves, maybe nausea. "Did she give you any hint what the news was?"

"No. No. We'll know soon, Katie."

"But this has got to be a mistake. Please," Molly said into the phone, late Friday afternoon in her office. She had the door closed, because there was always a chance someone could walk in, and she did not want this news to get out around Itasca, not one hint of it.

"I mean, I was trying to accept it, that my grandma didn't show up as my grandma, and I was about to try to convince my mom that we should ask her to confirm if my mom's adopted—but then we just got an email today saying my grandma has three new DNA matches, a biological child and two potential grandchildren!" Caden had called Molly from school with the news. "If this isn't evidence that the samples were mixed up, I don't know what is. It's as if some other family sent in their DNA at the same time we did, and my grandma's sample must've got confused with the sample of the grandmother in this other family."

The representative was kind but firm. "If you'll recall the process of entering the activation codes. You did that yourself, you said? And the connections between you and your mother and your son all came out as expected? And it's only your grandmother's sample that shows unexpected results?"

Molly swallowed. "Yes, that's true. I did enter the codes myself."

"Then, we advise people to understand that secrets sometimes do come out, and that the best thing to do is to ask your grandmother what she can tell you."

Molly hung up feeling helpless, flailing in the strangeness of the possibilities. Grandma Cecily not only wasn't her biological grandma—but she had some other family somewhere? How was that even possible? Molly tried to think what her father might say. *Family is family is family,* she imagined, for some reason—but what did that even mean?

Clarissa went to the Food Lion. They needed to pass the time somehow, and it gave her a feeling of normalcy to pace the crowded aisles, select the tomatoes and greens and sweet corn and crabmeat, price-compare the various brands of paper towels. When she got back to the condo, Kate had dough rising for monkey bread, and insisted on prepping the crab cakes, corn, and salad for dinner, though it seemed unlikely anyone would be hungry. "You just relax, Mom," Kate said.

Clarissa went out to the deck and tried to read last month's *Atlantic.* When her phone dinged, she grabbed it instantly, thinking it would be Lana, texting with some problem or delay—but it was Monty, with another dinner invitation. *Your timing is terrible,* Clarissa typed back. *My other daughter's coming tonight.* On impulse (she couldn't have said why; loneliness, terror, excitement?) she added, *We're in the middle of a bit of a family crisis.*

The phone was silent. She set it down and tried to concentrate on reading an article about the science of superstition. When she couldn't, she flipped to one on Hillary Haters. Haters! When Clarissa hadn't thought, in her lifetime, that she'd see any woman with an actual shot at the White House—

The phone dinged.

She picked it up and read Monty's text: *I used to be a therapist, in my other life back in Raleigh. Call me if you want to talk about anything.*

Ha ha, Clarissa wrote instantly, but her finger was wavering over the Send button when the phone dinged again.

Or go for a walk.

She considered this a moment, deleted the *ha ha,* and texted a thumbs-up emoji.

After a second, she added, *Thanks.*
No reply.

Then, finally, Lana was on the doorstep, big purse slung over her shoulder, snapped-shut laptop flailing in her hand, eyes gleaming and makeup streaked, as if she'd been crying while she drove. "Mom," she said, grabbing Clarissa into a hug. The laptop hit Clarissa's back. "Your biological mother is alive!"

Clarissa stiffened, stepped away. "What do you mean? That's impossible."

Lana shook her head, grinning. "Her DNA is in the system. It's a sure thing, Mom. Your mother is alive!"

It was really too much to comprehend, all at once.

As Lana pointed to the laptop screen, Clarissa and Kate, seated on either side of her on the sofa, leaned in and squinted at the charts and numbers, and Clarissa's vision blurred.

"See here, Mom, you're forty percent African! You have ancestors from Senegal, Mali, Cameroon/Congo, and Ivory Coast/Ghana. You're also three percent French, seven percent English, and about fifty percent Irish and Scottish." She made a couple of quick clicks. "And, look, I'm twenty-four percent African, and Kate is nineteen percent African! We have about half your DNA, Mom, and half Clayburn Montgomery's." Another click. "See here, Clayburn's two daughters who've sent in their DNA show up as 'close family,' so that means we're half-sisters to them, and Kate and I show up as 'immediate family' to each other, so that means we're full sisters." A warm look at Kate. "That's the good part of this. Plus, it seems we've got an African American grandparent on your side, Mom, which pretty much explains everything!"

"This doesn't make sense," Clarissa said. "How . . . ?" She could find no words to say.

Lana clicked back to another screen. "And, look here, Mom, this woman with the username *CLarson*, administered by *CadenB*, shows up for you as a parent/child match, with extremely high confidence. And she shows up for me and Kate as 'close family,' which can be a grandparent. That has to be your mother, Mom. It says she lives in Minnesota. And if we go to the next screen, here, you also have a half-sister, *RHarris*, living in Chicago."

Clarissa tried to let all this sink in. A mother, alive in Minnesota? A half-sister in Chicago? It did not seem possible. "No," she said. "This is not happening." She got up and went to the slider and looked out at the darkness, the shining white of the waves rolling in. These people had given her up. Maybe sold her. They didn't want her.

Behind her, she heard Kate: "Can we look at my results? There's something I want to see."

A click of the computer, as Lana said, "What are you looking for?"

"Just—anything unexpected."

Lana laughed. "All this isn't enough for you?"

Clarissa finally said they should eat and get some rest—Lana was ebullient and talking a mile a minute, Kate dejected and quiet—but, though Clarissa was exhausted when she crawled into bed, she couldn't sleep much, and they were all up early again on Saturday morning, poring over Lana's laptop some more, eating Kate's monkey bread and drinking strong black coffee to sustain them.

Clarissa had passed the night wondering not just about all that the test results had revealed, but also about one particular thing they had not: whether her biological father, ancient though he'd be, could still be alive. He would only show up, Lana said, if he had ever submitted his DNA. "We can certainly contact your half-sister and ask!"

Clarissa flinched. "I think that would be an imposition. I'm sure they know nothing about me. About us. If my biological mother is still alive, that would mean she was very young when she had me.

Chances are, he would've been young, too. I was something that happened before he had his real family, I bet." She had concluded that he was Black, and her mother white, because it was obvious the McNaughton Home wouldn't have taken in a pregnant Black girl, and she didn't want to say the worst possibilities in her mind. It was racist, of course, to think: Had what happened to Kate possibly also happened to Clarissa's biological mother? But how uncommon would a relationship between a Black man and a white woman have been in 1935?

What if Clarissa's existence was a source of pain for this woman who was her mother? She could not inflict herself on the woman, so late in life, could she?

Anyway, this was a woman who had *sold* her. As well as, obviously, lied about who the father of her baby was, because no way would Jack and Lola have purchased a child known to be half Black, and that doctor probably wouldn't have risked selling Clarissa, either. Not in the 1930s in the American South!

Lana shrugged. "We don't know anything till we ask. I could phrase it gently, you know. Aren't you curious?"

Clarissa took a deep breath. "I need some air. I'm going for a walk." Would she text Monty? Maybe. She needed a friend, and everything felt upside down, anyway.

But: "Can I keep you company?" Kate said, and Clarissa nodded and said of course.

Lana, nose in the laptop screen, barely waved goodbye as they grabbed their sunhats and went out. They were quiet walking downstairs, as Clarissa tried to order her thoughts, her emotions. She reminded herself: no matter what she was going through right now herself, she needed to be present for Kate.

"Are you all right?" Clarissa asked, when they got down to the sand.

Kate was hugging herself as she walked. "Yes, I think so." She laughed a little. "Are you?"

Clarissa nodded. "Confused. Spinning a bit. But, yes, I'm all right."

Kate smiled. "You have a mother. And a half-sister! Do you think you'll try to meet them?"

Clarissa took off her sunhat, ran a hand through her hair, and put her hat back on. "My mother didn't want me. She gave me up. Sold me."

"Mom, it might not be true that she didn't want you. And it definitely isn't true that she sold you. Remember, that article said that the mothers had to pay to be there at the Home, and they didn't know that doctor was selling their babies. They thought they were just being adopted into good families."

Clarissa let that sink in. *Okay. Right.* "I just can't fathom that any of this could be true. My father was Black? And how old would this woman have had to be when she had me, in order to still be alive today?"

"Fifteen, like me," Kate said quietly. "That would make her ninety-four now."

Clarissa felt chastised. *Of course. Fifteen.* They walked a few steps in silence.

"When you're fifteen, you don't have much of a choice about these things, Mom."

Clarissa swallowed. "I know, honey."

A few more steps in silence. The sun was bright, angling and sparkling across the water, the slow waves rolling in.

"I guess he hasn't had his DNA tested," Clarissa said.

"No. I guess not."

A few more steps.

"Maybe he used one of the other companies," Clarissa said. "You could always try sending your DNA to those."

"Maybe."

Another few steps.

"Or maybe he'll get a test done in the future, and you'll be here waiting for him!"

Kate kicked through the sand.

Clarissa sighed. She wished she could solve everything for her daughter, but she could solve nothing at all. For any of them. Except: "Do you think we should tell your sister about him?"

Kate looked over at Clarissa then. "Yes. Probably. I think we probably should."

And Clarissa saw in her daughter's eyes that pain was not a simple proposition; that it was tied up with desire, and failure, and striving, and love.

CHAPTER 41

Saturday, April 18, 2015
Itasca, Minnesota

*M*om, we don't want to upset you," Liz said to Cecily, late Saturday morning at The Pines. Cecily had on a smear of lipstick again and was dressed in her purple tracksuit. Liz was red-eyed, clutching a tissue in her fist, her capacity for denial evidently wearing thin. "But something has come to light that we need to ask you about."

Sitting beside Liz, looking at Cecily stretched out atop her bed, Molly prayed that what Liz was about to say wouldn't end up setting back Cecily's recovery. This morning on the phone, when Molly had told Liz, reluctantly, about the new email and her latest call with Ancestry, they'd finally agreed enough was enough. *We just have to ask her.* "I'll meet you at The Pines in an hour," Liz had said.

Now Cecily looked at Liz, an expression of mild interest on her face.

"Mom, we . . . we wanted to surprise you for your birthday, and Caden had this project for school, so we . . . we all sent in DNA samples. We sent one in for you, also, I mean."

Cecily's eyes widened quickly, then narrowed. "You sent in my DNA without my permission?"

"We . . . we just thought it would be fun! For your birthday. And then, it showed—"

"Whatever it is, it's not true," Cecily said.

"That I'm not your daughter."

Cecily looked at Liz for a long moment, and there seemed to be a sadness in her eyes. Then, she blinked and folded her hands over her belly. "Well. There must have been a mistake made. I would get on the phone with customer service."

"We tried that, Grandma," Molly said. "They stand by the results."

Cecily said nothing.

"It also shows that I don't have any Norwegian in me, Mom," Liz said. "And I thought you always said that Dad was a hundred percent Norwegian. And that you thought you were probably Irish and French, and the DNA result that came back as yours confirms the Irish, although, if it's really you, you also have a large percentage of English and Scottish. No French. But mine shows I'm Northwestern European—German—almost exclusively. No Norwegian at all. Or English or Irish."

Cecily had been biting her lip, and now blurted, "It certainly sounds as if the whole thing is a mistake! Your sample must have been mixed up with someone else's."

"Mom, if you swear it's a mistake, we will go back and check with Ancestry again. But it isn't as if another sample has turned up as my mother to indicate that there really was a switch made! And Molly and Caden show up as my matches, and not as yours. It's very confusing. I know it seems impossible. But the test shows I have three first cousins out in Rhode Island, and some cousins in North Dakota? And I know I was born in Rhode Island, and you said it was when Dad was still working at the sanatorium?"

Cecily licked her lips. Then, slowly, closed her eyes. "I'm not feeling very well," she said. "May I have some water?"

Molly reached for the pitcher on the bedside table and poured her a glass. Cecily had had Liz bring her favorite blue tumblers from home, saying she wasn't a child and didn't require plastic, she was not going to drop things, for God's sake. But now, as Cecily opened her eyes and sat up slightly again to drink, Molly saw her hand was shaking.

"Mom, I know this is hard," Liz said. "But, Mom—if I had a different biological mother, or if Dad wasn't my dad, I deserve to know the truth. Please."

Cecily set aside the water glass, lay back again and closed her eyes.

Liz wiped away a tear, shot a heartbroken glance at Molly—impossible not to notice: Cecily was not denying it—then pressed on. "There's something else, Mom. Just yesterday, Caden got an email alerting us that the DNA showed you—or, anyway, the person whose DNA showed up as yours—they have a living biological child. Someone born in 1936."

Cecily's eyes snapped open.

"Since the result just showed up, it seems this person—the child, I mean—just recently submitted their DNA, also. Ancestry has assured us that these parent-child relationships are definitive as revealed by the DNA. So, if you didn't give birth to a child in 1936, the year you turned sixteen, then that would definitely prove the sample's not yours—that they mixed them up somehow."

"A *living* child?" Cecily said.

CHAPTER 42

May 1936
Wilmington, North Carolina

Cecily woke up in a strange bed, wearing an unfamiliar nightgown, hearing rain outside.

It came to her instantly: *My baby is dead.*

The room she was in was tiny, with sloping ceilings and one small dormer, sprinkled in raindrops, letting the twilight in. She tried to sit up, but, between the pain and her severed stomach muscles, couldn't, and she sank back down.

She remembered: she had walked from the McNaughton Home as far as she could manage, wanting to find the train station. From her arrival weeks ago, she knew it couldn't be more than a mile away—she just didn't know in which direction. She'd stolen six dollars from Millie's petty cash in the kitchen, and figured she could get somewhere on that. Maybe even out of state, where they wouldn't be looking for her.

But the train station would probably be the first place they'd look. And she was exhausted. In pain. Bleeding. The sky had clouded over and a light rain begun to fall. She sat down—just for a moment, she'd told herself—underneath a large shrubbery at the back of a block containing a very large, elegant house. No one would ever see her, she thought, stretching out under the greenery, and though for a moment she'd thought, *What if they send dogs after me?*, she was asleep almost instantly, or maybe she'd just passed out.

Now a woman's voice said from the shadows, "Welcome back, little runaway."

Cecily was instantly on guard. She hadn't imagined things could get any worse, but it was now clear they absolutely could. She was at some stranger's mercy, just when she'd made up her mind never to be at anyone's mercy again. And someone had undressed her! But her bra was still on; she felt Lucky's picture inside it, against her tender skin. Thank heavens. If someone had seen it, there could've been bad trouble. She worked her mouth, then managed, "What makes you think I'm a runaway?"

The woman moved into the gray light that slanted through the dormer and put a finger on her chin, as if playing at thinking. She was sharp-featured, blond, wearing bright red lipstick and a slim dove-gray skirt, plus a crepe georgette cap-sleeved blouse with tiny pleats, a Peter Pan collar, and covered buttons. She was the most elegant woman Cecily had ever seen. "My gardener found you under the shrubbery in the rain," she said, then laughed. "Listen, you're safe here, all right? I'm not going to turn you in. You must be running from whoever cut you up like that. A skillful job, but that doesn't mean you wanted it done." She cocked her head slightly. Her voice softened. "Did someone take a baby out of you?"

Cecily tried to glare, to scowl. But it took everything she had not to start crying.

The woman shook her head, hands on hips. "I bet it was at the Mc-Naughton Home. You know, actually, I don't even want to know! A little kid like you. It makes me sick, the things that happen to girls." She let out a breath, brushed her hands together and smiled, as if that settled that. Her moods seemed to change as quickly as the sky on a partly cloudy, very windy day. "Anyway, I'm making you my pet. I don't want you to worry about a thing. You'll stay here until you're better."

"I can't stay here!"

"You most certainly can, and you will. Now, I'm going to bring you some soup." And the woman turned away and was gone.

ℒ

It seemed Cecily was going to have to plan another escape, but the mere idea of trying made her so tired. She'd been thinking for months about running away, and then she'd finally done it, and freedom had lasted all of an hour.

Anyway, the woman seemed almost nice. And this room—it was papered in tiny forget-me-nots. Even the sound of the rain was pleasant, from in here.

Though this was just the kind of thinking that always got Cecily into trouble. Not being aware until it was too late that no one actually had her best interests at heart.

A big orange cat padded into the room and jumped onto the bed with her. She smiled at the sight of him, scratched him behind the ears. She almost hadn't realized how lonely she'd been. He nudged her hand a few times, then lay down beside her and purred while she stroked his soft flank. A thousand thoughts tumbled through her mind—Tommy was dead, maybe Lucky had never loved her at all, she would never see Prince again, she would never in her life have another child—and settled in a new arrangement. Tears streamed down her face, and she petted the cat, letting his purr vibrate through her hand.

"Oh, George, are you making a nuisance of yourself?" the woman said, when she came in, carrying a tray. The tray had a flower in a bud vase on it. "You can push him away, if he's bothering you."

"I like him," Cecily said, wiping her tears from her face with the flat of her hand.

"Oh, you poor kid," the woman said, standing there holding the tray. There was nowhere to put it, on account of the cat. "George, honestly." The cat looked up briefly, then snuggled deeper into Cecily's hip. The woman shrugged. "Well, he's adopted you." She began unloading the contents of the tray onto the small bedside table. The bud vase, a bowl of soup, a cup of tea. "Hortense makes French onion soup to die for, I promise you. Do you like French onion soup?"

Cecily, who had never heard of French onion soup, narrowed her eyes.

The woman smiled, as if to say she would indulge Cecily for a little while. "Well, anyway, you're in for a treat. Here, let me help you sit up." She did so gently, then handed Cecily the bowl, a linen napkin, and a spoon, then pulled up a ladderback chair and sat down. "Now, tell me your name."

The soup smelled delicious. It was a rich, buttery-brown color and had a slice of bread floating in it, and the bread was covered in melted cheese. The sight and smell distracted Cecily, weakened her defenses. "Cecily," she blurted, then looked up, surprised by the sound of her real name. She had almost decided she would not be Jacqueline DuMonde ever again, but—not quite. Not till right this minute. And the decision felt very final now, suddenly, and a little bit frightening.

"Cecily, I'm Grace. It's nice to meet you. Now, your body has obviously been through quite an ordeal. I didn't examine you thoroughly, but I saw your stitches when I got you out of your wet clothes. So, you're going to need plenty of rest and time to heal. I'm afraid if you had tried to get much farther today, it might have killed you."

Cecily could hardly believe this was true; didn't want to, in any case.

"Now, the important thing is that my father never knows you're here. He would insist on reporting you to the police or some such nonsense. I don't think we'll have that problem for now. He's even sicker than you are, one floor down and on the other end of the house. The servants won't say anything. Now, I do know a doctor I think we could trust. Do you want me to call him to come take a look at you? I would pay for it, of course."

"No!"

One thin eyebrow arched. "I didn't think so. However, my guess is that this happened pretty recently?"

Cecily swallowed. Not answering didn't seem to be an option. "A week ago."

Grace nodded. "Here's what we're going to do. I'm going to take care of you—even cut your stitches out, when it's time—unless you develop a high fever or other signs of infection, in which case I will call this doctor, all right?"

Cecily nodded—Grace had an authority that was impossible to ignore—though immediately she thought she should say that it would have to be a doctor other than Dr. Addington. But Grace had already guessed about the McNaughton Home, and obviously wasn't in favor, so chances seemed good that Dr. Addington was not her friend.

The soup was beckoning Cecily. She'd had a little cooling in the spoon, and lifted it to her mouth.

Heaven.

But she needed to stay on guard—

"Do you have parents who will be looking for you?"

"No!"

Grace narrowed her eyes, then nodded. "I suppose I might as well believe you, but if I find out that's not true, I will be very unhappy with you."

"It *is* true! I'm an orphan. I have been all my life, almost."

Grace appeared to be making the calculations: An orphan, at the McNaughton Home? If true, then a scholarship girl. (Cecily thought then that Grace must know everything about everything. Did she know about Wayward?)

But Grace just gave another brief nod. "I'm sorry to hear that."

Cecily let out her breath. "Thank you."

A tiny smile showed that Grace also knew just how much she was overlooking, just how charitable she had decided to be. But Cecily's hunger overtook her. She spooned up another bite of soup.

"Just so you know," Grace said, "you don't have to worry. I do know what I'm doing. I was a nurse in the war, which scandalized my parents, but wasn't my father happy when it meant he didn't have to pay for a nurse, either when my mother had her cancer or when he had his stroke?"

Cecily looked up.

Grace's mouth tightened. "Mother was sick for three years, and then she died. My brothers died in the war. So, now it's just me and my father." She pointed her chin at the cat. "Plus George, whom you've met.

And we have Hortense in the kitchen; Rilla, our housemaid; and Paul, the gardener. He's the one who found you and carried you upstairs. As I said, none of them will say anything. They don't even go into my father's room, except Rilla, to clean, once a week. I bring him his meals and take care of him. He's getting better." Grace laughed sharply. "To be honest, I liked it better when he couldn't speak."

Cecily cocked her head. It seemed to her that people too often took their fathers for granted—even if these fathers didn't always do the right thing. She thought briefly of the prayer card she had left behind, then quickly reminded herself: she was done praying for impossible things.

Grace sighed. She leaned toward Cecily. "Listen, Cecily, I know the things that can happen. Believe me, I do. And, whatever happened to you, I want you to know that it wasn't your fault. I'm saying that to you because I wish someone had told me that, twenty years ago, when I was your age."

Cecily licked her lips, nervous again. She didn't want to trust Grace—but what choice did she really have? "Did you have a baby?"

Grace's mouth twitched. She looked at her hands. "No. I didn't. They wouldn't let me." Her eyes flashed up. "But I always thought it was a little girl."

Tears sprang to Cecily's eyes, as she remembered Isabelle's knitting needle.

Grace sat up straight and smoothed her skirt. "Now everyone thinks I'm an odd old maid. I *paint*. Do you think it's a cliché?"

Cecily didn't know what to say. Grace laughed and went on. "I dream of studying with Georgia O'Keeffe. I don't even know if she takes students, but, after my father dies, I intend to go to New Mexico and camp out in her yard till she agrees to take me on. Well, who knows? But I'll tell you one thing, I am never going to marry. My father hates me for it. But I made up my mind, after what was done to me. It's the only way to keep your sovereignty, as a woman, is not to marry."

Cecily thought she should know the word, but she couldn't remember its meaning just now. "Your what?"

Grace laughed, softly this time. But it seemed like she was laughing at herself, not at Cecily. "Oh, we'll have plenty of time to talk about all this. I don't mean to throw you in over your head. All I want you to begin thinking right now is, *It's not my fault.*"

Cecily blinked back tears again. She set her soup bowl back on the bedside table, her middle aching with the movement.

"You need to eat," Grace said, not unkindly.

"My baby died." The words, too terrible to speak aloud, came out a whisper.

"Oh, Lord! I figured someone stole him, or told you you couldn't keep him, or maybe you ran away from him. He *died?*"

Cecily began to tremble. "I would never have left him. He died. Because I couldn't give birth to him properly. Because I was not equipped. That's what the doctor said. I—"

"Oh, you poor, poor kid!" Grace stood and rushed out of the room, like she just couldn't stand the pain within it.

Cecily closed her eyes, her face hot with tears. With one hand, she stroked the cat. The other, she curled around under her arm, pressing the snapshot to her aching skin.

CHAPTER 43

Saturday, April 18, 2015
Itasca, Minnesota

Liz would not have begun to believe her mother's story at all—of the circus, the reformatory, the Home, the woman Grace who'd rescued her from under the shrubbery—had she not seen that photograph in Cecily's drawer that day two months ago when Cecily had fallen. The handsome young man in profile: *Lucky.* The father of Cecily's child!

"You had a baby," Liz said now, "and they told you it died, and then you found out they had *sterilized* you?" True, she'd had her suspicions that her mother may have given a baby up for adoption. But *this*? (This—this unequivocally meant *Cecily was not Liz's mother!*)

Liz could not accept it. No. No!

Cecily's lipstick had worn off. She was sitting up in bed, a hopeful look on her face. "Is my baby really alive?"

"It seems that may be true," Molly said, her voice sounding, to Liz, very far away.

And then came Cecily's voice: "Where is he? Do you know where to find him?"

"Wait," Liz broke in, as if trying to wake from a bad dream. "Mom. How could this be? Why—you're not my mother! What on—I don't . . . Why would they have *sterilized* you?"

"They did it to a lot of girls at the time. Girls who were considered low-class or 'feebleminded.'"

"But—but you're not feebleminded!" Liz—even as her head pounded in a steady, skittering rhythm (*my mother is not my mother; my mother is not my mother*)—was beginning to understand why Cecily had not wanted to share her story. Why she'd seemed almost desperate not to.

Cecily's mouth was thin. "Yes, well, they didn't like for girls to have sex outside of marriage, and any girl who 'couldn't control her impulses' was defined as feebleminded. Plus, in my case, the court had it on record that I'd slept with a Black man. Which was against the law. Once a girl crossed that line, she was considered irredeemable."

"God! How horrible!" Molly said.

Liz could not catch her breath. *My mother is not my mother.* "But wait. Then how did you end up in Rhode Island? What happened? If you loved this 'Lucky' so much, did you ever really love Dad?"

Cecily's eyes crumpled. "Of course I loved your father. Please, won't you tell me about my baby?"

It flashed in Liz's mind, then, the pie chart of her DNA: *92 percent German, no Norwegian.*

(Is my father truly not my father?)

"I'm sorry, Mom, but this just doesn't make sense!"

Cecily sat up straighter, temper flaring. "It was the height of the eugenics movement, Liz! You know, the idea—which some people actually believed!—that it would be a good thing to engineer society to create citizens with so-called 'desirable' characteristics. So, state governments would sterilize the people who they didn't want to procreate—it was what inspired the Nazis!"

"I'm not talking about history, I'm talking about you. You lying to me all my life and telling me that you were my mother!"

"Mom!" Molly objected.

Cecily sank back into her pillows, blinking away tears. "I am your mother, Liz. And you are not being very nice to me right now. I need to hear about my baby."

Liz glanced at Molly, who was looking at her aghast. *Right*—Liz needed to get a hold of herself. Trying, she turned back to Cecily. "Mom, please, I'm sorry," she said, wiping away tears of her own. "But this is a shock. I need for you to tell me everything."

CHAPTER 44

Summer 1936
Wilmington, North Carolina

I t was a hot, bright day in the middle of August when Grace hugged Cecily goodbye at the train station. "Promise you'll write to me," she said, and there were tears in her vivid green eyes. "And tell me where you are, and that you're all right, and whether you've found him?" She had given Cecily ten dollars, plus bought her a train ticket to New York City (Cecily had no idea how much that cost, but probably more than twenty). However much the ticket had been, Cecily understood that Grace, on top of probably saving Cecily's life, had given her what amounted to a small fortune.

Cecily, at some point during her convalescence, had woken with a start, realizing that whatever money she'd had in her account at the Bank of Sturgeon Bay in Wisconsin had been used to pay the expenses of the Sax & Tebow Spectacular last summer—that Isabelle, who was joint holder of the account (or maybe, for all Cecily knew or had paid attention, the sole holder), must have written a letter authorizing Mrs. Sax to make the withdrawal and bring the cash down to Manitowoc that day everybody first got paid. Not that it would've been enough to keep the circus afloat all summer, but it must've gotten them over some hump. Why Cecily hadn't realized it before, or why she was so certain of it now, she didn't know, but what she did know was that there was no reason to try to go back to Wisconsin, and that, from all her years with Sax & Tebow, there was nothing left, nor any reason ever to speak or think of it again. Anyway, to think of Prince, Isabelle, or anyone else, let alone the life she'd had then, would break her heart into so many small pieces that only dust would be left.

All she planned to keep—all she hoped for—was Lucky. She had the snapshot tucked inside her bra again, for safekeeping. She was wearing a hand-me-down dress of Grace's that Grace, who was much taller than Cecily, had tailored to fit her exactly. Cecily was almost back to the size she'd been before Tommy; the scar on her belly was a bright pink ridge.

"I promise," she told Grace now, though she didn't believe she deserved the kindness. All she'd done was *take* from Grace, and she didn't plan to ask for anything more, nor get in touch, until she had something to offer in return. She had never shown Grace Lucky's picture. She had told her only that the boy she loved had never known about the baby, and that she thought he might be in New York.

But neither she nor Grace knew if she'd have any luck—on any front— once she got there, and it didn't seem fair to expect Grace to care about the outcome, after everything she'd already done. Anyway, Cecily didn't trust that anyone could be as good, or as selfless, as Grace made herself out to be. Selfishness and greed would emerge eventually, and Cecily was glad to be getting away in time, before it had risen to the surface in Grace; before Grace had decided how she might make use of Cecily, with or without Cecily's consent. "I can't thank you enough, Grace. I really can't. I don't know what I'd have done without you. I'd have died, I bet."

Grace touched Cecily's face. "I'd keep you if I could. You know that, right?"

Within the past week, Grace's father had started to walk again. Grace feared it was only a matter of time before he discovered Cecily in the house. Grace said, knowing him, he'd call the police on Cecily and disown Grace entirely.

Knowing him, she said, he was going to live a hundred years, just to spite her.

"Goodbyes are terrible," Cecily said. "Let's just say good luck, all right?"

Grace nodded and stepped back. "Good luck, Cecily. I love you."

Cecily bit her lip, not believing her, hugged her again, and boarded the train.

On the steps of the library on 124th Street in Harlem, Cecily asked every person passing by if they knew Moses Washington Green, if they knew Lucky, and held up the snapshot for them to take a look. Some people just glanced and shook their heads. Others grabbed it out of her hand and stared closely for a while, squinting.

Nobody once said yes.

"Little girl, you been out here two months asking that same question," a man finally said to her, one afternoon in the rain. "You are never going to find this boy. You might start thinking he may not want to be found."

Cecily was hungry, tired, soaked through, and cold. She had been sleeping in Mount Morris Park near the old fire watchtower, climbing the winding stairs each night as if she could spot Lucky better from up there. She'd shown the snapshot to probably a thousand people. The money Grace had given her was almost gone, and the weather was getting colder. There wasn't work to be found in New York City, at least not that Cecily had found out about; at least not anything that would pay enough to rent a place for the winter, if she even had the first idea how to go about finding one. She was in no shape to try to become a bareback rider again; it had been a year since she'd been limber and strong. Anyway, circuses weren't hiring these days, either.

She had made up her mind to stop praying for impossible things.

"I just thought you might be interested in where she's been all these years," Cecily said to the pale, gray-mustached man sitting on the opposite side of the large oak desk.

There'd been only one thing she could think of to do. Once she'd made it to Providence by train—she was down to her last dollar—she'd walked straight to the library and looked up William Cahill, Senior, in

the city directory. The maid at his home had let her in almost immediately, once she'd said she had news of his long-lost daughter, Betsy. "I
thought you might like to send the police to fetch her home."

He laughed. "Oh, you did, did you?"

"Yes, sir."

His bushy eyebrows and mustache danced like caterpillars on his
face. "How do I know you're telling the truth?"

He didn't seem to her like a bad man. He was just someone who'd
done a few things wrong. She told him everything she could remember
about what Isabelle had said—the stepmother, the baby on the way,
stowing away on the circus train—then added, "From there, I guess
you'll just have to trust me."

Mr. Cahill tented his fingers. "I don't have a job for you," he announced. "I had to close the mill. I'm down to bare bones in my household. Hard times, you know."

Cecily swallowed. "Sir, I'm desperate. I don't want to have to tell you
what Isabelle—what your daughter, Betsy—did to me. But she ruined
my life. She really did. And she stole all my money, too."

"I don't see why any of this is my concern," Mr. Cahill said. "Even if
you're telling me the truth, whatever she did to you was clearly outside of
my control. She hasn't been under my roof—or even in communication—
in more than fifteen years."

Cecily sat up straighter. "Because, sir, if you had loved her enough
back then, back when she needed you to, everything would've turned out
different. And that's just a plain fact."

His caterpillar eyebrows came together in a frown.

"I have a letter of reference from your friend, Mr. William Cahill in
Providence," Cecily said to the dark-haired man seated behind another
ornate desk, this one inside a brick mansion in Newport. "He gave me
your address and said I should ask if you're in need of a housemaid. He
said you owe him a favor."

CHAPTER 45

Saturday, April 18, 2015
Itasca, Minnesota

So you never found him? You never found Lucky?" Liz asked, aghast at her mother's story, sorry for her grief—and wishing desperately that Cecily would get to the part of the story where *Liz* came in, because she needed to know: Had Cecily ever—missing Lucky, grieving her lost child—truly loved *her*? Truly loved Sam? Nonsensical to wonder, maybe, after a lifetime of evidence that she had—but Liz had lost her bearings! Her whole family was a lie? And what had happened to Liz's biological parents? Why had they given her up? (She had never been anybody's first choice, it seemed!)

"No," Cecily said. "I worked in Newport for a couple years, until the hurricane. Mr. Winthrop was visiting friends over in Westerly, and he was killed, and the house was damaged, and Mrs. Winthrop let half the staff go. I was glad to go, let me tell you. But I ended up back in Providence, and I couldn't find a job, so I was living on the streets for a few weeks, and everybody was desperate. The place had been flooded so badly that everything was damaged and smelled horrible—moldy and salty and slimy. Awful, you know. Then I got sick with TB, and I got sent to the sanatorium, where I met your father."

Cecily let out a long sigh, closed her eyes for a moment in obvious exhaustion—*oh, God*, Liz thought, *what if she can't go on?*—then opened them again and continued. "Of course, it was years before we got married, but he was the central figure in my life from the moment we met. But I truly thought he wouldn't want to marry me because I couldn't have children. And I had trouble trusting in love, or anything, or anyone, in general—perhaps you can understand."

"Grandma," Molly said, in a hollow, shell-shocked tone. "You never told me you'd ever lived in Newport, not in all the years that I lived there. And you never told me that you'd lost a baby—or, I mean, that you thought you had—even when I lost four of them!" She got up and walked over to the window. Liz, worrying, watched her looking out, arms folded, shoulders trembling. Outside, tiny snowflakes poured from a matte gray sky.

"In Newport right now," Molly said, "the daffodils are in bloom." And Liz understood it—the wish to be *elsewhere*. Anywhere but here, facing this, hearing this truth after a lifetime of lies. But the truth—Liz *needed* it now. Molly turned. "Grandma, didn't you think it would *help* me to know? To know that you had gone through something similar?"

Cecily shook her head. "But it was a secret, dear. I had kept it a lifetime. It had nothing to do with you. Only—I had to keep it to save us. To keep us *intact* together. Don't you see that everything I've done, I've done because I love you and your mother so very much?"

"But, Grandma, you *lied*," Molly said, and she turned to look back out the window, and Liz was suddenly shaking her head, too, as if to say, *no, no,* or as if the motion could clear her head of this muddle, make everything make sense. She needed food, sleep, something to set her right. (Would anything set her right, ever again?)

"I didn't mean—" Cecily started.

"But, Mom," Liz blurted, interrupting. "Where did I come in?" She could not bring herself to say: *If I was not born to you, did I at least belong to Dad?* "How—how did you come to be my mother?"

Cecily blinked again. "Oh, honey. It's too much. It's just too much. My baby. He's all right? He *lived*? He's still alive?"

Liz bit her lip to keep from saying, *It's a girl, a daughter.* "Please, Mom. I need you to tell me everything. About *me.* This is *my* life. I need the absolute truth. After all this time, I think I deserve that, at the very least."

Cecily's eyes crinkled. "Yes. Yes, of course you do." She sighed.

Folded her hands. Took a deep breath, maybe to calm herself, or decide where to start. Liz tapped her foot, trying hard to be patient; failing. Molly was still looking out the window, her back to the room.

"Well, yes," Cecily said, finally. "Well, honey, your father and I, we— well, you see, we just always considered you our gift from God—"

"So Dad isn't my biological parent, either?"

Cecily frowned, shook her head slightly.

Liz felt sick. Could hardly breathe.

"But we always *felt* you were ours completely! And we—we didn't want to complicate things for you by saying we weren't your biological parents. We just wanted everything to make perfect sense to you. For everything to be easy for you. The way nothing was ever easy for me!"

"But, Mom, now *nothing* makes sense! You adopted me? Who were my biological parents? Do you even know? How old was I when you got me?"

"You were about five months old," Cecily said quietly, looking at her hands, and Liz suddenly realized: the scar. The cut down Cecily's midline. It was from this *other* baby—not from Liz at all.

Liz had never before known what it was to be truly *speechless*, to have no words.

Cecily's eyes flashed up again. "Honey, this is a lot for one day. Would you just tell me, please—my son? My son is alive?"

Liz looked at Molly, and Molly, blinking back tears, nodded. "You have a daughter, Mom," Liz said. "Other than me, I mean."

By the time Kate and Clarissa got back from their walk, Lana had crafted emails to the half-sister, *RHarris*, and the biological mother, *CLarson*. "Wait," Clarissa said, and she had to sit down—her vision was swimming, suddenly.

What if they wanted nothing to do with her? Did she want anything to do with them? Did she really want to know why her mother had given her up, or how much money she'd got for her?

No. Not really. She didn't.

Except (Clarissa had to remind herself): As Kate had pointed out, the woman would have been a young girl at the time of Clarissa's birth. She probably hadn't had choices, and it was probably only the doctor who'd profited—

"Mom, are you all right?" Kate said. "Do you want some more coffee? Water? Maybe we should think about lunch."

"Let's just try your biological mother first, then, Mom," Lana said.

Clarissa looked at Kate, folding her hands to stop them from shaking. "It's too soon. I'm not acclimated to all of this."

"But, Mom," Lana said, "your mother's bound to be really, really old. Don't you want answers, before it's too late? Don't you want to know what happened?"

"Lana," Kate said. "If Mom says it's too soon, it's too soon!"

Lana frowned. "It's always been the two of you together, and me the odd man out. I'm tired of it, to be honest."

"You're *pushing* too *hard*," Kate said, in a heavy, strained tone.

"I'm not wrong. You always try to make me wrong."

Kate let out a little scream and headed for the kitchen, where she began opening cupboards, one after another after another, too quickly. "Damn it, can't a person get a *drink* around here? It doesn't seem like too much to ask!"

Clarissa and Lana exchanged alarmed looks. Quietly, Lana folded her computer closed and set it on the coffee table. "Katie?"

Kate let out another little scream, slapped her hands to her head, then snatched up a half-full blue glass tumbler off the counter and hurled it at the wall. It shattered, heavy pieces raining to the floor, water spattering the paint. "Kate!" Clarissa hurried toward her, skirting the broken glass, as Kate sank to the floor, leaning back against the cabinets, sobbing, head in her hands.

With effort, Clarissa got to her knees beside her. Lana was close behind. "Katie, Katie," Clarissa said, trying to gather Kate up, but Kate was pushing her away, saying, "Damn it, damn it, damn it," through her tears. "Leave me alone, leave me alone!"

"We're not going to leave you alone," Clarissa said, trying again to hold her. Lana had a hand on Kate's knee.

Finally, Kate surrendered to Clarissa, though she began crying harder, too. "Oh, Katie," Clarissa said.

"I had a baby," Kate said, through her tears. "Lana, I had a baby! When I was fifteen and I went to the goat farm!"

Lana drew back. "What?" She looked at Clarissa. And all Clarissa could do was lower her eyes, take a breath like she was about to go underwater, and nod.

CHAPTER 46

Saturday, April 18, 2015
Itasca, Minnesota

Molly had suggested an early supper at the Thai Garden—"I think we need some comfort food," she'd said—but Liz said that would hardly do any good. She needed to go home, try to get some rest. No, she did not want to explore the biological matches that had shown up for her on Ancestry, all those Rhode Island and North Dakota first cousins; no, that was the last thing she wanted right now. And no, she didn't want company, she was not going to check on Cecily's house, and Molly didn't need to, either.

She'd been worried about Molly, before, up in the room, back before *everything* had come out—but all she could think of now was trying to save herself. How—or *if*—she was going to manage it.

Then Molly said she had something to tell Liz.

Oh, Lord, Liz thought, and, because she felt she could not handle even one more tiny thing, she snapped, "What?"

"Evan's coming tonight."

From the tone of Molly's voice, and the slight pink in her cheeks, Liz thought maybe this was a different kind of visit than the last one; that maybe something had unfolded between them at a distance. "Good," Liz managed to say. It probably was good, for Molly. Liz would hear about it another day. All she wanted now was to get home to the lake.

But the relief of her arrival there was short-lived. The house felt quiet and strange. She flipped on the TV, thinking a *Law & Order* marathon might be just what the doctor ordered—something normal, for God's sake—but the light of it, too bright and flashing, started to make her nauseous, so she clicked it off. There was laundry and cleaning to do, but—why bother?

She brewed a fresh pot of coffee and carried a steaming mug through the sucking mud down to the lakeshore, to the Adirondack chairs she'd never managed to bring in last fall. (Dean never would've let such a chore go undone, and, yes, now they would need to be repainted.) She left her jacket unbuttoned; it was the time of year when forty degrees felt warm. The lake was thawing, gray slushy ice spotted with intermittent still pools. Liz sat for a moment, looking at it, trying to be grateful for the life she'd had. Even if her MRI results came back showing that the cancer had spread, even if she died six months from now, it would have been a good life.

She *was* grateful. But—still. For God's sake.

She was not who she'd always thought she was?

She was not who she'd always thought she was.

So, who was she?

Cecily had pleaded exhaustion, said to come back tomorrow. But Cecily wanted Molly to email the biological daughter right away, tonight, to explain what had happened, to say how thrilled Cecily was that the daughter was alive, that Cecily had always, always loved her, had grieved for her all her life.

All her life! While playacting the role of *Liz's* mother!

Liz could not help wanting to hate this woman, this unknown "daughter" who'd been born to Cecily. Who had *Liz* been born to? Why had they given her up when she was five months old? Was "Liz" even her real name?

(Did cancer run in the family, and, if so, did they tend to survive it?)

She lifted her coffee cup to her lips and let the steam warm her nose and decided that she was unsettled to the exact proper degree that any-

one would be, finding out that her parents weren't her parents and had
lied to her all her life. And she found herself remembering some things
she had tried to forget. One, a summer afternoon when she was twelve.
Angry about some small thing, she'd stormed out of the house without
a word and walked downtown to Ben Franklin. She was browsing the
craft supplies, exhilarated and nauseated by the freedom she'd claimed
(stolen, it felt like), when, confirming her guilty feeling, a police officer
came for her. He drove her home in his squad car, and Cecily came
running out, gathering Liz into her arms, saying, "Thank God, thank
God, I thought I'd never see you again! Never, ever do that again, please,
please, please!" As if Liz had hopped a bus to Florida and been gone a
month, not walked downtown for an hour!

This although, once, when Liz was about five, she woke in the
night calling for Cecily, and Sam came in to comfort her. "Your mother's out for one of her walks," he said, and, when this made little
Liz cry harder—who'd ever heard of a mother who went for *walks* in
the middle of the night? She did it *all the time?*—he added, "She has
trouble settling down, sometimes, but we just have to trust that she'll
be back. She likes to go down and see the trains." This did not make
Liz feel better. (The *trains?*) From then on, she would keep her ears
pricked, even in sleep, for the sound of the back door down below her
room squeaking open, then, some hours later, squeaking shut again.
*Your mother has trouble settling down sometimes. Your mother has trouble believing
in me. Though she always, always believes in you, so don't ever worry about that, all
right, honey?*

Well, maybe it all made sense now. These odd little shadowy things
about bright-light Cecily. The abandonments and betrayals she'd suffered must have made her nervous to try to hold on, must have made it
hard for her to trust, to *stay*.

But, God, what Liz had learned today: it was too much. Too much.

And she could hardly bring herself to think: her father was not her
father. *He* had lied to her all her life, too.

"Dad," Liz said out loud. "What the hell?"

"Dad!" she screamed, and the word echoed in the stillness.

"Thank God you're here," Molly said, when she opened the bungalow door to Evan, and she hugged him tight, pressing her face to his chest, taking comfort in his old familiarity.

"Hey, Moll," he said, and his voice rumbled in her ear in a way she remembered, in a way that felt like home.

They sat down together with Caden, and Molly explained what Cecily had revealed that afternoon, and how Cecily wanted them to email her biological daughter.

"That's wild," Caden said, finally—he seemed almost relieved; there had been no problem with the science, after all—and Molly was relieved, in turn, that he didn't seem upset, or even, really, shocked. Thank God, in the end, for the teenaged *whatever*. "Sure, let's email her right now," he said.

Molly swallowed. It had been a very long day. "Grandma Liz is having a hard time with this." She didn't want to say that she wasn't having the easiest time with it, herself. Much as she liked to believe there was a reason for everything, it was extremely hard to think what the reason could be for all of *this*. "I think maybe we should check with her before we actually reach out to this woman. Anyway, it seems we might be rushing into it—"

"Mom, seriously? Grandma Cecily's been looking for her kid for, like, eighty years. Or she would've been, if she'd known she was alive, right? I don't think emailing her tonight is rushing it. Grandma Liz will be fine. She always is, right?"

Molly took a deep breath. She didn't feel at all ready to dive into this particular pool. And *would* Liz really be fine?

But Caden cocked his head, imitating the way she sometimes scolded him. "Don't you always say, whatever Grandma Cecily asks of us, we do, because she's always done so much for us?"

Molly started, then, after a beat, nodded, sharing a glance with Evan, proud of their boy.

Caden, smirking slightly, went to get his computer.

"Oh my God," Lana said, when she opened up her laptop again. It was nine o'clock, after dinner. They'd calmed things down, they'd hashed things out, they'd argued and shouted and cried. Lana had threatened to leave and been talked out of it; they'd cleaned up the broken glass. Around five, they'd all put on their swimsuits and walked out into the ocean, as if that could wash them clean, and maybe splashing around in the chill and salt of the waves actually had, and then Kate had cooked them up a feast—salmon, scalloped potatoes, a big salad—and they had eaten, and laughed, and cried a little more, together. They had kept the prayer card in the center of the table.

"Mom! Mom, come and look at this," Lana said. "Katie, come look!"

CHAPTER 47

Saturday, April 18, 2015
Itasca, Minnesota

Cecily lay awake in the darkness Saturday night—it would always be *the day she'd been found out*—in a state of equal parts exaltation and regret.

Her baby was alive!

Hadn't she *known* there was something wrong with the McNaughton Home, with Dr. Addington? If only she'd been brave enough to question him (had he *wanted* her to look at her file, to read it, so she *would* truly believe his giant lie?), to ask for *proof*. Life could've been so different then!

But. Her life was her life. And, yes, the years after her baby's death—no, after her baby's *birth*—had been a decade-plus-long nightmare of grief and wandering. The loss had left a hole that nothing had ever filled.

Still, she would not have traded Sam, Liz, Molly, Eric, Caden, her life in Itasca—

Oh, but she wanted it all! She wanted her baby! Her baby *girl*, whom she'd thought of all these years as Tommy. She wanted not to have suffered so—

Not to have been betrayed by the only "sister" she'd ever had—

Not to have lost her first true love—

Well. Certain things you couldn't dwell upon, if you hoped to continue to survive.

(Was there any chance Lucky could still be alive? He would be ninety-seven years old! Would these DNA tests be able to tell her *where he was*, after all this time?)

"Sam, I'm sorry," she whispered out loud. "I'm not going to come to you, not yet. I want to meet my daughter!"

And she thought she heard Sam say, *I understand. But you have to tell Liz the truth now.*

"I will!" Cecily said. She sighed. Should she be angry that Liz and Molly had *stolen* a DNA sample from her? Probably. She would not have chosen for her secrets to come out this way. She might not have chosen for them to come out at all—though the miracle of learning that her baby was alive meant she couldn't wish these events away.

But now Liz was so angry. Cecily wished Sam were here to sit down across from their daughter and help Cecily explain. Should they have done so fifty or sixty years ago? Sam had thought so, but Cecily'd said no. If she hadn't been so frightened—if she'd known better. If, if, if.

And she found herself thinking of Grace. Long dead now, certainly. Cecily had always hoped that Grace had made it to New Mexico. She'd tried writing her, a year after marrying Sam and moving to Minnesota, finally feeling she had something to *offer*; or, at least, that she wouldn't need to *take* so much anymore.

She wrote that she had named her new baby after Grace, and that she had taught herself not only to cook and keep house (*I am a bona fide "doctor's wife," can you believe it?*), but also to make a cake of fifteen thin little layers, in the old Southern tradition, and that everyone in Itasca, when they talked about Cecily, would mostly begin and end by shaking their heads over the spectacle of her cakes. *Although they certainly seem to like them, too!* Cecily wrote. *I think it's good to be known for something particular, in a very small town, don't you? Because they will find things to say about you, regardless, so you might as well put something front and center, and let them think that they are the ones who've chosen what you're known for.*

She did not mention that, with each little layer she poured into her old-fashioned hoecake pan to quickly cook atop the blazing stove, she thought of Lucky's grandmother, and, as she watched the batter brown around the edges and turn into something solid and sweet, she thought, *Lucky*. She did not mention (or maybe didn't even realize, perhaps not till years later) that her cakes were the one way she let out the steam of her grief and loss and acknowledged her past; that, without this release, she might not have been able to uphold being the Cecily Larson she'd wanted to be; or that each little layer was a tiny prayer: that Lucky was safe, and well, and loved, wherever in the world he was.

That, when people ate Cecily's fifteen-layer cakes, they were ingesting actual love.

She wrote to Grace twice more after that. Never received an answer.

Grace, who had saved her life, made everything possible, had never written Cecily back.

Cecily had pictured her in Taos, painting the mountains, a flower, a bone; the spectacular light.

CHAPTER 48

February 1947
North Smithfield, Rhode Island

S am, look out! Look out!" Cecily pointed through the flying snow
at the taillights in the ditch ahead. Sam was a careful driver, even
more so in these stormy conditions, and he eased the Chrysler to
a stop on the edge of the road, angling slightly so his headlights were
pointed toward the trouble. The storm had caught them by surprise, or
they would've left the San and the Valentine's Day party much earlier.
Sam was driving Cecily back home to her Providence apartment; she
had handmade 102 valentines for friends old and new on the wards,
especially the single girls who didn't have anybody visiting them.

Up till the moment Cecily cried out, they'd been quiet together in
the car, lost in a feeling of bittersweetness, because they knew it might
be one of their last parties at the San. Sam's father had recently died;
Sam had not attended the funeral, saying only that he was too busy at
work. Cecily had been offended, on principle, but he said she didn't
know the full story, and, anyway, his patients needed him. A week later,
a letter had arrived from his mother asking Sam to come home and take
over his father's practice. *Itasca needs you, Sam. I know how you love to help people, and people here need help. People out there have other doctors, don't they?*

Cecily felt her throat constrict every time she thought of him leaving, but he hadn't asked for her opinion, nor for her to go with him, nor
proposed marriage again since she'd told him about Lucky and Tommy,
months ago. Anyway, if he had, she would've said no. She loved him,

of course, but she knew love didn't last forever, not even close, and she wasn't going to hang her hat on it, no, sir.

Still, sometimes she woke up crying, and, if Sam was there—if he ever had two days off in a row, he'd stay over at her apartment, making sure the neighbors didn't see him come and go—he held her and didn't say a word. He would run his finger over the ridge of the scar on her belly, give it a gentle kiss. They never spoke of it, of what it signified. She had let him see it—see her fully—only recently, only after she'd told him about Tommy. Even as her doctor, back at the San on his rounds, he had never seen her scar, and it had evidently not been noted on her chart, because, the first time he'd seen it, in the cool darkness of her bedroom, he'd flinched, drawn his breath sharply in—though, knowing the story, he shouldn't have been surprised.

Traveling through the darkness with Sam quiet beside her, Cecily's mind had had plenty of time to wander over such things. They'd seen no other cars on the road, as if everyone but them had known the storm was coming.

But now this car, in the ditch, smashed into a big oak in a patch of forest, a good quarter mile from the last house they'd passed.

"It looks like it just happened!" Cecily said. Sam nodded, and the two of them jumped out of the car.

The snow was blinding, cutting. Cecily shielded her eyes. Her over-shoes did no good at all; the snow slid inside her short boots, cold at first, then instantly wet. The snow was deep, off the side of the road, and she struggled to get through. Sam, with his much longer legs, was ahead of her.

"Hello?" he called, plowing through to the driver's side. There was no answer, no sound at all, just the whirling of the snow and the red of the taillights, the glow of Sam's headlights across the scene. The car was a black Chevrolet. "Hello?" Sam leaned to peer in the window, then held out his hand for Cecily to stop. "Don't come any closer."

"Why, what's wrong?" Cecily asked, though she should've known, and she was already at the window so she saw: A man slumped over the steering wheel, his head smashed and bloody, neck obviously broken. She staggered.

"I'm going around!" Sam blurted, careening back toward Cecily, and she was startled at first, confused, until her mind's eye reconstructed the scene: there'd been a woman, doubled over in the passenger seat, head against the dash. Cecily had not been able to take it all in at once, all that she had seen in a glance.

"Oh, God, Sam, help her!" she cried, as he struggled past, brushing Cecily's elbow on the way, as he always did whenever he was near, as if to reassure her, *I'm here, yes, I'm still here,* and if anyone could save this poor woman it was Sam, who'd been an Army surgeon at the front lines all through the war. Cecily didn't breathe as she watched him fade behind the scrim of blowing snow, hearing the rapid *crunch* of his feet punching through the snow crust as he made his way to the passenger's side and wrestled open the door, which creaked and scraped through the drift.

She heard a strange sound, then. A sort of a mewling moan. Oh, the poor woman! "Sam? Sam, do you need help?"

No answer. It was hard to see through the snowy haze, but he was leaning over where the woman was—

"Cecily!" he yelled. "Cecily!"

It couldn't have been three minutes later, she was back in Sam's car, the baby in her arms. The baby, who was, miraculously, seemingly, unhurt.

Who had been riding, perhaps, in the arms of its mother, its mother who had shielded it from the impact that had killed her and the baby's father both. Sam said there was no question. Neither had a pulse. They were already growing cold. "This baby would've died, too, if we hadn't happened along," he said, flexing his hands on the steering wheel. His eyes flashed to meet Cecily's, and she didn't know what he meant to say. What she knew was that, the instant he had placed this baby in her arms and she had carried it to the car through the blinding, whirling snow, this baby had become hers to take care of, to look out for, to keep safe. Forever.

"We could get married," Sam said. "We could go to Minnesota."

"Yes, all right," Cecily said.

Sam closed his eyes for a moment, then looked at her with a tiny smile, though his eyes were very serious. "We'd better call the police first. Go through the right channels, you know?"

Cecily felt the flush of disappointment; the nearness of the crime she was ready to commit. She did not want to let the baby go, not for an instant. She did not want to chance it being taken from her.

But Sam was right, of course. They had to go through the proper channels. "All right," she said. "Yes."

Sam drove slowly, carefully, away, leaving the red of the taillights behind them. They went to the nearest farmhouse and pounded on the door, asked to use the telephone. While Sam drove back out to meet the police at the site of the accident, Cecily sat in the warm kitchen, holding and crooning to the fussing baby. The lady of the house had made coffee, and sat across the table from Cecily, watching with a kind of longing. Her own children were asleep upstairs; almost grown, she'd said.

"I'm going to adopt this baby," Cecily said.

"Lucky little thing," the woman said, and sipped her coffee, as Cecily blinked back tears.

The baby was a gift from God, Cecily decided, and, when a policewoman came to the farmhouse in the morning and took the baby out of her arms, she started to cry and couldn't stop. Sam spoke quietly to the policewoman. "We want . . . soon . . . please," was all Cecily heard, and the policewoman in her skirt was a black triangle against the white of the new-fallen snow, carrying the baby out to the waiting police car.

Cecily cried for a week. Day by day, Sam would update her. The baby's name was Mary Elizabeth Myer. Little Mary's father, Paul, had been in the Navy, stationed in Newport. The night of the accident, he and his wife, Helen—plus baby Mary, of course—had been driving back to Newport after visiting Helen's aunt and uncle, who had raised Helen and her younger brother from the time they were orphaned, when Helen was ten. (*"What?"* Cecily said, looking up, and Sam just shushed her, caressed her hair.) The heartbroken aunt and uncle had not hesitated to take in the baby of their beloved niece—but perhaps, the policewoman had whispered to Sam, they would consider giving little Mary up for adoption. They were both sixty-five years old, the uncle had crippling arthritis, they had so little money and no hope of earning more. Helen's younger brother was only twenty years old, unmarried, stationed in Okinawa.

A letter had been written to the family of little Mary's father in Bismarck, North Dakota.

"If we get married," Sam told Cecily, "we'll have a better chance."

Three days later, a courthouse wedding. And a visit to the aunt and uncle, who lived in Burrillville, near the San.

It took ten visits, over the course of two months. It took Cecily, after she and Sam had befriended the couple, staying three weekends to help care for little Mary. (The aunt, Mae, and uncle, Arnold, were exhausted, grateful for the help. They saw how much Cecily loved the child. Arnold, especially, did not enjoy having a baby in the house, though he tried his best, but little Mary was his wife's sister's grandchild, and Arnold had devoted his life already to raising his wife's sister's children, and his arthritis had him in constant, excruciating pain.)

It took a letter arriving from North Dakota, saying that little Mary's father's family could not take her in. The grandfather was a widower, managing a large farm on his own, with his sons all away in the service.

The adoption was rushed through by a Rhode Island state official who was pleased to think that the orphaned baby would not become a drain on the state's strained resources. Mae cried when she signed the papers, but she hugged Cecily and said she knew it was for the absolute best.

The baby gripped Cecily's finger, and, Cecily was sure, smiled.

Sam finished out two final weeks of work. Cecily set her mind to learning how to cook, to shop for groceries, to scrub out little diapers by hand. She danced around the Providence apartment with the sweet baby in her arms, singing: "M-M-M-Mary, beautiful Mary, you're the only girl that I adore!"

Of course, they had decided not to call her Mary, though they would keep Elizabeth, out of respect for her birth parents. "A fresh start for a new life!" Cecily had insisted. (Deep down, she was terrified. Mae and Arnold could change their minds! A North Dakota relative could show up on the doorstep and demand that the baby be handed over! Cecily woke up at night in cold sweats; the sound of the baby crying was always such a relief. A new name was, in Cecily's mind, a *safety measure.*)

A new birth certificate arrived in the mail; the original would be sealed away in some dusty file drawer in the Providence courthouse. It was standard practice in Rhode Island for an official birth certificate to be created listing the adoptive parents just as if the child had been born to them originally, and so the certificate read: *Elizabeth Grace Larson,* born to Cecily DuMonde Larson and Samuel Eric Larson on September 15, 1946 (which was, indeed, the child's true birthday). Cecily pressed the document to her heart. "We're official!" she told little Liz, who blinked in seeming approval.

Cecily convinced Sam: they would tell everyone in Minnesota, in their new life, that they'd been married a year and a half already, and that the baby was theirs by birth. It would save poor little Liz such heartache, in the future, if she never had to know the way her birth parents had so tragically died!

"Are you sure?" Sam asked Cecily, more than once.

"Yes! Because I know what it's like! Not to know where you came from! To feel unwanted and heartbroken! And *you* know what it's like to be disappointed and hurt and grieving for things you've lost, or things you never had but should've! We don't want her to experience *any* of that, do we?"

"No, that's true," Sam said. "Though it isn't as though her parents wanted to give her up. You don't think it would be all right for her to know that her mother died trying to protect her?"

"No," Cecily said. All Liz need ever know, Cecily imagined, was that she was wanted, and loved, and wanted, and loved, and loved, and loved, and loved, and that would be the beginning and the end of everything. Anything else was too heartbreaking, too altogether *much*, for any child just starting out in life.

She managed to convince Sam: even his mother didn't have to know the truth! Sam was famously reticent, and did not write to his mother often. It would be just like him to get married and have a baby and not think to mention it.

She and Sam were laughing together, a little nervously, about this, as they set out for Minnesota in the Chrysler, all their worldly possessions—they didn't have much—inside. Sam drove, in his careful way. Cecily held the baby, little Liz, in her arms.

They didn't have much, but it was more than enough. They had everything.

CHAPTER 49

April 2015
Itasca, Minnesota

C an you ever forgive me?"

That's what Cecily had said to Liz.

"I have been desperate for your love, all along. That's why I never told you. I was so afraid I would lose you!"

"—It's going to take me some time, Mom."

That's what Liz had said back.

And Cecily had shaken her head quickly. "You see, the instant I held you, in the middle of that snowstorm, I knew what I was on this earth for. What everything I'd been through to that point was *for*. So that I could take care of you! Does that sound overdramatic? Well, it's just the truth!"

"But you're saying my mother died with me in her arms. She died protecting me?"

"She did! It was a terrible tragedy. Terrible. We were heartbroken to see—your father—he was so brave, you know, and he tried, he would've saved them, but it was already too late—and then, you see, you needed me! And you *were* love to me, you understand. You were the only doorway I had in!"

And Liz had swallowed back the bile in her throat, finding herself wondering—though she'd been just five months old—how could she have no memory of the accident, her parents dying in the car where she was riding in her mother's arms? And how could she have any prayer of knowing, at this point, what was true? "What does that even mean, Mom?"

And Cecily had blinked, as if surprised. "Well, honey, your father—he told me later that, when he put you in my arms, I—well, I changed *physically* before his eyes. And he saw that this was the way that he and I could be together for the rest of our lives. To keep you, to make you ours. You see, I wouldn't have been able to marry him without you. And I loved him so much. But I would've been too afraid. I would've missed out. And he—he loved me far more than I understood. More than I was able to understand for decades, to be honest! And we just—we always wanted to spare you the pain of knowing. That's all, Liz, honey. We wanted you to know only love. Not grief, or loss, or sorrow—not just starting out!"

Liz had put her head in her hands. And still Cecily had gone on, though her voice had sounded distant and strange: "And I have tried and tried—your father and I *both* did—to do as much as we could to help others. To make up for . . . for whatever might have been wrong about the way we went about things. Not telling Mae and Arnold where we went, for example. But I was so afraid of losing you! For years, I woke up in the middle of the night, terrified! But—building the hospital—that was in honor of your parents, in our hearts. The performing arts center, too. We were so grateful to them! They had done such a marvelous thing, creating you! I never forgot them. I always wanted only good to come out of this—"

And Liz had sat up straight again. "You were love to me, too. You always have been. You and Dad."

"Oh, yes! Your father loved you entirely. We have loved you so much, all your life!"

"I know, Mom," Liz had said, and sighed, and looked out the window to watch the snow fall.

But it was hard—no, impossible! To think of her parents—her biological parents—dead on the side of the road; of Cecily and Sam driving off to Minnesota pretending that Liz had been born to *them;* of the absolute *extravagance* of the lies that Cecily had told over the years—"You get your height, your eyes, your big sturdy bones, from your father!"; "I always love this scar, because it's from you!"

Impossible.

And it was impossible, too, to think of sweet, good Sam, if he were still alive—how would he explain such omissions of fact, such *lies*? ("I think it's in your *blood*, being a doctor!" he'd told Liz once, with an uncharacteristic sort of glee, when she was eleven or so and he'd caught her poring over his *Gray's Anatomy*.)

You were love to me.

You were my only doorway in.

Liz was scheduled for a lumpectomy and radiation. The cancer had not spread. Her chances of survival were 99 percent. A bullet dodged. All she had to do was *get through* it: the surgery, the recovery, the treatments, the next few weeks. Cecily would stay at The Pines, for the time being; Liz needed the ability to come and go from her, as she was ready, day by day.

"Wow, it's you!" her biological uncle—eighty-nine-year-old Joe Myer in Bismarck, North Dakota—had said, when Liz finally got him on the phone. "We had no idea what had happened to you!" Extremely cogent for his age, he explained: Liz's parents had married shortly after the war. Liz's father, Paul Myer, Joe's oldest brother, had been stationed in Newport, where he had met Liz's mother, Helen. "So, none of my family had ever met your mother. Paul hadn't even been home to North Dakota in years, on account of the war. He was just about to get out of the service, in fact. The last letter he ever wrote me, he said he was trying to convince your mother to move back to Bismarck with him.

"But then, the two of them got killed—" Here, Joe's voice broke slightly. He cleared his throat and went on. "And, since my mother had passed away, my father certainly wasn't equipped to take you in, and all of us boys were away in the service. Then we were told that

Helen's family had given you up for adoption, and that was the last we ever heard. We always hoped you were all right. We always hoped we'd hear from you."

Liz sighed, picturing Cecily and Sam driving away with her. Renaming her. Erasing her true origins entirely. Yes, she might've frozen to death had they not come along. But they still could have told her the truth, left it an option for her to keep in touch with her blood relatives, instead of doing everything they could to make sure the opposite was true. "Will you tell me about my father?" Liz asked.

Joe sighed, then, after a moment, said, "He was a good big brother. A little in his own head. Quiet. I'll tell you one strange thing I remember. We had no money growing up, you know. But Paul was itchy to create things. So, anything that broke into pieces—glass bottles or old china or crockery, things like that—he started fashioning into a mosaic on the side of the chicken coop. And we didn't even know what a mosaic was, back then, to be honest. It would catch the light in the morning, all those pretty pieces of broken colored glass, and make my mother so happy while she was looking out the kitchen window. A bit of beauty, in the middle of those dusty Dust Bowl years, you know." Joe sighed again. "It was all so long ago."

A Rhode Island first cousin on Liz's biological mother Helen's side, Frank Schneider, barely remembered that his father had had an older sister who'd died in a car crash a decade before Frank was born, and he'd certainly never heard there was a baby who'd survived that same crash. "How about that?" he said, when Liz told him her story, and about what Joe Myer had said, but Frank could shed no light on anything about Liz's biological mother. And Frank's father, who would've at least had stories from growing up with Helen, had died years ago.

"How strange," Molly said, when Liz told her all this. "The whole time I was living in Newport, I was living where my biological grandparents had met. Where you lived when you were a baby." She blinked and swallowed; her eyes teared. Evan reached for her hand, and she felt the comfort of it, and the strangeness. He'd been absent for so long, yet, still, he was *permanent*. "No wonder I always felt at home."

Eric called Liz, finally, from the airport in Seattle. With the climbing season over in Patagonia, he was on his way to Alaska to spend the summer leading packrafting expeditions. He was calm and good-humored about the DNA results—Liz guessed she should've predicted it, but she hadn't, perhaps because she was still so upset herself. But Eric said, "Sounds like, if Grandma and Grandpa hadn't happened along, you'd have frozen to death in that car, and none of us would be here at all."

"But they *lied* to me!" Liz said. "They lied to everyone! For almost seventy years!"

"They saved you. Saved *all* our lives, and only did what they thought was best for you," Eric said definitively, as if he'd been thinking about the question for years rather than three minutes. "Listen, Mom, my flight's boarding. I'll call you when I can, okay? I'm going to Ketchikan first, not sure what the signal's like there."

She hadn't told him about the cancer; found she was glad to have an excuse not to. "Oh, all right, then, honey. You be safe out there."

"Always am, Mom. Hey, funny to think: I'm half German!" He laughed, said, "Love you," and hung up, leaving Liz looking at the blank screen on her phone.

Liz (*Mary?* No—she was still just Liz; it was simply too late for anything else) got a big cardboard box up from the basement storage room, and, on a muddy, sunny first-day-of-spring-feeling day, a first few hardy daffodils beginning to bloom alongside the garage, she swept Dean's golf shirts into it and put the box into the Grand Cherokee to take to Goodwill. Dean would've wanted someone to get some use out of those shirts. She'd been selfish, she guessed, hanging on to them, when she already had so much of him: in Molly and Eric, in Caden, in the house Dean had bought for her, the studio he'd had built to her specifications. "So you can do your art!" he'd said, grinning. "That thing that makes you *you*, my dear!"

She had known love in her life. Indeed, she had. She was lucky. She just had to keep remembering it: she was maybe the luckiest person in the world.

"Hello?" Cecily said into Molly's cell phone, which Molly, standing beside Cecily's bed at The Pines, had handed over. "Hello? Clarissa? Oh, I love you! I love you! Can you hear me? I love you! Hello!"

CHAPTER 50

May–September 2015

C larissa had a mother.

Clarissa had a mother!

"Why does it break my heart so badly?" she asked Monty, walking the beach, as they did together sometimes now. They still hadn't gone to dinner, but she'd told him all about what she'd been going through—and, to her surprise, this act of unburdening herself had actually helped. So, she had just kept on doing it. He'd suggested she join a support group for people who'd had DNA surprises—more and more groups were being created, he said, as this kind of event was becoming more and more common—but, so far, she'd found talking to him enough. "My chest will not stop aching! Shouldn't I be *happy?*"

"Well, you hadn't known, until now, what you were missing. And now you can imagine what you lost, not having her, all these years. You can imagine the pain she might've spared you."

That was true. Oh, so true. The pain of Lola, of Jack Duncan, of Clayburn Montgomery; of all the years of feeling she belonged no-where, was *from* nowhere, connected to nothing.

Now, at age seventy-nine, she actually had a mother!

And Cecily was a delight. A pure delight! They talked on the phone for hours. (Each time they hung up, Clarissa cried and cried, and Kate would bring her a cup of tea, a homemade peanut butter cookie.) Kate had long conversations with Cecily, too, as much as Cecily's energy allowed. And, though Lana was back in Raleigh, busy teaching, Clarissa knew she'd spoken with her several times, as well. Lana was *interviewing*

Cecily, in fact, having received her blessing for the book she was writing that would be the story of all of them—beginning with Cecily and Lucky.

A bareback rider. A roustabout. Clarissa's parents! Her brave, foolish, beautiful parents. What a relief, and a joy, to hear Cecily speak of Lucky—her first love, her first true heartbreak.

Cecily's granddaughter, Molly, had emailed a scan of a photo of him, of Clarissa's father. The only photo Cecily had! The resemblance to Lana was uncanny.

"I am so sorry," Clarissa found herself saying to Cecily, when Cecily explained how broken she'd been when Lucky had left without even saying goodbye. ("I bet," Cecily had said, "that if he'd had the first inkling of *you*, he would've found some way for us to be a family!")

And Cecily said, "What are you sorry for? You're the beauty in this story. You're the whole reason why we loved each other, in the end—we loved each other so that you would come to be. I wouldn't change a thing. Do you hear me? I don't regret one thing."

Cecily had, from the start, been champing at the bit to find out about Lucky—what had happened to him, and was there any chance, at age ninety-seven, he was still alive? So, pretty quickly after their first contact with Cecily, Lana had emailed the half-sister, *RHarris*.

RHarris had been suspicious at first—she had no knowledge of any additional children of her father's, thank you very much—but, finally, when Lana emailed her the whole story that Cecily had shared, of the summer of 1935 and beyond, *RHarris*—Reyna Green Harris, daughter of Moses Washington Green—agreed to talk with her biological half-sister, Clarissa.

"God, no, we never knew our father had worked for any circus," Reyna said. (It turned out: Clarissa had one more half-sister, plus a half-brother! The two just hadn't ever submitted their DNA to Ancestry.) "Much less anything about a baby!"

"Oh, even he didn't know about me," Clarissa assured her. "But my mother, she tells me, loved him very much. They were each other's first loves."

"Huh," Reyna said. (She was sixty-five years old, a grandmother herself. To think of her father as a young man, before her, before her mother—in love, and with a white girl, making a baby in the middle of a circus—was a million miles away from anything she wanted to imagine.)

"Will you tell me about him?" Clarissa asked.

Reyna sighed. "Oh, he was a good man. A good, good man. A good father. Reliable. We had a happy family. But we lost him way too young. He passed in 1972. Only fifty-four years old. Heart attack. I was twenty."

"Oh!" *Clarissa's father. Dead.* Not a shock, exactly, but she felt it like a punch to her kidneys.

"He was a good businessman," Reyna went on. "Had what he called an 'empire' of ice cream stores. Eleven franchises all over the city, called Lucky's. Giant neon signs on top, you know. And that wasn't easy for a Black man to build in those days. He had served in the Army during the Second World War and never even got the GI benefits the white guys got. I mean, the government had *all* kinds of ways to lock the Black men out from those opportunities. Regardless, my father managed to build up his empire." She gave a warm laugh then, and it was clear her shell was breaking down. "He said you just never knew when somebody might be on the lookout for ice cream—that you always had to be ready."

When Clarissa told Cecily all of this, Cecily laughed and cried. She told Clarissa about the poem. "'Let be be finale of seem.' That was what we said to each other. We were going to make the world be exactly what we wanted it to be . . . and we did, for a very short time."

Clarissa blinked back tears, her phone hot against her cheek. "You really think he opened those ice cream stores in hopes you'd find him?"

A sigh. "He went to Chicago looking for me, I bet, because I'd told him that was where I was from. And I went to New York looking for him." Cecily sighed again, then her voice came across the line, sounding tiny and young and brokenhearted. "1972, you said?"

When Clarissa hung up, she cried and cried again.

"You see, Mom," Kate said. "You *were* wanted. You *were* loved. And your parents loved *each other*. You come from love. And you were always, always loved."

"Oh, honey." Clarissa sighed, and laid a hand against her daughter's face.

Kate had a far-off look in her eyes, these days, but a new serenity, too. She'd started talking about going back to Florida. She thought she was ready. She was going to check with the rehab center about buying Ransom.

And Clarissa thought: *It's true*—they really all were going to be all right now.

It was September when they all met in Chicago. Cecily was not really well enough to travel, but insisted. She could *sit in a car*, for heaven's sake, she said. (*Yes, even for nine hours!* she said.)

Liz did not want to go—she was through the worst of her radiation treatments, but hadn't fully come to terms with everything yet, and didn't feel up to a trip, besides—so it was Molly, Evan, and Caden who piled into the Mazda with Cecily, Molly driving, Cecily and Caden in back. (Because Caden was continuing a special study of genetics this year, independently with Mr. Rasmussen, this trip amounted to research, or so Molly and Evan had claimed to the school, laughing together afterward when the school had actually bought it.)

The four of them were used to each other's company these days. Yes, Caden had spent three weeks in August with Evan in Newport and Maine, and he'd also gone to hockey camp in Brainerd in late July. But Evan now spent a week or two each month in Itasca, too, and, in the early summer, with the lease up at the blue bungalow, Molly and Caden (and Evan) had moved into Cecily's big white Victorian, after, with Liz's blessing, converting Sam's old office into a downstairs bedroom for Cecily, allowing Cecily to move home from The Pines.

Molly felt that, unlike Liz, she had come to terms with the lies Cecily had told; with her reasons for telling them. But she also knew that forgiveness was far easier from where she was sitting, because Cecily had never taken anything from Molly, the way that, in Liz's view, she'd taken Liz's identity and biological family—the truth of who she really was. To Molly, Cecily had only given, and given from her heart. She would always simply be Molly's beloved Grandma Cecily.

Meanwhile, Evan was arranging for his business partners to buy his share of the Newport brewery, and planning to start a micro-brewery in northern Minnesota. He thought there could really be a market, given all the Northwoods towns, Duluth, the Twin Cities. Evan and Molly would keep the Newport house for summers and holidays, maybe rent it out the rest of the time, and Molly hoped this would, someday soon, give her an opportunity to meet some of her biological relatives who lived in Rhode Island, the family of Liz's biological mother, Helen Schneider Myer.

Sure, there was a lot still to figure out—logistically and, of course, between her and Evan. Would they get married again? Molly wasn't sure. What she did know: she was not going to let him go again. It was really forever, this time. For her sake, his sake, and Caden's. And, once the Newport business was sold, Evan wanted to buy a place of their own in Itasca.

But there was no real hurry on that. Cecily was going to need help for a while, and, for the time being, at least they had the upstairs to themselves. (Cecily had insisted Molly use the master bedroom—but, God, those purple walls! They made Evan groan and laugh every time he walked into the room.) Molly would go back to full-time practice soon, but for now she'd been scheduling client sessions just three days a week, allowing her to help out Liz through her cancer treatments; giving her more time with Cecily, too.

Through all of this, Cecily's friends from the Prayer and Action Circle, other committees, and book clubs were in and out, helping with this or that errand or chore, bringing over another hotdish, staying for a cup of coffee at the kitchen table. The story—that Cecily'd been a circus bareback rider and had a long-lost daughter whom she'd always believed had died at birth; that Liz wasn't actually Sam and Cecily's biological child—had circulated around town, of course, but hadn't caused as much of a ripple as Molly would have expected. (Most people said they weren't even sure whether to believe it; others grew quiet, like they had secrets of their own.) The Prayer and Action ladies, though, when left with Cecily one-on-one, would grill her gently, trying to reconcile what they'd believed of Cecily for decades with what they'd just learned, until finally Evan or Molly would step in and say, "All right, ladies. Cecily needs her rest."

Honestly, Molly thought that they should all simply do what Cecily had described doing after she'd been arrested: only look ahead, and not back.

She thought they were getting a good start on that now. For the long weekend in Chicago, long anticipated and carefully planned, Clarissa, Kate, and Lana were flying up from North Carolina and staying at an Airbnb near the one Molly had rented, which was near where Reyna Harris and her family lived, in the Austin Village section of the city that bordered Oak Park.

"Are you nervous?" Molly said to Cecily over her shoulder, as they set out, leaving Itasca behind them. It was a gorgeous, golden, September blue-sky day. Tall pines lined the highway. "To meet your daughter? And Lucky's other children?"

"Excited!" Cecily said.

Molly smiled over at Evan, and he grinned back. They'd talked at length about synchronicities, chains of events, all the parts and pieces that had had to come into play for Cecily to find her biological daughter, for Evan and Molly to get back together, for Liz to discover her cancer so early on. Even Cecily, overhearing them one day, had agreed that, as painful as the events of her early life had been, the outcomes seemed by grand design. "Kate says my daughter saved a thousand lives with that domestic violence center she ran," she'd told Molly. "And your grandpa and I saved your mother's." *Not to mention breathed life into this whole town*, Molly had wanted to add, because she knew now that Cecily never would've ended up in Itasca at all, if it wasn't for Lucky, the lost baby, little Liz on the side of the road.

Molly did understand why Liz was angry, but she had to believe that, one day very soon, Liz would begin to appreciate the patterns of all these intersecting lives as some of the most beautiful artwork imaginable.

"I'm hungry," Caden said. "When are we gonna stop for lunch?"

"Let's at least try to make it to Duluth, bud," Molly said, laughing.

An hour and a half later, they were all unwrapping giant sub sandwiches from Erbert and Gerbert's as they crossed the mile-long high bridge from Duluth over into Wisconsin—the expansive view from way atop it always gave Molly the appealing feeling of being set free from the limits of her own, earthbound life—when Cecily sighed. "This is where I first kissed Lucky," she said. "Superior, Wisconsin."

"Grandma?" Molly said, with a nervous glance in the rearview mirror, a sidelong glance at Evan. This did not seem like it could be true. Was Cecily losing her grip on reality? Were they going to have to turn around?

"July fourth, 1935," Cecily went on. "During the fireworks. We were here on the circus train. I never could stand to come back here. All these years living so nearby! It was always too painful. I thought—of all places in the world that Sam would be from, why did it have to be less than a hundred miles from here? Because, you know, the moment I first kissed Lucky was the moment I knew I loved him, and it was the moment I started to lose him, too. I didn't know that at the time. But now, I look back, and I see him just . . . evaporating, the way a dream does when you wake up." She sighed, looking out at the blue expanse of Lake Superior. "We just never had a chance."

Molly blinked back tears. Evan reached over to squeeze her hand atop the steering wheel. Even Caden was quiet.

"No, Grandma," Molly said. "I guess you didn't. I'm so sorry. I'm so very, very sorry."

"Oh!" Cecily said, from the back, when she spotted the three women standing on the steps of the former orphanage, as Molly pulled into the circle drive. Two women—the taller, paler one, in a white belted dress, had a gorgeous mane of chestnut hair; the other, in a red dress, had darker skin and beautiful black curls—flanked a petite, white-haired lady who (yes, there was no mistaking it, even at this distance) looked just like Cecily. "Oh, stop, let me out, let me out!" Molly parked, and Evan hurried to help Cecily, who would've leaped down from the SUV, if given an instant more.

It was Lana who'd managed to figure out—from what Cecily remembered of how the place had looked, and of that taxi ride with Tebow down to Union Station—the name and address of the orphanage where Cecily had spent three years of her early life. The old mansion still existed—now as a law office—and, with the lawyers informed of and happily consenting to the reunion, Cecily and Clarissa had agreed that this was where they would first meet.

"There you are! There you are!" Cecily said, holding out her arms to Clarissa, moving as quickly as she could toward her.

It was like looking into a mirror, looking into those sapphire eyes.

Finally, Clarissa thought. *I'm home.*

"This is where my mother left me," Cecily said, after some moments, after they'd hugged and cried and hugged some more, with Kate and Lana taking turns, too. Cecily was trying to catch her breath. She could not believe it, could not believe it! She would've sworn she re-membered the tiny mosaic tiles of the front stoop, the stained-glass fleur-de-lis in the door, from the day she was four years old. "And now, it's where I find you. Oh, thank God, thank God!" She hugged Cla-rissa again, then Kate again, and Lana, then Clarissa once more. She wanted never to stop. The DNA tests had revealed no close relatives that could tell her about her parents, about Madeline and Thomas McAvoy. This, now, was the only biological family she had. The only biological family she'd *ever* had.

Lana tapped her shoulder and showed her a small picture frame. "Remember this?"

"Oh, my word," Cecily said, taking the prayer card in her hands.

They met Lucky's daughters, Reyna and Gwen, and his son, Langston, plus their spouses and eleven of Lucky's grandchildren and great-grandchildren, at Lucky's grave at Oak Woods Cemetery on the South Side. Cecily briefly touched the stone, tracing her fingers over the let-tering, which read simply, *Moses Washington Green, 1918–1972*—but then, there were so many people to meet! The introductions and hugs were awkward but heartfelt. All around, Cecily heard voices young and old, high and low, a chorus of: "And you are . . . ? And you are . . . ? And that makes you my . . . what . . . ?" Finally, everyone was laughing. They set-tled, some of them, into the grass surrounding Lucky's grave—he was buried beside his wife, and her children joked she might just be rolling her eyes and giving Lucky what for about all this—and others stood by chatting, getting to know one another.

Reyna came over to Cecily with a soft smile, pulling a tiny notebook out of the deep pocket of her blazer. "My father had a whole stack of these little notebooks," she said, "and I finally read them all a few years ago, after my mother died. I thought you'd like to see this." She opened to one of the last pages. "I remembered it because I didn't know who 'Cecily' was, so of course I wondered."

Cecily looked, and there was Lucky's familiar handwriting, the thick strokes of pencil:

May 8, 1936—Chicago

CECILY.

Around every corner of my dreams, I hear you calling out my name
(If I could find you to tell you once more
I love you
Would I stop aching like this?)

Cecily looked up, blinking at Reyna. "He wrote this on the day that Clarissa was born, and he was already here in Chicago?" These facts together were so astonishing that all Cecily could do was close the little notebook and look at its cover, as if that would help her make sense of everything. And then she realized the cover seemed oddly familiar. And though she realized, too, that Lucky might've owned countless notebooks like this one (but maybe not!), she flipped through it, the early pages, until—yes.

There was her handwriting.

"Oh!" she told Reyna. "I wrote this! This was me!" *Exquisite, sanguine, oblivious, incandescent.* She was brought back to the stable tent; the scent of hay; the warmth of Prince nearby. Tears blurred her vision.

Reyna leaned in to look. "Really? Wow." She leaned back. "You know, that was the only place in any of his notebooks—I mean, from his whole life, because I read through all of them—the only place where there was different handwriting. I had forgotten about that. It was you?"

"It was me!"

"And he had left you? He didn't know you were going to have a baby?"

Cecily shook her head, wiping at her eyes. "He didn't know. He was trying to protect me, I think. He was worried we'd get caught. I thought he loved me, and then I doubted it, and now I know he did. He did love me." Tears were streaming now; she looked back down at the notebook—*exquisite*—and remembered the note he'd slid under Prince's bridle the day he'd left: *Bittersweet*. "We were writing a poem together," she said.

Reyna smiled in a comforting way and reached to squeeze Cecily's hand, and she looked around at the gathered crowd, the two families, which were really one. "Yes," she said. "Well, it seems as if you did that, the two of you."

Cecily smiled, wiping away her tears, and then one of the grandsons caught her eye. How had she not noticed him right away? "Who is that, Reyna? He looks exactly like Lucky. Like Lucky when I knew him!"

"That's my grandson, Elijah. He's fifteen right now."

Elijah was chatting with Caden in that offhand, cool way of teenaged boys, and Cecily blurted, "It's like a miracle, seeing him. Will you introduce me?" Reyna nodded, took Cecily's arm, and guided her carefully over across the grass to where he stood. After a short conversation—Cecily hoped no one would ask her what Elijah had said, because all she could see, all she could think, was *Lucky*—Cecily asked the young man to promise to write to her, and he smiled the way Lucky would've smiled—that same bright, mysterious, knowing smile—and said he would, and it suddenly broke her heart and confused her that Lucky had never had the chance to meet this boy, his own great-grandson, and here Cecily was, standing here with him, talking to him, in real life, in real time. None of it made any sense, and it made her tired to realize how very old she was, how long Lucky had been really gone.

And somehow, then, Cecily was at the edge of the circle, as everyone else hugged again to say goodbye, and Clarissa came over and linked her arm with Cecily's. Cecily blinked back more tears, as happiness and gratitude flooded her again. "Speaking of impossible things," she said, watching everyone hugging and laughing and promising to stay in touch, and Clarissa smiled, watching, too.

"How do you think that doctor ever lived with himself?" Clarissa asked. "The one who told you I had died? How do you think he got away with it, not just in the case of me and you, but over and over again?"

Cecily sighed. "I don't know. I don't like to think about him."

"Oh—of course," Clarissa said, seeming chastised.

Cecily hadn't meant to make her feel bad—would never want to do that. This was her *daughter*. Her daughter! "But, dear, in a way, we have to admit, he's responsible for *all* of this. The good as well as the bad. For *all* of these people here existing. So, we have to just say 'all right.' We have to just accept it. The criminal and the insane and the selfishness and greed. And the munificence of everything, too. You know?"

Clarissa nodded, blinking back tears. For the lost years, Cecily knew—and oh, God, don't think Cecily didn't feel the weight and grief of those lost years, too.

And yet.

"I wish Lucky could've seen this," Cecily told their daughter, and she showed Clarissa the poem Lucky had written on the day that Clarissa was born. "You see, don't you? How much we loved each other?" Clarissa was nodding, with tears rolling down her cheeks, pressing the little notebook to her heart, and Cecily looked back around at the gathered families. "Isn't it beautiful? I wish my husband, Sam, could be here, too." *And Liz*, she thought. "I wish everyone could be here," she said softly.

But Liz would come around, Cecily had to think. Liz had told Cecily what Eric had said, and Cecily had wanted to cheer, to call him, to send an extravagant gift to wherever he was in the world. Because she could see: Liz was on the verge, the absolute *verge*, of forgiving her.

Yes, Cecily had to think this was true.

Cecily reached to squeeze Clarissa's hand, and Clarissa squeezed back, and Cecily realized suddenly that, in the end, maybe she really never had stopped believing in impossible things.

That maybe she never would've survived to make it here, if she had.

The Scent of Mulberry

May 15, 1936
Wilmington, North Carolina

When Jacqueline DuMonde did not appear at the table for lunch, Ethel Oglethorpe realized with a start that she ought to have paid closer mind when she'd seen the girl go out to the garden with her book this morning. She wasn't well yet, still bleeding—it was a travesty, Ethel thought, that Rachel Peters was insisting on picking her up tomorrow and bringing her back to Wayward.

Picturing little Jackie slumped in a faint and bleeding on the ground, Ethel excused herself—it was important to maintain a calm facade for the girls—and hurried out through the kitchen, ignoring Millie's quizzical look.

Out in the garden, the only sounds were the singing of birds, the slight rustle of leaves. The heat made Ethel begin to sweat immediately; her corset pinched her (there was no question she'd been putting on weight this past year, alas) as her heels clicked down the brick path to the stone bench, encircled in shrubbery, where she knew Jacqueline had enjoyed reading.

There was no sign of the girl.

In the air was the scent of mulberry.

Then, Ethel saw the book, abandoned on the bench. She went to pick it up. A mud-spattered *Sense and Sensibility*.

"Jacqueline?" she called out, though she supposed she already knew.

A bird whistled in return.

Ethel flipped through the pages of the book. *I will be calm,* she saw was underlined. *I will be mistress of myself.*

A lump rose in Ethel's throat. *The poor, sweet child. Never had a chance.*

Out fluttered a printed card. It fell to the path.

With effort, Ethel bent to pick it up.

A picture of a bearded saint. *Hope begins with Saint Jude. The patron saint of lost causes.*

Now real tears came to Ethel's eyes, though she couldn't have explained why. Except—usually, this job was full of rewards. Everyone was made happy. The girls were well cared for and glad to know their babies would go to good homes. The adopting couples were pleased to pay well for a beautiful child. Usually, the couples were older, and would not have been allowed to adopt through usual channels. Usually, they had tried everything to have a child, typically for many, many years, and they were so grateful. Many operations of this nature were not so ethically, so happily, run.

And Ethel liked to think she was providing a service. Making dreams come true. Besides that, she managed everything with the utmost discretion. Even taught the girls manners. Most ended up marrying well—better than they might have without Ethel's tutelage—with no one the wiser.

But Ethel did not like when things didn't go according to plan. She did not like what Dr. and Mrs. Addington had decided to do in the case of Jacqueline DuMonde. Telling her that her baby had died! What cruelty! And then to follow the recommendation of the state eugenics board without even the girl's knowledge, making it so poor Jacqueline would never have another child in her life, when Ethel would've sworn that Jacqueline was about the furthest thing from feebleminded any girl could be, let alone a prostitute or potential murderess, the way her file claimed. (And, yes, it had been Ethel's job to convince Jacqueline to surrender the child, and Ethel had failed at that, so she did feel some culpability. But, still. She felt there had to have been another way to ensure that the child was available to the adoptive parents. She felt that efforts could have been made following the birth—but Dr. Addington had said they couldn't take any chances.)

So, Mrs. Addington had whisked the healthy baby girl away in the night, while poor little Jacqueline was still unconscious, and Mrs. Addington had been caring for the child at the Addingtons' home. Tonight, the adoptive parents would arrive from Kentucky, pay their six thousand dollars (never knowing they were being charged a thousand dollars extra, on account of the mother having been a scholarship girl), and take the baby away.

Rachel Peters would clear five hundred dollars personally—more than two years' salary, for her.

Ethel looked around the garden, wondering how far Jacqueline could have gotten in the two hours since Ethel had seen her. With the state of health that the girl was in, Ethel should make sure she was found. She should call the police.

But she could envision how that would play out, she could see it all the way through: it would mean state prison for the girl.

Would Ethel lose her job if Rachel Peters arrived to find Jacqueline DuMonde had escaped?

But what would Rachel Peters care? She'd get her five hundred dollars. If she had to account to anyone for a missing inmate—seemingly, it had bothered no one that Wayward had been one girl short, the past couple of months—she would think of something, clever woman that she was. Chances were, she could make Jacqueline DuMonde disappear altogether from the records.

The girl deserved a chance, Ethel thought. Especially after what the Addingtons had done.

Then she had a wild thought. A solution.

She looked around the garden once more. *Yes*, she thought. The girl was a survivor.

All she needed was a chance.

L

That afternoon, Ethel—she had told the girls that Jacqueline Du-Monde's family had come early for her, that she'd been heartbroken not to get to tell them goodbye—prepared the birth certificate for Jacqueline DuMonde's little girl. Henceforth, the child would be known as Clarissa Ann Duncan, daughter of Jack and Lola (*née* Breckinridge) Duncan of Lexington, Kentucky. Ethel would report the birth to the county registrar as if Jack and Lola were the biological parents; as if Jacqueline DuMonde had never existed at all. The registrar received a hundred dollars per month from Dr. Addington to accept whatever information the McNaughton Home submitted as gospel fact, so there would be no question why the well-to-do couple from Lexington had traveled to Wilmington for the birth of their daughter.

As usual, where the form asked for "place of birth," Ethel made no entry. Dr. Addington was a forward thinker, and did not want the grown babies, years in the future, getting too curious about the McNaughton Home. "No good could come of that," he said. It was the girls who'd given birth he was protecting, he said, as well as the adoptive parents.

Next, on McNaughton Home stationery, Ethel typed a short narrative of the child's biological background. This was rarely done, but, in cases like Jacqueline DuMonde's, where the baby had emerged with a slightly darker skin tone, Dr. Addington required it. These girls kept some secrets even from him, and he didn't want couples showing up a year or two down the road questioning a child's purity and demanding their money back. "People believe what you tell them," Dr. Addington always said, and Ethel, who had no idea of Jacqueline DuMonde's background, let alone the baby's father's, enjoyed the imaginative exercise—the father being "from an old English family long in the U.S." was a particularly nice touch, she thought—picking out the letters on the typewriter's sticky metal keys, leaving room for Dr. Addington's signature at the end.

Next, she prepared a death certificate for Jacqueline DuMonde, getting a secret little thrill as she wrote in the cause of death in her neat cursive: *Complications from childbirth.* This, she would not send to the state—because Jacqueline DuMonde, after all, had never been at the McNaughton Home, nor given birth; Lola Duncan had—but to Miss Peters. Ethel was counting on the fact that Miss Peters would not want to file it, so as not to shed light on her lucrative arrangement with the McNaughton Home. Miss Peters would certainly have a new certificate drawn up with a different cause of death and signed by someone at Wayward, showing that the girl had died in custody there.

The important thing was that Miss Peters would believe that Jacqueline DuMonde was no more; that Miss Peters would make Jacqueline DuMonde disappear entirely.

At three, Dr. Addington arrived as scheduled, stopping at Ethel's office first. True to form, he signed every paper she set in front of him without bothering to read it, chatting lazily about the weather. He trusted her that implicitly; they had been working together so long.

While he went off to give the girls their examinations, Ethel folded Clarissa Ann Duncan's birth certificate into one envelope, labeling it as such. Into another, she folded the typed narrative and the prayer card Jacqueline had left behind. (This was a bit of a risk, suggesting as it did that the baby's parents were Catholic, which the Duncans might protest. But a part of Ethel was in rebellion against so thoroughly erasing Jacqueline DuMonde from the earth; at least, she felt sending Jacqueline's little keepsake along with the child was the right thing to do.) This envelope she labeled, *Background information (if desired).* Perhaps it would never be opened. A lot of parents didn't want to know. They wanted their baby to have literally dropped from heaven. A stork delivery, like greeting cards showed. It made Ethel laugh, the things that people would believe, just in order to live with themselves.

She put the two envelopes together into a large brown envelope, and, when he came back into the office, handed the package to Dr. Addington. He would pass it along to Jack and Lola Duncan tonight. Dr. Addington's eyes were bright, the way they always were when he had a big payment coming. (But, Ethel reminded herself, Dr. Addington was generous in his care of the girls. Dr. Addington provided well for his employees. Dr. Addington was a good-hearted man, or Ethel would not have worked for him all these years.)

By the time he left, it was getting late, but Ethel still had time. She sealed the death certificate into an envelope, addressed it to Miss Peters at Wayward, then put on her hat and gloves. ("Look at the fine lady!" Millie teased, as Ethel strolled out through the kitchen; Ethel so rarely left the Home for any reason.) She went out to the garage to her scarcely used Buick. The lightest rain was falling. Ethel drove carefully over to the train station and parked. She covered her hair with a scarf. Resolutely not keeping an eye out for Jacqueline, who, after all, might at this very moment be boarding a train, Ethel dropped the envelope into a postbox, then hurried through the drizzle to the Western Union office and filled in a telegram blank.

To Rachel Peters, NC Reformatory for Wayward Girls

UNFORTUNATE TURN OF EVENTS STOP J DUMONDE PASSED AWAY THIS AM FROM DELAYED COMPLICATIONS STOP NO NEED FOR YOU TO COME STOP YOUR FEE WILL BE FORWARDED STOP SIGNED DR JOS ADDINGTON

Ethel counted out the fee from her own pocketbook.
All the girl needed was a chance.

September 2019
Kure Beach, North Carolina

Kate got in from riding Ransom feeling good and with just enough time to spare. She was going to meet Lana, who was down visiting from Raleigh, and their mother and Monty for dinner at McGillicuddy's to celebrate: Lana had just gotten a publication contract for her book, *Lucky: How DNA Solved the Mystery of My Biracial Identity and Gave Me a New Family.*

Kate took a quick shower, not washing her hair, and picked a red sheath out of the closet, her favorite pair of sandals. She still looked good for sixty-one, she thought, as she let down her hair and assessed herself in the mirror, and she hadn't had a drink in three years. Life was good. Almost better than ever, in fact—except for the fact that it was missing Mark. But she'd come through to a place of gratitude for the years she'd had with him, and for the fact that she'd found reasons to go on living without him, and living fully, soberly, happily. She was closer to her mother and sister than she'd ever been; she had family in Minnesota now, too. She had more hope for the future than she'd ever had, and if that was strange, at her age, she didn't care.

Though she hardly had time—maybe it was just habit—she sat down at her computer (she loved the desk in her new home, which overlooked the white sand of Kure Beach) and clicked on her email.

Her stomach lurched when she saw two emails from Ancestry. (She'd long ago taken over management of her own account from Lana; no way did she want her sister acting as go-between on all her communications, which had turned out to be many.)

You have a new DNA match!

And: *You have a new message!*

Okay, well, maybe another of her Montgomery half-sisters had sent in her DNA and reached out? Tricia had written Kate a while back, and now they were in touch every month or so; they'd even met once. And Kate had spoken to Clayburn on the phone, before he'd passed away last year. Lana had, too, once. (Clarissa had not.) To Lana, he had said, "I never once thought of you as mine," which, of course, had sent her screaming back to therapy and given her two chapters' worth of material for her book. She'd taken to referring to him as "the sperm donor"; to Lucky as her "spiritual father."

To Kate, Clayburn had said, *I'm sorry, Katie. I was wrong.*

Not as satisfying as she'd have thought, but better than nothing, in the end. (Of course, she hadn't told Lana, and never would.)

Kate clicked on the message, anticipating a half-sister or some distant cousin. She'd trained herself, after all this time, not to hope for more. But then she saw the username—*MattK*—and she knew.

Her vision blurred as she read:

Hello,

    I apologize for dropping in out of the blue like this, but it seems from the DNA that you must be my birth mother. I was born June 1, 1973, at Good Samaritan Hospital in Portland, Oregon. I hope it's all right that I'm contacting you. I would really like to get to know you, if you're agreeable. I've always known that I was adopted, but never knew anything about you. I hope that this is not an unwelcome message. I look forward to hearing from you, and, I hope, to getting to know you.

Sincerely yours,
Matt Kowalski

And a phone number! He had given her his phone number! Kate was laughing and crying. She picked up the phone and called her mother. Clarissa didn't answer, and Kate left a bubbly voicemail, probably incoherent, finishing it, "I'll see you—I'll see you very soon, at the restaurant!" Then she quickly dialed Cecily in Minnesota.

"Cecily, Cecily, you won't believe it!" And Kate told her the news.

"Oh, my dear, that's wonderful." Cecily sounded tired but happy. Kate had already talked to her at length about her fears surrounding telling her son—in the event he ever contacted her—the details of his conception, and Cecily had advised the truth. *Tell him that light comes out of the darkness; that without darkness there could be no light,* she'd said. Now she said, "Please, call him right away. Right away! That's my great-grandson. My and Lucky's great-grandson. I want to meet him. I've stayed alive for the chance, I think!"

Kate was crying as she hung up and dialed the number Matt had written below his name.

"Hello?" It was his voice! Her son's voice!

Kate had to swallow hard before she could speak. "Um, hello? Matt? My name is Kate Montgomery. I—I just got your message. I was so happy to hear from you!"

"Kate Montgomery?" His voice was thick with emotion.

Tell him, Cecily had advised, *we never stopped praying for impossible things.*

Tell him that, thanks to him, and you, and your mother, a long-ago love lives on.

"Yes, Matt. Yes. I'm Kate Montgomery. I'm your mother."

ACKNOWLEDGMENTS

Thank you first and foremost to the incredible Kate Nintzel for her passionate work on this book and for seeing straight through to the heart of every line to help each scene become the best it could be. A profound thank-you to my fabulous agent, Deborah Schneider, for believing in this book and in me, and to Brian Lipson and Cathy Gleason for their enthusiasm, hard work, and support. Special thanks also to the amazing Molly Gendell and the entire team at Mariner for all their wonderful work to bring Cecily to the world: Lindsey Kennedy, Allison Carney, Stephanie Vallejo, Renata DiBiase, Mumtaz Mustafa, Kate Falkoff, and Marleen Reimer.

Thank you to my brilliant friend Terence Sullivan, who makes so much possible and who supported me through and lent his incredible intuition and genius to the final edit and to so much else. Thank you to Lara Zielin and Molly Holleran for reading early drafts and providing helpful and essential feedback and encouragement. Thank you to my parents, Marya and Bob Farrell, and brother, Bill Brown-Farrell, for reading early drafts and cheering me on. Thank you to Dustin Black for his optimism and faith. And huge thanks to my author friends Lesley Kagen and Brian Freeman for helping me along the road.

Thank you to Dave and Beth Moulton for showing me life in Vero Beach, and to Christopher Daly for overall inspiration and support. Thank you to Alphonzo Heath for being the genesis of so much in my life and my writing. Thank you to Mark and Kim Jespersen for their extraordinary support over the years, and to all my friends and extended family—especially Christine Skorjanec, Carrie Sutherland, and my aunts Sonya Christensen Steven and Nadia Christensen—and the Maine friends who've become my chosen family—Joyce Jones, Knight

Coolidge, Audrey McGlashan and Rich Hurlbert, Megan Kelley, Andrea Vassallo, and Erica Berman, in particular—for the wide net you've provided under the tightrope of my life this past decade and beyond. This book simply wouldn't have been possible without all of you.

This book came to me like a dream, and then I needed to fill in the details! I'm incredibly grateful to Ann Fessler for writing *The Girls Who Went Away*, which I read years ago and which never left me, and to Dani Shapiro for writing her brilliant memoir *Inheritance: A Memoir of Genealogy, Paternity, and Love*, which so gracefully explores and explains the emotional impact of an unexpected DNA result. For the world of the 1930s circus, I drew inspiration from the beloved novel *Water for Elephants* by Sara Gruen, and, for the exact details I needed, relied on the amazing depth of information available on the website circushistory.org, as well as specifically the article "Logistics of the American Circus: The Golden Age," published in *Production and Inventory Management Journal* (Vol. 46, No. 1, 2010) and written by Vincent A. Mabert and Michael J. Showalter. For Cecily's time at the sanatorium in Rhode Island, I relied on the documentary film *On the Lake: Life & Love in a Distant Place*, directed by David Bettencourt and produced by G. Wayne Miller.

To create Cecily's time at the fictional "Wayward," I leaned heavily on the nonfiction book *Bad Girls at Samarcand: Sexuality and Sterilization in a Southern Juvenile Reformatory* by Karin L. Zipf (Louisiana State University Press, 2016). Though I changed some details about life in the reformatory to fit my story, and invented the McNaughton Home so Cecily would have a chance at escape, Cecily's story, unfortunately, hews closely to the facts of what was happening in the U.S. in the 1930s and beyond. In North Carolina between 1929 and 1950, more than two thousand girls and young women were involuntarily sterilized, often without their knowledge or consent, and, between the late 1920s and mid-1970s, this was the fate of more than sixty-four thousand nationwide. Most often, these girls and young women were BIPOC and/or classified by the standards of the day to be "feebleminded" or "immoral." Often, they had been victims of rape or incest. For detailed information, I recommend the University of Vermont website https://www.uvm.edu/~lkaelber /eugenics and Linda Villarosa's 2022 *New York Times Magazine* article "The Long Shadow of Eugenics in America" (https://www.nytimes .com/2022/06/08/magazine/eugenics-movement-america.html).

Any errors or distortions of fact I invented to fit the story are, of course, my own.

Finally, a profound thank-you to my readers, and to the heroic booksellers and librarians everywhere who champion the love of fiction. You are, in the end, what makes this writing life of mine and this book possible. I could not be more grateful.